TENDER TORMENT

Adam leaned closer. Even with scratches on her face and blue circles under her eyes, Niki was beautiful. She had never looked lovelier to him than she did right now. He reached out and pushed a dark tendril from her cheek, letting his hand linger for just a moment on her silken hair. Reluctantly, he drew it back, then got to his feet. Yet he couldn't make himself go, not yet. He wanted to stay on, waiting to see if she would need anything. If she awakened, he should be near.

He couldn't fool himself any longer. He loved her. He didn't care about anything in the past. He loved her and wanted to be with her. True, she *was* feisty and quarrelsome. She *did* make him angry and frustrated, but it didn't matter. Perhaps these were even some of the reasons he loved her. What he did know was that he didn't want to lose her. Seeing her now—hurt, helpless —he knew he wanted to take care of her for the rest of his life.

Adam bent down and kissed her lightly on the mouth, whispering, "I love you, Niki O'Hara, like it or not!"

Also by Robin Lee Hatcher:

STORMY SURRENDER
(THE SPRING HAVEN SAGA, VOLUME I)

HEART'S LANDING
(THE SPRING HAVEN SAGA, VOLUME II)

THORN OF LOVE

ROBIN LEE HATCHER

LEISURE BOOKS   œ   NEW YORK CITY

To my husband,
Gene,
whose unfailing love and support sustains me;
to my editor,
Jane Thornton,
whose enthusiasm for my books encourages me;
to my readers,
who have been so generous with their praise.
I appreciate you all.

A LEISURE BOOK

Published by

Dorchester Publishing Co., Inc.
6 East 39th Street
New York, NY 10016

Printed in the United States of America

CHAPTER 1

Niki O'Hara lacked none of the fire and temper attributed to her Irish ancestors. When she was angry, she was angry to the very core, and there was no doubt in the minds of anyone there in the living room that that was her present state.

"I don't care what you think. I'm going to New York and I'm going to be an actress!"

"Niki, be reasonable. You don't know what you're saying."

Niki glared at her mother, violet eyes snapping in defiance. "Of course I know. I'm seventeen, Mother. Not seven."

"Oh, yes. I'd forgotten. You *have* reached a ripe old age." Sarcasm laced Brenetta O'Hara's words as her own temper flared. She took a deep breath, trying to calm herself before she said something she would later regret. "Niki, please listen to me. You don't know what it would be like. You've hardly set foot off this ranch. Things are different in the city. You wouldn't like it, I assure you. You belong here."

"How do you know what I'd like?" Niki protested. "You're not me. We're not at all alike."

That wasn't entirely true. When Brenetta was hardly more than Niki's age, she had tenaciously pursued her own dreams, no matter what the odds. Perhaps it was the memories of dreams shattered that made her so determined to keep her youngest child at home, safe from the hurts and disappointments that the world outside could heap on the unsuspecting.

Niki looked toward her father, her anger melting into a plea for understanding. "Da, can't you see it's time you let me go?"

Wordlessly, Rory came across the room and stood before her. He raised a work-roughened hand and caressed her cheek. Black eyes stared deep into her own, looking at her so intensely that Niki felt he could see inside her soul. She knew he couldn't understand her desire to leave Heart's Landing. He had told her often enough that the years he had spent away from this ranch had been the bleakest of his life. He'd hated the city. To him, there was no place more suitable to live than here. This ranch, these Idaho mountains, his family—that was his life, all he needed to be happy.

"I love you, Da," she whispered. She kissed his brown cheek, then turned back toward her mother. Here was the real opposition.

How was it that two people who loved each other as Niki and Brenetta did could be at constant odds? It had always been so. Niki never saw her mother lose her temper with Starr or with her brothers, BJ and Travis, but it seemed as if Niki was always in hot water. Truth was she was Brenetta's favorite, though Brenetta would have protested and sworn she had no favorite among her children.

Niki moved across the thick carpet, her mind working rapidly to form the right words. "Mother, remember when we went to San Francisco and you took me to that play? I was too young to understand much, but I knew right then that that was what I was going to do. I wanted to be behind those footlights and become someone else, say someone else's words. I wanted to hear the applause and take my bows." She sat down beside Brenetta on the couch. "I've got to go, Ma."

"No, you do *not* have to go. You're too young."

Anger exploded again. Niki jumped to her feet, tired of pleading, tired of trying to make her mother understand. She wasn't going to waste words any longer. "Well, I *am* going, whether you like it or not. You can't keep me a prisoner here. This place can go to the devil for all I care. I'm going to New York."

"That's enough out of you, Kathleen Nicole!" Brenetta was on her feet too. "You

9

speak that way about our home and I'll take the strap to you that you've needed for a long time."

Niki uttered a startled gasp as she stepped backwards. "Why did I think you'd understand? You don't love me. You don't care what I want. You only think of yourself and . . . and . . ." Tears began to blur her vision, but before she let them spill, she spun on her heel to leave the room. "I hate you! I hate you!" she cried as she disappeared up the stairs, leaving behind stunned silence.

In her room, Niki threw herself across her bed and succumbed to her misery. Finally, tears spent, she drifted into a troubled sleep.

Heart's Landing Ranch had been carved from the Idaho wilderness by Niki's grandparents in the late 1860s. Her paternal grandfather, Garvey O'Hara, had worked for Brent and Taylor Lattimer, Brenetta's parents, and had died while saving Brenetta from a forest fire. Her family's roots had grown so deep in the Idaho soil that it seemed there had always been O'Haras and Lattimers living here. Both of her grandfathers were buried at Heart's Landing, alongside several nephews and one stillborn sister. Her parents grew up here and were married in this very same house.

A special love existed between Rory, the strong, silent half-breed, and Brenetta. A love that had survived separation and betrayal and the schemes of others. A love that had joined them together and forged a dynasty to rule a fiercely beautiful land. The O'Hara children had thrived, honed by the oft-times harshness of nature, yet instilled with its gentleness too. And though alike in their stubborn strength, each were individuals.

Starr, the oldest, was fair and lovely. Her blonde hair and light blue eyes set her apart from the other O'Hara children. She was actually not Niki's sister but the daughter of Brenetta's cousin, Megan. No one ever talked about Starr's real parents. All that Niki knew was that her father had been married to Megan before he married Brenetta and that he had always considered Starr his own, in love if not by blood. Starr had married Reuben Levi when Niki was almost nine, and they lived about fifteen miles away on a small spread of their own. Though Niki was fond of her adopted sister, the difference in their ages separated them more than the distance between the two ranches.

Niki's oldest brother, Brent Jefferson—better known as BJ—was also married, but he lived just the other side of the paddocks in the new house he'd built for his bride, Gwen. Although BJ was taller than his father, he had the same darkly handsome features of Rory's Cheyenne mother, White Dove. He also had inherited his Indian grandmother's quiet, thoughtful nature and the love she'd had for the earth and the beauty of all God's creations. BJ had finished his education in the East but had come home as soon as he could, letting it be known that it would take a miracle to drag him away from Heart's Landing again.

Travis O'Hara was a different story. He, too, had been educated in the East, but he had chosen to stay. His great-grandfather, David Lattimer, had established the Lattimer Bank and Trust Company, and both Brent Lattimer and, later, Rory O'Hara had made their own fortunes following in his footsteps. But Brent and Rory were men meant for the wilderness and had fled the smoky board rooms with gladness. Travis, however, loved the world of finance and was happy to stay and take up his rightful place as David Lattimer's heir.

And then there was Niki. It wasn't that she hated country life or that she thought she'd like city life better. But what she wanted could only be found in the city. She wanted fame and glamour. She wanted to hear the applause and accept the roses and take her bows. She wanted to be cloaked in fabulous gowns and gems as she strode across the stage, speaking lines written perhaps centuries before by great men. It made no difference to her that she didn't know anything about what it would take to *be* an actress. Anytime Niki wanted something, she went after it with great zest and determination. This would be no different.

When Niki awoke from her troubled sleep, she got up from her bed and went into the bathroom where she splashed away the tear stains with cold water. Catching a glimpse of herself in the mirror, she wondered if she was pretty enough for the stage, especially now with her eyes reddened and puffy.

Just an inch or two over five feet tall, she had a slender, almost boyish figure. She had inherited her dusky complexion from her father. Her eyes were the same deep blue as her Grandmother Taylor's, with just the right dash of purple to give them their unusual violet lights. Her hair was a rich, dark-chocolate shade of brown, worn long, the riotous array of curls cascading around her shoulders. Not being given to vanity, she was unaware of her own beauty and could only seem to find defects.

Still looking in the mirror, she suddenly threw her arm up against her forehead as her eyes grew wide with horror. "But, sir, if you turn me out of my house, whatever shall become of me?" Her narrow, arching brows were drawn together in a sinister frown as she laughed wickedly. "Why, my dear, you do not need to be turned out. Come live with me. I'll take care of you." She held palms against her cheeks. "I should rather die!"

"Bravo! Bravo!"

Niki whirled around to find her grand-mother standing in her room. She blushed scarlet. "Oh, Gram. I didn't hear you come in."

"How could you? You were in the midst of being propositioned by that scurrilous landlord of yours." Taylor smiled. "And glad I was to hear you have enough sense to send him packing. Gives me a sense of peace when I think of you living alone in New York or London or wherever it is that fame will take you."

"Gram, you believe in me, don't you? You know I can do it."

Taylor sat down in the rocking chair next to the window. She nodded slowly as she pushed the chair into gentle motion. "Yes, Niki. I believe you'll do it, and I believe you'll be just fine while you're making your dream come true. That is if you can control that fiery tongue of yours. It will get you into more trouble than anything else if you don't."

"But I . . ." She swallowed her protest. Her grandmother was right. She did speak without thinking, especially when she was angry or excited—or when it came to her mother. "You're right, Gram, but how can I make Ma see that this is what I must do? I don't want to just be someone's wife or to live on a ranch like this one in the middle of nowhere."

"Oh my," Taylor said with a sigh as she laid a blue-veined hand on Niki's head. "How things have changed. When Brent and I came here, the peace of this nowhere, as you call it, was just what we wanted. And now here you are, chomping at the bit to escape the refuge we so carefully built. Oh my." She closed her eyes, and Niki knew that she was drifting off to another time, lost somewhere in over six decades of memories.

Taylor's ageless beauty and healthy body belied her sixty-six years. Her hair was now silver instead of black, but her face was unlined and her mind was as sharp as ever. Niki loved to hear her speak. Taylor's melodic southern accent had always soothed her and made her long to see her grandmother's childhood home and meet the people she had heard her speak of so often.

"You must understand something, Niki," Taylor said suddenly, causing the girl to look up into her eyes. "Your mother is only trying to protect you. She loves you terribly and doesn't ever want to see you hurt. She'll have no way of protecting you when you're so far away."

"But I don't need protection, Gram.

Good heavens! You were married to your first husband *before* you were seventeen. I've heard you tell the story myself."

"That was different, dear. I *was* married. It was what was expected of a girl of my generation." She chuckled. "I'm sure your parents could understand better if it was a mad passion for a man that was about to take you away from them instead of the lure of the stage. They would probably be glad to see you safely married."

"Married! Why ever would I want that?"

"Goodness, Niki. Don't make it sound like such a terrible institution." Seeing Niki about to protest, Taylor continued. "Oh, I know you didn't mean it that way. You have a goal to reach first. It's exciting and adventuresome and mysterious. Women of means, as you are—or rather, as you will be —didn't ever think of working in my day. That was only for the poor and the widowed." A twinkle flashed in her eyes. "But I think, if I were young again, I'd be tempted to do something like this too. Unless, of course, Brent was alive."

"You and Grandfather had something very special, didn't you, Gram?"

A sad-sweet smile fluttered across Taylor's lips. "Yes, yes, we did. I wish you could have known him, Niki. I wish he could have lived to see his fine grandchildren. You know, it's been twenty-six years since Rory brought Brent's body back from the mountains, and yet sometimes I still expect to see him walking through the front door." She shook herself. "Heavens, I didn't mean to get so sentimental. I just wanted you to know I'll do what I can to help you, but you've got to promise to hold that tongue of yours around your mother. Agreed?"

Niki nodded.

"Good. Now, I must go and see what the cook is preparing for supper. BJ and Gwen are joining us tonight." Taylor brushed her lips against Niki's forehead. "We'll talk more later."

Despite her resolve, the next few days saw more flare-ups between mother and daughter, and the atmosphere at Heart's Landing began to resemble an armed camp. It didn't matter that mother and daughter loved each other. Neither of them seemed able to speak their feelings. The words were imprisoned behind a wall of misunderstanding. Niki's heart ached until she thought it would burst, yet she couldn't and wouldn't back down. She was determined to leave, even if she could never return home again. And Heart's Landing was her home. She did love it, even though she couldn't confess it to Brenetta just now. She didn't want to be estranged forever from her family, but even if that's what it would cost her, she was going to be an actress. She would never give up her dream.

True to her word, Taylor was at last able to arrange a truce. On a bright spring morning, Niki listened apprehensively as the details of the agreement were outlined to her. Occasionally her glance darted to Brenetta who was standing near the doorway of her grandmother's sitting room, her eyes averted and her mouth pinched with disapproval.

"Niki, I'd hoped I would find a solution to the unhappiness in this home, a solution that would end the division between my daughter and my grandchild. I don't seem to have achieved that yet, but I hope I'm making a little progress. Your mother has agreed to let you accompany me on a trip to Spring Haven. I've talked often of going, and before I die or get too old to travel, I want to see my old home and my surviving friends and family one more time."

"Gram, you're not anywhere near ready to . . ."

"Hush. I didn't mean I was ready to lie down tomorrow. I just mean I want to take this trip." Taylor cleared her throat. "Now, as I was saying, your mother has agreed to let you go with me. We'll stay at Spring Haven until your eighteenth birthday, and then I'll take you to New York and arrange for you to study in the theater for one year."

Niki sat forward, beginning to take more of an interest in this plan.

"Mind you, Niki, you won't be able to take any part that isn't a direct assignment by your acting coach. Nothing for pay or for glory. Only for study."

"I don't care. It sounds wonderful, Gram. You'll see. I'll do whatever they tell me, and I'll become the best actress . . ."

"One thing your grandmother hasn't mentioned," Brenetta interrupted. "During your trial year in New York, if you appear in any unapproved play or if you break any of the rules your grandmother and I set down for you or . . . or if your behavior is less than respectable in any way, then you'll have to return home. And if you refuse to come home, you'll be on your own. There'll be no financial help from your grandmother or anyone else in the family. Your trust fund is tied up until you're twenty-five, and I'll see to it that the bank is unavailable to you as well. Do you understand?"

Tears stung Niki's eyes as Brenetta's icy words pierced her heart, yet she refused to let them be seen. Her heart pounding in her ears, Niki replied with feigned calm, "I understand, and I agree to your terms. If I can't abide by them, then I'll happily starve before I'll ask for help from you or your precious bank. I'll make it on my own or I'll die trying, but I don't ever want anyone to say I made it because I had it easy or because someone bought it for me." She turned her blurry vision in Taylor's direction. "When do we leave, Gram? I can be ready any time."

Before Taylor could answer, Brenetta left the room. Staring at the empty space where her daughter had stood, Taylor sighed deeply. "Oh, Niki. I wanted us to go with your mother's blessings. I didn't want it to be like this. Not like this."

Cattle dotted the green valley that stretched westward from the two-story main house. Tree-studded mountains surrounded the pastoral scene, mountains harboring deer and elk, bear and wolf, chipmunks and snakes and eagles, mountains that were at times white with snow or splashed with the pinks and purples of sunset or sprinkled with bright wildflowers amid the dark greens of the pines or the chartreuse leaves of the whispering birch and aspen.

Niki was in the window seat, her chin resting on folded arms as she stared out across her vast homeland, when her father entered her room. She lifted her head to look at him. Rory's face was etched with worry and sadness. He closed the door with care, then crossed the room to sit beside her.

"Kitten."

She went into his arms, tears bursting forth. She shook with sobs, hardly understanding her own emotions. She just wanted to be rocked in her father's arms and told that everything would be fine, all the problems in her world would go away. Daddy would kiss the hurt and it would disappear as it always did. She cried herself out, and still he held her tightly.

Finally, Rory pushed her away just enough to give her his handkerchief. She dried her eyes and obediently blew her nose. Still sniffing, she said, "Why is it that I've got to make everyone so miserable to get what I want?"

Her father shook his head. "Breaking away is never easy. You're leaving everything familiar, and your mother and I are having to let you go. It's a necessary part of children growing up, but I can't say I care for it."

"Da, I love you both. Really I do."

"We know that, Kitten."

"Are you sure Ma knows it?" Niki stared out the window, forcing the quiver from her voice.

Rory's hand ruffled her hair. "Yes."

"We leave tomorrow morning. I don't suppose she'll come into town to see us off?" Niki looked hopefully at her father but knew deep inside what his answer would be.

"Don't count on it, Niki. Your Ma's having a hard enough time knowing you're leaving. I don't think she could bear to say her goodbyes at the station."

Niki wanted to believe that that was the reason. Yet with all the angry words that had been hastily spoken still forming a barrier between them, she couldn't bring herself to accept it. Hurt feelings and stubborn pride blocked her view of her mother's side. "Well, I suppose it doesn't really matter. Things'll be a mad rush at the station anyway."

She sensed the sadness in her father's touch but couldn't bring herself to meet his gaze. She was rescued by a knock at her door. BJ entered without waiting for her summons.

"Good morning, you two. I came to see if Niki wanted to take one last ride before she goes. I've got to round up a few strays. Are you interested, Niki?"

Niki quickly nodded. "I'd love to, BJ. Give me a few minutes to change. I'll meet you by the barn."

"Come on, Da. You can help me saddle the horses."

Niki kissed Rory's cheek, then hurried to her closet and began sorting through her clothes. She didn't turn again until she heard the door close behind her father and brother.

Taking a bright red riding habit from its hanger, she tossed it across the bed and began unfastening her dress. By the time she was pulling on her black leather boots, she was feeling a little better. She was determined not to shed another tear over leaving. Da was right. It was a natural process for the young to leave home. Perhaps she wasn't going about it the way most proper young ladies did, but she wasn't like other young ladies.

"I'm most likely not even proper," she said aloud, a smile tweaking the corners of her mouth for the first time in days.

BJ was waiting for her alone, sitting on the hitching post. Two copper-colored geldings stood patiently nearby, their tails swishing rhythmically at buzzing flies.

"Sorry I took so long, BJ."

"No problem, sis. I already know where the strays are." He offered a hand up into the saddle as he spoke.

Niki's horse, Raja, was one of three that belonged to her, but he was her favorite. He was the only horse she had trained all on her own. Her father presented the two-year-old colt to her on her tenth birthday, and it had been love at first sight. They had grown up together, spending long afternoons racing through meadows and splashing in icy streams. Now, Raja nickered his hello as she settled herself over his back. She patted his neck in return.

BJ swung into his own saddle. "Up Silver Canyon," he said as he turned his horse's head around.

Brother and sister rode in silence for over

an hour as they climbed their way higher into the mountains, leaving behind all evidence of the ranch. When they stopped to rest their horses before going on, Niki sat beside a birch tree, twisting a sliver of grass in her fingers.

"Are you ready to leave?"

Niki looked up at her brother. She nodded.

"Been a bit tough on all of you, hasn't it?"

"I don't think Mother likes the idea of an actress for a daughter."

BJ laughed. "Don't imagine so, but she'll back you all the way once she gets used to it. Ma's never been one to worry what other folks think once she gets it in her head it's right."

Niki sighed. "I just can't figure her out, BJ. Why can't we ever seem to get through to each other? She's always told me I can be anything, do anything, that I shouldn't let other people stop me from reaching for the stars. Then when I do . . ." She shook her head despondently.

"Sis," BJ said as he sat beside her, "even you should be able to see that the two of you are too stubborn to see eye to eye right now. Later, after you've had some breathing room, when you've grown up a bit more and she doesn't see you as her baby, then you can be friends again."

"We weren't ever friends *before*, BJ."

BJ's arm tightened around her shoulder. "It'll happen, Niki. I promise."

"So everyone keeps telling me."

BJ smiled as he nodded. Suddenly, he chucked her under the chin, then jumped to his feet. "Well, let's get up and get going. The day's wastin' and lost cattle don't care if they're caught by cowpokes or actresses."

CHAPTER 2

Adam Bellman stood in the middle of the long, oak-lined drive, hands clasped behind his back and a frown furrowing his brow. The acres and acres of lawn—filled with magnolias, cedars and pines, and perfumed by violets, pansies, honeysuckle and roses—had grown shabby for lack of enough money and caring hands to tend them. Still, he couldn't sell off any of the land surrounding his home. No matter how sensible it sounded, it would be unthinkable.

His glance shifted ahead to the two-story manor house. White Grecian columns, in need of paint, lined the portico. In fact, the entire building needed paint. Still, it was beautiful, a whisper out of the past, telling of another time, another way of life. Adam had grown up listening to people talking about the way things used to be, hearing the stories so often he sometimes thought he knew more about the world before the Civil War than now. He knew so well how Spring Haven must have looked back then

—noble, regal, affluent.

He shook his head, looking again at the signs of financial hardship that plagued him daily. He had no time for daydreaming. He had to be practical. Everyone was depending on him.

Erin stepped into the doorway as he approached the house. She lifted a hand in greeting, then brushed away the loose tendrils of strawberry blonde hair that had escaped the confines of her kerchief. "I've just taken two apple pies from the oven. I was hoping you might be along soon."

Adam smiled despite himself. His aunt Erin always made him feel good. A tiny woman of thirty-three, she made him think of a pixie out of some fairy tale with her emerald green eyes, her pudgy nose covered with freckles, and her hair the color of peach preserves. Although not truly pretty, she had charm, and she always seemed to find something to smile about, no matter how gloomy the circumstances.

"To be honest, Aunt Erin, I was sitting in my office, daydreaming about apple pies, and something told me you must be baking one with my name on it. So I put away all my papers and headed for home."

"Good. Come along then. I've already called Pop, and he just might eat them both before you get sat down." She hooked her hand through his arm and they walked together toward the back of the house.

Pop Montgomery was sitting beside the small kitchen table, quietly smoking his pipe as he eyed the cooling pies on the nearby counter. "I'd begun to think you'd never get here. Do you know what a cruel woman your Aunt Erin is, my boy? She calls me in and then tells me I can't have a bite until you're here too." He clucked his tongue as he shook his head. "Pure spite, that's what it is. Regular meanness."

Erin laughed as she kissed his wrinkled cheek. "Well, you survived and now you can have *two* pieces if it will make you feel better."

"That it would. That it would."

Adam took his seat across from Pop as he listened to their friendly banter. He'd grown up hearing the two of them teasing and joking with each other, and he enjoyed it as much as they did.

Pop and Erin were all the family Adam had ever really known. His mother died shortly after he was born, and his father, Martin Bellman, died before Adam turned six. He had a few vague memories of the tall, thin man with large brown eyes who used to take him riding in the evenings, but it was Erin who he remembered tucking him in at night or cleaning up his skinned knees or scolding him for being late to supper. And Pop, Martin and Erin's step-father, (whose Christian name was Alan Montgomery) was the one who had taught him how to fish and how to ride. It was Pop who had labored long hours to keep food on the table and to send Adam to college so he could become a lawyer as was expected of the eldest Bellman male of each generation.

Erin placed a plate in front of Adam, the slice of pie still steaming, filling the air with tangy sweetness and making his stomach growl.

"Look at that! She even gives you the first piece," Pop cried before Erin could serve him. He shook his balding head again, his green eyes laughing. "You'd think she'd at least give preference to me as the best looking of us two men . . ." he winked at Adam " . . . if not because of the proper respect she should be giving to the elderly."

"Elderly, my foot." Erin pulled his chair close to the table, grinning as her eyes darted between her men. "Enough of your silliness. I have some important news to share. I've heard from the family in Idaho. They're coming for a visit."

"Who? When?"

"If you'll wait a moment, Pop, I'll tell you. Aunt Taylor. And she's bringing one of her grandchildren. Brenetta's youngest, I think. I was so excited when I got the call that I can't remember exactly who she said. They'll arrive in Atlanta next Friday."

"Bless my soul. Taylor Lattimer." Pop leaned back in his chair. "How many years has it been?" he asked himself softly.

"Must be near twenty."

Adam took a bite of apple pie as he watched and listened. He'd heard often enough in his life about the wonderful and beautiful Taylor Lattimer, but he'd given up thinking he would ever actually meet her. When Grandmother Marilee was still alive, she would sit on the porch in the evenings and tell him stories about her childhood or about the war or about her children when they were still young and at home. Almost always, Taylor was a star player in the stories. Everyone seemed to love her—in spite of her marrying a Yankee before the war was even over. Now he would get to see for himself if she was all he'd been told.

"I must have been about thirteen when she was here last, Pop. It was the summer before Martin died. She came here before she went to Europe. What a wonderful summer. She and Mother . . ." Erin's voice faded.

Pop nodded. "They were a pair. All those years they lived thousands of miles apart, and they were still as close as ever. I know it hurt Taylor a great deal not to have been here for . . . for Marilee's funeral."

"Why didn't she come?" Adam asked, unconsciously seeking some flaw in this paragon of an aunt.

"Her own family was bereaved. Starr's baby was born prematurely. The child—a boy, I think—died at birth and Starr's life hung in the balance for a long time." Pop clapped his hands together as he sat up straight in his chair. "Here now. When did you say they'd be here? Are we to meet them in Atlanta? We'd best start making some preparations, don't you think?"

Erin laughed. "No, Pop, we're not to meet them in Atlanta. Aunt Taylor said they would be spending the night there and then would drive out the next day. I've told Mary to air the bedrooms in the east wing and to open the east drawing room. I don't know what else we can do until they get here and we know how long they're going to stay."

"Well, at least we must plan a feast befitting the occasion."

"I'll see to it, Pop."

Adam forced a smile. "While you two are making all these plans, I'm going to excuse myself. I've got some briefs to look over and then I need to take a ride to look over the south field."

"But you haven't finished your pie," Erin protested.

"Save it for me. I'll have it after supper."

Adam escaped to his study before the frown was evident on his brow. Where on earth were they going to get the money to entertain these people? They'd just barely scraped by with last year's crop, and at this point, his law profession was more a liability than an asset. He was too new and untried. His name meant something in Bellville because he was a descendent of the founding family, and besides, there had almost always been a Bellman attorney in town. But in Atlanta, where he must prove himself before he could succeed, he was just another new lawyer.

He sank into the chair behind the large desk, then swiveled around to face the window. Why did he try to fool himself? It wasn't just the lack of money that plagued him. He didn't *want* to be a back-country lawyer in Bellville or even someone important in Atlanta. He wanted more. He wanted to join a firm like Houseman and Cheavers, or Clemons, Smith and Horace in New York and work with brilliant men of business and finance whose daily decisions affected the lives of millions.

Even as his pulse quickened at the thought, he felt ashamed of himself. He ran his fingers through his brown hair as he turned his chair back around, then held his head in his hands as he leaned his elbows on the desk top. After all that Pop and Erin had done for him, how could he think of deserting them? Was he really so heartless?

"They'd never understand," he said aloud.

And how could he expect them to? They had given themselves completely to assure him a wonderful childhood and a sound education. Now it was time for him to give something back. He'd just have to forget his dreams and learn to be content with what work he would have here. Being a big city attorney wouldn't ever be worth hurting the only two people he cared for in the world.

The days leading up to Taylor and her granddaughter's arrival flew by. Adam had never seen Erin and Pop in better spirits. He was even a little jealous over their undisguised zeal.

The motorcar that bumped its way up the long drive in the early afternoon on that Saturday of May 1908 was one of the few ever to do so. The chatter of the engine not only drew the family but every field hand and house servant into the front lawn to witness the unusual event. The driver stepped out and carefully offered a hand to the two ladies still inside. Adam watched from the doorway as they alighted and turned to face the family waiting on the portico.

Both wore large hats, their motor veils hiding their faces from view. The taller was dressed in a light blue blouse and darker linen skirt. The smaller was wearing a violet-colored traveling dress made of fine lawn. Without being able to see their faces, Adam was hard pressed to guess which was the older and which the younger of the two, but Erin seemed to know. She rushed down the steps, her arms held out to the woman in blue.

"Aunt Taylor! We're so happy to have you here again."

Their hands clasped a moment.

"Come in. Come in. You must be weary. Our roads aren't exactly made for motoring out this way."

"So we discovered," the voice said from behind the veil.

As Erin led the way up the steps, Taylor and granddaughter unfastened the netting from around their necks in unison and lifted them over their hats. Adam stared at the youthful looking woman who he knew was several years older than Pop. He couldn't believe she could look so young.

"Taylor, my dear. It's so good to see you." Pop took her hands and leaned forward to kiss her cheek.

Her smile showed genuine affection. "And you, Alan. You look wonderful. It's been so long . . ." She turned to the girl standing quietly behind her. "I want you to meet my granddaughter, Niki. Niki, come say hello to your Uncle Alan and Cousin Erin."

Niki stepped forward. "Hello, Uncle Alan."

"Pop. Just call me Pop. Everyone does." He held her face between his hands. "I'll be if she isn't the prettiest one yet. Taylor, she even outshines you, and I sure never thought that would happen."

"Move over, Pop, and let me get to meet her. I'm Erin. I can't tell you how wonderful it is to have you and your grandmother here. I must have been about your age when Taylor was here last. How old are you, Niki?"

"I'm seventeen."

"Honestly? But you're so tiny, I never would have guessed."

Adam had only been listening with half an ear ever since his eyes had locked on Niki. She was indeed beautiful and so small she reminded him of one of Erin's old porcelain dolls. She looked as if he could break her in half with one hand. Her heart-shaped face with dark, smooth skin and full, pink mouth was lovely, but it was her violet eyes that drew his attention. He stepped forward, wanting a clearer look at this Dresden doll.

Erin saw him and reached out to take his arm, drawing him even closer. "Aunt Taylor, this is Adam. Just look at how he's changed since you last saw him!"

Reluctantly, Adam broke his gaze to greet his aunt. Taylor's expression was somewhat wistful as she took his proffered hand. "Adam. I can hardly believe it. You're the image of my father, the first Martin Bellman, your great-grandfather. How proud he would be to see a man like you at Spring Haven."

"Thank you."

She smiled, letting her eyes sweep over everyone on the veranda. "I can't tell you how wonderful this place looks to me. No matter how old I get or how long I stay away, it's still home."

"Then let's get inside so you can look around," Erin said as she took her once again by the arm. "Of course, things are a bit run down. We're not the richest members of this family, but we do all right and stay happy." Her chatter faded as they disappeared into the house.

Adam turned again toward Niki, but Pop was already offering his arm to her. "If you don't mind keeping company with an old badger like me, I'll be glad to show you around, Niki."

"Thank you, Uncle . . . Pop. I'm very eager to see everything, and I'd love to have you be the one to show me."

"Come along, Adam," Pop said to him.

For some unexplainable reason, Adam was feeling irritable. "No thanks, Pop. You go on. I've got a lot of work to go over in my study. I'll see everyone again at supper."

"Suit yourself."

Niki loved everything about Spring Haven. In her eyes, there was no shabbiness, only an elegant aging. Taylor had a story to go with every room, and Niki was drawn into the past with ease. She could see the drawing room filled with girls in hooped skirts, dancing and flirting with young men who would soon be off to war. She could envision her grandmother as a beautiful young bride, gliding down the curved staircase, dressed in white satin and pearls. She sensed the sadness of death and the joy of new life that had touched the house through the years. She knew without a doubt that she was going to love her stay here, even if it was a delaying tactic before she could reach New York.

Taylor and Erin were still in the nursery as Pop escorted Niki back down the stairs and into the east drawing room. "Tell me about your parents. How are Rory and Netta?"

"They're well. Da works hard but they both love the ranch. My brother, BJ, and his wife help out too."

Pop scratched the bald spot on top of his head. "It's hard for me to imagine the two of them with children of their own. As grown up as you are, I mean. Your mother was about your age when I last saw her. What a sad time it was when she left here. Rory married to Megan and Brenetta brokenhearted because of that scoundrel, Stuart Adams."

"Mother was in love with another man?" Niki couldn't believe it. Her parents were too perfect together.

"Well, maybe I shouldn't have said anything."

"But you must tell me now."

Pop looked uncomfortable. "Suppose I should make you ask Taylor."

"Pop!"

"All right. It shouldn't be a secret. Your mother was engaged to Stuart Adams, a fellow from over Charleston way. Loved him, she did, 'til she found out he was only after her money. Like to broke her heart, but she did a smart thing in turning him out. She could've married him anyway." Pop shook his head. "And then there was Rory, in love with Brenetta but tricked into marrying Megan."

Niki was intrigued. "How was he *tricked* into it?"

"What are you two so intent about?" Erin asked as she and Taylor entered the room.

"Gram, is it true? Was Da in love with Mother but tricked into marrying cousin Megan?"

Taylor's eyes widened as she turned her gaze on Pop. "Alan, have you been spreading family gossip to Niki already?"

"Well, I . . ."

"I can remember when you were the quiet newcomer. Never much to say. Why, remember when Brent and I arrived to meet you that first time? I liked you right off. You and that lopsided grin of yours."

"Gram," Niki interrupted, "you're changing the subject."

"It's true, Niki," Taylor answered with a sigh. "Rory was very much in love with Netta, but your mother still thought of him as an older brother. Megan got him drunk —you know he never drinks—and tricked him into proposing marriage. Being an honorable man, Rory wouldn't have considered not keeping his end of the bargain. That's really all there was to it."

"That might be all there was to it, Gram, but it's something I didn't know before. I think our visit here could be very enlightening. Just think of all the family secrets I may be able to uncover during our stay!"

Taylor laughed. "Knowing you, Niki, whatever you can't uncover, you'll probably imagine."

Everyone else laughed, too, and the conversation wandered in another direction. When the subject became cotton crops, Niki couldn't keep her mind from straying elsewhere, and when Pop mentioned Adam's name, her thoughts stayed with her cousin even as their words continued.

Niki had grown up around more men than women. Her father, her brothers, the ranch hands—she was no stranger to the male sex. But there was something about Adam that had made her feel strange and unsure of herself from the first moment their eyes met. There was nothing unusual about his light brown, wavy hair which he wore neatly trimmed and parted on the side. She liked the way his light blue eyes had looked at her, and his smooth-shaven, tanned complexion was attractive, but neither of these attributes was extraordinary. Certainly he was handsome. Yet there was more to it than that. Perhaps his height was a factor. He must be nearly a foot taller than she was, and his shoulders were broad, the muscles of his arms well-defined beneath the white shirt he had worn. Her eyes glanced toward the doorway as she wondered where he was now.

Soft candlelight flickered, casting a gentle glow over the family as they gathered in the dining room for supper. The long ebony table had been polished to a high sheen, and its surface reflected the warmth of the gathering.

Adam took his place at the head of the table. Erin sat to his right with her step-father seated beside her. Taylor was seated on Adam's left, and Niki sat across from Pop.

"Adam tried to tell me that I deserved the place at the head of the table," Pop said as the food began to be served, "but this table is so long I felt lost at the other end. I like this arrangement much better."

"I agree with you, Alan," Taylor said, "but I also understand what Adam was trying to say. The Bellmans owe a great deal to you for what you've done at Spring Haven. You've poured your life into it."

"Taylor, my dear, I didn't do anything unusual. I loved Marilee and I love Spring Haven. I just did what needed to be done. Heaven knows, without your financial help, we would have lost it years ago."

"It was never enough. Philip, Marilee, you, Martin—every one of you was too stubborn to let me help the way I wanted to."

"You know how the Bellmans felt about Yankee money," Pop answered with a shrug.

Taylor's voice was tinged with sadness as she replied, "The war ended years ago, Alan."

"But it hasn't been forgotten."

There was a long silence, fraught with sensitive undercurrents. Niki glanced from face to face.

"Goodness," Erin interjected at last, "we're letting our meal get cold. Pop, pass Niki some of this gravy. I'm sure she's never had anything so good back in Idaho." As the bowl crossed the table, she added, "Tell us about Heart's Landing, Niki. We've been regaling you with stories about Spring Haven all day. Now it's your turn."

Niki smiled, glad to talk about something she knew so well. "I don't really know what to tell you. It seems so new and rugged after seeing this place. I've always felt that Heart's Landing was my family's past, that that's the farthest you'd have to look to know about us. Even Gram's stories didn't make me realize what it would be like here." Erin's look encouraged her to go on.

"Our house is large but nothing like this. It's two stories high and made of logs, but it's a far cry from what most people think about as a log cabin in the mountains. There are lovely carpets and picture windows. Of course, what Heart's Landing really is is a ranch. We raise beef cattle and horses. You really should visit us sometime so you can see for yourselves. The country's so different from what you see around here."

"You sound as if you love it very much," Pop said. "You'll probably be homesick before long and glad to get home."

"Oh, I'm sure I'll miss it, but it will probably be quite awhile before I get back there."

"Adam, that reminds me." Erin turned away from Niki to look at her nephew. "I forgot to tell you the good news. Taylor and Niki are going to stay with us until next spring. Isn't that wonderful? Now we'll have a whole year to show them off!"

Although Adam's reply was polite, Niki thought she detected something less than unbridled joy at the news, and suddenly, her own pleasure was snuffed out.

43

* * *

Adam Bellman was not a man prone to introspection. He didn't try to analyze why he felt his life was being invaded by his young cousin; he just knew he wasn't happy about her becoming a daily member of his family. The truth was, except for Erin, Adam was suspicious of all members of the gentler sex. It hadn't always been so. He had been raised in a home filled with love and laughter. His natural instincts had always been to trust people and to share himself openly. That had changed after he met Christina Medloe.

It was his first year at college, and his roommate introduced him to Christina. She was pretty—dark brown hair and eyes, full red lips, a dainty figure. He fell in love with her, and when she told him she loved him too, he thought the rest of his life would be perfect. It was, until he took her home with him in the spring. Seeing his home through her eyes was the first time he realized that it wasn't as beautiful as it could be, as it once had been. That, in fact, his family came close to being poor when compared to people like the Medloes. Their days at Spring Haven were strained, and when Adam took Christina back North, he knew it was over between them. She accused him of lying to her, of making her think he had a magnificent Southern plantation and that, as his wife, she would have been someone of importance in Atlanta, but the cruelest blow came when she accused him of using her to get to her father's money.

"Why, everyone must be laughing at me," she'd said to him that last night they were together. "I'm the only one that didn't know you were a fortune hunter. Thank goodness we hadn't announced our engagement. I would have died of shame."

He'd been fooled. She hadn't ever loved him. She'd been caught up in the romantic notion of what it would be like to live on a great plantation in Georgia. She hadn't cared about him or his family or his home, just the fact that he wasn't wealthy, that he wasn't what she had imagined him to be.

Adam had sworn then that he would never trust another woman, that he would never give one more notice than courtesy required. He'd poured all his energies into his studies, determined to become the best lawyer he could be. And that's just what he'd done. He had excelled at his studies and was recognized as the most dedicated and determined law student ever to come out of the law department. Only his friends who had known him in his first year of college recognized how he had changed, how he no longer laughed or knew how to relax.

Despite his secret desire to practice law in New York, he had come back to his family and the safety of his home. There was no danger of being proved a fool here, and he could always trust Erin and Pop.

He hadn't counted on his home being invaded by this attractive little cousin of his. He didn't like the way Niki made him feel. The way he was aware of how she talked with her hands. The way he noticed her smile and her bubbling laughter. The way her perfume stayed with him even when she was nowhere near. He had shut himself away from females like her—like Christina —choosing instead an unfettered association with women of what was commonly called "easy virtue."

Now here was Niki. She was cheerful and friendly, apparently innocent and—worst of all—obviously very wealthy. He couldn't take the chance of caring for someone like her again. No woman would ever again revive the hurt he had felt after Christina.

CHAPTER 3

"**A**dam, may I disturb you for a moment?"

He looked up from the papers on his desk. Erin had opened the door just enough for him to see her face. He motioned her in.

"I know you're trying to get some work done, but I really felt I must speak to you." Erin sat in the high-backed chair across from him. "Aunt Taylor and Niki have been here two weeks already, and we haven't done anything special for them. I think it's time we planned a party." She paused a moment and then added, "And I think it's time you were a little more friendly, too. What's gotten into you?"

Adam frowned. "Nothing's 'gotten into me,' as you so quaintly put it. I've just been busy." He cleared his throat. "As for the party, if you feel it's something we must do, then by all means, do it. Just be careful of the money you spend. I'd like to impress them as much as anyone, but money is one thing we do not have a lot of at the moment."

"Why, Adam Bellman. I've never heard anyone sound so much like Dickens' Mr. Scrooge in all my life. It certainly isn't money that will impress Taylor Lattimer."

"I'm sorry, Aunt Erin. I guess I'm a bit worn out from going over these accounts. I didn't mean to take it out on you . . . or on Aunt Taylor."

Erin got to her feet and came around to the back of the desk. She laid her hand on his shoulder before kissing the top of his head. "I think you worry too much about everything, Adam. Why don't you forget these papers for a little while? Take a ride down to the river. Kick your shoes off. Go wading. Quit acting like an old man, Adam. You're allowed to have fun some of the time."

"Someone's got to worry about us, Aunt Erin."

"Well, it doesn't have to be you right now." She kissed his forehead one more time, then left him alone in the study.

Adam stared at the closed door. Perhaps she was right. Maybe a ride would clear his head. He'd been staring at the same sheets of paper for hours and didn't know anymore what they said now than when he'd begun.

He got to his feet abruptly and left the house, heading for the barn. Most of the stalls stood empty, a silent reminder of the days when Spring Haven bred the finest horses and had one of the largest stables in

Georgia. He opened a stall door and brought out the chestnut gelding, leading him toward the tack room. Once the animal was saddled and bridled, Adam leapt onto his back and rode swiftly out the door.

Away from the house, he nudged his willing mount into a gallop. Man and horse became like one as the wind rushed by them, pounding hooves raising clouds of red dust. By the time he began pulling back on the reins, the fresh air had whipped away the tension from Adam's neck and shoulders. He stopped and dismounted at the river's edge and stared across to the opposite bank.

Erin was right. He did need to get out. It had been a long time since he went riding just for the fun of it and not as a means of getting him some place to do more work. Maybe she was right about more than one thing. Impetuously, he sat on the bank and removed his shoes and socks. Picking up a few flat stones on the river's edge, he stepped into the chilly water and waded out a short distance. He took careful aim, then began skimming the rocks across the surface of the water, counting the number of times each one bounced before it finally disappeared.

His last stone sank to its watery grave after nine skips, and Adam felt quite pleased with himself. Suddenly something skimmed over the surface beside him, bouncing and skipping again and again before it sank. He looked around to find Niki at the water's edge, her skirts hiked up in one hand, her other hand on her hip.

"BJ taught me to do that when I was about seven years old. Did a pretty good job, didn't he?"

"Seems so." Adam made his way back through the river to the bank. "Here. Let me help you out," he said, offering her a hand and pulling her up onto shore.

"I've been out exploring. Everything is so different here. It makes you feel . . . oh, I wish I knew how to explain it. Settled. No, that's not it. Peaceful and important. Maybe even immortal." Niki smiled at him, her cheeks pink with pleasure, her expression one of shared joy. "You must know what I mean?"

For a moment, he knew exactly what she meant. He'd felt it himself, yet had never tried to put words to the feeling. As he stared at her, she blushed and dropped her eyes to his hand which was still holding hers. He let go.

"I've got to return to the house. I'm sure you'd prefer to walk back alone." He hadn't meant to sound so unwilling to spend time in her company.

"Yes. I would prefer to walk."

"See you at supper."

"Of course."

* * *

Niki vacillated between surprise and anger. What had she done to make him dislike her so? She watched him riding away, his back so rigid, and then thought of him as she'd seen him only moments before, pant legs rolled up, standing in the middle of the river, skimming rocks like a school boy instead of a respected young attorney. She liked him much better as the boy.

She reached down to pick up her shoes. As her fingers touched the cool ground, she remembered how he had held her hand and the odd feelings his touch had aroused in her. Even at the memory, she felt a strange fluttering in her stomach and her cheeks burned.

She shook off the unwelcome feelings. The day was too beautiful to spend worrying about her disagreeable cousin. Taking up her shoes, she started her walk back to the house.

Niki found Taylor and Pop sitting in the shade on the portico, drinking tall glasses of iced lemonade.

"There you are," Taylor called to her as she came up the steps. "Erin has been looking for you. She's all excited about a party she's planning for us."

Pop motioned to the chair at his side, and Niki sat down. "It's about time we had a party in this old house. It was made for them. These last years have been all too dismal for my liking."

Taylor patted his hand in understanding.

"You know the party I liked most of all?" Pop continued. "It was the costume party Marilee gave for Brenetta. I guess you and Brent weren't here, were you, Taylor? Still in London with Carleton. Say, how is that boy?"

Taylor laughed gaily. "He's no boy anymore, Alan. He's a doctor in Boise and has a large family of his own."

"Niki! Where have you been?" Erin cried from the doorway. "Come with me. I need your help."

Niki obeyed instantly, catching the excitement in her cousin's voice.

"You'll never guess what has happened! Adam says he wants us to give you a party. I'm so pleased and excited. It's been so very long since we even thought of entertaining. Of course, all my life money has been a bit of a problem, although we certainly are better off than a good many people." Erin smiled as she hooked her arm through Niki's and led her up the stairs. "You simply must help me plan everything even though you are the honored guest. I've never done anything like it."

Erin entered her own bedroom, Niki in tow. "Mama gave a few small affairs after Martin died that I can still remember. Most of them were to try to find me a husband, but I was much too plain to suit anyone. Besides, I was happy to stay here and take care of Pop and Adam.''

"Why, Erin. You're not plain at all.''

"Don't try to flatter me, Niki. I'm much too old for that nonsense.''

Niki would have said more in protest but was stopped as Erin threw open her closet door, revealing a multitude of dresses, many of them ball gowns made of fine satins and rich taffetas. Some even had hooped skirts.

"Amazing, isn't it?'' Erin asked as she pulled out one of gowns. "Aunt Taylor bought most of these for Mother. When pride wouldn't let her take any more money from your grandmother to help in the running of Spring Haven, then Aunt Taylor would send word to a dressmaker in Bellville and have her make up some new dresses for my mother. They meant so much to her, too. She did love pretty clothes.''

"But they all still look new.''

"Oh, some of them were never worn. Others she wore maybe once and then put them away . . . to keep for nice, she'd say.''

Niki took the midnight blue gown from Erin and walked to the mirror that stood near the closet door. She held the dress in front of her, the billowing fabric hiding her own simple white blouse and brown skirt. "My goodness, Erin. It's like stepping back in time.''

Erin sat on the edge of her bed, her face

alight with pleasure. Niki turned away from the mirror and looked at her. She had protested earlier when Erin called herself plain, and now she could see that what she had said was really true. While her cousin wasn't pretty, there was something unique and pleasing about her appearance at this moment.

"That's exactly what I thought," Erin said, disrupting Niki's musings. "Why not have a ball from out of the past? Any of Aunt Taylor's friends that are still alive probably remember the years around the Civil War better than they do yesterday morning. And any young folks that come would enjoy it too, if only as a lark. What do you think?"

Niki joined her on the bed. "I think it sounds wonderful, Erin. What can I do to help?"

They spent the afternoon together, furiously planning what they referred to as "the party of the century," and came down to supper with their spirits still soaring.

"Good evening, everyone," Erin said as they entered the dining room. "Wait until you hear all that we've planned!"

Niki stepped to her usual place and was surprised to find Adam holding her chair for her. She nodded to him, her eyes meeting his for only a moment before she turned to sit down. "Thank you," she whispered. The ridiculous fluttering started again in her stomach. When she looked up, she found Taylor watching her with a strange half-smile that Niki didn't understand.

"So, Erin, tell us what it is you're so excited about."

Erin was only too happy to pour out the details from their afternoon, and Pop and Taylor listened attentively. But when Niki looked toward Adam, she found him watching her instead. He wasn't smiling or frowning. His gaze seemed to ask a question that she didn't comprehend. There was nothing for her to do but drop her gaze as she'd done before.

The house had long since fallen silent, but Niki was still unable to go to sleep. With an exaggerated sigh, she shoved aside the sheet and got out of bed. She walked to the French doors that opened onto the balcony outside her room, and pushed them open, allowing the silver glow of the three-quarter moon to spill into her dark room, bringing with it a refreshing breeze. She stepped outside. The cool wood slats of the balcony floor felt good on her bare feet. Her loose-fitting nightgown whipped delightfully against her skin.

Reaching the railing, Niki stopped, staring up at the moon. "What are you looking at, Old Man?" she whispered to the luminescent orb. "Do you see us better than we see ourselves?" She smiled at her own silliness. Talking to the moon now. What next?

She allowed her mind to go blank, simply standing in the friendly night, sensing more than hearing the song of the river in the distance and the occasional call of a bird. She liked it here. She liked it here a lot. If she couldn't be in New York . . .

New York. It wouldn't be long until she was there. It was *really* going to happen. Someday she would walk out onto a stage to the acclaim of hundreds, maybe thousands, of people. Her imagination took over, and she bowed to the moon, her own personal spotlight. Of course, after her triumphant appearance at the theatre, there would be parties and dancing.

She curtsied to her imaginary partner. Taking a corner of her nightgown in her right hand, she began waltzing around the balcony, her eyes half-closed as she twirled and swayed to the music in her mind.

"I believe this is my dance."

"Oh!"

Her eyes darted open as her feet stopped their merrymaking. Adam stood before her, his face expressionless. He held out his arms for her, and she was drawn to them as if by a magnet. His eyes never left hers as he began guiding her expertly around the balcony. Her head began to spin as she returned his gaze, his face towering above her from his seemingly great height. She was incapable of thinking clearly. Time was meaningless. She had no idea how long they glided and twirled to the ghostly melody.

He stopped abruptly beside her open doors. Niki could feel her heart racing, yet she didn't seem able to draw a breath. When his arms released her, the breeze that had earlier seemed refreshing now felt cold, and she shivered. Adam placed one finger under her chin and held her head motionless as he lowered his lips to meet hers. There was a moment of surprise before a strange but sweet warmth flowed through her veins, making her knees weak.

His hand left her chin and his mouth released her lips as he stepped away from her. Unconsciously, she lifted her fingers to touch her mouth. Then she drew her breath in a tiny gulp, suddenly very much aware of the thinness of her nightgown and the nearness of Adam.

"Oh!" she gasped again and fled into her room, closing the door behind her before falling weakly onto her bed, so completely drained that she was asleep before she could begin to try to sort out what had just happened.

"Niki? Are you awake yet?" Taylor poked her head inside.

Niki opened her eyes slowly, motioning with one hand for her grandmother to come in. She sat up and stretched, then leaned against the fluffy pillows at her back while she lifted her hair off the back of her neck before letting it fall in a tangled disarray over her shoulders.

"I've never known you to sleep so late. I was afraid you were ill."

"Is it that late?" Niki asked, surprised.

"Indeed, yes. We've all had our breakfast and Adam has left for Atlanta."

Adam! The memory of his kiss hit her like an electric shock. "Atlanta?"

"Yes. It seems he had some sudden business come up, and he won't be back for several days."

"Gram? What do you think of Adam?" She tried to make the question sound casual.

"Think of Adam? Well, I certainly like him. He seems to be a very fine man."

Niki twirled a lock of her chestnut hair, staring hard at the reflected light in the dark shafts. "Sometimes he seems even older than Pop."

"He takes his responsibilities very seriously, Niki. He's got the plantation to take care of and a legal practice to establish. It can't be easy for him. And remember, he's grown up without brothers and sisters . . . or parents. He hasn't had the luxuries that you've had." Taylor gave her a stern look. "Is something wrong?"

"No," Niki replied as she shoved aside

the covers and dropped her feet to the floor. "I'm just curious about everyone here." She walked over to the closet and pulled a dark purple skirt and lavender blouse from the rack of clothes. She stepped behind the closet door and lifted the nightgown over her head, saying as she did, "Erin says she's never married because she's too plain. I think she believes she is, but I never think of her that way."

"No, I don't think many people would, though I suppose it's true. It's Erin's joy of life that makes her appear more attractive than she is. It was the same way with Alan. Maybe that's why the two of them are so close." Taylor paused long enough to walk over to Niki who was now seated at her dressing table. She took the brush from her granddaughter's hand and began untangling her thick mane. "Erin has always been so devoted to Adam, too. I can't imagine her wanting to leave either of them, even for a husband and family." Taylor looked at Niki's reflection. "She would certainly never want to step out on her own like you're planning."

Niki laughed aloud. The thought of Erin living alone in a big city seemed somewhat incongruous.

"Niki? Why haven't you told anyone about your plans?"

"I started to one of our first nights here, while everyone was at supper, but then I was interrupted and it never seemed to come up again." She twisted in her chair to look up at Taylor. "I decided it might hurt their feelings if they thought I'd just come as a means of getting to New York. Perhaps when we're ready to leave next spring, I'll tell them. I think I'd rather just let it be for now. Okay?"

Taylor nodded and placed the hairbrush back on the dresser. "It's your decision."

Niki got to her feet, feeling a special closeness with her grandmother. She raised her arms to hug Taylor and then planted a kiss soundly on her cheek. "You're terrific, Gram!"

"Why, thank you, Niki. I think you're terrific, too."

Over the next two weeks, Erin and Niki kept busy with the plans for the summer ball. They settled on a date in mid-June and began addressing invitations. Erin spent lots of time on the telephone, learning names of people who she should invite, old friends of Taylor's and young people who would have something in common with Niki. Carpets were hauled outside and the floors polished to a bright sheen. Taylor hired some gardeners to work on the lawns and more house servants to help with the cleaning. Even Pop got into the act at the supper table, arguing with everyone over the food that should be served. They were weeks of frenzied activity.

Niki had been so busy that she hadn't had time to think of Adam or the kiss he had left her with before going to Atlanta. In fact, the memory of it had dimmed until she almost believed it had never happened.

She was sitting in the shade of the veranda when he cantered up the long drive late in the afternoon. She saw him pull his horse to a sudden stop and then stare at the painters as they brushed a new white coat on the beautiful old manse. She saw his jaw stiffen.

Adam hopped from the saddle and strode toward her, taking the steps two at a time. "What on earth is going on here?" he demanded.

"They're painting." It seemed obvious enough to her.

"I can see that," he grumbled. "Where's Erin?"

"She's with Gram. They've gone into Bellville, but I expect them back soon."

Adam walked slowly down to the ground and turned to look up at the men on the balcony above him. He shaded his eyes with one hand, his mouth growing grimmer by the minute.

"What's wrong, Adam? Aren't you pleased to see the house being painted?" She couldn't begin to fathom what had upset him.

"What's wrong? Just *who* do you think's going to pay for it?"

"Gram, of course. She wanted to do it."

That only seemed to make things worse. Adam shot her a look akin to loathing, then grabbed his horse's reins and led him off to the stables.

Adam would have had a difficult time trying to explain why he was so angry and why he was taking it out on Niki. He'd wanted to get the place painted for so many years now, but there just hadn't been the extra money. The sacrifices had seemed to make sense when he was in law school. But now . . . now things should be getting better, yet they weren't. Maybe they never would.

He began brushing his gelding with vigor, muttering to himself all the while. Little by little, the anger faded until finally he sat down on a bale of straw with a sigh. "You know what, Banjo?" he asked the tired gelding. "My problem is envy. I'm jealous because Aunt Taylor can decide the place needs painting and just hire someone to do it . . . just like that." He snapped his fingers for emphasis.

That wasn't his only problem. There was Niki. He couldn't shake the memory of her, standing on the balcony, wearing that thin white nightgown, the breeze shaping the fabric to fit her lithe figure and the silver rays of the moon lighting the beautiful angles of her face and the soft, feminine curves of her body. From the moment she'd arrived, he'd been all too aware of her—the way she laughed, the way she talked, the way she moved. He was no pimple-faced, inexperienced bumpkin that she should be affecting him this way. Yet affect him, she did, until he could think of almost nothing else. He hated himself when he growled and grumbled at her, but it seemed to be his only defense against her natural charms. He wished he'd never kissed her. He had caught her by surprise, and the kiss had been innocent. Yet he had sensed the fire inside her, waiting to be kindled.

Well, it didn't matter. He would have to stay his distance. Adam Bellman had learned his lesson with women. He wasn't going to risk that kind of hurt again. She might seem innocent, but he had been wrong before. Besides, he had too much of his father and his grandfather in him. Pride was the family curse. Even if Niki did care for him and even if she weren't concerned that his side of the family wasn't wealthy like hers, he couldn't bear to have people thinking that he was only interested in her because of her money.

He couldn't help wondering, though, if things were different, if there just might have been something between them.

CHAPTER 4

Niki stood in front of the mirror in her grandmother's girlhood bedroom as the colored maid finished buttoning her dress up the back. She could almost imagine that she had been transported back through time, so complete was her transformation from twentieth century, independent young woman to a gentlewoman of the antebellum South.

Her dark hair was drawn back from her face, then fell down her back in tight ringlets. Scarlet ribbons were twined through the curls. Her matching red gown was cut low over her breasts and had such a tiny waist, Niki wondered if she dare breathe. The skirt was full, supported by what seemed like dozens of stiff petticoats. She had wisely refused to wear a hooped skirt, fearing she would sit down and find her skirt popping up over her head, revealing her undergarments to half the county.

"Niki, you look spectacular!"

She turned toward the bedroom door where Taylor was standing. "Thanks,

Robin Lee Hatcher

Gram. So do you." She looked at the mirror again. "I'm a bit nervous. I've been thinking how very secluded my childhood was. I've never been to anything like this before."

"Why don't you just think of it as opening night?" Taylor's smile was reassuring. "Come along. We should be with Erin when the guests begin to arrive."

Niki nodded. One last peek in the mirror, a lift of the chin, and she was ready to go.

Together they walked along the hallway and then descended the curving staircase. They were a striking pair, Niki in her bright red gown and Taylor dressed in blue, the same color as her eyes. Taylor had foregone the ringlets, choosing instead to wear her hair up, a diamond and sapphire tiara crowning the simple styling. Her gown was less full, and it showed to advantage her still youthful figure.

Pop and Erin were waiting for them in the shimmering entry hall. Electric lights had been banished for the party, and the tiled floor reflected the flickering candles that were burning everywhere. They had a few moments to compliment each other on their appearances before the first guests arrived.

Niki stood between Pop and Taylor, greeting stranger after stranger, until she was convinced that everyone, young and old, who lived within a hundred miles must have come. Music was playing in the west drawing room; it mingled with the buzz of conversation, creating a festive atmosphere.

Niki thought everyone must finally be inside, when Erin cried, "Here's Adam at last."

"Aunt Erin, Pop, you remember Melina Howard. Melina, this is my aunt, Taylor Lattimer, and my cousin, Niki O'Hara."

"We're pleased to meet you, Miss Howard," Taylor said as she took Melina's hand.

Niki only nodded, uncomfortably aware of her instant dislike of this woman leaning on Adam's arm.

A golden-haired beauty of about twenty-two, Melina stood at least six inches taller than Niki. Her brown eyes were rimmed with long, dark lashes that kissed her cheeks whenever she blinked. The bodice of her bright yellow gown was covered with sequins and cut to accentuate her voluptuous bust, and the silky folds of the skirt clung to her hips in a somewhat suggestive manner. She had obviously chosen to dress to please the men who would see her rather than in keeping with the nostalgic theme of the party.

"I'm happy to meet you, Mrs. Lattimer. And Niki, you're every bit as cute as Adam told me you were." She turned accusing eyes on Adam. "But, really, darling. She's much more grown up than you made her

sound. She's hardly a child any more."
Turning to Niki again, she added, "We
must find time to chat later. If I can ever
get a moment away from Adam. He *does*
like to monopolize my time."

Niki blanched, then reddened. "Of
course," was all she could say in reply.

Adam nodded to Niki and Taylor, then
escorted Melina into the west drawing room
where couples were beginning to dance.
Niki's gaze followed them, her eyes
shooting darts of hatred at the departing
woman's back.

"Miss O'Hara? May I have the pleasure
of a dance with you?" A young man she had
met earlier stood beside her. He bowed
gallantly from the waist.

She took his proffered arm without hesi-
tation. "I'd be delighted."

As soon as they entered the drawing
room, Niki's eyes found them. Melina was
pressed tightly against Adam, her head
tilted back so she could stare adoringly at
his face as they glided around the floor.
They moved as if they had danced together
many times before. Niki didn't know why
that thought made her even more angry,
but it did.

She forced herself to smile at her partner
as she tried to remember his name. His
hand on her back helped to guide her as
they, too, began to move to the soft music,
but she couldn't keep her mind on the

music or her partner. Fortunately, she had been well-schooled in the art of dancing, and she didn't have to concentrate to follow him, thus managing to keep from embarrassing herself by stepping on his toes or tripping over her skirts.

Every time she caught a glimpse of the woman in yellow, twirling around the room, her anger boiled anew. No longer a child, indeed! Is that what Adam had told her? And her so snide and self-assured, hanging on his arm for dear life. Even to someone as inexperienced as Niki, Melina's meaning had been clear—Stay away from him. He's mine.

Well, Niki certainly wasn't after *him*. She'd given him nary a thought in days. Who cared who Adam spent his time with? *She* certainly didn't, but she wasn't about to stand by and let that hussy put her down that way. Somehow she'd let Melina Howard know that she, Niki O'Hara, wasn't afraid of her.

The dance ended and Niki's partner escorted her back toward some chairs lining the wall. She thanked him and he left her without her ever remembering his name. But there was no shortage of dance partners for Niki. She was immediately asked to dance again, and every time a song ended, she found another gentleman waiting to take the last one's place. Finally, to escape them, she pleaded exhaustion and slipped outside.

The fresh air felt good. She hadn't realized just how stifling it had been inside. She leaned against one of the massive columns and closed her eyes, sighing.

"It can become tiring, can't it? Being fawned over by men, I mean."

As Niki opened her eyes to look at Melina, she wondered how she could learn to hate so quickly that soft, southern accent. She had always loved it in her grandmother.

"Even as much as I love to be in Adam's arms, I can only stand it so long before I need a breath of air." Melina stepped closer.

"Are you enjoying the party, other than that?" What else could she say?

"Oh, I think it's a very quaint idea. All these old folks remembering how it used to be. The South can't quite ever get over that. I wonder if we'll ever get into the twentieth century."

Niki felt trapped into making conversation. "Have you lived here all your life?"

"Oh, yes. I grew up in Atlanta. My father's a judge, and he's been very helpful to Adam. He knows a bright young man when he sees one. Adam is going to go a long way in his profession. Of course, it doesn't hurt him to have the daughter of a respected judge by his side either."

"I'm sure it doesn't."

"It's been awfully difficult for Adam,

these past few years. He's had to finish his studies and try to keep this old place from falling down around his ears too. It's been quite a millstone around his neck, I can tell you." Melina leaned forward, whispering in a confidential tone, "I've tried to tell him he should get rid of it and move into the city where he can associate more often with the people who can help him with his career."

Niki moved off down the steps, putting some distance between them. She stood with her back towards Melina. "But what would become of Erin and Pop? This is their home."

Melina sniffed. "Adam certainly can't be expected to worry about them the rest of his life. Besides, I'm not going to live out here once we're married, and they're not going to live with us in Atlanta. They'll have to take care of themselves, no matter what."

The pain in her chest was very real. "I didn't know Adam was engaged."

"Well, we haven't ever formally announced it, but there's been an understanding between us for several years. Simply everyone in Atlanta knows about us."

"I see."

"Adam, darling. I knew you'd come looking for me before long."

Niki turned back around to find Adam standing beside Melina at the top of the steps. She was thankful for the darkness of the night for there were unexplainable tears in her eyes.

"Niki," Adam said, a touch of a question in his voice, "everyone is looking for you inside."

"I'll be in after a while. I just needed some fresh air."

Melina took hold of Adam's arm with both hands, then leaned forward to kiss his cheek. "Let's join the party, Adam. I think Niki wants to be alone just now."

Adam hesitated a moment, then allowed her to lead him back inside. There was something about the way Niki had looked and sounded that bothered him. She had seemed so small, standing there in the shadows of evening, and her voice had had a forlorn quality to it that nagged at him. He kept looking back over his shoulder to see if she'd come back inside yet.

"Adam, really! Stop being a mother hen over that girl."

He looked at Melina, not bothering to hide his irritation.

She lifted one very attractive eyebrow. "Why, Adam. I realize that girl has all the money in the world you would need, and of course, I couldn't blame you if you went after some of it. No one would. But she couldn't possibly be of the help to your career that my daddy can be." She stroked his jaw with her finger, a suggestive smile on her lips. "I'd get worried, but I've always known you weren't looking for a rich wife, no matter how young and pretty."

"Melina, you really are unpleasant."

She leaned closer, letting her breast brush against his arm. "Only sometimes, love. Only sometimes."

He wheeled away from her, angry strides carrying him quickly to the back of the house where he took refuge in his study. He would never have thought it possible for him to come so close to striking a woman, no matter how good the reason. If only what she'd said hadn't been true. He *was* interested in his cousin—and more than just a little so. Avoiding her didn't do any good; he just daydreamed about her. But Melina was right. Folks would say he was after her money, and his pride wouldn't allow that.

"So how much pride do I have now with Melina?" he asked himself aloud, and was disgusted with himself as he faced the truth.

Melina's virtue, or lack of same, was no secret in Atlanta, but her father was a prestigious judge, someone who could make or break an attorney's career in Georgia, and when Melina set her cap for Adam Bellman, Judge Howard had let his approval be known. A woman like Melina was no danger to Adam's emotions, so it had been easy for him to comply. He had fallen into the pattern of calling on her whenever he was in Atlanta. There were no risks with her; they understood each other. He provided her with a respectable escort, and she provided him with her body without emotions clouding the issue. Besides, his relationship with Judge Howard's daughter wasn't hurting his career any, either.

Adam sank into the chair behind his desk, dropping his head into his hands as self-disgust washed over him. And he thought he had so much *pride*.

"Adam? Is something wrong?"

He straightened at his aunt's voice. He cleared his throat as he stood up. "Not anything I don't plan to change." He had the feeling as he looked into her eyes that Erin knew exactly what—or rather, who—he was referring to.

"You know, dear, that Pop and I are always proud of you. There's nothing you could do to make us love you more or love you less."

"Aunt Erin, I think I've been wrong about a lot of things for a long, long time."

She met his gaze, her expression serious, then smiled in satisfaction. "Come back out and join us, Adam. We've missed you."

Niki excused herself while the party was still in full swing, telling her grandmother that she wasn't feeling well.

"Do you need me to come with you?" Taylor asked.

"Heavens, no! It's just a headache, Gram. I'll go to bed and be fine in the morning. You stay and enjoy yourself with all your old friends."

She climbed the stairs, her shoulders bent forward in total fatigue, an emotional exhaustion that was something new for her. Though she didn't realize it, her headache had begun the moment Adam and Melina went back into the house, leaving her standing alone in the dark. When she finally forced herself to come back inside, she couldn't keep herself from looking for them, but they were nowhere to be seen. She hated to imagine where they might have gone.

Niki spent a restless night, tossing and turning, pulling the covers this way and that, too warm, then too cool, until daylight finally crept into her room, allowing her to get up at last, more exhausted now than when she'd gone to bed the night before. Her spirits were still very low, and she gave little care to what she pulled from the closet to wear. She ran a hasty brush through her hair, then went downstairs to see what could be found to eat.

It was amazing how much work the servants had accomplished while everyone else was abed. Everything was in its usual place. There was no sign left of the great crowd that had milled through the house only a few short hours before.

Niki wasn't the first one up, however. She found Erin already seated at the dining room table, sipping a cup of hot coffee.

"Good morning, Niki. I didn't think I'd have any company so early."

"Neither did I." Niki helped herself to a cup of coffee, then sat down across from her cousin. "Did many guests choose to stay over with us?"

"No. Everyone left last night except Melina, and Adam took her home this morning."

"Already? But it's so early. Besides, I thought she would be staying longer."

Erin smiled. "So did she."

Niki's face came alive as she returned Erin's smile with one of her own. Suddenly, the day seemed to promise better things than her restless night would have led her to believe. "I think I'll take a walk."

"All right, dear. Enjoy yourself."

The azure expanse overhead was trimmed with lazy white clouds. The sweet, melancholy phrase of a meadowlark wafted through the trees as if to bid her good morning. She walked with enthusiasm down the long drive, her arms swinging at her sides. Once she held her arms out, as if to embrace the world, and laughing at her own foolishness, she threw her head back and began twirling around and around until she was too dizzy to continue.

She loved him. It was that simple. Why had she been so blind to it? She'd thought she understood all about men, just because she'd grown up around so many of them. But brothers and ranch hands couldn't prepare a girl for this kind of feeling. She hugged herself and resumed walking.

How could she have misinterpreted her own feelings so completely? Just like last night. Niki had thought she didn't like Melina because Melina had treated her like a child, when the real problem was that Niki was jealous. She didn't want to see Adam dancing with someone else, especially someone as beautiful and sophisticated as Melina. She wanted to be the girl he danced with. She wanted to be in his arms, just like that night when they'd danced on the balcony outside her room.

Her discovery could have left her sad, remembering the things Melina had said about her and Adam, but something had gone wrong or he wouldn't have taken her back to Atlanta so early in the morning. Niki was new to this game, but she was a quick learner and she was stubborn. When she wanted something, she went after it with a singleness of purpose. The next time she saw Adam, she would see him with different eyes, and she would learn what she needed to do to make him notice her.

* * *

"Gram, how did you know you were in love with Grandpa?"

Niki and Taylor were riding in the surrey down a shady lane. Taylor had been spinning tales of her girlhood, pointing out places of memory to Niki as they moved along, the friendly clip-clop of the horse's hooves on the dusty road making it easy to forget that things were so different now, that in the cities the streets were filled with noisy motorcars and telephones rang in homes all over the country.

"How did I know?" Taylor pondered the question.

"Did you know him very long? Did you just like him to begin with or was it love at first sight?"

Taylor laughed. "No, Niki. I don't think love at first sight would be an accurate description. Oh, we were attracted to each other, but we seemed to disagree on everything. We argued so often." The smile faded as she continued. "Perhaps I loved him long before I knew I loved him. It's rather hard to remember. It seems like I just woke up one day knowing he was the man I would always love."

"But how did you know what love *felt* like? It can't be the same as loving your parents or your brothers."

Taylor turned her alert blue eyes on Niki. "Is there a reason for these questions?"

"Gram, I'm going to be an actress. I've got to know about love, and since I've never been in love, I've got to ask someone." Her voice rose in protest. "Do you realize I've never had a beau? I've been on cattle drives with men galore. I've served them meals and washed their scrapes and bruises and mended their shirts, but I've never walked hand in hand with someone in the moonlight. I . . ." She stopped, appalled at her outburst.

"Niki, my dear, you're right. I hadn't given much thought to it. You haven't had many opportunities to meet suitable young men. Perhaps we should go in to Atlanta to stay for a while, give you a chance to meet more people your own age." Taylor pulled back on the reins, stopping the surrey. "I forget that I'm an old woman, happy to sit around and reminisce about the past while you'd rather be living in the present."

"No, Gram. I really don't want to leave Spring Haven right now."

"Well, we'll see." Taylor clucked to the horse, and they started forward again. "We'll see."

When they returned home, they discovered Adam in the drawing room with Erin and Pop. It had been five days since the party, days of anxious waiting for Niki until he returned from Atlanta.

"Adam." She felt both joyful and shy as she spoke his name in greeting. Her hand went to her hair, nervously checking to make sure all was in place.

Niki didn't notice her grandmother's shrewd observance and quick assessment.

"We've missed you, Adam," Taylor said as she sat down in a chair near the window. She looked absentmindedly around her lap and at the floor as she spoke, then turned toward Adam. "I seem to have misplaced one of my gloves. Adam, would you mind checking the buggy to see if I left it there? I would hate to lose it."

"Of course, Aunt Taylor."

As soon as he'd left the room, Taylor stood up and looked around again. On the seat of the chair was the missing glove.

"How silly of me!" she cried, shaking her head. "I really am getting old. Niki, go tell Adam I found it. I don't want him out there searching for something I had all the time."

Niki complied at once. She hurried out of the house and across the yard toward the stable. She found Adam searching under the seats of the surrey.

"Adam! Never mind. Gram found it."

He straightened up, turning to face her.

"She must have dropped it as she was sitting down. It was on her chair."

They stood looking at each other.

Adam nodded. "I'm glad it wasn't lost."

"So am I."

Again the silence.

"Niki . . ."

She liked the way he spoke her name.

" . . . I never did tell you how lovely you looked the night of the party."

Niki felt a rush of pleasure. "Thank you, Adam."

"I had hoped we'd get to dance together."

"I'd hoped so, too," she answered a bit breathlessly.

"There'll be other dances. You must promise to save the first one for me."

Her heart sang at his simple request. So this was what it felt like to be in love!

CHAPTER 5

I t wasn't easy for Adam to change his thinking about women. He had been convinced for too long that they were better thought of only in passing, something pretty to behold and play with and then be forgotten. Melina certainly hadn't been the one to tempt him to change his ways. Now there was Niki, and he wanted to be different. He wanted to trust her. He wanted to care, even if he was proven a fool once again.

Still, he had to proceed with great caution. He was unsure of his own judgment in matters of the heart. Besides, Niki seemed so different from anyone he had ever known before. She was young and inexperienced. He didn't want to frighten her. So he pursued her affections with great care, afraid that he might scare her away if he moved too fast, never dreaming that he had already won her love.

The summer months proceeded slowly for Niki, tortured as she was by uncertainty.

Adam sought her out often. They went for walks together. He showed her his favorite boyhood haunts. He even took her to his secret fishing hole. They shared stories, learning about each other's growing years. They were often heard laughing, but there were also times when they sat in silence, learning to read each others' moods. Sometimes Niki was convinced that his feelings for her were special. At other times, he seemed to hold himself away from her, leaving her to wonder what she had done wrong or if he really cared at all.

Worst of all were the days when he went into Atlanta. She would wander around Spring Haven, a forlorn look on her face, as she imagined him dining with Melina. She could just see that blonde wench batting her eyes seductively at him over a glass of wine while her father, the noble judge, excused himself and went to his study, leaving poor Adam to fight off Melina's advances.

There was no telling how long things might have continued in this same pattern if Taylor hadn't decided to take matters into her own hands.

Autumn had arrived, sweeping away the warm, rose-colored hues of summer and replacing them with blazing oranges, crimsons and golds. Mornings were crisp, the days clear and mild. Crops were being harvested. The scent of new-mown hay lingered delightfully in the air. Fields were turned under to await the spring planting. Adam had been in Atlanta for nearly two weeks, and with each passing day, Niki became more maudlin and snappish.

They were at the breakfast table when Taylor announced that they were going into Atlanta. "All of us," she added emphatically. "This family needs an outing. Pack your best things, Erin. We'll take in some plays and the opera while we're there."

"When do we leave, Gram?"

"We ought to be able to leave by Wednesday, don't you think, Alan?"

Pop knew he was trapped. "I don't suppose this place will fail if I'm away a few days. I expect I can have things in order by then." He leaned toward Taylor, whispering, "You're a sly one, you are."

"Thank you, Alan. I'll accept that as a compliment."

Atlanta was a city of the old and the new. Fiercely proud of its past, yet ready and willing to meet the future head-on. A growing, metropolitan city, it was still a country town, drawing its strength and character from the red clay hills, the forests and the mountains, from the very land that gave it life. A city that had refused to die, even when ravaged by war. A city that had risen again from the ashes.

Niki watched her grandmother's face as

the motorcar puttered along Peachtree Street. Occasionally she would speak, telling them about houses that had once stood there and the families that had lived in them. There were new houses, large, beautiful houses, but they were not the same.

"I've never gotten over it," Taylor said, turning her eyes away. "No matter how many times I've come back here, I still expect to see the Mason home standing in that spot, with its white fence and rose-filled lawn and Sophia Mason in the doorway, waving her kerchief at me. I guess it's true. The older you get, the more you live in the past."

"Don't be silly, Gram. You're not old."

"Thank you, dear. I'm forever grateful for your devotion." Taylor patted Niki's hand and chuckled, her good spirits returning.

A young man with sandy hair and spectacles was waiting for them outside their hotel. "Mr. Montgomery. Miss Bellman."

"Hello, Sam," Erin replied in greeting. "I didn't expect to see you here."

"Mr. Bellman asked me to wait for you and see if there was anything you needed. He can't get away from court right now. Big case, you know. He said he'll meet you here for supper."

"No, Sam, there's nothing we need,

except to freshen up from our drive." Erin turned toward Niki and Taylor, extending her hand toward them in introduction. "Sam, I'd like you to meet my aunt, Mrs. Lattimer, and my cousin, Miss O'Hara. This is Sam Mitchell, Adam's clerk and a good friend of the family."

"Pleased to meet you, Mrs. Lattimer, Miss O'Hara. Here, let me help you with your luggage."

"Thank you, Mr. Mitchell," Taylor replied, and led the way into the hotel lobby.

Sam didn't set down the bags for a bellboy to bring up, instead carrying them himself into their suite. "Are you sure there's nothing I can do for you until Mr. Bellman arrives?" he asked, looking at Niki hopefully.

"What? Oh. No, there's nothing." Niki's reply was far from attentive as she looked around the pleasant sitting room.

A bit dejected, Sam turned to go. "Well, if there's nothing, I'll get back to . . ."

Niki turned suddenly. "Did Adam say what time he'd come?"

"No, Miss O'Hara. Just that he'd come as soon as he could."

"Oh."

Taylor came out of one of the bedrooms. "Niki, if you don't want Adam to get here and find you still covered with road dust, you'd best get a move on."

Niki glanced down at her rumpled skirt and knew her grandmother was right. She wanted to look her very best for Adam. Without so much as a goodbye for Sam, she rushed into the other bedroom and began sorting through the dresses she'd brought with her.

Taylor was alone in the sitting room of their suite when Adam arrived. Though she had heard sounds of activity, and even anxiety, coming from Niki's room, she had not seen her granddaughter in over two hours.

"Sit down, Adam. I'm sure Niki won't be much longer. I think Alan lay down to rest until you got here, but I'll ring Erin and tell her you're here."

"Why don't you wait, Aunt Taylor? No point in making Pop get up until Niki's ready."

Taylor had been about to reach for the telephone but agreed with Adam. "You're right. No need to rush." She settled back in her chair and fixed an interested gaze on Adam. "How is that trial of yours going?"

"It's difficult to tell," he replied with a shrug, but the frown on his brow revealed worry.

"Who is the judge?"

"Judge Howard."

"I thought as much by the look on your face." She chuckled as he looked at her, then ran a hand over her silver hair. "I didn't earn this gray hair without learning to be a little perceptive, Adam Bellman. You *have* stopped calling on Miss Howard, haven't you?"

Adam nodded.

"And the Honorable Judge Howard is not pleased. No doubt his daughter has had a few unpleasant things to tell him about your treatment of her."

"No doubt."

Taylor leaned forward, her expression very serious. "Tell me truthfully, Adam. What is this going to mean to your career?"

"It won't help it any," Adam answered, his voice grave. He got to his feet and walked over to the window looking out on the busy street below. "I suppose most of my work will be what I can get in Bellville after this is over. If that's not enough to keep me busy, there's always a million things that need to be done at Spring Haven."

Taylor followed him across the room and stood by his side. She gazed outside, letting silence take the place of conversation and giving her nephew time to think about what he'd just said. Finally, she sighed, "You know, Adam. I've lived a lot of years, seen a lot of things, known a lot of people. I've made more than a few mistakes of my own, mistakes I hope I've learned from. Somewhere along the way, I also learned to pay attention to my intuition about folks. I could be wrong, but I have a feeling you want more from life than an office in Bellville and overseeing the plantings and harvests at Spring Haven."

"I love Spring Haven!" Adam protested.

She placed a hand on his arm. "Of course, you do. So did I. I still do. But my life had to be lived elsewhere for me to find real happiness. I don't mean I couldn't have been happy at Spring Haven, but if I'd refused to leave there, for whatever reasons, I wouldn't have led the wonderful life I did." Despite his dark frown, Taylor wasn't about to let the matter drop. "Adam, I'm not just an old busybody with nothing to do but pry into your private feelings. I care about the happiness of my family, and you *are* family to me, no matter how distant." She paused, then asked, "Why don't you tell me what you'd really like to do, if you were on your own and Spring Haven didn't exist?"

Perhaps it was the softness of her voice, the genuine concern written in her face, or the wisdom shining in her dark blue eyes. Whatever it was, the frown disappeared from Adam's brow as he began to speak. "If it was just me . . . Well, I guess I'd be in New York. I've always liked that city," he smiled at her, "even if it is filled with Yankees. I was in law school with the grandson of Jonathon Houseman of Houseman and Cheavers. He offered to ask his grandfather to consider me for a spot with the firm, but . . ."

"Gram, I . . ."

At Niki's voice, Taylor and Adam turned around. She had stopped in the doorway, her eyes on Adam. Her dark blue evening gown of satin and draped chiffon had an empire waistline and a fitted skirt with a long train, showing to advantage her slim, feminine figure. The bodice revealed only a modest amount of throat and shoulders. Around her neck was a simple gold locket. Her dark brown hair was hidden beneath the enormous brim of her hat made of moonlight blue satin with a deeper blue under-brim and crowned with blue and violet ostrich feathers and a pale blue buckle.

Adam came forward and bowed deeply from the waist. "Miss O'Hara." He offered her his elbow. "Will you do me the honor of dining with me this evening?"

A pink blush brightened Niki's cheeks. "I would love to, Mr. Bellman."

"I'll let Erin know we're ready," Taylor said, though she knew neither would hear.

Niki was in a state of euphoria throughout supper. Adam was attentive and charming, telling her lighthearted stories about bumbling young attorneys and dour old judges. She ate little, too captivated by his nearness to be hungry. It was the best night of her life.

But Niki's evening of joy was not to be a long one. Their meal was only half over when she noticed Adam stiffen as he looked across the room. She followed the gaze. Entering the dining room on the arm of a distinguished, white-bearded gentleman was Melina Howard.

Her gown of gold lame clung to her ample bosom and rounded hips. She held the end of the gown's train in one hand, revealing gold slippers and a well-turned ankle. The brim of her fashionable hat exceeded the width of her shoulders and was topped with towering masses of gilded feathers and flowers. She paused a moment, letting her eyes sweep over the diners until they rested on Adam. A lazy smile lifted the corners of her mouth, and she nodded in his direction.

"Scandalous," someone hissed behind Niki, but she didn't hear them. She was only aware of Adam and his gaze that followed Melina as she crossed the room and took her seat at a table.

Time began to drag as Niki fought to keep herself from looking in Melina's direction. When she couldn't resist any longer, her gaze was met by one of victory in the eyes of the woman across the room.

"Excuse me, sir. Are you Mr. Bellman?" the maitre d' asked as he stopped at their table.

"Yes."

"There's a call for you, sir. If you'll come

with me, I'll show you to the telephone."

"Thank you." Adam got to his feet, saying to the others, "I shouldn't be long." Adam followed the headwaiter through the tables and into the foyer.

The maitre d' pointed to a far wall. "Over there, sir. The one on the right."

Adam picked up the receiver. "Hello?"

There was no reply.

"Hello?" he said again. "Hello."

"Is there a problem, darling?"

Adam stood still a moment, then placed the receiver back in its cradle. "Is this some sort of joke, Melina?" he asked as he turned around.

"How else was I to get to talk to you?"

"I think we've already said everything we have to say to each other. I told you months ago that we're through. We were all wrong for each other, Melina. I'm sorry. It was my fault. I never should have let things go as long as they did, but there's really nothing more to be said. If you'll excuse me, I'm going back to my family."

Melina took hold of his wrist. "Adam, my love, don't you think you should reconsider what you're doing? Besides the fact that you have disappointed my father a great deal—and everyone knows it's not wise to do that—you have hurt my feelings terribly. But I am willing to forgive you." Her arms snaked up around his neck. "Very willing, darling," she whispered before she pressed her lips to his.

Adam simply waited, unmoving, until she released him. Then he pulled his handkerchief from his pocket and wiped his mouth with deliberation. "Excuse me, Miss Howard." He stepped around her and started back toward the dining room.

"Adam Bellman, don't you *dare* leave me like that!" Melina cried, but he ignored her and kept going. "You'll be sorry for this. My father will see that you regret it."

He was smiling as he approached the table. It had felt good, walking away from her as she sputtered like a wet hen. No matter what happened with Judge Howard, it had been worth it.

"Ladies, I'm sorry I kept you waiting," he said as he resumed his place at the table.

There had been a moment when she was ready to admit defeat as she watched Melina leave the dining room, the confident sway of her hips making Niki feel childish and inadequate. But meek acceptance of defeat was not something she was prone to. Perhaps he did only see her as his little cousin. Perhaps she had misread him, putting meaning into his words, his expressions, that weren't really there but which she wanted to be there. Still, if she was woman enough to pursue a career of her own, she was woman enough to try to win Adam's love. She might be proven a fool, but she wouldn't quit until she knew she'd lost.

"Excuse me a moment," Niki said.

She left the table in a hurry, not giving anyone a chance to ask where she was going. Winding her way through the tables, she tried to think of something to say to Adam that would explain why she had followed him. As soon as she entered the foyer, she knew she wouldn't have to say anything to him. They stood together at the other side of the foyer, Melina standing on tiptoe as she kissed Adam. Niki whirled away, anger erupting in her heart. Nothing she had ever experienced before had made her feel this way, know this kind of rage. She could gleefully scratch out the woman's eyes, and would, if she ever got the opportunity.

"I'm sorry, Gram," she explained as she returned to the table. "I thought I saw someone I met at our party this summer, and I wanted to say hello."

"Who was it?" Erin asked.

"No one. I was mistaken."

She looked up as Adam approached them. He was smiling, and she wasn't sure who she was angrier with, Melina or Adam.

They finished supper in silence, and then Adam ordered a cab to take them back to their hotel. Niki was the last one to be helped from the horse-drawn vehicle.

As he handed her down, Adam asked,

"Niki, would you like to take a walk with me before retiring?"

"Go ahead, dear," Taylor said before Niki could answer for herself, "but don't get chilled." After that, she couldn't very well refuse, even if she'd wanted to.

The moon and street lights dispelled the darkness, and they walked together in silence. Niki kept trying to think of something to say, something that would let Adam know that she was a woman that he could love, that she had more to offer him than Melina, but she was tongue-tied.

As they turned a corner, Adam stopped beneath the shadows of a large dogwood tree. His hand touched her upper arm. Her heart fluttered as she looked up at him, but she couldn't see his face. Standing so close to him in the dark, her heart pounding in her chest, she had a sudden vision of Melina kissing him and the smile he'd worn when he returned to the table.

"Niki, I'd like to ask you something."

Her heart skipped a beat, and the vision of Melina disappeared.

"We've become . . . good friends these past few months."

Was that all? Just *good friends?*

"Your grandmother said something to me this evening that made me think about some changes I need to make in my life. I'm hoping you'll tell me how you'd feel about it."

"About what, Adam?"

"I've been thinking of going to New York . . ."

"New York?" She couldn't believe it. It would be perfect if Adam could be in New York too. Then she would have everything in the world her heart desired.

"Yes. I've thought about it for a long time but with Melina . . . Well, the time wasn't right. Now things are different."

Melina! So that was it. He and Melina were going to New York. How could he? The anger she had felt when she saw Adam and Melina embracing was nothing to what she felt now.

"What do you think about me leaving here and going to New York?"

She could barely hide her fury as she fought to preserve some of her wounded pride. "What on earth makes you think I would care whether you stayed here or went to New York? I certainly can't advise you."

There was a long pause. She sensed Adam stiffen and then he stepped away from her. "I thought . . ." His words trailed away into silence.

She had thought he cared for her, but all the time he was just being kind to his little cousin. Friends! She didn't want to be his friend. He could go the the North Pole—or to the devil himself—for all she cared.

His voice was hard, tinged with bitterness when he spoke again. "I guess I *would* be better off to decide on my own. I've never found anyone I can trust as well.'' Adam took her elbow and turned them back toward the hotel. "It's getting late," he said gruffly.

Niki didn't reply.

CHAPTER 6

Stubbornness and tenacity were two of Niki's greatest assets, as well as two of her greatest faults. There was no way anyone was going to change her mind, and within a month, her grandmother had given up trying. They left for New York four months ahead of schedule.

Niki had never seen so many people in one place before. The train station was noisy, the people rushing in all directions. She looked around in amazement, her heart racing to keep pace with the pulse of her new city.

"Gram! Niki!"

She turned around at the familiar voice, her eyes searching the crowd until she spied Travis working his way toward them. Niki had been twelve when she had seen him last, and although he looked different in his dark business suit than he had in his denims and boots, which was how she remembered him, she had no problem recognizing the familiar dusky skin, dark hair and black eyes which were so like their father's.

"Travis!" She waved to him enthusiastically, and when he finally reached them, she threw herself into his welcoming arms with delight.

He kissed her cheek, then held her back from him. "Niki, I can't believe it. If you hadn't been with Gram, I'd never have known you." He released her and hugged Taylor. "Gram, you don't know how good it is to see folks from home." He offered an arm to each lady. "Come on. Let's get you out of here."

Niki couldn't stop staring as they drove through the streets of New York in Travis' handsome, chauffeur-driven Thomas Flyer. They were surrounded by motorcars, double-decker buses, and buildings taller than she had ever imagined.

"I've taken a home for you on Fifth Avenue. It's not as large as most of its neighbors, but I think you'll like it better than living in a hotel. Of course, I didn't expect you until spring so I didn't have a lot of time. If its not what you want, we'll find something else."

Taylor squeezed his hand. "Thank you, Travis. I'm sure we've put you to a great deal of trouble, coming so suddenly. I have every confidence that we'll be pleased with our accommodations."

Compared to many of the enormous and ornate residences they had passed, the three story, white brick house seemed a lit-

tle out of place, but both Taylor and Niki
were charmed. It had style and grace, something that was all too often overlooked by
the excessively wealthy.

The staff was waiting for them in the
entry hall, the women wearing black
dresses, white caps and aprons, and the
men in dark suits. The housekeeper, Mrs.
Mulligan, was a short, grim-faced woman of
about forty who looked like she could keep
an army in line. In contrast, Max Cohen,
the butler, was very tall and thin and wore a
tight, welcoming smile. Agnes Tiffany was
in charge of the kitchen and was, Travis
told them, the greatest cook in all New
York. His compliment was followed by a
pleased blush on the older woman's face.
Two maids, both in their early twenties,
were the last of the female members of the
staff. Pearl was the prettier of the two with
abundant auburn hair, dark green eyes, and
a smile that revealed straight, white teeth.
Fiona was obviously shy, her mousy-haired
head bobbing a hello as she lowered her
eyes to the floor. Last of all was Roger
Williams, the chauffeur, a pleasant but
rather nondescript fellow in his early
thirties.

Introductions completed, Travis led
Taylor and Niki into the drawing room of
their new home. The overall color scheme of
the room was white with accents of gold
and silver. French Antique sofas and chairs

covered in white satin, the fabric shot
through with silver thread, were everywhere, and a thick white carpet covered the
floor. Ornate silver statues, large and small,
stood in corners or rested on tables. An
enormous gilded mirror covered one wall,
making the room feel much larger than it
was. Overhead, the crystal chandelier hung
from a cherubim and seraphim frescoed
ceiling. At the windows, full panels of
brocatelle frame lace curtains were backed
by white sheers.

Niki looked around, her mouth slightly
agape. While the outside had seem unpre-
tentious in comparison with the surrounding residences, the glitter and shine of this
drawing room was fascinating to someone
used to a simpler elegance. She would soon
learn that this decor *was* considered simple
by their new neighbors.

"A bit different than home, isn't it,
Niki?" It was obvious Travis enjoyed
playing his role of debonair New Yorker for
his little sister. "Don't worry. You'll get
used to it in no time at all."

Taylor took a seat by the large window
and removed her hat. Placing it on the sofa
beside her, she let out a long sigh and then
smiled. "Tell me, Travis, about your life
here. It obviously agrees with you."

"Very much so, Grandmother. Not that I
don't miss Heart's Landing sometimes. I
do. But this is where everything is happen-

ing. You only have to look at the homes lining Fifth Avenue to know that's true. This is where people come when they've made their money, and I'm a part of it, helping them make their decisions, advising them where to invest." Travis sat in a chair near Taylor, holding his hat on his knee. He grinned openly as he confessed, "Not that too many of these old men listen to a fellow they consider still wet behind the ears, but the day will come."

"Of course, it will. You've got your father's good sense for business. Rory may not have liked living here, but he knew what he was doing."

"You needn't remind me of Da. I can't do anything without someone saying 'I remember when your father . . .' " He lifted his eyes toward the ceiling in exaggerated futility. "Sometimes I wonder if I'll ever be able to match the old man's wizardry."

"Wizardry?"

"It must be that, Gram. Everyone old enough to remember Da *or* Grandfather Lattimer seems to be under a spell." He twisted in his chair, looking for Niki who was still wandering around the room, picking up knickknacks and staring at paintings and statues. "What brought you to New York ahead of schedule?" he asked Taylor. "I thought Ma had everything detailed and outlined."

"She did, but she wasn't counting on Niki

falling in love."

"Niki?"

"Don't sound so surprised. In case you haven't noticed, your sister is no longer a child."

"Well, of course I noticed, but . . ."

Taylor waved him silent as Niki crossed the room to join them.

"I had never imagined living in a place like this, Travis," she said, "but I love it. Thank you for finding it for us."

Taylor got to her feet. "Why don't we have a look at the rest of the house, and then I think I'd like to lie down awhile. It's been an exhausting week thus far, and I'm ready for a rest."

"I'll show you around, Gram, and then I'll be going. I'll come round again tonight and take you out for supper."

Niki glowed with excitement at the prospect but was disappointed when her grandmother shook her head.

"Thank you, Travis, but I'd rather dine in tonight. Tomorrow will be soon enough for us to get acquainted with the city." She motioned for Niki to follow along, then started for the stairs, Travis at her side. "I hope you'll join us for supper. There's so much I still want to ask you, but I'm just too weary."

"I'll be here, Gram. Nothing could keep me away."

* * *

Niki reclined on the chaise longue, sipping a cup of hot tea. She had a feeling of sublime contentment, and she sighed with pleasure as she placed the cup on the table at her side and leaned back.

Her bedroom was large and airy and much to her liking. The desired effect of the furnishings was to suggest a room in an ancient French house. Toile wallcoverings, curtains, upholstery, and even the bed-spread were uniform. The enameled Louis Seize furniture was new, though it was meant to look antique. Besides the chaise lounge, there was a sofa and two chairs and, of course, the large bed. Pearl had already emptied Niki's trunks into the enormous armoire, which had been painted to match the expensive French-style furniture.

Though their evening was to be a quiet one, Niki knew that the days to come would be filled to the brim with new sights and new faces. Taylor had said that one of their first orders of business was to find a dress-maker to make them some new clothes. She would look up her old friends and acquaintances, and they would begin doing some entertaining, albeit on a small scale. Niki had been told before they departed Spring Haven that the theatre would be avoided until her birthday arrived. In the meantime, she would become well-acquainted with this exciting city of her dreams.

A light rap interrupted her train of thought.

"Yes?"

Pearl stepped into the room. "Miss O'Hara, I was wondering if you'd be needing me to help you dress for dinner."

"No, thank you, Pearl. But you could lay out my things for me. My silk blouse, I think, and a dark skirt."

With a nod, Pearl went directly to the wardrobe. Niki sat up and stretched, then picked up her cup and finished her tea. Still holding the cup in her hand, she stood up and walked to the windows where she pushed aside the sheer curtains and looked down on the avenue below.

Dusk was spreading its gray tint across the sky, and there were few pedestrians left strolling along the sidewalks. But the street was still busy with automobiles, businessmen on their way home from their offices in the heart of the city, couples on their way to an early supper before an evening at the opera or perhaps the theatre. As she stood there, she recognized Travis's car as it pulled to a stop at the curb in front of their house, and she knew she had better hurry.

The conversation at their table that night was delightful. Niki had forgotten how charming and funny Travis could be. He reminded her of scrapes they had managed to get into together as children and told stories of his days at Harvard. Niki was enjoying herself immensely until he asked about Adam.

"Say, you haven't told me a thing about your stay at Spring Haven. How's Adam? Did you know I met him when he was here in New York a year ago? I thought he was rather a swell fellow, though from what I could see he needs to learn how to let loose and have fun sometimes."

Niki had succeeded quite well until this moment at putting Adam entirely out of her thoughts. Now his face came rushing back at her, and she didn't like the way his memory made her feel.

"Everyone is well at Spring Haven, Travis," Taylor answered. "You're right about Adam. He's far too serious about things, and if I've read him right, he doesn't trust many people either. I've known a few others like that in my life, and usually there's a big hurt in their past somewhere." She wore a thoughtful expression. "From what I hear, Adam is a brilliant attorney. I have no doubt that he's going to be terribly successful once he's given the chance to prove himself."

Erin stood at the table in the entryway, looking down at the return address on the envelope—*Houseman and Cheavers, New York, New York.* She knew it must be an offer of a position with that firm, and she also knew that she must somehow make Adam accept it.

When Taylor had told Erin what Adam

said, about wanting to go to New York but that he wouldn't because of her and Pop, she had wanted to cry. Didn't the boy know that everything they had done for him was because they loved him and wanted him happy, not to have someone to look after them? Of course she would prefer to have him close to home, but not if he would be happier elsewhere. Ever since he'd returned from law school, he'd been far too serious; he'd grown cynical about people, and often it seemed he had forgotten how to laugh. Something had happened to change him and being involved with Melina Howard hadn't helped matters. He needed to get away from Spring Haven. He needed to get a new perspective on his life.

Besides, Niki was in New York now.

Taylor wasn't the only one with insight. Erin had seen what was blossoming between Niki and her nephew. She didn't know what had happened to make them both so miserable, so sad and angry that Niki had run away rather than trying to make things right, but she did know that Adam should go after her. He had to ignore all the excuses his practical mind could think of and listen to his heart. He needed to throw caution to the wind. This letter just might contain his chance to do just that.

Tapping the envelope against the palm of her hand as she nibbled her lower lip, lost in deep thought, she turned toward Adam's study. There was no time like the present for action.

"Adam," she said firmly as she entered the dark-paneled, masculine room, "I really must talk to you about something."

He looked up from his papers as if he would try to put her off for a while, but the determined look on her face convinced him otherwise. "What is it, Aunt Erin?"

She sat in the large, leather-upholstered chair across from him, still tapping her hand with the envelope. "Adam, I know things aren't going well for you here, with your trouble with Judge Howard and all. No, don't try to deny it. I've lived in these parts too long to not know what's going on."

Adam sighed and leaned back in his chair but didn't speak.

"I know this is something I've said before, but you're getting old before your time. You've forgotten how much fun we used to have. Life should be a joy, not one big problem. Now I know you love the practice of law. You didn't become a lawyer just because it was tradition for Bellmans to do so. I think what you need to do is get away from here. Get away from Spring Haven and Atlanta and everything. Start a new page in your life, so to speak."

"Aunt Erin, how could I? Even if things aren't going well in Atlanta, you and Pop need me here."

Erin leaned forward, pointing a finger at him. "That's *just* the kind of thinking I'm talking about, Adam Bellman. Just who do you think did everything around here while you were growing up? And we still managed to have a good time at it. But you! You're one big frown all the time."

"I . . ." Adam bristled, not knowing how to respond to this unusual criticism by his aunt.

"Don't argue with me, Adam. Pop and I love Spring Haven, but if things go on like this, we'll have to leave just so we can smile again." She could see he was getting angry. Now she changed her tactics, speaking softer and appealing to his reason. "Adam, be honest. If you're worried about finances, wouldn't we be better off if you had a steady practice with a good law firm and could send us regular financial help than the way things are now?" She got to her feet and leaned across his desk to take one of his hands in hers. "It's not that I'm trying to get rid of you, Adam, but something's got to change."

What could he do but nod? She was right, after all.

"Then promise me something. If you were to get an offer from a prestigious law firm to join them, no matter where in this world they are, promise me you would take it."

"But . . ."

"No excuses, Adam. Pop and I want you to go. We want you to be happy, and you're not happy here. We won't sink with you away. We know how to run the place, and we've got a little money stashed away. Besides, Pop really does like to be in charge, and whether you realize it or not, things are better now financially than they were a few years ago." Her eyes pleaded with him. "Now, promise me you'll go if such an offer ever comes your way."

He shook his head in surrender, chuckling lightly. "All right, Aunt Erin. You win. It's rather a moot point anyway, since no *prestigious* firm is going to offer a position to some poor lawyer from the backwoods of Georgia."

"Is that right? Well, I may lose my dollar, but I'll wager one that that's just what they've done." Triumphantly, Erin dropped the envelope onto the desk in front of him.

Adam picked it up, his eyes staring at the return address, then looking up at his aunt. "Houseman and Cheavers? Why would they . . ."

"Open it, Adam. Open it and find out why."

Adam controlled his growing excitement. "It could be for any number of reasons, Aunt Erin. Whatever it is, it's most certainly not a job offer." With that, he slit open the envelope and removed the letter. His eyes scanned the page once, then again, and then again. He couldn't believe it. He looked up at Erin, then back at the page. It read the same, but he still didn't believe it.

"I was right, wasn't I?" Erin cried. "It *is* an offer!" She hurried around to the back of the desk and threw her arms around his neck. "What does it say? Tell me, Adam."

"It's an offer from Mr. Houseman himself. He wants me to come to New York for an interview. Aunt Erin, I can't believe it."

"Well, you'd better believe it, Adam, 'cause you're going. When does he want you there?"

He perused the page once more. "In the next week or so."

"Good. I'll have you packed and ready to leave by Friday." She kissed his head and walked out of his study before he could speak again.

As she closed the door behind her, she whispered, "Thank you, Aunt Taylor," under her breath, then went in search of Pop to tell him the news.

CHAPTER 7

Guests had already begun to arrive, filling the drawing room of the white house on Fifth Avenue with cheerful conversation. Most of the men were friends of Travis. Some of the ladies had arrived on the arms of their husbands, but many were young debutantes in the company of their mothers. Taylor and Niki greeted them warmly while they each mentally cursed Travis for his tardiness. It was a bit awkward to be the hostesses and not know a soul.

Of course, there was no lack of admirers for Niki. They were more than happy to introduce themselves to the beautiful young woman with the violet eyes that matched her gown of silk. Her hair was piled on top of her head and crowned with a purple ostrich feather. A necklace of large amethysts graced her white throat, and matching bracelets circled her wrists. Patches of pink brightened her cheeks as she blushed at the men's flowery compliments.

"Miss O'Hara," Joseph Claymore, the tallest of the three men surrounding her said, "we never would have guessed your brother had enough good sense to have you for a sister. Are you sure he's not adopted?"

"Indeed. You're much too beautiful to be related to that scoundrel," added Peter Cross.

"Is that why he's left you out West? Was he afraid we'd discover he's not really related to Rory O'Hara?" Oliver Samuels peered at her over the rim of his glasses as he spoke.

Niki glanced from one to the other, protesting with laughter. "No. No. I'm afraid I must claim him. He is definitely my brother, scoundrel though he may be."

"Well, he won't get away with keeping you hidden from us any longer, Miss O'Hara. If you'll allow me, I'd like permission to call on you one evening next week."

"That's very kind of you, Mr. Claymore, but I . . ." Before she could finish her reply, she heard someone call out Travis's name in greeting and turned toward the doorway. "Excuse me, gentlemen. My errant brother has arrived."

As she began walking toward the entry hall, she could see Travis removing his hat and coat and handing them to Max along with his gloves and walking stick. He turned back toward the door, speaking to someone all the while. She wondered who he had brought with him that had made him come so late.

"Excuse me," she said as she slipped past the last couple obstructing her exit from the drawing room. "Travis, what on earth . . ."

"Look who I've brought with me, Niki."

Top hat in hand, his wavy brown hair parted and slicked back, Adam nodded formally. "Hello, Niki. You look lovely tonight."

"Adam? You came to New York?"

"Great piece of luck, Sis. He's up here on business and decided to give me a call. I was just leaving to come here. I couldn't very well tell my own cousin that I was too busy to eat with him." Travis was smiling broadly. "I practically had to drag him here, but I told him you and Gram would've had my hide if I didn't make him come."

Niki had brought her quivering nerves under control now, and she held out her hand to him. "Travis is right, Adam. We would have been very put out with you both if you'd refused to come. Whenever you're in New York, you must consider this your home."

"Thank you. I wasn't sure I'd be welcome." He was watching her with steady blue eyes.

Taylor came out of the dining room just

then.

"Gram," Travis cried, "look who I found in New York."

"For goodness sake! Adam!" Taylor hurried forward and took his hand in hers, accepting his warm kiss on her cheek. "I'm so very glad to see you."

"Thank you, Aunt Taylor. It's good to see you, too."

"You've arrived just in time for supper. Our cook says we must eat before everything is ruined. Travis, would you please help me with your friends? They've all been terribly nice, considering their host's neglect."

Travis tossed Adam a forlorn look. "I'm always to blame, no matter what goes wrong. Come with me, cousin, and I'll introduce you while I'm rounding them up for dinner."

Niki stayed in the hall, but her eyes followed Adam's back into the drawing room. She had nearly forgotten how handsome he was. And so tall. He towered over most of the men in the room. She saw him nod and reply politely to introductions. She was aware of many pairs of feminine eyes watching him as closely as she was. Well, it didn't matter to her anymore. She was over her silly infatuation. She wouldn't be bothered by his presence. He was simply her second cousin from Georgia, visiting the family while on business in New York.

"Miss O'Hara? May I take you to supper?"

Niki nodded without looking his way. "Thank you, Mr. Claymore. I'd be happy to sit with you."

Throughout the meal that followed, Niki seemed unable to keep her eyes from drifting in Adam's direction. His attention was being monopolized by two very lovely females, but it was difficult to surmise from the expression on his face whether or not he was pleased with his circumstances. Several times she brought herself up short, returning her gaze to Joseph and forcing herself to make light conversation with him, smiling pleasantly on cue and laughing when she should at his jokes. And all the while she couldn't help wondering if Melina had come with Adam to New York.

They returned to the drawing room after supper, most of them gathering around the piano as Peter Cross began to play. A place was make for Niki on the bench at his side, and Joseph leaned against the piano so he could be close to her.

"Play something special for Niki," he said.

Peter's fingers danced lightly over the ivory keys. "I don't think there's a song been written that's pretty enough for her, but I'll try."

Niki blushed, enjoying the flattery, yet flustered by it. Her eyes dropped to her hands, folded in her lap. When she looked up again, her gaze met with Adam's. He was leaning against a nearby wall. His blue eyes seemed cold and there was a cynical twist to the smile on his mouth. She didn't like the look.

"What do you think of this one, Miss O'Hara?" Peter asked as he began to play. "Are you familiar with it?"

"What? Oh, no. I don't believe so."

Joseph laughed. "Confess, Pete. That's something new you've written, isn't it?"

Niki looked at Peter. "Did you really? It's very strange, rather haunting. What made you think of it?"

"I went to see Mrs. Fiske in *Salvation Nell*. I couldn't get over the scene when her lover killed a man and she sat on that stage for the longest time, just staring into space. When I got home, I sat down at the piano and wrote it."

Niki's pulse quickened. "Tell me more about Mrs. Fiske."

"She's marvelous. Have you ever seen her perform?"

"No, but I hope to soon. I've heard so much about her." She paused a moment, her eyes darting from Peter to Joseph before sharing her secret. "I want to be an actress. That's why I've come to New York."

"That's wonderful, Miss O'Hara," Joseph cried. "You'll be famous in no time at all, and I'll be your greatest fan."

"After me, that is," Peter interjected.

Smiling, she looked across to where Adam had been standing, but he was gone. The acclaim with which the others had greeted her revelation no longer seemed so bright.

"Excuse me," she whispered, getting up from the bench. "I must speak to Travis."

Niki wove her way through the guests gathered around the piano, looking for Travis. She didn't know what she would say to him once she found him. It had only been an excuse to escape everyone's watchful eyes while she rid herself of the strange heaviness that was strangling her heart.

"An actress! Travis, she's not serious, is she?"

"I'm afraid you're wrong there, cousin. She's very serious."

She heard them before stepping from the drawing room and stopped before she was seen. They were standing just the other side of the draperies that framed the doorway. Although they spoke in hushed voices, she could hear them clearly.

"But she can't know the least thing about the theatre. Where did she get such a crazy idea? Why hasn't your grandmother put a stop to this foolishness?"

Niki pushed aside the draperies as she stepped through the doorway. "I may not know anything about the theater yet,

Adam, but I usually know when something is none of my business. This is none of yours."

The hall was chilled by the looks they exchanged.

"You're right about that, Miss O'Hara," Adam said as he placed his hat on his head. "I really shouldn't concern myself with whether or not you make a fool of yourself . . . or whom you make a fool of yourself with. As I've already seen, you'll have plenty of men to choose from while you play your little games."

She could feel the color draining from her cheeks. "Mr. Bellman, I am not playing a game, and someday, you'll be forced to admit that you were wrong."

"Should that unlikely day ever arrive, I will publicly kneel before you and proclaim your greatness." He tapped the brim of his top hat with his cane. "Good evening, Miss O'Hara. Good evening, Travis. I'll catch a cab back to my hotel. Thanks for the interesting evening."

Niki stared at the closed door, then looked at her brother. "*Ooooh!* That man. That insufferable man!" With that, she spun around and returned to the drawing room, determined to forget that Adam Bellman even existed.

The motorcar stopped before a tall office building. Taylor stared up at it while she waited for Roger to open her door and help her out.

"Do you want me to wait here, ma'am?"

"Yes, Roger. I don't expect to be very long."

She smoothed the skirt of her tailored wool suit before walking toward the building. A doorman opened the door for her, bowing slightly as she went by him. An elevator carried her up to the fourth floor and the offices of Houseman and Cheavers.

"Mr. Cheavers is expecting you, Mrs. Lattimer," the pretty secretary replied when she'd given her name. "Come with me, please." The young woman led her down a long hallway, stopping at a large door at the end. She rapped lightly, then opened the door. "Mr. Cheavers? Mrs. Lattimer is here." As the secretary pushed the door all the way open, Taylor could see him rising from his chair behind his desk.

Conrad Cheavers was a tall, gray-haired man in his sixties. He had a close-trimmed beard and sharp gray eyes that sparkled when he smiled as he was doing now.

Taylor moved past the young woman and heard the door close as Conrad came toward her, his arms outstretched.

"Taylor." He clasped her right hand between both of his. "Taylor Lattimer, you look wonderful. I'd almost given up hope of seeing you in person. I'm so glad you called." He led her toward a sofa. "Sit down, my dear."

"I had to come, Conrad," Taylor said as she removed her gloves. "I had to thank you for your help."

"Nonsense. That boy is sharp. It's you who've done us a favor."

"Then Adam has agreed to join the firm?"'

"He has. He's gone back to Georgia to tie up some loose ends, and then he'll return to New York. Probably in a month or so."

Taylor sighed her satisfaction. She was glad her meddling had turned out all right. She hadn't been sure if she should interfere or not, but after hearing Adam's confession that night in Atlanta, she was convinced that he should at least be given a chance.

Conrad had been a close friend for many years, first of Brent's and then of hers, too. After Brent died and she brought their son, Carleton, back to the East to study to become a doctor, Conrad and his wife had taken her under their wing, helping her through the lonely days and months that followed. When Taylor returned to Heart's Landing, they stayed in touch through letters. Emily Cheavers had passed away five years ago and letters had dwindled to a halt, but the friendship was unchanged. When Taylor had called Conrad upon her arrival in New York, it was as if no time had passed at all since they'd last seen each other.

"You understand, Conrad, that no one must ever know I had anything to do with Adam being brought here."

He chuckled as he leaned forward and took her hand once again. "My dear Taylor, no one could drag that confession from my lips. I would much prefer everyone thought I was the brilliant person that brought his talent to the firm." He winked, then released her hand as he leaned back in his chair. "Now, that's enough about Adam Bellman. I want to know about you. Will you come to dinner with me one night this week so we can catch up on old times?"

Taylor smiled. "Yes, I would like that very much."

Niki was in a near daze as she walked beside her grandmother into the restaurant, followed by Conrad Cheavers. Ordinarily, she would have been looking around with interest, absorbing the sights and sounds of the packed establishment— the thick red carpet and gold and white walls; the people seated at the large, round tables covered with sparkling white table cloths, chattering noisily; women with colorful feathers in their hair and their throats encircled with blazing diamond necklaces; men in white tie and tails, their hair slicked back, their mustaches trimmed. Ordinarily, but not tonight. Niki had just come from the Shubert Theatre where she had witnessed Mrs. Fiske's ingenious portrayal of Nell, the noble scrubwoman, in *Salvation Nell.*

"Niki? Sit down, dear."

Returning to reality, Niki realized that Conrad was holding out a chair for her. Taylor was already seated and was smiling at her tolerantly.

"Thank you, Mr. Cheavers," she said as she slipped into her place at the table.

"You're quite welcome, Niki. I'm glad to see you enjoyed the play." He exchanged a glance with Taylor that admitted his understatement.

"Enjoyed it! Mr. Cheavers, it was too wonderful to believe. I knew she must be talented, but I had no idea . . . Oh, I want to be able to capture an audience like that. Didn't you feel like you really were in Hell's Kitchen? I did. Are the slums really so awful as that?"

"I'm afraid so, but let's not talk of slums tonight. Not while I'm with the two most beautiful women in New York." He turned his attention toward Taylor. "We've not had a moment to catch up. What have you been doing with yourself?"

Niki could see she wasn't necessary to this conversation. As Taylor began to talk of Heart's Landing and Brenetta, Rory, and all the others, Niki turned her attention elsewhere. Their table was in a shallow alcove which provided a view of the room while still giving them some privacy. Niki took advantage of this view, letting her eyes roam from table to table. She was immediately aware of the lifted gazes and the silent conversations, and she looked quickly toward the source of disturbance. Standing at the top of the stairs that led down to the main floor of the restaurant was Minnie Maddern Fiske with her husband, Harrison Fiske.

"Gram, it's *her,*" she whispered in awe.

She was wearing a creation of blue chiffon velvet with a chemisette and hanging oversleeves of black French lace. Her head was topped by an enormous black and blue hat with sweeping ostrich feathers. She wore a black fox stole around her shoulders and carried a matching black fox muff upon one arm. She nodded slightly, acknowledging the admiring stares, then started down the steps on her husband's arm.

Niki's gaze never left her until she disappeared into a private eating chamber. "Isn't she something?" she whispered to no one in particular.

The waiter came with their supper. Niki wasn't very hungry after all the excitement, but she dutifully ate a few bites while allowing herself to remember Mrs. Fiske's performance one more time. She was oblivious to Conrad's remarks to the waiter or to his and Taylor's conversation throughout dinner.

"Niki, Mr. Cheavers asked you a question."

Her grandmother's mild rebuke brought her back to the present once again. "I'm sorry. I'm afraid I didn't hear you. What was it you said, Mr. Cheavers?"

"Your grandmother has told me about your aspirations for the stage. I was just wondering what your plans are."

"I'm going to study acting this next year. It's a sort of trial period to see if I really have any talent, but I know it's what I want to do, and if I want it bad enough, I just *must* have some talent, don't you think?"

He smiled at her warmly, nodding his head. "Most certainly, my dear. And who is your coach going to be?"

"I don't know." Niki looked at Taylor. "Gram, have we even tried to find someone?"

"Not yet," her grandmother replied, "but we're not in any big hurry. We have another month or so to enjoy ourselves before that starts."

Conrad patted his mouth with his linen napkin. "Perhaps I can be of help. I know a few people in the theatre."

"Honestly, Mr. Cheavers? Do you know Mrs. Fiske?"

"I certainly do. Have known her for quite a few years, as a matter of fact. She might be able to tell us of someone to help you get started. Why don't we ask her? Here she comes now."

Niki turned in her chair to follow his gaze. It was true. Mrs. Fiske was making her way through the tables in their direction, pausing now and then to exchange a few words before moving onward. Conrad rose from the table and held out a hand in her direction.

"Conrad, how nice of you to invite me over," Mrs. Fiske said as she accepted his hand.

"It is you who should be thanked, Minnie," he replied. He held out his free hand toward Taylor. "I'd like you to meet a very good friend of mine, Taylor Lattimer, and her granddaughter, Niki O'Hara."

"I'm pleased to meet you both."

"The pleasure is all ours, Mrs. Fiske," Taylor said. "Won't you sit down for a while?"

"Thank you. I'd like to very much." Mrs. Fiske looked at Niki. "So, you are the young lady Conrad says wants to be an actress?"

Niki found it nearly impossible to reply. "Y . . . yes."

Mrs. Fiske lifted Niki's chin with her fingers and studied her closely. "Well, you're very pretty. Have you had any stage experience?"

"No."

"That's a pity. It's good to start early, but you're still young. You'll learn fast enough."

"I'm very eager, Mrs. Fiske."

The actress nodded, a knowing smile on her lips. "I'm sure of that." She patted Niki's hand. "You just listen to what your coaches and directors tell you, and you'll do fine." She paused thoughtfully, then added, "But don't ever be afraid to think for yourself either. Don't become a mindless puppet. You've got brains, too." With that, she stood up.

Conrad got to his feet as well. "Thank you for coming over, Minnie. I hope you and Harrison will find time to join me for supper some time soon."

"Thank you. We'll certainly try. It was a pleasure meeting you, Mrs. Lattimer. Miss O'Hara, I'll be watching for you."

Niki watched her walk all the way back through the busy restaurant before turning around in her chair again. "Gram," she whispered, "I never would have believed this could happen. Mrs. Fiske . . ."

Taylor shook her head, chuckling softly. "Come back down to earth, Niki."

"Miss O'Hara, if you'll permit an old geezer like myself to say so, someday *you'll* be the one dropping by tables and giving advice to your hopefuls."

Her violet eyes sparkled as she replied, "Thank you, Mr. Cheavers. I hope you're right!"

CHAPTER 8

Mrs. Whitman shook her head emphatically. "No. No. That's not right, Nicole. Anyone sitting past the fifth row couldn't hear you. You must *project*. Even a stage whisper must be heard."

"I'm sorry. I'll try again."

"Not today. Our time is up. Besides, I understand you have an important engagement tonight." At least Mrs. Whitman was smiling as she walked toward the stage. "We'll take this up again in the morning."

Niki sat on the floor, too weary at the moment to think about the birthday party her grandmother and brother had planned for her. "Do you think I'll *ever* get it right?"

Mrs. Whitman clucked her tongue. "My dear Miss O'Hara, I have told you before that you have wonderful stage presence and a great deal of talent, but that doesn't mean you don't have much to learn. Don't allow yourself to get discouraged. With time and hard work, you'll do fine." She picked up her hat from a chair in the front row and placed it on her head, pinning it securely in place. "Be sure to tell Fred when you leave so he can lock up. Good day, Nicole."

Niki watched her leave, not moving from her spot in center stage. It was hard to follow her coach's instructions about not becoming discouraged, especially when they had been going over the same scene and the same lines for hours. She heard the outside door close, the sound echoing through the theatre for a moment before the auditorium was cloaked in silence.

"I like this place," she whispered, looking out over the rows and rows of seats and imagining them filled with people.

When Conrad Cheavers had brought her here several weeks ago and introduced her to Mrs. Whitman, Niki had known at once that she was going to like working in this place with Mrs. Whitman as her teacher. The theatre was owned by Mrs. Whitman and her husband but had not been used to put on a play since Mrs. Whitman retired from the stage.

"Some day," Mrs. Whitman had told her, "if the right material came along, we might try reopening it."

Niki got to her feet and walked around the smooth boards of the stage. She sniffed the air. The place smelled of old leather and dust. It pleased her.

"George, I cannot bear to have you go,"

she said, trying once more to make herself heard in the back rows, while still sounding as if she whispered.

"If George is smart, he won't leave you."

"Oh!"

"Sorry. Didn't mean to frighten you."

Niki looked at the man as he came down the aisle and stepped onto the stage. He was a short, good-looking fellow in his mid-twenties with sandy hair and faded blue eyes. His pin-striped suit was worn, and the hat in his hands was beginning to fray around the brim.

"There wasn't anyone at the door, so I came in. I'm Harry Jamison. I'm looking for Mr. Whitman."

"I'm afraid he isn't here today. Mrs. Whitman just left."

He had a very pleasant smile. "Are you rehearsing for a play?"

"Just practicing some lines."

"Would you mind if I listened?" He stepped down from the stage and sat in the front row.

"Well, I . . ." Niki didn't want him to stay. The silence of the theatre that she had been enjoying just moments before now made her nervous. Her eyes darted to the doorway at the end of the long aisle, then back to Harry Jamison. She wondered where Fred was.

"Please. I won't stay long."

"Hello! Niki, are you ready to leave?"

Travis stood in the doorway where seconds before she had glanced.

A relieved smile lit up her face as she grabbed her wrap from one corner of the stage and scurried down the steps. Harry got to his feet and bowed slightly as she went by him, then followed after her. She could see Travis's puzzled frown as she approached him. She took him by the arm, feeling suddenly very childish for being frightened.

"Travis, this gentleman is Mr. Jamison. He stopped by to see Mr. Whitman and caught me rehearsing."

Travis offered his hand. "It's a pleasure, Mr. Jamison. I'm Travis O'Hara."

"The pleasure's mine," Harry replied, shaking hands with Travis while still looking at Niki.

His watchful eyes brought back her original nervousness, and she tugged at Travis's arm. "Come on. We really must be going." She looked back toward the darkened wings of the theatre. "Fred! I'm leaving now. You can lock up." She hoped he'd heard her. She didn't want to wait around any longer to find out.

The car was waiting for them outside. Travis opened the door for her, helping her inside, then went around to the driver's seat. Cocking his head toward the theatre where Harry still stood watching them from the doorway, he asked, "Who is he, Niki?"

"I don't know. An actor, I suppose."

As the car pulled away, she twisted in her seat to look back. Harry was tipping his hat to her in farewell, still smiling. She had a strange feeling that she would be seeing him again.

"So, little sister," Travis said, drawing her attention away from the diminishing Whitman Theatre, "do you feel any older?"

Niki shook her head. "Not a minute, but it's good to know that I am. Despite what Gram said, I'm afraid Mother would have been furious about my startng my lessons early, even if it was only a few weeks."

"I think Mother would have understood. After all, Mr. Cheavers went to all that trouble to find a good coach for you."

"I'm not so sure, but it doesn't matter now. I'm eighteen. In another year, I'll be able to pursue my career in earnest. I can hardly wait."

They fell silent as they drove along Fifty-Ninth Street toward Fifth Avenue. Niki watched the people in Central Park, remembering how recently she had gone ice skating there. She was glad March had come at last. She had enjoyed herself since they'd arrived in New York, but she was ready to get to work.

Travis stopped the car in the drive at the front of the house. Before he could get around to Niki's side, Roger was there to open the door.

"Take it around back, will you, Roger?"

Travis said. He crooked his arm for Niki. "Come on, birthday girl. Let's get ready for your party."

Mrs. Mulligan had certainly done her job that day. The house shone from hours of cleaning and polishing. Delicious odors wafted through the hall leading from the kitchen. The table in the dining room was already set with china and crystal, the silverware reflecting the light from the shimmering chandelier overhead.

Niki left Travis downstairs and went up to her room. Her clothes had been laid out across the bed, and water was being drawn for her in the bathroom. Niki sank into the tub with an exaggerated sigh, closing her eyes and enjoying the warmth of the perfumed bath water. She was glad she had convinced Taylor that she wanted a quiet dinner party at home instead of a larger affair at the club. The last few months had seen a series of social gatherings, and Niki had grown tired of the whirl of activities.

She got out of the tub, wrapping herself in a large, soft towel. Barefoot, she returned to her room. She dropped the towel on the floor and slipped into her satin bedrobe, then moved to the window of her room. She leaned her forehead against the glass and looked down at the street below. A strange meloncholy enveloped her as she remembered other birthdays, all of them at Heart's Landing.

Da never worked on her birthday. He'd always said that's what he had a foreman for. Her mother baked the cake herself, chocolate with chocolate icing—Niki's favorite. BJ and Travis, when they were still at home, always made her a special present. The year Da had given her Raja, her brothers gave her a homemade, leather tooled headstall. How she treasured that gift. It was the next year that she'd broken her arm on her birthday, falling off her horse while racing Travis back from Starr's place. After the doctor left, Brenetta had sat by her bed all night long, reading to her when she was awake, giving her cold drinks of water when she was thirsty, making her as comfortable as was possible. Funny how that memory made her homesick when nothing else had these past ten months.

She was interrupted from her thoughts by Fiona's rap on the door.

"Your guests will be coming soon, miss. Are you ready for me to help you dress?"

"I'm ready."

Her gown was a gift from her grandmother. It was made of mediterranean blue satin and lace. The bodice was snug, and the skirt fell in a straight line to the floor, accentuating the gentle curve of her hips. Around the shoulders and over the bust were tiny feathers, dyed blue to match the color of the gown. Niki was pleased with her reflection in the mirror as Fiona fastened the clasp of the diamond necklace around her throat. Except for teardrop earrings, it was the only jewelry she wore.

"Thank you, Fiona," she said as she turned one more time before the mirror, then walked to the door. "Tell my grandmother that I've gone down."

Ringing door chimes greeted her as she stepped into the hallway. Her guests were beginning to arrive. She hurried toward the stairs, male voices and laughter drifting up to meet her.

"I can't believe it. This is too much." Travis laughed again. "Wait until Niki comes down."

She stopped midway down the stair. Her brother was right. She didn't believe it. She had certainly never expected to see Adam standing in the entry hall, hat in hand, after his departure several months before.

"Sis, look who's here. This is the friend Marc said he was bringing with him."

Niki had met Marc Houseman nearly two months before while waiting for her grandmother at the offices of Houseman and Cheavers. He had been calling on her quite persistently ever since. When he asked if he could bring along an old college chum that had just joined his grandfather's firm, Niki had no reason to deny the request, especially when he told her how lonely the fellow was since arriving in New York.

Her gaze shifted to the pretty blonde on

Adam's arm. He didn't look very lonely at the moment.

Adam wore a wry smile. "It seems I'm destined to keep popping up here to surprise you."

Niki came on down the stairs. "It seems so, Adam. I hope this time we can bid each other a fonder farewell." She looked again at the woman at his side.

"This is Marc's sister, Anne Houseman. Anne, this is Niki O'Hara, my cousin and Travis's sister."

Anne nodded. "Thank you for letting me come, Miss O'Hara. May I say you have a lovely home."

"You may, and thank you. Please call me Niki." She turned toward Marc and took him by the arm. "Let's not stand here any longer. Come into the drawing room where we can be comfortable."

The others followed her lead, taking their places on the sofa and nearby chairs. Adam sat in a chair directly across from Niki, and he watched her in a most disconcerting manner.

Marc, seated beside her, looked from Niki to Adam to Travis. "Come on. Someone really must explain to me what's going on here. I feel very left out."

Max, the butler, brought in some champagne on ice, and Travis got up to pour. "I'm not sure any of us knows. Adam here is our cousin from Georgia. Niki and our grandmother were just down visiting the family there last summer. None of us had any idea Adam would be coming to New York."

"I've been after him to come for years, ever since we were in law school together. I'm just glad I was able to get my father to take note of him—and that Adam had the good sense to at least come up here to consider taking the job."

Niki met Adam's gaze then. "I thought Melina would be coming to New York with you." As soon as it was out, she wished she hadn't said it. For one thing, it showed an interest in Adam's personal life that she just didn't have. It really made no difference to her if he cared for Melina or not.

"I never had any intention of asking Melina to go anywhere with me. We had a parting of the ways long before I decided to come to New York."

There was a heavy knot in her stomach. "Oh."

Travis stepped in to cover the awkward silence. "Adam, have you met Mr. Cheavers yet?"

"Only for a moment when I came to interview with Mr. Houseman. He stepped into the office briefly."

"Well, Gram knows him, and he's taken quite a shine to Niki, too. He's even taken her to supper at Rector's and found her an acting coach. He'll be here tonight."

The information didn't seem to please Adam. He turned toward Marc, asking, "Did you know this?"

"Hey, my friend. Don't look at me like I've been setting anything up. I'm as surprised as you are."

Niki hadn't really been listening to anything that was being said. Not since she'd learned about Melina. She thought back to that night in Atlanta. Could she have been wrong about what she'd seen, about what Adam had said? She looked at him now, sitting across from her, and all the emotions that had seemed so real last summer came flooding back. Had she misjudged him?

He was turned in his chair, looking at Travis and affording her a good view of his handsome profile. She suddenly recalled a time last summer when they had gone fishing together. There he'd sat on a fallen log, his white cotton shirt open at the neck, his pants rolled up past his knees and his feet bare, an old straw hat, much too small for him, perched on his head. He dangled the willow branch over the water, the string making ripples on the glassy surface, and she sat beside him, silent, not daring to speak as she looked at him, memorizing every detail in his face to savor again later once she was alone in her room.

The muted colors of summer lent a dream-like quality to Adam's private fishing hole. Except for the occasional scolding from a bird in a nearby tree and the whisper of the river which was not far from this glassy pool, Niki could easily imagine that the world had stopped, that nothing existed except for this tiny corner of the earth, with Adam and her the only inhabitants. She liked the thought.

He had turned suddenly, catching her staring at him. "What are you thinking?" he asked.

"Nothing special. Just how nice it is here."

He had simply nodded, an understanding smile on his mouth, and turned his eyes back to the lazy water, allowing her to study him further. A tiny bead of sweat trickled down the side of his face. His hair, damp from the heat and humidity of the day, clung to his forehead, and she had to suppress the desire to reach out and push it back, knowing instinctively that the gesture would be much too intimate. If only she could be sure what he felt for her . . . but she wasn't sure and so she stayed her hand.

"Adam Bellman! Whatever are you doing here?" Taylor's exclamation brought Niki abruptly back to the present.

The men got to their feet as Taylor came into the room. After hugging Adam and greeting Marc, Travis introduced her to Anne.

"It's so nice of you to join us, Miss Houseman. Travis told me you and your escort would be coming, but you can't imagine how surprised we are to find that your escort is Adam." She turned toward Adam. "Why didn't you let us know you were coming? How long will you be in New York?"

Adam looked a bit sheepish. "I'm afraid I've been here for several weeks, Aunt Taylor. I'm working here now."

"And you didn't let us know?" Taylor cried in dismay. "Good heavens, Adam. I thought you knew how welcome you are in our home."

Adam looked over Taylor's shoulder at Niki. His eyes seemed to ask her if what her grandmother had said was true. Did Niki want him here?

The door chimes saved her from having to search herself for an answer to the unspoken question.

"That must be Conrad," Taylor said as she slipped away from Adam and walked toward the entry. "Conrad. Come in. Everyone is waiting. And we've had a most wonderful surprise. My nephew is here, just in time for Niki's birthday."

Adam was silent in the car on the way back to his apartment. The evening had been an uncomfortable one, and his sour mood had afflicted the others with him. He knew Marc must be puzzled by his obvious displeasure at finding himself in his cousin's home. In addition, he had thoroughly spoiled the evening for Anne.

It had seemed a good idea when Marc asked if he'd like to join him for a quiet dinner with some good friends. Since coming to New York, he'd been working hard to prove himself to Mr. Houseman. He put in long hours every day at the office, taking thick briefs home with him at night, researching and studying into the wee hours of morning, long after most of the city had the good sense to be in bed. Marc's invitation had been a welcome break from his routine.

Adam's schedule did not allow for meeting and socializing with young ladies, and so he was glad to oblige when Marc suggested he escort Anne to the party that evening. She was attractive, though a trifle shy. He'd had no wish to ruin her evening or hurt her feelings, but he knew he had done both. She would have to be a complete fool not to know that for most of the evening Adam scarcely knew she was alive.

The car rolled to a stop in front of his building. He stared for a moment at the door leading into the lobby, trying to think of something to say. He wasn't very good with words at times like this. He took a deep breath and reached for the door handle, turning his eyes toward Anne. "Thank you for going with me, Anne. I'm sorry I wasn't more entertaining."

A hint of tears glistened in the corners of her eyes as she smiled bravely. "I was very happy to go with you, Adam. I hope we can do it again sometime."

"We shall then." He stepped out of the motorcar. "I'll see you at the office tomorrow, Marc. Goodnight, Anne."

He walked toward the door, not turning around until he heard the car pull away from the curb. Then he stopped long enough to watch it disappear into the darkness before making his way up two flights of stairs to his small apartment. He threw his hat onto the sofa, then sat down in the wooden chair beside the kitchen table, angrily cursing himself. He ran his hands through his hair. What was wrong with him? The entire evening had been a disaster.

He couldn't believe that the sight of Niki could throw everything off balance for him. If her rejection of him in Atlanta hadn't been enough, his last visit to her house on Fifth Avenue should have proved that she wanted nothing to do with him. She had certainly shown his thoughts about the feminine gender to be true. You couldn't trust them. They were only concerned with themselves. There were a few exceptions to the rule—women like Aunt Erin and perhaps Aunt Taylor—but Niki was not among them.

Still, he couldn't shake her from his

thoughts. She was so beautiful, so confident. Oh, sometimes he caught a glimpse of confusion, a shadow of doubt in her eyes, but those times were few. There had been a day when he'd hoped to see much more hidden in those violet orbs . . .

"Damn!"

Adam got up from his chair and went to the icebox. He stared inside but there was nothing there he wanted. Turning around, he walked across the living room to the window, opening it to the cool night air. On the sidewalk below, a young couple had paused, their heads close together. After a moment, the man stole a quick kiss and the woman's nervous laughter drifted up to where Adam stood watching. He closed the window.

CHAPTER 9

"Gram, I don't know why you think you have to include Adam in everything we do. You know how much he enjoys picking a quarrel with me." Niki pulled her hat ribbon snug under her chin as she turned from the mirror on the wall.

Taylor shook her head, showing an innocent smile. "But, my dear, he *is* family."

"Oh, poppycock!"

"My goodness, Niki! Such language!"

Niki tossed her head. "Humph," she snorted indignantly. She pivoted back toward the mirror, her violet eyes snapping and her mouth turned in a practiced pout. "He's a true blackguard, that's what he is," she whispered to her reflection.

She didn't know what possesed her grandmother to torture her so. Ever since Niki's birthday party, Taylor invited Adam over to their house at least once a week. No matter how many others were there, even if the house was filled to the rooftop (which it seldom was of late), Adam always seemed to be nearby, ready to start an argument with her. It didn't matter what the topic was either. They were predictably at opposite ends of the pole. Often-times, she got so caught up in proving her point to him that she scarcely noticed anyone else who might be with them.

"I don't know why he has to be so disagreeable," she mumbled. Just thinking about him brought hot splashes of color to her cheeks.

Taylor took her by the shoulders and peeked at her in the mirror. "Did it ever occur to you, Niki, that you *enjoy* your arguments with Adam?"

Niki spun around. "*Enjoy* them! How preposterous!"

"I know, dear. It was just a thought." Taylor pulled on her gloves as she headed for the door. "Roger is waiting with the car. Come along or we'll miss the fun."

Niki was looking forward to today's outing. A day with friends—Travis, Marc, Anne and all the others—a picnic in Central Park, horseback riding, boating on the lake. It sounded so delightful. For weeks she had been rehearsing with Mrs. Whitman, sometimes for as many as twelve hours a day. She got up so early in the morning and dropped into bed at night so exhausted that she hadn't even had time to notice the blossoming of spring. Niki intended to take advantage of her day off. She wasn't going to think of anything more consequential than being sure she kept her parasol between her delicate white skin and the burning rays of the sun.

At the designated site, Niki alighted from their automobile with enthusiasm. A large party awaited them, young and old alike, their blankets laid beneath the shade of spreading branches, their laughter as warm and friendly as the afternoon breeze.

"Niki! Gram!" Travis, wearing a white linen suit and straw hat, hurried to meet them. "I was beginning to wonder if you were coming." He took both ladies by an arm, calling back over his shoulder as he led them away, "Follow me with the food, Roger. We're starving."

"Is that why you invited us, Travis?" Taylor chided him. "Just so you could have some of Mrs. Tiffany's cooking?"

He hung his head. "You've found me out, Gram. Will you forgive me?" They all laughed.

They made their way through the crowd, stopping often to greet friends or make new ones. Before reaching Travis's group of intimates who had congregated near a grove of tall trees, Taylor chose to stop and spend some time with friends closer to her own age.

"You and Niki go on," she told them. "Just make sure you bring me something to eat before you young folks make it all disappear."

As they approached their destination, Niki looked around at the men and women already seated on the blankets. She knew almost everyone. Marc and Anne Houseman were there, Joseph Claymore and Oliver Samuels, Ruth Biddle, Louisa Smythe, Peter Cross and Virginia Croft. People who had become her friends since she'd arrived in New York, friends she liked to be with when her schedule allowed.

"She's come at last with the food," Travis called.

The announcement was met with cheers and more laughter.

Travis pointed to the blanket shared by Marc and Anne and a girl Niki didn't know. Travis helped her down, then knelt between her and Anne.

"It's good to see you again, Niki. We've missed you," Anne said with a warm smile.

"It *has* been a long while, hasn't it, Anne? I've told Gram we must have all of you over, but I've been working dreadfully long hours at the theatre." Niki turned her eyes toward Marc. "Perhaps we could have all of you over next week."

"Perhaps," he said softly. Then he motioned to the red-haired girl at his side. "Miss O'Hara, I'd like you to meet Sarah Wycott. Sarah, this is Niki O'Hara, Travis's sister."

There was something in the way he spoke Sarah's name that alerted Niki of a change that had taken place since she had last seen him. She let her gaze linger for a moment on the subject of Marc's adoration, waiting to feel at least a twinge of jealousy, but none came. Her smile was bright and genuine as she held out her hand toward Sarah. "I'm very pleased to meet you, Miss Wycott."

A warm blush spread up from Sarah's neck under Niki's scrutiny. She glanced at Marc, then smiled uncertainly as she accepted Niki's offered handshake. "The pleasure is really mine, Miss O'Hara. After hearing Marc . . . I mean, Mr. Houseman, and his friends talking about you, I've so wanted to meet you, too."

"I hope they've been saying kind things."

Sarah looked even more flustered than before. "Oh, of course, they were."

Niki let her gaze move to Marc, but he was watching Sarah, his heart in his eyes. She was actually quite relieved. There had been moments, when she wasn't too preoccupied to notice her own behavior, when she had realized that she wasn't being fair to Marc. Although she'd never indicated she felt anything other than friendship for him, neither had she purposely discouraged him from pursuing her affections. She felt much better seeing him with someone who obviously adored him as much as he did her.

Travis cleared his throat as he got to his feet. "Excuse us, everyone. Anne and I are going to take a boat out on the lake." He reached down and effortlessly pulled Anne up from the blanket. "Don't eat without us."

"We may not want to wait that long," Marc called after them. He chuckled. "Probably couldn't hear me."

Once again Niki became aware of a change in relationships. She had had no idea that Travis was seeing anyone seriously, yet by the looks of things, he and Anne had become an item while she was slaving away under Mrs. Whitman's tutelage. Until this moment, Niki had never given any thought to her brother's love life. At any of the gatherings at their house, he had always come alone, leaving her the impression of a totally unfettered bachelor. This new Travis was a bit of a surprise.

The couple retreated, Travis in his white suit and Anne in her bright yellow dress. Niki continued to stare off into space long after they had slipped from view. She thought about Anne and the first time she had seen her at Adam's side. She hadn't been sure she was going to like her at that moment, but now she thought of Anne as a good friend. From the way Travis and Anne had looked at each other just before they left for their boat ride, Niki thought they

might soon be more than good friends.
They might be sisters.

"It looks like no one's thinking of eating
just yet," Marc said, interrupting her
musings. "Sarah and I are going to take a
walk. You don't mind, do you, Niki?"

"No. Go right ahead."

Around her, reclining on bright colored
blankets, were so many people . . . and
almost all of them in pairs. Niki sat there,
suddenly aware of just how alone one could
be in a crowd. There was an unpleasant
feeling of panic, a quick question of her own
ability to attract men. Caught in this web of
uncertainty, she didn't see Adam's
approach.

He stopped a short distance away from
her. The puzzled expression on her face only
added to her beauty. Her normally arching
eyebrows were drawn together in thought,
and her lips were puckered, forming a tight
circle with her mouth. Her legs were tucked
at her side, her ankles peeking from beneath the hem of her pastel pink gown. Her
abundant chestnut hair had been piled high
on her head, and a matching pink hat
perched to one side.

Try as he might, Adam couldn't resist
any opportunity that came his way to look
at her or be with her. There was no fighting
the attraction he felt for her. Deep down, he
must have known that he no longer thought
of her as a scheming, untrustworthy

female. When he thought of Niki, he thought of sparkling eyes and fiery words, sudden laughter and blazing tempers. She made him glad and angry at the same time. She delighted and confused him. Whatever it was he felt for her—and he still doggedly denied that he could love her—he always wanted to be around her.

And, of course, there was his perverse delight in starting an argument with her. She fought so bravely and with such firm conviction. He just couldn't help himself.

Niki became aware of someone watching her. Her eyes snapped up to meet his. She couldn't stop the sudden smile that brightened her face. She was no longer alone.

"Adam! I was beginning to wonder if you really had accepted Gram's invitation to join us today."

He tipped his straw hat in greeting, then walked over until he was standing very close, causing her to bend her head back to look up at him. "I didn't think you cared if I accepted or not," he said, a cock-sure grin turning the corners of his mouth.

She turned her head away, shrugging to show her disregard. "Well, I certainly wouldn't think of *forcing* you to come where you'd rather not be." She plucked at a loose thread in the blanket. "But, of course, Gram's feelings would be hurt if you didn't join us."

Still close, he knelt down. There was no

ignoring the nearness of his broad shoulders, but she kept her eyes averted from his face. Her pulse quickened. She tried to muster her usual anger or—barring that—her total disregard of his presence.

"Before we find the topic we want to fight about today, Niki, what do you say we take a ride and enjoy the pleasant day?"

His remark was so unexpected and so candid that she broke into laughter, her eyes darting up to meet his. She found his gaze brimming with mirth as well.

"I think it's a perfectly wonderful idea, Mr. Bellman. I'm sure there's a vast wealth of subjects we haven't broached with each other, and a ride just might stir some of them up."

Still chuckling, Adam helped her up, then tucked her hand beneath his elbow as he led the way through the picnickers. Niki was keenly aware of Adam's strong body and good looks. She knew there were more than a few sets of envious eyes watching them and felt a stinging sadness that they didn't really have something to be envious of. Not that she actually wanted *Adam* for a beau— she knew better than that—but she did wish she had someone. It didn't occur to her that she could have had her choice of men if she ever paid anyone beside Adam any real attention.

The Carson Smythes had provided horses from their vast stables for those at the picnic that wanted to spend some time riding. Adam chose a perky little black mare for Niki, setting her up on the side-saddle as easily as if she were a feather. His own steed was a lanky chestnut-colored animal that pranced anxiously, eager to stretch himself beneath the saddle.

As they started down a bridle path, Adam broke their silence. "Did I forget to tell you, Niki, that you look particularly pretty today?"

She kept her eyes straight ahead. "Yes. I think you *did* forget to say it, but thank you for saying it now."

"I'm surprised that someone as pretty as you hasn't snagged yourself a husband by this time."

The pleasure of his compliment ebbed. "It's not my intention to *snag* myself a husband at any time!" She nudged her horse with the heel of her shoe.

"Wait. I didn't mean . . ."

Niki looked over at him, for once believing that he hadn't meant to start a quarrel. She was about to smile, but just at that moment, a barking dog pounced from behind a shrub beside the path. Darting and ducking with great agility and skill, he nipped at her horse's fetlocks. The little mare crow-hopped from one side of the path to the other; she kicked and spun but could not rid herself of the offensive beast at her feet.

"Get away," Niki yelled at the dog, fighting at the same time to control her mount's growing panic.

Adam tried to drive off the dog with his riding crop, but the path was too narrow. With Niki's horse spinning and rearing, he had no room to strike at the animal. Sensing that time was running out, he reached for the mare's bridle, but he was too late. The little horse had had enough. The whites of her eyes showing in her black face, she bolted, nearly unseating Niki in her race for freedom. The menacing canine tried to give chase but was unequal to a horse driven by terror.

Niki had no time to worry whether or not the dog was still chasing them. Her steed had taken the bit in her mouth and was racing pell-mell down the bridle path. There was little she could do but hang on. The wind whipped her hat from her head, and tree branches stung her arms and face. She tugged with all her might on the useless reins, fear beginning to cloud her thinking.

Up ahead the path turned to the left and the right. Niki gripped the saddle pommel with one hand and tangled her other hand in the mare's thick mane, wondering which way the horse would veer. Then she felt the animal gathering for flight and she knew she was in trouble. Though she had been riding since before she could walk, she had never had much use for the sidesaddle in her Idaho mountains. She was comfortable enough in it for quiet city riding, but she knew she would be unseated if her horse tried to jump the fast approaching hedge.

She parted company with the wild-eyed mare just before the animal's front hooves reached the turf. She hit the ground rolling, covering her face with her hands as she tumbled down a slight incline. She came to rest with a jolt against an old tree stump. A wave of blackness washed over her, sucking her into a sea of oblivion.

"Niki! Niki!" Adam called as he crashed through the shrubbery and ran toward her unconscious form.

Her skin was covered with tiny cuts and her face was a ghostly white. His own breath caught in his throat as he bent over her, his face close to hers; he let it out with a sigh as he felt warm air from her mouth brushing his cheek. She looked so small and broken, her dress torn and tattered, her hair tumbling free from its pins. He was afraid to touch her and afraid not to.

"Niki," he whispered again.

A weak groan escaped her parted lips.

"Niki!" He slipped an arm under her neck, bringing his face close to hers again. "Niki?"

"Adam . . ."

"Thank God," he said under his breath. "Niki, can you open your eyes? Look at me, Niki."

Her eyelids fluttered as she tried to obey him. Everything still seemed to be spinning, falling, twirling. She wanted it to stop. She raised her arm, trying somehow to halt the terrible sensation, and her hand was quickly taken by Adam and held in his comforting grip.

"Come on. Open your eyes so I'll know you're all right. Don't be stubborn, Niki."

She was able to force them open, but his face was only a blur above her. "Adam . . . I . . ."

"Shhh. You've taken quite a spill. Just lay there a minute and get your bearings." There was real concern in his voice.

Niki blinked. The dizziness was leaving her, the haze lifting from her eyes, and she was beginning to be able to see his face. She noticed his frowning brow first, then his tousled hair. She tried to smile. "I really am . . . a better horsewoman . . . than that."

A relieved smile replaced the worried frown as he nodded. "I know." He paused, the smile disappearing as he gazed into her eyes. "Perhaps we can try again another day."

"Okay."

"Are you ready to sit up?"

"I . . . I think so."

She wasn't expecting the searing hot flash of pain that swept through her as she tried to sit up. She cried out, then slumped back into his arms as she fainted once again.

"Nothing to worry about, Mrs. Lattimer," the doctor said softly as he closed the door to Niki's room. "I've taped her ribs. She's going to be a very sore young woman for quite some time. No strenuous activities. No horseback riding. Bed rest will do her good, but when she's able to get up, let her. Just don't allow her to overdo it too soon."

The doctor took Taylor's elbow as he spoke and led her down the stairs. At the bottom, Adam and Travis were waiting, Adam worrying a path in the floor as he paced back and forth from the steps to the drawing room. Hearing their voices, Adam darted back to the railing leading up to the second landing.

"How is she?"

Doctor Sears patted Adam's shoulder. "She's going to be fine, my boy. Cracked rib and bruised from head to toe, but there's nothing wrong with her that time and a bit of common sense won't cure."

"May I see her?"

"Me, too?" Travis added.

The doctor looked thoughtful a moment, then nodded. "I gave her something to help her sleep, but I think it would be all right for you to look in for a moment. Just don't stay too long."

Adam headed up the stairs. Travis was

set to follow when Taylor's hand alighted on his arm.

"Travis, see Dr. Sears to his automobile before you go up, will you, please."

He was about to protest, but the stern look in her eyes warned him against it. As he glanced back at the stairs, understanding dawned. "Certainly, Gram," he said in a conspiratorial tone, adding a wink.

Taylor ignored him, turning once more toward the doctor. "Thank you so much for your help, Dr. Sears."

"Not at all, Mrs. Lattimer. I'll look in on her again tomorrow. You just make sure she rests and she'll be back to normal in no time."

The drapes were drawn, throwing the shadow of evening over Niki's room. Adam closed the door behind him and looked toward the bed, waiting for his eyes to adjust to the dim light before walking across the room.

Niki lay very still, her dark brown hair spilling across the white satin-covered pillow like an ink blot on clean, white stationery. She seemed so terribly pale, her eyes sunken in bluish circles. Adam stood beside her bed and stared down at her, blaming himself for the pain he saw etched on her face. If only he'd acted sooner . . .

She opened her eyes and looked directly at him, as if she had sensed he was there.

"Adam . . ."

"How're you doing, Niki?" He knelt beside the bed.

"Not so bad . . . but I've been better."

She smiled so valiantly, it only made him feel worse. He reached out and clasped her hand, bringing it to his lips for a kiss. "I'm sorry. I wouldn't see you hurt like this for anything."

She chuckled, then grimaced in a fresh wave of pain. "Don't be silly. It wasn't your fault." She gave his fingers a weak squeeze. "I blame you for all kinds of things . . . when we argue, but this . . . wasn't . . . your . . . fault . . ." Her eyes closed involuntarily as her words faded. The medicine was working. She was asleep.

Adam leaned closer. Even with scratches on her face and blue circles under her eyes, she was beautiful. She had never looked lovelier to him than she did right now. He reached out and pushed a dark tendril from her cheek, letting his hand linger for just a moment on her silken hair. Reluctantly, he drew it back, then got to his feet. Yet he couldn't make himself go, not yet. He wanted to stay on, waiting to see if she would need anything. If she awakened, he should be near.

He couldn't fool himself any longer. He loved her. He didn't care about anything in the past. He loved her and wanted to be with her. True she *was* feisty and quarrelsome and headstrong. She *did* make him angry and frustrated, but it didn't matter. Perhaps these were even some of the reasons he loved her. What he did know was that he didn't want to lose her. Seeing her now—hurt, helpless—he knew he wanted to take care of her for the rest of his life.

He bent down and kissed her lightly on the mouth, whispering, "I love you, Niki O'Hara, like it or not!"

CHAPTER 10

Inactivity bored Niki to tears. She was not a spoiled society matron who liked to lounge about and eat grapes—or whatever it was they did with themselves. She was ready to return to her lessons with Mrs. Whitman, whether her grandmother was ready to release her or not.

"I swear I know how many little flowers there are on this infernal wallpaper," she muttered to herself as she stood at the window and stared down at the street. "I've certainly had enough time to count them all!"

Roger was just returning with the car. She watched him park it beside the house, then walk around the rear entrance. He had taken Taylor into the city to have lunch with Conrad Cheavers. Apparently, Conrad had promised to see that she got home and Roger had been sent on his way.

"Well, then. Why don't I give him something to do?"

Decisively, she turned away from the window and crossed the room to her closet.

She pulled the first dress within reach from its hanger, then carried it, along with her silk undergarments, over to the bed. She slipped her bedrobe off her shoulders, letting it slide down her back and drop in a pile on the floor. She looked down at her wrapped torso, wrinkling her nose in distaste as she fingered the bandages. She winced. She was still tender.

Dressed in a ruffled summer gown of finest lawn, she left the house followed by Mrs. Mulligan's vocal reprimands. Roger helped her into the motorcar, his expressionless face hiding his own thoughts about her venture outdoors so soon after her accident.

"Take me to the Whitman Theatre," Niki said as they backed down the drive.

"Yes, ma'am."

Niki leaned back against the seat with a sigh. She was glad to have escaped the house. Confinement didn't suit her in the least. She was anxious to get on with her lessons. One day the right part would come her way, and she had to be ready for it. Mrs. Whitman must be terribly disapproving of her incapacitation. After all, the show must go on, mustn't it?

They arrived without delay at the theatre only to find the doors locked and no one about. Niki was disappointed. She had had her heart set on working for at least a little while with Mrs. Whitman, just to get herself back into the swing of it.

Roger got back behind the wheel. "Where to now, Miss O'Hara?"

"Just drive for a while, Roger. I don't feel like going home quite yet."

"As you wish, ma'am."

Niki stared out the window, watching the buildings and people move past her. So many people. So many lives being lived in this city.

She began to think about what Travis had said when he came to dinner a few weeks ago. He was talking about all the Europeans coming to America. Thousands of immigrants pouring through Ellis Island every day, looking for a better way of life. She wondered how many of them found it, a better way. Sure, along the streets she traveled, everyone was dressed in fine attire, clothes to keep them warm in the winter, iced drinks to keep them cool in the summer. They had plenty to eat. Nice houses to entertain in. Soft beds to sleep in. But what was life really like for the immigrants, these people who came with little more than the clothes on their backs and their secret dreams?

"Roger, take me down to the Lower East Side."

The chauffeur stepped on the brake and turned to look at her with raised brows. "Miss O'Hara, are you . . ."

"Do as I say, Roger!"

He turned around, the stiffness in his shoulders showing his feelings in the matter, and pressed his foot down on the accelerator. They jerked forward, then rolled smoothly down the street toward their destination.

The teeming tenements were a new sight for Niki. The streets were narrow and crowded with milling people, pushcarts, vendors. Ragamuffin children raced through the streets or played in open fire hydrants, their laughter and yelling only a part of the cacophony that filled her ears. Lines were strung overhead, and newly washed clothing seemed to fill the space between buildings.

Niki stepped out of the car and stood on the curb, gazing around her.

"Paint yer pitcher, miss?" someone inquired.

"What?" She turned with a jerk, startled by the voice so close at her side.

The raggedy old fellow was holding a pad and paint brush. Nearby, an easel was set up, the artist's chair a rickety wooden crate and his selection of paints limited to five colors. But she liked the twinkle in his eyes and the warm twist at the corners of his mouth, and she decided she wanted to see what he could do with his brush and limited colors.

"Thank you, sir. I would like that very much."

"Would you take a seat over here, miss?" he asked, pointing toward the doorway of a building.

She shook her head, common sense asserting itself for once this day. "No. I'd rather you painted me right where I stand."

The old man frowned but nodded, then turned back to the tools of his craft. Niki leaned against the automobile, seeking a comfortable position. Her side was beginning to throb, sharp pains shooting up and down her back, but she forced herself to ignore it, concentrating instead on the strangeness of everything around her.

An inkling of just how fortunate she was had taken root. Things she had always taken for granted were now seen in a new light. The family back in Idaho hadn't had a chauffeur, for instance, but had they wanted one they could have had one, automobile or no automobile. She hadn't always had as many fancy clothes as she had now, but if she had been so inclined, she could have ordered twice as many without giving the cost a single thought. When she thought of having less than someone else, it was never in the sense that the people around her in this Lower East Side had less.

It was a strange sensation to be suddenly aware of the enormous gap that separated her from so many thousands of people. It made her uncomfortable to have to look at so much poverty when she knew she would be driving back to the luxury of her home on Fifth Avenue.

A group of screaming youngsters sped by her, some of them shirtless, all of them with bare feet. In a moment, they were back, circling her car. The one in front—the littlest—suddenly grabbed her skirts and hid behind her. It wasn't until then that she realized this wasn't a game. The others were chasing him, and their intent didn't look too pleasant.

"Here now," she demanded. "What is this?"

"Give 'im to us, missus. He's got comin' what he's got comin'."

Niki looked at the boy wedged between her and the car. She supposed he was about eight or nine years old. His face was smudged with dirt and soot, but she could see clearly enough the black eye he sported. There were more bruises on his neck and arms. He wore what could loosely be called a shirt, but she guessed if it were removed, she would find more bruises on his back.

Taking him firmly by the arm, she pulled him out in the open. "Now, tell me what this is all about."

The child shook his head and struggled to be free of her grasp.

"I'm not going to let you go." She read the fear he was trying to hide from her in his wide brown eyes. Looking at the band of boys waiting with clenched fists, she said,

"Go on. All of you! I'm not turning this one over to your justice, whether he's got it coming or not!"

There were a few exchanged glances, but none of them moved to leave.

"Roger."

The chauffeur jumped quickly from the car and came around to where she stood. The boys moved back a few steps when they saw him.

"Open the door for me, Roger. We're going to give this child a lift home."

The lad didn't seem to appreciate her rescue. He still fought to escape her grip on his arm as she pushed him into the motorcar before her. Roger shut the door, then went around to the driver seat. Before he could pull away, however, the street painter tapped on the window, holding up the portrait for her to see.

"Your pitcher! Ain't ya going t'pay me fer your pitcher?"

Niki reached into her reticle and brought out several dollars. "Here. I hope that's sufficient." She exchanged the money for the painting, then nodded to Roger to drive on.

Looking at the portrait for the first time, she was surprised at how good it was. The background was little more than a gray wash, the car behind her a quick sketch, but the old artist had captured Niki on his cheap canvas. It wasn't just that the likeness was so good that intrigued her. There was a special look in her eyes, an adventuresome lift to her chin. Did she really appear like that to the world? How she hoped so.

But she had other things to see to now besides admiring her own portrait.

She tapped on the glass separating her from Roger. "Take this up beside you, please. It's still wet."

Roger pulled over and came around to her door to take the painting. With that out of the way, Niki turned her attention back to the street urchin at her side.

"Do you want to tell me why those boys were after you?"

He shook his head, refusing to look at her.

"All right. You needn't if you don't want to. Just tell me where you live, and we'll take you home."

Still he was silent.

Niki couldn't stop the smile that crept over her mouth. The boy's brave facade, though transparent, was certainly stubborn. There must be some way to get the information from him. She couldn't just turn him loose in the streets again. Those bullies would probably be lying in wait, expecting that to happen.

"Will you at least tell me your name? Mine is Niki O'Hara. My friends call me Niki."

She could see his inner struggle written on his dirty face. He tipped his head up, eyeing her suspiciously. "Eddie," he said.

"Eddie what?"

His hands clenched on his knees. "Ain't nothing more. Just Eddie."

Niki nodded her head as she turned to look out at the passing streets. Roger was driving around the same blocks, staying in the neighborhood, waiting to be told where to let the boy out.

"I really do want to help, Eddie. Why don't you tell me where you live so we can take you there? Then you won't have to worry about those boys chasing you again."

"I'm not afraid of them," he blustered.

"Of course not. That's not what I meant at all." She patted his knee. She waited expectantly for him to tell her their destination.

Eddie's mouth formed a stubborn line as he dropped his gaze to the floor of the automobile. It was apparent that he was through talking.

Niki sighed audibly. "Well, if you won't tell me, I guess there's nothing to do but take you to the nearest police officer so that he can find your parents."

This drew his attention back to her. There was more fright written on his thin features now than when that whole pack of boys were chasing him. "Don't do it, miss. I ain't done nothin' wrong. I ain't got no parents. I ain't got no home. Just turn me out anywheres and I'll be out o' your way."

Niki hadn't been prepared for his outpouring. No parents. No home. Surely he must be lying to her. He was just a little boy. Children his age didn't live alone in a city like this. At least he must live in an ophanage. "Where do you stay at night since you have no home?"

"Under stairs. Sometimes in doorways. Once I found a room in an old building that nobody lived in no more, but some men came along and threw me out. They kept my only blanket, too." He was watching out the window. "Here!" he cried. "Let me out here."

Niki took the boy by the shoulders and twisted him around toward her. Then she lifted his chin with one of her fingers, forcing him to look at her. "Eddie, are you telling me the truth? Do you really live all alone like that?" Somehow she knew he was. A million questions seemed to plague her as she gazed into that street-wise face. How did he eat? Where did he get his clothes? How did he keep warm in the winter?

She tapped on the window. "Take us home, Roger."

Eddie's eyes became truly panic-stricken when he heard that. "Let me out o' here!" He grabbed for the door, but Niki stopped him.

"Just sit quietly, Eddie. I'm going to take you to my house. We'll get a good meal in you and some new clothes for you." Her look was stern but friendly. "I promise we won't call the police. Will you trust me just for a little while, Eddie? If you don't like it, I'll have Roger bring you back and drop you off at any corner you like. I promise."

After a moment's consideration, her promise seemed to satisfy him. He relaxed against the seat and returned his gaze to the changing scenery outside the car window. Niki relaxed too. Her side was throbbing from exertion and tension, and she knew she was going to pay dearly in pain and soreness for today's adventure.

As soon as the car pulled into the drive, the front door opened and Taylor and Adam stepped outside. They waited on the steps while Roger came around and opened the door. Niki got out, the renewed pain in her side making her move stiffly, carefully. She glanced at Taylor, hoping her grandmother was going to understand. She turned back toward the car and held out her hand. There was a long pause while a decision was made, then Eddie took hold of it and slid across the seat and out of the car.

"Don't be afraid, Eddie," she whispered, noting his nervous, wide-eyed stare. "They're very nice people." With a firm step that belied her physical pain, she led the orphan up the walk.

Taylor and Adam were both staring at

Eddie, glancing every now and then at Niki in utter confusion. She gave them both a smile in return as she half-led, half-towed Eddie up the steps, passing her staring relatives, and into the house. She noted when they stopped that Eddie was standing even closer to her now than he had when he was hiding from that gang of boys.

"Gram, this is Eddie, a friend of mine. I've asked him to join us for supper." Her look pleaded for cooperation.

She needn't have worried. Taylor was all smiles as she held out her hand toward Eddie. "Eddie, I'm very pleased to meet you. We're delighted to have company for supper." She waited until Eddie, somewhat reluctantly, accepted her offer of friendship and shook her hand.

"Roger's bringing in a few things I had him pick up on our way home. Send him right up to my room when he comes in. I'm going to take Eddie upstairs so he can wash and change." Niki glanced down at Eddie, then added, "Perhaps you should ask Max to come up, too."

Eddie was in a state of disbelief. He had never seen any place like this. He continued to look around as they climbed the stairs, glancing behind him nervously, memorizing where the door was in case he was forced to leave in a hurry. Niki opened the door to her room and ushered him inside. His gaze moved slowly around the room, taking in the carpeted floor, the big bed, the chairs and chaise lounge.

His gaze moved up to Niki's face as he found his voice. "How many families live here?"

"Families? Why, only one, Eddie."

"No. Not in this room. I mean in the whole building."

Niki knelt down on the carpet beside him, sensing the vast differences that separated her world and Eddie's. "Only one family lives here. The whole building is our home. This is my bedroom. This is where I sleep at night."

"You mean all you do is *sleep* here?"

She nodded. "That's right."

Roger and Max stepped into the room, the chauffeur carrying the boxes of clothing she had purchased for the boy on the way home.

"Just put those things on the bed," Niki told him. "Max, this is Eddie. Max is our butler, Eddie. He's going to show you where you can take your bath and then he'll help you get dressed."

"Bath? I don't need no bath."

"Why, of course you do. You'll feel much better at supper once you've bathed and changed."

Eddie was scowling, not the least pleased by this bit of news. "I don't need no bath," he repeated.

Niki wasn't about to argue with him. She

stood up again, the glance she gave Max a firm order to see that the boy bathed—with *soap*—whether he liked it or not. "Bring him down to the drawing room when you're all through, Max. Roger, you'd best stay and help Max."

Neither of the men commented as they looked at the glowering, scruffy urchin that stood between them. Niki left them and went down the stairs, as reluctant to face her grandmother and Adam as Eddie was to face the horrifying specter of a bath.

Taylor was standing in the same spot Niki had left her in. Their gazes met as Niki descended the staircase. Niki paused uncertainly, but then Taylor smiled, and she knew it was all right.

"You seem to have had quite an afternoon, Niki," Taylor said as her granddaughter paused on the final step. "Let's go sit in the drawing room and you can tell us all about it."

Niki hadn't let herself meet Adam's eyes since she'd arrived home. Somehow she knew he would be disapproving, and she didn't want to deal with him at the moment.

"Now, my dear," Taylor settled into a chair. "Tell us what mischief you've been up to."

"Not mischief, Gram. I was so terribly bored after you left. All this sitting around was driving me up the wall. When Roger came back with the car, I decided to take a drive. I thought I'd go down to work with Mrs. Whitman for just a little while, but she wasn't at the theatre. When we started driving again, I remembered what Travis was saying the other night about all the immigrants coming to America and so I had Roger drive me down to the Lower East Side." She paused a moment, drawing a breath, unconsciously holding her side as the pain worsened. "Gram, I had no idea how those people live. And when Eddie came running . . . Why, he was being chased by a group of hooligans twice his size. Did you see his eye and his other bruises? When I learned he's an orphan and has no home, I just couldn't bear to . . ."

Pearl stepped into the room. "Mrs. Lattimer. There's a telephone call for you."

Taylor looked undecided if she should take the call or not.

"It's Mr. Cheavers."

"I'll be right there, Pearl. Excuse me a moment, Niki, Adam."

Taylor was hardly out of the room before Adam jumped to his feet, drawing Niki's gaze at last. His face was black with anger as he began pacing back and forth across the room.

"What kind of idiot are you, Niki O'Hara, going into the slums alone? Haven't you any common sense or is your brain just something to keep the space wider between those cute little ears of yours?"

"Now, you wait just one minute, Adam Bellman," Niki cried as she jumped to her feet.

"No," he growled, stopping in front of her. "*You* wait. Do you know what kind of people live down there? Do you have any idea what could have happened to you?"

"Well, I . . ."

"Of course, you don't. What do you know of poverty and what it can drive people to do? You could have been raped or killed, Niki! Someone could have stuck a knife in your ribs."

"But . . . " she began to protest.

Adam grasped her shoulders, drawing her up to her tiptoes. "How would your grandmother have felt then?"

"But nothing *happened*, Adam, and maybe . . . just maybe, I've done something good. Maybe I'll be able to do something to help relieve some of that poverty."

"How? By bringing home some dirty little waif to be treated like a stray cat. Sure. Clean him up. Give him some warm milk and stroke him a few times. See how pleasantly he purrs. But what about tomorrow or the next day when you return him back into the streets? Then what? How is that going to help him live with the ugliness that surrounds him?" He gave her a little shake before letting go.

She winced as shards of pain cut at her

sides, a slight groan escaping through her clenched lips.

Seeing her pain only seemed to make Adam angrier. "Sit down, Niki, before you fall down. You can't even take care of yourself, let alone some street brat."

"That's enough!" Fury erupted inside Niki. "What business it is of yours what I do? Even if I did get myself killed down in the slums, it's none of your concern. Why don't you go poke that lawyer's nose into someone else's affairs and leave me be. If I want some advice, I'll ask someone for it . . . and it sure won't be you I ask."

"Fine. I'm going. And if I'm ever stupid enough to come back here, it certainly won't be to see *you* or give *you* any advice. Say goodbye to Aunt Taylor for me. I won't wait."

Her anger unabated, Niki followed him to the door. She stood beside it as he went out onto the porch, then stepped into the doorway. "I'm sure Gram will miss you. She loves her family no matter how muleheaded they are. Goodbye, Mr. Bellman."

He paused and looked back at her. "Miss O'Hara, you could drive a man to drink. Lord have pity on the man who is fool enough to fall in love with you!"

"*Oooh!*" Niki cried in frustration, slamming the door in his face. "Good riddance!"

CHAPTER 11

Niki was pleasantly surprised by Eddie's transformation following his bath and the donning of his new clothes. Under the weeks and months of accumulated dirt that had been caked on his skin, Eddie was a nice looking boy—sandy hair with an obstinate cowlick and very round brown eyes. He was thin and bruises still marred his skin, but good food and time would cure both those defects. When she'd brought him home, she hadn't thought any further into the future than rescuing him from that band of bullies, putting some decent clothes on his back, and feeding him a good hot meal or two. But after Adam left—as much as she hated to agree with anything he said—she knew he was right about Eddie. She couldn't just turn him loose again. She'd started something and she was going to finish it.

They were sitting at the supper table. Fiona was serving their meal, starting with steaming bowls of clam chowder. Eddie gawked at the tableware and the chandelier and the gilded picture frames and mirrors on the wall. Even after Taylor and Niki began eating, he continued to stare all around him, ignoring the bowl of soup Fiona had set in front of him.

"Don't you like clam chowder, Eddie?" Taylor asked gently.

He looked at the bowl, then at Taylor, saying, "I don't know. Never had any."

"Aren't you going to taste it and find out?"

He paused thoughtfully. His hands were hidden under the tablecloth, but Niki could tell he was wringing them. He glanced at her, then turned to answer Taylor's question. "I don't think I should touch your nice things. I might break them."

Taylor's glance was warm and reassuring. "Eddie, my dear boy, it won't matter to me in the least if you break my dishes. I'm much more concerned with getting some good food into that stomach of yours. Now go on. Pick up that spoon and give it a try. Go on."

Hesitantly, he obeyed her. He leaned low over the bowl and slurped the soup noisily off the spoon. The utensil at eye level, he pondered the taste, brows frowning in contemplation. Then he took another spoonful, this one followed by a satisfied smile before he began eating with gusto. Niki and Taylor exchanged a pleased look and then returned to their own meal.

Fiona came to remove their bowls. Judging by the look on his face, Eddie had thought the meal was over. His amazement was clear as the maid brought in platters of roast beef, corn, potatoes, and gravy.

"Fill his plate high, Fiona," Niki said.

"You mean I can eat as much as I want?"

"Until you're too full to eat any more."

"Wow!"

Niki couldn't restrain the idea that had been forming in her mind any longer. She leaned forward. "Eddie, how would you like to stay here with us for a while? You could have a room of your own and plenty to eat everyday."

The pause between bites was barely noticeable. Niki wondered if he had even heard her. She looked toward her grandmother, afraid, now that it was too late, what her reaction to this suggestion would be.

In response, Taylor said, "I think that's a fine idea. Would you like that, Eddie?"

The boy looked up from his food, his eyes darting back and forth between the two women. His gaze was wary, studying them for some angle, some trick. No one he had ever known had given him something for nothing.

"Of course, we'll have to clear it with the authorities, make sure you have no family anywhere that might be looking for you," Taylor added.

"Ain't got no family. Last folks I remember was a brother, but he died a few winters back. Don't remember my ma or pa at all. Guess I never had any."

"Then will you stay with us?" Niki asked again.

He was still suspicious but he nodded slowly. "Guess it won't hurt nothin' to stay a day or two."

Niki beamed. Though she earnestly wanted to help Eddie, she couldn't help but think what Adam would say when he learned she hadn't thrown the boy back where he came from. She was going to prove him wrong in this just as she was going to prove him wrong about her acting.

Niki would never know just how lucky she had been when it came to Eddie. A boy of the streets, living by his wits, he had become adept at stealing and lying to survive, but somewhere in his past—perhaps the older brother he remembered or perhaps the parents he *couldn't* remember—someone had taught him some basic honesty. Besides, he was bright. He might not have an education, but he knew when he'd found a good thing. He didn't plan on blowing a set-up like the one he'd just fallen into. As long as Niki and Taylor played fair with him, he would play fair with them. He didn't even object when Niki told him they were going to hire a tutor. Actually, he had always had a secret yearning to know how to read and write.

As for Niki, she enjoyed Eddie a great deal. Once she was back working with Mrs. Whitman, she found it very refreshing to come home and listen to Eddie as he told her what he had seen or learned that day. Sometimes he would share his stories about growing up in the slums, an ugly side of life that made her shudder with horror at the same time as it made her grateful for the life she'd known. He also helped her to see the world through fresh eyes, seeing and experiencing things for the first time.

Their lives settled into a comfortable pattern. Niki spent her days at the theatre, then came home to a quiet evening with her grandmother and Eddie. She turned down Travis's invitations to join him and his friends, content to pour all her energies into her acting. Except for Conrad Cheavers, who came over to dinner on a regular basis, they did no entertaining of their own. Niki felt a twinge of disappointment that Adam didn't call or drop by, but she snuffed it out, refusing to admit that she missed him, even in the slightest.

Summer slipped away, shedding its coat of green for a costume of orange and russet.

The wind whipped her ankles with its icy tentacles as she pushed the door closed behind her. Niki shivered as she began unfastening the buttons of her coat, reluctant to remove the fur collar from around her neck. However, she had arrived late—one of Mrs. Whitman's taboos—and she wasn't going to risk drawing any more attention to herself by dawdling while she tried to get warm.

"Sorry I'm late," she called as she hurried down the aisle.

"Quite all right, Miss O'Hara. I just came in the back myself." Tucker Thorpe offered his hand to help her up onto the stage.

Niki and Tucker had been working together for several weeks now, both on serious drama and on comedy pieces. Tucker was a pleasant fellow, about her own age, with auburn hair and green eyes. Niki thought he was terribly talented and a lot of fun to work with.

"Very generous of you, Mr. Thorpe," Mrs. Whitman said as she walked onto the stage from the wings, "but it is not all right with me. I expect my students to be on time . . . *both* of them."

Tucker raised his eyes to the ceiling, but only Niki could see him. She suppressed a giggle.

"I have important news for you two. If you're ready to work harder than we've ever worked before, Mr. Whitman and I have decided to open the theatre for a real production . . . starring Miss Niki O'Hara and Mr. Tucker Thorpe, of course."

Niki was struck dumb.

"Well? Haven't you anything to say?" Mrs. Whitman was enjoying herself, grinning from ear to ear.

Tucker was the first to respond. "What production? When?"

"We've found a delightful little script. A musical comedy. I think it's perfect for your debut."

"A musical? Oh, Mrs. Whitman, do you really think I can handle a musical?"

"Niki, I think you can handle anything I tell you to handle. You're a natural." She pointed to a couple of wooden chairs on the stage. "Sit down and let me tell you about it."

And so it began. If Niki had thought she was working hard before, she was in for a surprise. Her days started before sun up and ended after the sun had set. While rehearsing, she felt filled with energy, but as soon as she stepped into the automobile, she succumbed to the exhaustion that overwhelmed her. She never complained. Tired though she was, she loved every minute of it.

The schedule called for the show to open the first of December. Niki looked forward to that day with great excitement and formidable trepidation. One moment she knew this was her great chance to prove to herself and everyone else that she was born for the stage. Other times she was convinced that she would fail miserably, that she would forget all her lines and the play would be a flop—all because of her!

Like a giant orange ball, the sun rested on the treetops. Birds sang their evening songs and squirrels scurried from limb to limb in the dying rays of daylight. Somewhere on the lake, two lovers floated idly, their laughter floating away from them on the gentle summer breeze.

She rode beside him in silence, her heart racing for some unexplained reason. Then there was the dog. It jumped from the bushes, nipping at her horse. The horse was spinning, rearing, kicking, but still it didn't leave. Any moment now, her mount would bolt down the path. She knew it. And she knew what would happen once it did. She would fall and the pain would start all over again.

But this time was different. Adam reached out and pulled her from the saddle. He held her safely in his arms as her horse raced away, riderless. The dog was gone too. Everything was still. She was aware only of his eyes as they stared into hers. Ever so slowly, he bent his head toward hers. He was going to kiss her. In a moment, she was going to feel his lips touching hers! She waited breathlessly.

"Young man, just what do you think you're doin'?"

Niki sat up with a gasp, her eyes wide open and her heart pounding in her ears. A dream. But it had seemed so real. And so strange. Why was she dreaming about Adam?

"Put that down and get into your room."

Her room was dark, but a light shone under her door. Niki got quickly out of bed. She slipped her robe over her nightgown, then hurried to find out the cause of the disturbance in the hallway. She pulled open the door just as Taylor did the same across the hall. In unison, they looked toward the stairs. On the top step was Mrs. Mulligan, wearing a plaid robe over her high-necked, cotton nightgown, her head covered in a white nightcap. Eddie stood beside her, the housekeeper's heavy hand on his shoulder.

"Mrs. Mulligan, what's the trouble?" Taylor asked.

"I found him sneakin' about the house. Probably stealin' you blind while you sleep, if you were askin' me. Look! See what he's picked up tonight!"

Clenched in his hands, Eddie was holding a miniature bronze horse.

Taylor moved toward him, her kind features undisturbed. "Thank you, Mrs. Mulligan. You may go to bed. We'll handle this."

"To bed, is it?" Mrs. Mulligan mumbled as she turned to descend the stairs. "How can I sleep with such trouble in the house?

191

Mark my words . . ." Her voice faded away as she turned a corner and disappeared from view.

"Would you like to tell us your side of it, Eddie?" Taylor asked softly.

"I wasn't stealin' nothin'."

"We didn't think you were." She, too, placed her hand on his shoulder, but Taylor's touch was worlds apart from that of Mrs. Mulligan's. "What *were* you going to do with it, Eddie?"

He raised his chin defiantly. "I . . . I wanted it in my room. I'll put it back."

"No need to. You may have it."

Eddie's mouth fell open, the defiance disappearing, replaced by confusion. He loosened his grip on the small statue in his hand. "You mean for my own?" he whispered in awe.

"Yes. It's yours. You may keep it in your room or wherever you like." Taylor bent and kissed the top of his head. "Now let's all go back to bed."

As she turned, Eddie grabbed at Taylor's waist to give her a spontaneous hug, something he had never done in his entire life. In his exuberance, he tripped and fell against her, knocking her off balance. Niki watched in horror as Taylor tumbled over Eddie and rolled down the stairs.

"Gram!"

Niki raced after her, her heart in her throat. Her grandmother was lying in a crumpled heap at the bottom of the stairs.

"Gram!"

Taylor didn't move.

"Pearl! Mrs. Mulligan! Max!" Panic rose in giant swells, threatening to sweep Niki out of control.

"I didn't mean to," Eddie whispered from the top of the stairs. "I didn't mean to. Mrs. Taylor, I didn't mean to hurt you."

Mrs. Mulligan whisked around the corner, then ground to a halt. "Mrs. Lattimer! Lord have mercy, what's happened here?"

"She's fallen. Quick. Call the doctor. Don't just stand there. Call Dr. Sears at once."

Mrs. Mulligan hurried for the telephone as Niki knelt down on the floor, cradling Taylor's head in her lap.

"I knew it," the housekeeper called back to her. "I knew there'd be trouble with the likes o' him in the house."

Niki paid no attention to her, concerned only with the terrifying stillness of her grandmother. She was unaware of Eddie, tears streaking his cheeks, as he paused at the open door of the house to look back at the two people who had been so kind to him. Then he closed the door behind him and disappeared into the night.

"It's not good, Miss O'Hara. Your grandmother should probably be in a hospital but she refuses to go. I'm sending a nurse over to stay with her." The doctor shook his head as he slipped on his coat. "Mrs. Lattimer is a very healthy, very strong woman, but she's no spring chicken. Broken bones and sprains don't heal as fast when you get to be her age. If she doesn't take care of herself and do just as I say, she may find herself unable to walk again."

"I'll see that she does just as she's told, doctor."

He smiled as he shook his head. "You weren't exactly a model patient, my dear girl. Are you certain you can handle someone older and even more stubborn than you?"

"She won't be allowed to move more than her little finger."

"Well, she won't want to move even that for a day or two," he said as he put his hat on his head. "I'll check on her again in the morning. Goodnight, Miss O'Hara."

"Goodnight, Dr. Sears. Thank you for coming so quickly."

Niki leaned against the door with a sigh as she glanced up to stairs toward her grandmother's room. She knew the doctor was right. Taylor would be a difficult patient. She was no more fond of inactivity than Niki.

"Miss O'Hara?" Max was watching her from the doorway to the dining room. "How is she?"

"Her leg's broken, Max, but she's going to be all right."

"Miss O'Hara, did you think to call Mr. Cheavers? He'd want to know."

"Mr. Cheavers?" It hadn't occurred to her to call anyone besides the doctor. "I can't call him in the middle of the night."

The butler shrugged his shoulders. "Whatever you say, miss, but he'd want to know, no matter the time."

Niki considered his comment for a moment and knew he was right. She would have to be blind not to know that Conrad Cheavers was courting her grandmother. He would indeed want to know, no matter the time. "I'll call him at once." As she walked toward the telephone, she added, "Max, would you check on Eddie, please? I haven't seen him since Gram fell. He must be hiding in his room. Poor kid. He must have been scared to death. And he was so happy about the horse, too."

"I'll do it, miss." Max went up the stairs.

The telephone rang at the other end, then a sleepy voice answered, "Cheavers."

"Hello? This is Niki O'Hara. I need to speak to Mr. Cheavers. It's important."

The voice on the other end was indignant. "Miss O'Hara, do you have any idea what time it is? Mr. Cheavers is in bed and I suggest you do the same."

"I don't care what you suggest," Niki snapped back. "And if you don't want Mr.

Cheavers showing you the door, you'll wake him. Mrs. Lattimer has had an accident."

There was an anxious pause. "Oh, my. Yes. Yes, I'll get him at once."

Conrad must have rushed instantly to the phone for Niki didn't have long to wait.

"Niki? Niki, what's happened?" There was no trace of sleep in his voice.

"Mr. Cheavers, I'm afraid Gram has had an accident. I thought you should know. She's taken a bad fall and broken her leg. She's going to be all right but . . ."

"I'll be right there, Niki." The line was dead.

Niki placed the receiver back in its cradle, then started for the stairs. The doctor had said Taylor was sleeping, but Niki wanted to be at her side in case she awakened and needed something. The nurse the doctor had ordered wouldn't arrive until morning.

Niki pushed her unruly hair back from her face as she climbed the stairs. What a terrible night.

"Miss O'Hara?" Max met her at the top of the stairs. "Eddie's not in his room. He doesn't seem to be anywhere in the house."

"Not in the house? But, Max, where could he . . ." She placed her hand over her mouth as her eyes grew wide. "Oh, no. Max, you don't think he . . ." But, of course, it was true. The boy thought the accident was his fault, that he had hurt Taylor. "Max, get Roger and go looking for him. You *must* find him! You must!"

"We'll do all we can, miss."

CHAPTER 12

Glenrose, Conrad's estate on Long Island, was secluded. Just the sort of place to see that Taylor got the necessary rest the doctor had ordered. When Conrad insisted that they bring her grandmother here, Niki hadn't been able to say no to him. He was a very forceful person when he felt strongly about something, and he definitely felt strongly about Taylor Lattimer. Mrs. Whitman had been very understanding when Niki explained her need to be away for a few days while Taylor got settled in at Glenrose.

"You have your part almost to perfection, Niki," her director had said. "You go on with your grandmother. We'll use your understudy while you're away so the rest of the cast can rehearse. Don't give us another thought. We'll see you on Thursday."

Niki could see she wouldn't really be needed at all at Glenrose. Conrad had enough servants to staff a small hospital, let alone take care of one patient who had brought along her own nurse. Besides,

Conrad had also accompanied them, and he doted on Taylor in a most amusing way—amusing to Niki, at least, for she was young and had never considered that people her grandmother's age could be so openly and demonstratively in love.

More than Taylor's actual injuries, she knew her grandmother was worried about Eddie. He had disappeared without a trace, and they both knew he had left carrying the blame for Taylor's mishap. Although Max and Roger had searched the streets for several days, there had been no sign of their little orphan. Niki had notified the police, just in case they should see him, but she knew that was futile. The city was filled with boys that could fit Eddie's description, and since he had not broken any laws, the police would be little help in tracking him down. She hated to think it, but she would probably never see Eddie again.

Glenrose was a beautiful, tree-studded estate with over sixty acres of lawn and wooded countryside. The brick manor itself had nearly a hundred rooms in its three stories. It was an experience just finding ones way from bedroom to dining room to drawing room. Niki spent her days, in between sitting with Taylor, exploring the mansion. It was the ballroom that fascinated her the most. The enormous room had two walls paneled with mirrors from ceiling to floor. The outside wall was glass, exposing a stone terrace, manicured formal gardens, and a pond complete with lighted fountain. The one remaining wall was covered with a bejeweled and gilded fresco. The painting showed twirling dancers in the very same ballroom, an orchestra against one of the mirrored walls, and lovers outside, strolling hand in hand in the gardens.

"Gram," she asked Taylor the same day she first discovered the ballroom, "have you ever been to Glenrose before?"

"Once, when your grandfather was still alive. We came to a gala party here one night."

"Then you've seen the ballroom."

Taylor frowned thoughtfully, then nodded as remembrance brought a smile to her lips. "Ah, yes. It's something, isn't it? Brent and I danced until nearly dawn. It was a wonderful night. We were returning from Europe. Your uncle Carl was able to see at last, your mother was over her broken engagement, and we were on our way home to Heart's Landing. The world seemed very bright that night."

"Gram? Are you still in love with Grandfather?" The question popped out without invitation.

"What a strange question, Niki," Taylor said, but she didn't look disturbed by it. In fact, she seemed to be considering it quite seriously. "Why do you ask?"

There was no point beating around the bushes. She had started it. She might as well finish it. "I was wondering because of Mr. Cheavers."

"Conrad?"

Niki studied her grandmother, her silver hair pulled neatly back into a chignon, her blue eyes as expressive as ever. Could she be so perceptive of others but not Conrad? Niki took hold of one of Taylor's hands and squeezed it affectionately. "Gram, how do you feel about Mr. Cheavers?" She paused a moment, then added, "He's in love with you, you know."

"Conrad?" Taylor echoed herself.

They were interrupted by Taylor's nurse, Mrs. Smith, as she entered the room. "Miss O'Hara, there's a telephone call for you."

"For me?"

"Yes, miss."

Niki stood up, bent forward to kiss her grandmother's forehead, then whispered, "I'll be back later."

Niki walked along the wide hallway, following the curved staircase down to the main floor of the manor. Just off the entrance hall was the study. It was here that she took the call.

"Hello?" she said in the receiver. "This is Niki O'Hara."

"Niki? It's Mother. Can you hear me?"

"Ma? Ma, it's great to hear your voice." It was true. It really was wonderful after so many months. Although Niki had been writing to her family in Idaho regularly, she had remained stubborn about talking to her mother until she had achieved her goal. "How did you know we were here?"

"We got your telegram about Mother's accident. When no one answered at your place, we called Travis. He told us you'd taken Mother out to Conrad Cheavers' place on Long Island." There was a lot of static on the line and the reception was weak. "Niki, how is she? I know your telegram said she was all right, but I want to be sure."

Niki nodded as if Brenetta could see her. "She really is going to be fine, Ma. You know Gram. She's a tough one. A broken leg isn't going to keep her down."

"Well, I'm glad to know you're with her anyway. How long will the two of you be staying out there?"

"I think Gram will be here until she's completely recovered. Mr. Cheavers will see to that. I'm going back to the city on Wednesday. I've got to be back for rehearsals on Thursday."

There was a pregnant pause on the other end of the line. "Niki, you can't be serious?" her mother's incredulous voice asked. "I want you to stay with your grandmother until she can return to New York with you."

"But, Ma, I can't do that. We have a play

opening in just a few weeks. I've told you in my letters that I have the lead. I can't throw that away now."

"Kathleen Nicole, you'll do just that. Your grandmother is more important than any play . . . and you'll stay with her." Brenetta's stern tone boded ill for Niki if she chose to argue.

But argue she did. "I'm sorry, Mother. Gram doesn't need nor expect me to stay, and I have to go back to New York before she's able—whether you like it or not." Her own temper was showing, her voice rising in anger.

More crackling lines, befitting the moods of the participants of the conversation.

"Niki, remember the terms of your stay in New York. If you disobey me, you'll have to return to Heart's Landing. And don't think your grandmother will come to your rescue. She's promised to abide by the rules, too. She may be extraordinarily fond of you, but she'll stand by her word."

Niki held the receiver away from her ear for a moment, pondering her mother's demands. She knew what Brenetta was saying was true. Her grandmother would be bound by her promise. If Niki refused to obey her mother's wishes, she would be forced back to Heart's Landing or she would be on her own. The decision took only a second to make.

She placed the receiver to her ear once

more. "I'm sorry, Ma. I can't hear you any-more. I'll give your love to Gram . . . just before I go back to the city." Then she hung up.

Niki sat staring at the phone for several minutes. She would have to tell Gram what had happened. No. She wouldn't do that. It would only worry her. She would simply go back to New York and move out of White House. She had enough money to last her for several months, and by that time, the play would be a success. Mrs. Whitman had told them that if the play was a hit, they would no longer be considered students but actors and would be paid accordingly. That would take care of her income. Of course, she wouldn't be able to afford any more lessons, but then, she wouldn't need them after playing on Broadway.

The telephone rang again. She hesitated, certain it would be Brenetta calling back, then picked it up.

"Hello. Conrad Cheavers' residence."

"Hello. This is Adam Bellman. Is it possible for me to speak to Mrs. Lattimer? I believe she's a house guest of Mr. Cheavers."

Niki considered identifying herself but decided against it. Instead, she disguised her voice. She was quite adept at accents, a talent she had discovered since working with Mrs. Whitman. "I'm sorry, Mr. Bellman. Mrs. Lattimer is unable to come to the telephone."

"Listen. Can you give her a message, please? Tell her I've been on business in Philadelphia for several weeks and have just learned of her accident. Give her my love and tell her I'm thinking about her."

"Yes. I'll tell her, sir."

"Oh, miss. Is Mrs. Lattimer's niece there also?"

Niki's heart skipped a beat as the dream she had had just before Taylor's accident suddenly flashed in her mind. "Yes, sir. She's Mr. Cheavers' guest, too." She felt a little breathless. "Was there a message for her?"

A pause. "No. No message. That's all."

"Very good, sir. I'll tell Mrs. Lattimer you called."

"Thanks."

The line went dead.

Adam sat back in his chair. He wished he had asked to talk to Niki. Even if they had argued, it would have been good to hear her voice. He missed Niki so much even the servant that answered the telephone had sounded like her. If he wasn't so blasted stubborn, he would have gone back to Niki's the day after their last argument, even if he *had* sworn he'd never be back.

"Lord have pity on the man who is fool enough to fall in love with you."

Those had been his last words to her, and

truer words were never spoken. He was, indeed, to be pitied for he did, indeed, love her—and was miserable in his unrequited love. He *would* have gone back. He would even have asked Niki's forgiveness for what he'd said to her that night, but Jonathon Houseman had chosen just that time to assign him to one of the most difficult and lengthy cases of his career, a case that would keep him in Philadelphia for several more weeks to come.

Adding to his misery was the realization that Niki thought him a heartless ogre over the matter of Eddie. He hadn't meant to give her the impression that she shouldn't try to help the boy, but he had seen too many wealthy folks trying to assuage some inner guilt by dropping a few dollars into the vast sea of poverty, never really giving heed to the cries of the desperately needy that surrounded them in the slums of New York. He knew that Niki wasn't like that. She wasn't going to dress the boy in new clothes only to turn him back on the streets. Yet Adam had made her believe that's what he thought she would do. He had really messed up.

So what else was new?

Taylor lay in her giant-sized bed, propped up by a preponderance of goose down pillows. Sunlight spilled through the large, ivy-framed windows, belying the cold

November day that left frost wherever shadows lingered. A fire crackled cheerfully in the fireplace across from her four-poster bed.

She was in a pensive mood. Conrad had just left her bedside. After what Niki said to her, she had been watching him with new eyes, and now she had to admit it. He was in love with her. Not just a good friend. In love with her.

"I'm a blind old bat," she muttered to herself, silently calling herself several kinds of a fool.

So, what was she to do about it? She had never thought—not once in all these years —that someone besides Brent might love her . . . or that she might love someone else. Yes. That's what was really bothering her. Could she be falling in love with Conrad, too? Was it possible, when she'd known she would love Brent the rest of her days, that another man had won her heart? She felt disloyal at the very thought.

"All these years, Brent," she whispered, "and you're as real to me as if you were in this room with me right now."

Time hadn't erased her memories of him —so tall and handsome with his dusky brown hair and tawny eyes. Sometimes she saw him as she'd seen him that very first time, his jacket covered with a thick layer of red Georgia dust. Or sometimes he was wearing his Union uniform, like he was the day he galloped up the drive at Spring Haven, returning to make her his bride. And sometimes he was dressed as a wrangler. That's how she'd liked him best, his shirt open at the neck, a wide-brimmed hat worn low over his forehead to keep the sun out of his eyes. No, time hadn't erased her memories, but had it freed her to love again?

Taylor gazed into the orange-red flames, the flickering light almost hypnotic. Perhaps the mesmerizing dance of the fire put her into a sort of trance, or perhaps she was searching her soul so hard for answers that she was dreaming while wide awake. Or maybe—just maybe—he was there.

"Brent," she whispered to the apparition she now saw leaning against the mantle of the fireplace. "Brent, would it destroy what we had together if I loved another man? Am I just a very foolish old woman?"

He smiled, and that smile said more than a thousand words could have hoped to say.

"Thank you, Brent. You know he'll never have the part of my heart that belongs to you. He'll never take away the memories, the past we shared, but it would be wonderful to love someone again and to be loved. I would so like to be loved the way you loved me."

He disappeared, fading back into the firelight as suddenly as he had come, and Taylor drifted off to sleep.

* * *

"Gram, you do what your nurse tells you or I'll be back in a flash to make sure you do."

Niki was wearing a traveling dress and a long, fur coat. A warm hat was already tied snugly over her head, and she was holding a fur muff in one hand as she sat beside Taylor, saying her goodbyes.

"You quit your fussing over me, Niki, and be on your way. You'll be getting home after dark as it is."

Niki laughed merrily. "Look who's looking out for whom!" She glanced toward Conrad who was standing on the other side of the bed. "You're going to have your hands full, Mr. Cheavers. She's getting feisty already."

"I think I can handle her." There was a twinkle in his eye as he glanced at the patient, looking as lovely as ever in a periwinkle-blue, chiffon bedrobe, her silver hair swept up from her neck and held in place with sapphire combs.

Niki kissed her grandmother's cheek. "I'm going to miss you, Gram," she whispered, her voice choked with suppressed emotions. If only she could tell her about Brenetta's phone call. If only . . . but she couldn't. Gram would try to reason with her, tell her to wait until she could talk things over with Brenetta. Niki couldn't wait. If she didn't go back, she would lose the part to her understudy. This was her chance and she couldn't let it slip from her grasp.

She stood up and held out her hand toward Conrad. He walked around the bed and clasped it warmly as they exchanged an understanding glance, sharing the knowledge that they both loved the woman in the bed a great deal.

"You go back and prepare to be the best darned actress that ever appeared on Broadway, Miss O'Hara. We'll be there in the front row to cheer for you on opening night. You can bet on it."

"Thank you, Mr. Cheavers. I know you'll see that Gram behaves."

Taylor's eyes darted back and forth between them. "Would you two quit talking about me as if I weren't here? It's most annoying."

Everyone laughed, and Niki bent over the bed to kiss her grandmother one more time before leaving.

"You call me if you need me, dear," Taylor told her, a tear glistening in the corner of her eye. "I'm going to miss you."

"I'll miss you, too, Gram. Be good to Mr. Cheavers." She sniffed back her own tears. It hurt more than she could say to deceive her grandmother this way. She hoped Taylor would forgive her when she learned of Niki's disobedience.

"See you on Broadway," she called over

her shoulder as she disappeared through the bedroom door. And to herself she added, "Look out, Broadway, 'cause here comes Niki O'Hara!"

CHAPTER 13

Niki stretched languidly, then sat up in bed. Light was just beginning to peek through the window curtains, and she knew Fiona would soon be bringing her a cup of coffee to help her wake up. She got out of bed, padding barefoot across the floor, and pulled open the curtains, letting in the pewter gray light of early dawn.

Staring down at the deserted street below, she realized this would be the last morning she would be looking out this window. This afternoon, after rehearsals were over, she would go in search of an apartment. She planned on taking her packed suitcases with her when she left for the theatre. She would tell the servants she was going to be staying with friends until her grandmother returned. That way no one would be calling Taylor and upsetting her. Niki would call her herself in a few days, once she was settled, and tell her what had happened. She felt that once she was in her own place, she wouldn't be as susceptible to Taylor's reasoning powers.

A quick rap on her door announced her morning coffee.

"Come in."

Fiona entered, carrying a tray with a small silver coffee pot and china cup in its center. "You're up already, miss. I hadn't expected it after you got in so late last night."

"I've got a big day ahead of me, Fiona. After being away, I'm a bit nervous about rehearsals. Suppose they've found my understudy to be a better actress than I am?"

"Not a chance, miss!" Fiona cried in earnest as she set the tray on the table near the bed. "Now, come have your coffee before it's too cold for drinking."

Niki took the cup with her to her dressing table where, in between sips, she began vigorously brushing her hair, bringing out the sheen in its deep chocolate strands. She felt so alive this morning. Excitement made the very air vibrate around her. Today she would be back on the stage. It seemed weeks instead of days since she had been at Whitman Theatre. She could hardly wait!

A large suitcase in each hand and a smaller one under each arm, Niki watched as Roger drove away in the car. After rehearsals, she would hire a cab to take her in search of her apartment.

She struggled with her suitcases as she

attempted to open the door in a lady-like fashion, but it was impossible. Glancing quickly around her, she turned her back to the door and gave it a push with her rump, backing inside as it flew open. The lobby was empty, the theatre quiet.

"Hello? Anyone here yet?"

No one answered.

Niki was surprised. She had thought she was running a little bit late and had dreaded Mrs. Whitman's disapproval.

She put the suitcases down near the door and went on into the auditorium. It was dark. "Hello? Mrs. Whitman?"

She heard footsteps backstage.

"Mrs. Whitman? Are you there?"

Lights flicked on, then Fred, the doorman, stepped onto the stage.

"Who's out there?" he asked, squinting his eyes toward the back where she stood.

"It's me, Fred. Niki O'Hara. Where is everybody? Isn't there a rehearsal today?"

"Haven't you heard, Miss O'Hara? The play's closed. Ain't no more rehearsals."

She felt as if someone had punched her. "Closed?" She walked toward the stage. "What do you mean, *closed?*"

Fred shook his head and clucked his tongue. "Would've thought somebody would've let you know." He scratched his shaggy sideburns. "Mr. Whitman's had a heart attack. Don't look too good for him, it don't. I don't expect there'll be another

Whitman production here. Mrs. Whitman's not left his side, and won't as long as he's alive. If'n he dies, I don't think she'll want to come back, either."

Niki sagged into a seat, her eyes wide with shock. It was terrible about Mr. Whitman. Really terrible. But what was she to do now? She couldn't go back to White House. If she did, she would soon find herself on the train heading for Idaho.

Seeing her white face, Fred came slowly down the steps from the stage. "I'm sorry I gave you such a jolt, Miss O'Hara. I shouldn't of sprung it on you like that."

"No. That's all right, Fred. I . . . I'm just surprised." She looked up at him. "Would you get me a cab, Fred? I sent my car home."

"Right away, Miss O'Hara. Right away."

The three room apartment, a second story walk up in Greenwich Village, was small but quaint, and the price fit her pocketbook. Niki paid the landlady the first month's rent and closed the door. She walked across to the couch and sat down, the springs squeeking beneath her. Her eyes trailed around the room, memorizing the sparse furnishings of her new home. Everything seemed so still, so silent. She was on her own. For the first time in her life, she was really on her own.

For one second, she allowed fear to sweep

through her, leaving a chill in its wake, like ice in her veins. Then she thought of her grandmother. Taylor had taken care of a plantation in the midst of the Civil War. Niki's own mother had helped build Heart's Landing to be one of the greatest ranches in the Northwest. It wasn't in Niki's blood to give in to fear.

"Well, then, I'd best start doing some planning," she said aloud, breaking the silence. "First, a job. I'll have to find out who's holding auditions and get a part in a play. It may not be a lead like I'd hoped, but it'll feed me until that lead comes along."

But parts were not that easy to find. Niki felt as if she'd seen every director and every agent in the theatre district of New York. She walked more streets and knocked on more doors than she would have thought possible, and still no one showed any interest.

"Check back with us later, miss."

"Naw, we got nothin' now, but if you'd like to drop by my place . . ."

"You're a cute kid. You just might turn into somethin'. Come back in a couple years and we'll see about it then."

"Mrs. Whitman? Oh, sure. She was something in her day. Heard her husband died. Too bad. Well, you've had a good teacher. Sorry I got nothing for you."

Finally, she admitted she'd have to find

some other sort of work until something opened up for her on the stage, even if it was only in the chorus. She also knew it was time she called Taylor and let her know that she was all right and not to worry, but she didn't want to do that until she could tell her she had a job.

Several days later she found a position in the millinery department of an exclusive department store.

"Miss O'Hara, we have a fine clientelle here at The Baron's. We expect our employees to remember that they are here to serve our clients with utmost care. They are people of breeding, and you must *never* forget your place." Her new supervisor looked at Niki over the rim of her glasses. "You are a fairly attractive girl. Don't forget that we expect your personal life to be above reproach as well. No dating other Baron employees. Certainly no flirting with any of the gentlemen customers. Is that understood?"

"I understand, Miss Sherman."

"Good." Miss Sherman took her behind the counter. "Miss Jones, come here," she called to a tall, extremely thin woman at the other end of the counter. "Miss Jones, this is our new employee, Miss O'Hara. She's going to be working with you in Millinery. See that she knows where to put her things."

"Yes, ma'am."

Miss Sherman turned abruptly and walked down the wide aisle.

"She's really something, isn't she. You can call me Grace."

"Hello, Grace. I'm Niki."

"Put your hat and purse under here. Lunch too if you've brought it."

Niki removed her hat pins. "I didn't know if I'd find anything or not, so I don't have a lunch with me."

"If you like cold turkey sandwiches, you can share mine. My mother always packs more than I can eat." Grace's smile was warm, and Niki knew she was going to like working with her. "Come on. I'll show you the ropes."

By the time the day was over, Niki's head was filled to capacity with do's and don'ts, facts and figures, rules and regulations. Every time she waited on a customer, she had looked up to find Miss Sherman peering at her from behind a counter, a frown furrowing her pristine forehead.

"I feel like I'm being followed," she told Grace.

"Ah, just ignore her. You're doing fine."

"Thanks."

As Niki secured her hat in place and slipped into her coat, Grace stopped beside her on her way out. "I don't live far from here, Niki. Would you like to stop over for supper tomorrow night after work? I'd love to have you."

"That's awfully nice of you. I'd like to

very much."

"Super." Grace buttoned her coat up tight around her neck. "See you in the morning."

The November air was crisp, the clouds overhead promising snow. In fact, as Niki walked toward her apartment, a light flurry began to blow, stinging her cheeks and sticking to her dark lashes. She tucked her hands deep inside her muff and leaned forward, her pace quickening before the storm got too serious.

She was glad to see her building come into view. The streets seemed awfully dark and strange to her, out in them alone. She was eager to get into her own rooms and lock the door behind her. As she hurried up the stairs, she pulled her key from her pocket, then opened the door and entered as quickly as she could.

The room was nearly as cold as outside. She could feel heat coming from the steam radiator, but it wasn't enough to get rid of the chill she felt. Although a fire would have been nice, she was too tired to bother. Instead, she decided to go right to bed. She wasn't even hungry. She just wanted to sleep.

But sleep wouldn't come once she'd crawled between the cold sheets of the bed in her tiny bedroom. Different thoughts skipped through her mind in relentless procession, staving off the blessed release that sleep would bring her.

It began with how different this bedroom was from her room on Fifth Avenue. This one was so small, there was barely room for the single bed with its lumpy mattress and the dressing table. Faded wall paper covered all the walls, the once bright blue design now turned a dirty gray. Two pictures had once hung over the bed. Someone had removed one of them, leaving only the outline of the frame on the wallpaper; the other was a nondescript watercolor. A rag rug covered the floor next to the bed.

From there, she thought of Grace and how she had looked at Niki's fine coat and fur muff. With a start, Niki realized just how different she must be from all the other employees at The Baron's. She decided then and there that she must try to dress more like them, to not stand out with her fancy clothing. She didn't want anyone to know that she was more accustomed to being waited on than doing the waiting.

Of course, there were her thoughts of Taylor. She still hadn't called. Poor Gram. If she tried to call Niki and couldn't find her, she would be worried, even with the message that Niki had left about staying with friends. No, she had to call her and tell her what she was doing. Tomorrow. Tomorrow she was going to do it.

And, now that she was working, she must remember that her free time really wasn't free to be spent with new friends like Grace. She had to use it trying to find a way onto the stage. Selling hats and gloves to ladies from Fifth Avenue wasn't going to get her on Broadway, wasn't going to put her name in lights on the Great White Way.

As the wind blew around her window, whispering mournfully, Niki drifted into a troubled sleep.

"Hurry up, driver," Adam said impatiently, watching out the window as they drove down Fifth Avenue. Everything was covered with snow, a magic, fairyland white. "Can't you go any faster?"

"No, sir, I can't. Not on these roads. I'll get you there in good time."

But it wasn't fast enough to suit Adam. He wanted to see Niki. He hadn't thought of anything else for weeks, especially once he'd known things were wrapping up and he'd be coming back to New York soon. Now he was here and on his way to her house. It couldn't be fast enough when he'd waited so long.

"There! There it is, driver. Stop here."

He hopped from the car before it had come to a complete stop. He ran through the snow, jumping over drifts, nearly stumbling as his feet sank below the crusty surface. He reached the door, puffing, his breath turned to frost in the air, and rang the doorbell. Mrs. Mulligan answered the ring.

"Mrs. Mulligan. It's good to see you. Is Miss O'Hara in?"

She looked a bit surprised. "Why, Mr. Bellman, sir. Come in. It's colder than the North Pole out there." She pulled him inside and shut the door. "Here. Let me take your hat, sir."

"Thank you. Please tell Niki that I'm here and would like to speak with her."

"I'm sorry, Mr. Bellman. She's not here."

His heart sank. He'd been counting on her being at home at this hour. "Is she at the theatre?"

"No, sir," Mrs. Mulligan's reply was reluctant.

"Do you know when she'll be back?"

"Mr. Bellman, I think you'd best be talking to Mrs. Lattimer about the young miss," the housekeeper replied briskly.

Adam was alarmed. Something had to be wrong for her to evade such simple questions. "What is it, Mrs. Mulligan? What's happened to Niki?"

Mrs. Mulligan turned her back toward him as she placed his hat on the hall table. She paused a moment to draw a deep breath, then turned to face him again. "I'm sorry. I just don't know where she is, sir. After Mrs. Lattimer fell and that little street urchin ran away . . . I knew things would come to no good with him around.

Miss O'Hara, she came back to take her lessons but something went wrong there and she just up and left." She stopped and regained her stern composure. "I really can't tell you what's going on, sir. You'll have to call Mrs. Lattimer. She's still out at Mr. Cheaver's place on Long Island. Number's next to the telephone, if you'd like to call from here."

"Thank you, Mrs. Mulligan. I'll do just that."

Taylor was impatient for her leg to heal, especially now with Niki taking flight. The girl had been very evasive when she called.

"Gram, don't worry. I've got myself a very respectable job with some very nice people, and I found myself a nice little apartment. You'd approve. Really you would."

"Where *is* your apartment, Niki?"

"I can't tell you. Gram, I've got to do this on my own. Mother wouldn't let you help now anyway, not since I so flagrantly disobeyed her. Don't worry about me, Gram. I'm going to be fine. When I get that part on Broadway, I'll let you know."

A letter had arrived a few days after the phone call, but it hadn't told her any more than she'd already known. Taylor didn't want to force Niki back to White House. After all, there *was* the problem with

Brenetta—and she could be more stubborn than Taylor and Niki put together—but Taylor did want to know what Niki was doing and how she was getting along.

When Adam's call came, she was down in Conrad's library, trying to take her mind off Niki by reading a good book. It wasn't working.

"Aunt Taylor, what's going on? I came to see Niki, and Mrs. Mulligan seems to think she's disappeared."

"Not disappeared exactly, Adam. Let's say she's temporarily misplaced herself."

"What kind of answer is that?" Adam obviously felt this situation did not call for levity.

Taylor smiled to herself. Her great-nephew was so transparent in his feelings for Niki, but she wondered if he had yet acknowledged those feelings, even to himself. It was time that he did, as far as she was concerned. She couldn't think of two people who belonged together more than Niki and Adam, even if they didn't have the common sense to know it.

"Aunt Taylor, are you there?"

"Yes. Yes, I'm here. I was just thinking about something else." She cleared her throat. "Listen, Adam. Why don't you drive out here and we'll talk? I've been laid up with this leg, and I'm quite bored. Perhaps between the two of us, we can figure out where Niki has got herself to."

"Well, I . . ."

"Don't be stubborn, my boy."

"All right. I'll be there this afternoon."

"Good. Do you know how to get here?"

Adam replied, "I'll get directions from Marc. Goodbye."

"Goodbye, Adam." Taylor placed the receiver back in its cradle, still grinning.

Aloud to herself, she added, "Maybe this will do them both some good."

The gray skies had cleared, leaving behind an icy blue day. Adam's first view of Glenrose was picture perfect, the white blanket of snow sparkling and glittering in the sun's light, the temperature still too low to let any melting of the winter wonderland take place. Conrad himself opened the door in answer to Adam's ring.

"Adam. Come in. Taylor's been waiting for you." As Adam passed over his coat and hat, Conrad inquired, "How was Philadelphia? Have you tied things up there, or will you have to return?"

"Unless something slipped by me, which I certainly don't think it did, I shouldn't have to return, sir."

"Good. Good." Conrad began walking toward the salon. "Please call me Conrad. I'd like to consider us friends as well as business associates."

Adam nodded but had no chance to reply as they stepped into the salon, an enormous room filled with brocade and velvet chairs and sofas, Tiffany lamps, crystal chandeliers, heavy oak tables and ornate carpets. Taylor was seated near one of the three fireplaces in the room. Her feet were propped up on a stool, a blanket thrown over her legs for added warmth.

Her beautiful old face lit up when she saw him. "Adam, I thought you'd changed your mind. It was getting so late."

"Couldn't have kept me away, Aunt Taylor. I've missed you." He kissed the top of her silver-haired head. "I feel like I haven't seen you in years." He sat down in a chair beside her.

"It *has* been about six months." It was a gentle reproof.

Adam leaned forward, resting his arms on his knees as he stared into the fire. His handsome face looked troubled, his rugged jaw tense. "I know I shouldn't have stayed away so long. But this case in Philadelphia . . ."

"Adam?" Taylor's voice was hushed, forcing him to look up at her. When his wretched gaze met hers, she continued. "Adam, don't try to fool yourself, even if you must try to fool me."

A half-hearted grin lifted the corners of his mouth.

"My dear boy, why don't you just admit that you love the girl?"

He ran his fingers through his hair, a

gesture of impatience—or was it futility? "What difference would it make if I admitted it? The feeling is far from mutual."

"I wonder, Adam," Taylor whispered, her own eyes drifting to the fire. "I wonder. . ."

CHAPTER 14

Grace's apartment was really only one room—a small one, at that—with a tiny alcove that had been converted into a kitchenette. But she had made it uniquely hers. Grace was a lover of flowers and she had them everywhere—photographs, paintings, bedspread, curtains . . . even a few live ones. A daybed was against the outside wall beneath the lone window, and a table, used both as a night stand and for meals, was beside it.

The two girls sat on the daybed, eating some just baked cookies, slightly blackened on the bottom. Niki had just finished telling Grace about her acting ambitions. She had confessed that she had left home against the wishes of her parents, but withheld the true facts about her family.

"But, Niki, I think that's absolutely super! To think my new friend will someday be a famous actress. I just know it will be soon!"

"I hope you're right. It seems like I've been waiting so long already." Niki tucked her knees under her chin, her violet eyes growing dreamy as she thought about how her opening night might have been if Mr. Whitman hadn't fallen ill and died. Tucker and she would have *wowed* them all.

Grace leaned back against the wall. "I guess I've never had any greater goals than to find a man who could love a plain girl and then get married."

"Why, Grace, you're not plain," Niki protested.

Grace laughed. "You're sweet, Niki, but I know what I look like. I'm too tall and too skinny. My complexion is sallow and my hair is stringy."

Unfortunately, Grace's description of herself was quite accurate. Niki studied her friend from the other side of the daybed, puckering her lips in concentration.

"You know," she said at last, "if you'd use a little make-up . . ."

"*Make-up!* Good heavens, Niki. I couldn't possibly! My mother would disown me if she ever learned I was using make-up."

Niki scoffed. "How absurd. If it makes you look better, why would anybody think it was so terrible?"

Grace uncurled her legs and stood up. "Well, you couldn't make me look any shorter with your stage magic." A few steps took her across to her kitchen where she poured some more milk in her glass.

Turning, she leaned against the waist-high counter that divided the room from the alcove. "How are you going to look for parts when you work such long hours? Miss Sherman sure won't give you any time off for such nonsense. You have to be going to your own funeral to get any time off from The Baron's."

"As a matter of fact, I'm going to a reading tomorrow night. A friend of mine arranged it for me. Tucker says the part is perfect."

"Is Tucker your sweetheart?"

It was Niki's turn to laugh. "Tucker? No, not Tucker. I don't have a beau."

"Have you ever been in love, Niki?" Starry-eyed, enchanted by her own dreams, Grace wasn't really expecting an answer.

"I thought I was . . . once," Niki replied softly, the question bringing Adam's face clearly to mind.

How she missed him—aggravating, opinionated Adam. His wavy hair, his tall, lean body, so strong yet so tender. She missed his blue eyes challenging her, his laugh that had so often made her glad and just as often made her angry. She even missed every one of their silly fights. She tried to tell herself that she was just lonely, that she only missed Adam because he was part of all she had left behind. After all, she missed Gram and Conrad, too, and she had never once missed Adam when she'd still been with Taylor. Or had she?

She'd had the same dream about Adam several times in the past few weeks. It always stopped short just before he kissed her, and she always awoke, breathless and feeling cheated. She scolded herself for such silliness, but it didn't make the dreams go away at night. Nor did it eliminate their haunting memory during the day.

Adam was at the house on Fifth Avenue when Niki called again. It was only a few days before Christmas, and everyone was feeling the strain of separation.

"Gram, how are you? How's your leg doing?"

"I'm coming along just fine, Niki. It's you we're worried about."

"No need for that. I'm doing okay. I've met a very nice girl, and we've become great friends. We work together at . . ." She stopped herself. "Her name is Grace. She's helping me evenings, practicing lines and such."

Taylor's voice was gentle as she asked, "Any luck with a play?"

"No. No luck, but there's bound to be something soon." Another long pause. "Have you heard anything from Mother?"

"Yes. I spoke to her a few days ago. She wants you to come home."

Almost tearfully, Niki replied, "I can't, Gram. You know I can't. This is something

I have to do, even if it takes me years."

Taylor did understand. That was the problem. She wanted Niki with her for her own selfish reasons, but she knew this was a time of learning and growing for Niki that would benefit her the rest of her life. It wouldn't hurt her to struggle a bit.

"Yes, Niki. I *do* understand."

"Thanks, Gram. I love you!"

"I love you, too."

Adam had been standing over her shoulder the entire time. Now, he whispered, "Let me speak to her."

"Niki, someone else wants to say hello." She passed the phone to Adam.

"Niki? Niki, it's Adam. Where are you? I've got to see you."

There was only silence at the other end while Niki struggled with her warring emotions. She wanted to see him. She wanted to understand at last what she felt for him. Her nights were so often haunted by his image. But if she saw him, he might force her back to Fifth Avenue, and once she was there, it was only a matter of time before she would be at Heart's Landing. Besides, he had scoffed at her ambitions. She had to prove to Adam, above all, that she could do it.

"I'm sorry, Adam. I can't see anyone. Not until I'm appearing on Broadway."

"Don't be so damned stubborn. Don't you know what you're putting your grandmother through?"

Taylor grabbed his arm. "Shhh!" she hissed, trying to stop him, but it was too late.

"That's between her and me, Adam Bellman. I should have known you hadn't learned to mind your own business. Why don't you just let me live my own life?"

"You're being childish. Now tell me where you are so I can . . ."

The line went dead at the other end. He held the receiver away from his ear and stared at it mournfully.

"You two are quite a pair," Taylor muttered. She motioned for Max, who was standing in the background, to push her wheelchair into the drawing room. "Not a lick of sense between the two of them."

"All right!" Adam cried, slamming down the phone. "Maybe I *was* wrong. But how do you know she's not in some sort of trouble out there? She may not even be getting enough to eat."

"Adam, you astound me. Do you think I'm not trying to find out where she is? But, even when I find her, I'm not going to interfere, and if you know what's best, you won't either."

He followed her into the drawing room. "Then what am I to do? Just wait around? Aunt Taylor, I love her. I've loved her from almost the first moment I saw her at Spring Haven. I think it's time I told her."

"Not now, Adam." Taylor shook her head, her gaze warning him to heed the wisdom of her years. "There have been times when you should have, but now is not one of them. She wouldn't believe you if you told her, and you just might ruin your chances of winning her if you did. Give her a little time to succeed."

Adam could only shake his head slowly, not knowing who was right or what he should do. If only he could find her . . .

Christmas Eve. When Niki left The Baron's, the snow was just beginning to fall again. It was already dark. She couldn't bear to go back to her apartment, not just yet. Alone on Christmas Eve.

She hailed a cab and gave him directions, then sat back in her seat, letting depression settle over her like a shroud. She was so lonely. Grace had invited her to go home with her, but Niki hadn't wanted to butt in on her family's Christmas festivities.

If I weren't so stubborn, I'd be with Gram and Travis, she thought.

The cab slowed down. "Here we are, miss," the driver called back to her.

She opened the door herself. "Wait here," she told him. "I won't be staying."

Niki got out and stood on the sidewalk, staring up at the house. It was ablaze with lights. A green wreath decorated the door, and she could see people milling around the drawing room. Gram was probably still in a wheelchair, but she would be holding court, all the adoring men in her life making sure she was happy and comfortable. Conrad would be there and Travis and Adam. Anne would probably be there with Travis, and perhaps Marc and his fiance, Sarah Wycott, too.

"I love you, Gram. I love you, Travis," she whispered, tears filling her eyes. She brushed them away impatiently as she got back into the cab. "Take me back to The Baron's."

The store was closed, all the employees gone home to be with their families on Christmas Eve. Niki stood on the sidewalk as the cab drove away, staring at the darkened store windows. The wet snow clung to her face and mingled with her tears. At this moment, proving she could be an actress didn't seem so important.

She turned toward home, shoulders drooping. She passed no one for several blocks, and her depression deepened. It seemed that there wasn't a soul in the world that cared if she was alive or dead. She was close to the point of looking for another cab and heading back to Fifth Avenue when a dark form, huddled shivering in a nearby doorway, caught her attention.

Good sense should have told her to hurry on her way, but instead, Niki was drawn closer. Whoever it was, was small and slight, no danger to her. It had to be a child or a woman. She stopped a few feet away.

"Can I help you?"

He looked up, surprised that someone had spoken to him.

Niki couldn't believe it. *"Eddie?"*

He had been crying, just as she had been, and he wiped his eyes and nose on the sleeve of his raggedy jacket.

"Eddie, we looked everywhere for you!" Niki knelt beside him, ignoring the snow that already was making her dress wet. She held out her arms to him. She prayed that he wouldn't try to run away from her. "Eddie . . ."

Still choking back his tears, he slipped into her embrace as if he'd never been away. Niki held him close. She rubbed her cheek against his matted hair, murmuring his name.

Finally, she loosened her hold. "We can't stay out in the cold all night, Eddie. Let's go back to my place. It's just a few blocks from here."

The boy rubbed his eyes again, sniffing loudly. "A few blocks?"

"Yes. I've got my own apartment. Come on." She stood up and held out her hand for him to take.

Eddie stared at it a moment as if unsure of what he should do, but once he was sure, he moved quickly. He grabbed her hand like a drowning man would grab a life raft.

Together they walked through the falling snow, no longer alone on Christmas Eve.

The first thing she did upon arriving at her apartment was run him a bath. While he was soaking in the warm water, she put the kettle on to boil.

Poor Eddie, she thought. He had grown even skinnier and had seemed more the frightened waif now than when she'd first seen him last summer. She wished she had a gift of some sort to give him for Christmas. As for herself, just having him with her was present enough.

"The robe's a mite big," Eddie said from the door to the bathroom.

Niki looked up, then began to laugh. She had left him one of her robes to put on. As little as she was, it still was far too long for him, and it trailed behind him on the floor, the sleeves hiding his hands. Besides, the pink satin looked just plain silly on him.

"Come here and sit beside me," she managed to say as she controlled her mirth. When he'd done so, she asked, "Tell me where you've been? Why did you run away? We've missed you, Eddie."

He hung his head, his smile disappearing. "I couldn't stay after I hurt Gram that way."

"Oh, Eddie! That was an accident. No one blamed you." Niki put her arm around his shoulder. "Gram was so worried about you."

Eddie's brown eyes came up to meet hers. "Is she . . . is she all right now?"

"She's fine. She was up and around in no time," Niki said, stretching the truth. "She's still looking for you, Eddie. She loves you. We all do."

He fidgeted, struggling with words he had never said aloud before. "I love you, too."

Niki pulled him against her again, nuzzling her face in his hair. Time ticked away, unheeded in its passing, as she held him in silence. She couldn't help but think of the many times her mother and her father and her grandmother had held her just this way. She'd been so lucky. She had always been loved, always had somebody to take care of her. In Eddie she had been given the opportunity to share that love with someone who needed it desperately.

"Eddie?" she whispered. "Would you come live with me again? I'm here all alone, and I really would like your company."

He didn't look up. He just stayed nestled in her arms and answered, "Yes."

CHAPTER 15

It was difficult to look crisp and fresh when the temperature outside on this July day was nearing one hundred. The humidity made it difficult to breathe. Damp tendrils clung to Niki's forehead, and her blouse felt plastered to her back. She was counting the minutes until closing time when she could rush home and sink into a cool bath.

Miss Sherman marched by, pausing just long enough to give Niki a withering look. The woman didn't even have the decency to look warm in her dark skirt and jacket.

Niki's anxiousness for closing time wasn't just because of the heat. She had an audition tonight at the Stuyvesant Theatre on West Forty-Fourth Street. David Belasco, the producer, would be there himself. If he liked her . . .

"Excuse me, miss. I'd like to try on some of your hats."

Niki brushed back her hair from her face and automatically smiled. "Of course. Won't you take a seat right over here?"

* * *

The Stuyvestant was a magnificent theatre, containing the most sophisticated lighting system ever devised and a large elevator stage. It also, Niki had heard, included sumptuous apartments for Mr. Belasco and his stars, but Niki could only hope she would get to see them some time in the future. Her first worry was just to get through the audition.

Behind the bright lights, Niki could make out the forms of several men, the red glow of their cigars confirming that these shapes were men and not just her imagination.

Although it was cooler than earlier in the day, Niki was once again damp under the arms, this time from nerves. She had just finished reading the selected part and was awaiting a reaction. She hated the silence that dragged on and on more than anything. She told herself she mustn't get discouraged. This time she might just win a part.

Oh please, she prayed, *let me be chosen!*

She heard a man clearing his throat.

"Very well done, Miss O'Hara. Very well done."

"Thank you, sir."

"I believe you have a great deal of talent. Given the right property, you could make a name for yourself on Broadway."

She was holding her breath.

"However, I just don't think you're right

for this character. You're too young."

She released the air in her lungs, the all too familiar sinking sensation churning her stomach.

"If you'll leave your name and where we can reach you with my secretary, I'll keep you in mind for the future."

Niki didn't show her disappointment. She just nodded and smiled pleasantly. "Thank you for auditioning me, Mr. Belasco."

As she left the stage, she was passed by an older woman, sure to be right for the part. It was so unfair. She could have done that part. She could have made herself look older. She knew it. She knew she could have done it.

It was a long walk from the theatre on Forty-Fourth Street to her apartment in Greenwich Village, but she had grown used to walking. It was a good thing she liked to walk. Cabs were too expensive for a working girl. Besides, she didn't really mind. Though there were times she missed the ease of her life of a year ago, she still felt a sense of achievement living on her own. She had learned to shop for bargains and she had become a pretty good cook. At least, Eddie seemed to think so.

She smiled when she thought of Eddie. He was still with her, and she was very proud of him. She thought of him as a younger brother. Once again, he showed her the excitement of discovering new things, new ideas. Niki couldn't afford a tutor for him like Taylor had hired, so she taught him herself. He was an eager student, inquisitive and bright.

The months since Eddie joined her had passed quickly. She auditioned for every play she heard about, and she refused to let discouragement defeat her. Despite the rejections, she believed in herself. When the time was right, she would get her chance. It had to happen. Her job at The Baron's was pleasant for the most part. Grace, of course, made it easier to bear with her quick wit and wry humor.

Niki called Taylor once a month. Her grandmother no longer asked where she was living. Instead, she told Niki that she trusted her and was proud of her. Taylor was pleased that Eddie was living with Niki and always asked her to give the boy her love. She also passed along bits of family news. Travis was taking Anne back to Heart's Landing to meet Rory and Brenetta. It looked as if the two were planning to get married, although nothing had been announced. Rory was worried about Niki and wanted her to write. Her mother was also worried but was sticking to her guns about funding Niki's career efforts. Adam was at Spring Haven. Pop was ill, and Erin had asked him to come for a visit. Taylor was thinking of going down herself if Pop didn't improve soon.

Dusk was settling over the city as Niki walked toward home. She paused at a street corner before crossing. As she stepped off the curb, she dropped her purse. She picked it up and hopped back out of the street when she saw a delivery truck barreling toward her. As she did so, she caught a glimpse of a man leaning against the building on the corner. He looked vaguely familiar to her, but his face was turned away and she couldn't place him.

Shrugging mentally, she resumed her journey home. As each block passed, she became more and more aware of a disturbing sensation of being followed. She wouldn't allow herself to turn to look, afraid to confirm her suspicions. Finally, however, when she was still four blocks from her apartment, she couldn't bear it any longer. She cast a furtive glance over her shoulder. She was right. He *was* following her. The man she had seen earlier, whom she thought she should know from somewhere, was keeping an even pace with her, stopping when she stopped, walking when she walked.

Niki's breath caught in her throat as she tried to swallow back panic. Her steps quickened, her destination seeming so far away. She could hear his footsteps on the sidewalk. He was walking faster. He must be getting closer. Just when she thought she might start screaming in fear, her building came in sight. Grabbing her skirts, she broke into a run.

"Wait, miss!"

Niki bolted up the stairs, scrambling in her handbag for her key. She couldn't find it. She pounded on the door. "Eddie! Eddie, open the door."

"Please, miss. Wait. I don't want to hurt you."

Niki twirled around, her back flattened against the closed door. "What do you want?" she demanded.

The man was standing halfway up the stairs. He had removed his hat and was holding it with both hands. "Do you remember me, miss? I'm Harry Jamison. We met about a year ago at Whitman Theatre."

Her heart began returning to its normal rhythm. Yes, she did remember now. He had come when she was rehearsing alone. Come to think of it, he had frightened her then, too.

"I'd call you by name, but you never introduced yourself. Except I remember that the gentleman who came for you called you Niki. Am I right?"

She still eyed him warily as she replied. "Niki O'Hara. And, yes, I do remember you. But I don't think that explains why you were following me, Mr. Jamison."

"I apologize, Miss O'Hara, but I didn't know how else to make sure I would know how to find you."

"I beg your pardon?" She was searching through her handbag for her key, eager to get inside. Her fingers settled around it with relief.

Harry came up a few steps closer. "If you'd give me just a moment, I'll explain."

"You can explain from where you are, thank you."

He smiled, showing a row of straight, white teeth. "I'm going to be producing and directing a new play. I saw your reading this evening. I'd like you to be my leading lady."

Before she could stop herself, her mouth dropped open in surprise. She closed it quickly, but not before he had seen her shocked response and began laughing.

"Now, Miss O'Hara, if you don't trust me in your apartment, would you be kind enough to join me for supper so that we can discuss the particulars?"

"No, I . . . I mean, yes . . . I mean, come in, please, Mr. Jamison." She fumbled with her key before opening the door.

The apartment was dark and hot, the windows closed. She went immediately toward them and threw them open, hoping for a breeze to lighten the air.

"Please, sit down. Make yourself comfortable. I have some ice. May I get you some tea?"

"Not a thing, Miss O'Hara." He pointed to the chair. "Please. You sit down, too."

She obeyed him, realizing that she was stuttering and bumbling around like a fool. Some leading lady.

"Miss O'Hara . . . may I call you Niki?"

She nodded.

"I am not a wealthy man, but I love the theatre. I've been working toward doing my own show for several years now. Finally, I have enough money and the building to do just that. Of course, I can't pay my actors what Belasco or Shubert or the like can, but I hope it will be a profitable venture for all involved." Harry scooted forward to the edge of the sofa. "If I bring over the script, will you look it over and see if you're interested?"

Niki didn't need to think about it. She had nothing to lose. "Yes, Mr. Jamison . . ."

"Harry."

"Harry." She returned his grin. "I'd like to read it very much."

He got to his feet. "Good. I'll bring it by tomorrow night. Any special time?"

"After eight would be best."

"After eight, it is." He put his hat back on his head, still smiling, his faded blue eyes twinkling. "I'll see you then."

Before she could get to the door to see him out properly, he was gone. Niki watched as he disappeared down the stairs and out into the night. How quickly the disappointment and fear of this evening had turned to excitement and anticipation. A director wanted her for his play. She was going to be in a play. It was happening. It was really happening at last!

The telephone rang persistantly, jolting Taylor awake. She waited in her dark bedroom for the servant's footsteps outside her door, telling her what the caller wanted at this hour of the night.

The predicted footsteps were followed by a gentle knock on the door. "Mrs. Lattimer?"

"I'm awake, Mrs. Mulligan. What is it?"

The door opened, spilling light from the hall across her bedroom floor.

"Mr. Bellman's on the telephone, ma'am. He says he needs to speak with you."

Taylor was already getting out of bed, donning her bedrobe as she headed for the door.

"Adam? What's wrong?" she asked as she picked up the receiver.

The connection was poor and full of static.

"Aunt Taylor, can you get away from New York and come down here? Pop . . . Pop's dying and he wants to see you."

Tears sprang at once to her eyes. She'd been afraid of this call. "I'll be on my way in the morning. You tell him I'm coming." As she set the receiver down, she said to herself, "Hold on, Alan. Hold on 'til I get there."

* * *

The skies were black with their burden of rain, matching the gloom that had settled over Spring Haven. Taylor sat at the bedside of her friend, watching the shallow rise and fall of his chest, listening to the belabored breathing. He hadn't awakened since she'd arrived, but she refused to leave his side in case he did.

How many loved ones had she outlived? Too many. Too many.

"Maybe I've lived too long," she whispered, her thoughts drifting back through the years as she spoke.

David Lattimer, her first husband, had died in this very room. Dear David. How long ago that seemed. She was a child and he the much older, much wiser husband. He cherished her and, finally, he died to save her.

Jeffrey Stone, her second husband, fought and died for the Confederacy. He died on a battle field, far from those that loved him. Her sorrow was all the greater because she knew she had failed him. Though she loved him in her own way, she couldn't give him her heart. It already belonged to Brent—the Union officer, her former son-in-law . . . and the father of her child.

Brent. When she married him, she thought she would be happy forever, and there were many happy years. But Brent was snatched away from her too soon. The bullet that took his life left her wounded. Not a physical wound, but a wound nonetheless.

Her brother, Philip Bellman. He died in a fall from his bedroom window, haunted and pursued by demons. Marilee, his wife and Taylor's dearest friend. Megan and Martin, their children. So many. So many were gone.

"Taylor." Pop's hoarse whisper jerked her back to the present.

She took his hand. It was so thin and frail, so cold. "Alan, you old coot. What do you mean, lying around in bed like a man of leisure? There's not a thing getting done without your know-how."

He tried to smile, but it turned into a cough. Taylor reached over and tenderly wiped phlegm from the corners of his mouth. He squeezed her hand, his grip weak. His eyes thanked her for her caring touch.

"Taylor, my girl, I'm dying. There's no way around it, and every one knows it."

"Oh, Alan . . ."

"Before I go, there's something I've got to say." He coughed again, his strength ebbing even more. "You've been a good friend to me, making me a part of this family, and I've loved you for it. And you know I've loved everyone of Marilee's kids like they were my own. I never liked to see any of them unhappy."

"You were a good husband to Marilee and a good father to the children."

"Now it's Adam who's unhappy. He's got your granddaughter stuck in his craw and can't get her loose." Pop closed his eyes a moment, sinking into his pillow. Then he continued in his hoarse, faded voice. "You've got to do all you can to get those two together, Taylor. I don't know if they've got enough sense between them to know how to do it themselves." Again he gave her a pale smile.

"I'll do it, Alan. I promise."

"One more thing." He was growing weaker. "I've never told Erin about her mother and me. I think she knows, but I never found the words to tell her. Would you . . . would you tell her for me? Tell her how much I loved her?"

"Let me get her, Alan. She's been in here day and night. I had to threaten her to get her to leave to try to get some sleep. She's only been gone a little while. Let me go get her so you can tell her yourself."

"No . . . time. It's . . . been a . . . good . . . life . . . Taylor."

There was no corresponding intake of breath to the rush of air that hissed through his lips. Taylor held his wrinkled hand against her cheek as tears ran down her face.

"You're so right, Alan Montgomery," she whispered. "It's been a *very* good life."

After the funeral two days later, Taylor put Erin to bed. The woman was distraught and worn out, both physically and emotionally.

"I should be downstairs with our guests," she said in protest as Taylor tucked the blankets around her shoulders.

"Adam in managing just fine. Everyone down there will understand. You're allowed to grieve, Erin."

"Oh, Aunt Taylor, I'm going to miss him so."

She began to weep, and Taylor gathered her into her arms and rocked her like she would a small child.

"Of course, you'll miss him. Just as I missed my father after he died."

Sniffing, Erin pulled away. She dashed the tears from her cheeks as she lifted watery green eyes toward Taylor. "He *was* my father, wasn't he?"

This wasn't the time Taylor had planned to carry out Pop's request, but she couldn't duck the question.

"Yes, Erin. He was your real father. He wanted to tell you himself. He just never knew how. He asked me the night he died to tell you how much he loved you. How very much he loved you."

"I suppose I should be horrified to learn that . . . that I'm not Philip Bellman's child. After all, my mother and he were still married when I was born. But it just doesn't matter." She sniffed again. "I'm *glad* I'm Pop's daughter. I'm proud of it."

As she began to sob again, Taylor nodded in understanding. "You should be proud, my dear. He was a good man. I loved him, too."

"No, Miss O'Hara. Your grandmother's not here. She's in Georgia. That Mr. Montgomery passed on, and she's gone to be with the family."

Niki listened to Mrs. Mulligan's voice at the other end of the line, speaking so calmly of Pop's death. Poor Pop. He had been so healthy when they'd been there two years ago. Now he was dead. She couldn't believe it. Adam must be heartsick. Erin, too, of course, but it was Adam whose pain she felt. He loved Pop so very much, just as she loved Gram.

"Is there a message I can give your grandmother when she comes back?"

"Yes. Tell her I've taken a part in a play. I've got the lead. Tell her I've quit my job now that we're rehearsing, and I'll let her know when we'll be opening." She hesitated. "And, Mrs. Mulligan. If she calls, ask her to tell Erin and Adam how sorry I am and that I . . . I love them. Will you do that?''

"Of course, Miss O'Hara. I'll be sure she knows.''

CHAPTER 16

Taylor marched around the drawing room, hands behind her back and a thundering frown pinching her brow. Finally, she stopped behind the satin upholstered sofa and turned her stormy blue eyes in Conrad's direction.

"I've had enough of this nonsense, Conrad. I'm going to help that girl whether she likes it or not. And how can her mother be so stubborn? As if she didn't have everything she wanted at that age." She pointed a finger at him. "I've got a plan, and *you've* got to help me!"

He threw up his hands in a gesture of defeat. "I wouldn't dream of arguing with you when you get like this, my dear. I value my life too much."

Taylor ignored his jest. She sat down and motioned for him to do the same. "I can't be obvious about my assistance. She has far too much pride for that."

"What is it you plan to do?"

Niki had been working on Harry's play

only a few short weeks when his backer pulled out. The play folded, and Niki was out of work. She tried to help him find someone else to produce the play but to no avail. At first, she wasn't too discouraged; after all, she'd been disappointed before. But then she started running out of money and she still hadn't found a job. Niki didn't know that her grandmother had long since located her and had been keeping close tabs on her welfare.

When it looked as if she and Eddie would soon be starving, Taylor decided enough was enough. Her plan was two-fold. It would keep Niki from going hungry while still allowing her to continue her pursuit of an acting career, and it would bring Adam and Niki back together, something Taylor was determined to do. Later that November afternoon she put her plan into action.

Mrs. Fiske stopped before the secretary's desk. "I would like to see Mr. Bellman, please. I'm Mrs. Fiske."

The secretary was flustered. "I know. I mean, I'll tell him. Would you like to sit down? It will only take a moment. I'm sure he'll be right with you."

Mrs. Fiske nodded.

Betty, Adam's secretary, rapped on his door, then opened it without waiting for a summons.

Adam looked up from the stack of briefs

on his desk. "What is it, Betty?"

"Sir, *Mrs. Fiske* is here to see you."

"Mrs. Fiske?"

"*The* Mrs. Fiske. Mrs. Fiske, the actress! She's sitting out there right now!" Betty was awestruck.

Adam stacked his briefs and pushed them aside. As he rose from his chair, he said, "Please show her in, Betty."

"Right away, sir."

Adam stepped around to the front of his desk, checking his tie and suitcoat. As the famous actress entered his office, he held out his hand in welcome.

"Mrs. Fiske, this is a pleasure."

"Thank you, Mr. Bellman. I appreciate your seeing me like this. I hope I'm not intruding."

"Not at all," he assured her. "Won't you have a seat and tell me why you've come to see me?"

"I'm going to be brief, Mr. Bellman. I have had the pleasure of meeting Miss Niki O'Hara. I believe she's a relative of yours? Well, I've seen some of Miss O'Hara's work and have been very impressed. If that girl ever gets a good part in a good production, she's going to be a star."

Adam nodded, confounded by Mrs. Fiske's interest in Niki.

"Miss O'Hara has run into a bit of bad luck lately. The play she was cast in has folded, and she is apparently out of money with no work in sight. Now, I don't want to see her spending the rest of her life working behind the counter of some store sellng hats to old fuss budgets. She belongs on the stage."

"So she's always told me."

Mrs. Fiske smiled. "Mr. Bellman, I want to help her. I came to Conrad. He's an old friend of mine, but he said to let you handle it for me."

"Handle what, Mrs. Fiske?" He was rather apprehensive to hear her proposal.

"I want to become her benefactor, but my identity must remain a complete secret. Never, under any circumstances, is anyone outside of this room to know that I am doing this. Is that understood?"

Adam shifted in his chair. "Mrs. Fiske, I have no problem with keeping your involvement in strict confidence, but I still don't understand exactly what it is you want me to do."

"It's very simple. I will provide a monthly allowance for Miss O'Hara. An ample one that will allow her to live comfortably, though not extravagantly. She will then be able to expend all her efforts toward her work on the stage instead of earning her daily bread." She smiled at him again. "In addition, I will help fund any legitimate play she is in, if necessary. However, every penny will come through you and must be approved by you.

In other words, you will act as her business manager."

Different emotions were at war in Adam's breast. Although he hadn't shown it, the news that Niki was out of money and out of work had upset him. Knowing that she was in trouble made him want to rush to her aid as quickly as possible. It had been nearly a year since he had seen her, yet he couldn't rid himself of her image. It still haunted him. He wondered if he would ever be free of loving her.

At the same time, he knew he was asking for full-time trouble if he became Niki's business manager. They would be thrown together constantly. If they had argued before, they would argue even more with him advising her. He could foresee it.

"There will be a handsome fee for you, of course, Mr. Bellman. I'll ask that you prepare a monthly report along with any requests for additional funds and give it to Mr. Cheavers. He'll see that I get it." Mrs. Fiske stood up and extended her hand. "Do we have an agreement, Mr. Bellman?"

Common sense had no chance. If he had to fight with Niki twenty-four hours a day, it would be worth it just to see her again.

Adam got to his feet and shook her proffered hand. "It's a deal, Mrs. Fiske."

Niki had grown quite fond of her little apartment. She hoped she wouldn't be forced to move. What little savings she had, though, were quickly evaporating. She was especially worried about Eddie. He seemed to think her money problems were his fault. He kept saying he should leave and then she wouldn't have to think about moving. She couldn't bear to think of losing him. Street-wise, independent little Eddie was her family.

Harry had brought over some potatoes and onions along with a soup bone, and Niki had fixed a stew. After dinner, Eddie lay down on his cot in the corner of the living room to read a book Niki had given him, and soon he was asleep. Niki and Harry sat at the table, talking softly, their conversation, as usual, centered on the play they still hoped to do.

Although Harry had tried to interest Niki in a more intense relationship than what they had, she had declined. She liked Harry well enough, but she wanted no entanglements, no hurts and disappointments from a man in her life. It suited her better to have Harry as a friend and a director. It was enough.

"I still think we can interest Mr. Taylor in this script. If I can just get past that secretary of his, I know he'll go for it." Harry sighed. "That secretary of his watches him like a hawk."

"Harry, there's something you've got to know. If something doesn't happen soon,

I'm going to have to give up and go home. Eddie is beginning to think if he wasn't here, I'd be fine. He keeps talking of leaving. I can't let him do that. If I don't have some income, I'm taking him back to Idaho with me and giving up the stage."

"Give up! I never heard anything so preposterous. Why, you're the most beautiful, most talented actress ever born. Once these silly directors get a look at you . . ."

Niki leaned across the table and patted his hand. Her eyes twinkled and her smile was pleased. "Oh, Harry, you do flatter me. Whatever would I do without you to lift my spirits the way you do?"

"I'm not about to let you find out."

The knock on her door surprised her. She glanced at the clock, then at Harry, her raised brows expressing her puzzlement. "Who on earth . . ."

Niki got up from the table and went to the door, still wondering at the identity of the caller. She kept so much to herself, she rarely had any visitors other than Harry and Grace, and Grace was away right now visiting her parents.

She opened the door slowly. There he stood, hat in hand, wearing a dark winter coat over his suit, as tall and handsome as ever, his light blue eyes disturbingly observant, his mouth wearing the slightest hint of a smile.

"Hello, Niki."

"Adam!"

"May I come in?"

Niki stepped back, allowing him to enter. He stopped abruptly when he saw Harry, then turned around to look at her.

"It's been a long time," he said, his voice low.

"A long time," she echoed.

"You look well."

"Thank you." *Such trivial words,* Niki thought. Why did he make her feel so strange? "Please, Adam. Let me take your coat. Sit down."

As he sat on the sofa, Adam let his eyes wander around the small living room, stopping in surprise when he saw the boy asleep on the cot. He turned a questioning glance toward Niki.

"That's Eddie. You remember."

"That's the same boy?" He paused, then added with a note of urgency, "Niki, you've got to understand something. I never meant that you shouldn't have helped the boy. I'm glad you've given him a home. You . . . you're very special."

She basked a moment in his praise before replying, "Not really. He's done much more for me."

Harry cleared his throat and rose from his chair at the table.

"I'm sorry," Niki said, color brightening her cheeks as she realized she had forgotten him. "Harry, this is my cousin, Adam Bellman. Adam, this is Harry Jamison, my director."

"Your director?"

She laughed airily. "Well, we hope so. We've been working on a play, but we've had a problem or two getting it produced."

Harry sauntered over and stood behind the chair Niki was seated on, placing a hand possessively on her shoulder. "We've worked very hard together," he said.

Niki was too happy at seeing Adam to be aware of the tension sparking between the two men. All her dreams about him, about his embrace, about his kisses, came swirling back, assaulting her senses with a vengeance. She had missed him. She had known she had missed him. But this was more. This was so much more.

Could I be in love with him? she wondered, and was immediately aghast. No, she couldn't be. She had left behind that silly notion in Atlanta over two years before. She hadn't even seen him in a year. How could she think herself in love with him?

Adam was in no better position to be objective. Having long since admitted, both to himself and to Taylor, that he was in love with Niki, he couldn't help but fear the worst when he looked at this pair together. Just what was this Harry to her really? He certainly made himself at home in her apartment. Adam would have liked nothing better than to take Harry Jamison by the scruff of the neck and pitch him down the stairs.

Anger and jealousy made him sound stiff and formal when he spoke again. "Niki, I have a business proposition for you. I don't want to take up any more of your time this evening, so I'd like you to call on me at my office some time tomorrow." He got to his feet and reached for his coat. He had the terrible feeling that if he didn't get out of there, he was going to do something he would regret later.

The coldness of his voice and what seemed an abrupt order for her to make an appointment with him the next day threw icy water on the warm sensations she was feeling for him. She stood up, too, eyes snapping.

"I'm sorry, Adam. I can't promise anything about tomorrow. If you've got a business proposition for me, why not just tell me now?"

There she was again, getting her dander up, biting his head off when he'd done absolutely nothing. "I think this is a private matter and that we should discuss it alone."

"Anything you have to say to me regarding business can be said in front of Harry. I have no secrets from *him*, of all people."

Adam glared at Harry with ill-concealed hostility. "I'm sorry. I didn't understand."

He sat down again. "I have been approached by an individual who, for some unknown reason, has taken a liking to you. This person wants to become your benefactor but has stipulated two conditions. One, no one must ever know who that benefactor is, including you, and two, I must control the purse strings."

"*You?*"

"That's exactly how I responded, Niki. Don't ask me why, but I've been chosen to become your business manager. That is, if you choose to accept the offer."

Niki didn't know what to say. Was he telling her the truth?

Harry wasn't stricken with the same affliction. He wanted some answers. "Just what is this so-called benefactor willing to do for Niki?"

Adam ignored him as he watched Niki.

"Mr. Bellman?" Harry was not easily dissuaded. "Just what are the terms of this business proposition?"

"Niki will receive an allowance to live on while she pursues her acting. Should she need anything beyond the normal allotment, she will come to me," The next part was what he hated revealing in front of this fellow. "The benefactor will also help finance a production of her choosing should she not be cast in someone else's."

"Niki, love! Do you hear that?" Harry jumped to his feet. "We've got ourselves a

267

backer for the play. We can do it now."

It was Niki's turn to ignore Harry. She stared into Adam's eyes with open defiance. "What if I don't want you for my business manager? Isn't there someone else I can work with?"

"No." Adam got to his feet and put his hat on. "Think about it tonight and come to see me tomorrow if you want to accept the offer." He opened the door, saying, "Perhaps you and Mr. Jamison should discuss this before you make a decision. Goodnight, Niki."

The door closed.

Harry's eyes sparked with anticipation. "Niki, do you know what this can mean to us?"

"Oh, Harry, shut up," Niki snapped, still glaring at the closed door.

CHAPTER 17

December blanketed New York in a world of white. Snow fell relentlessly for several days before the temperatures plummetted, the accompanying hoarfrost turning the leafless trees into strange-shaped skeletons, their many arms reaching for the sky in silent cries for spring.

Niki had little time to notice the crystal beauty of winter. As the time for the opening of the play approached, she spent nearly every waking moment at the theatre, going over her lines again and again. She was anxious for the play to open, yet apprehensive, too. There was a nagging feeling in the back of her mind that something was wrong with the play, that changes needed to be made, but she kept her peace, not venturing to air her opinions to Harry.

And how exasperating *he* had become! Always he seemed to be sending her to Adam with requests for more money. From the moment she accepted her mysterious benefactor's offer, she wondered if she'd

done the right thing. Adam never inter-
ferred like she'd been afraid he would do. In
fact, the only times she saw him were when
she went to his office. He always greeted
her pleasantly, listened to her requests, and
then gave her the needed funds. It all
seemed too easy somehow . . . and too
formal.

A few days before Christmas, Niki found
herself once again waiting outside Adam's
office.

"Mr. Bellman is with a client, but if you'd
like to wait, he should be free shortly,"
Adam's secretary told her.

Niki nodded and sat down near the door.
She picked up a magazine, not bothering to
see what it was, and leafed through it
without seeing a thing as her thoughts
replayed this morning's events.

"Harry, this line just isn't working,"
she'd cried in exasperation.

Her leading man, Jeff Stokes, had thrown
up his hands as he turned away from her
and walked down stage toward their
director.

Harry had left his seat in the tenth row of
the auditorium. "It would be fine if you'd
just say it the way I've told you. Now, let's
try it again from Mr. Samuel's entrance.
Remember, Niki, you're in love with this
man. He's telling you he's leaving. Your
heart's breaking. Try to make it believable,
will you?" he'd finished, sitting down once

again, this time in the first row.

Niki closed the magazine as she mumbled her denial. "It's *not* the way I'm saying the line. The scene's all wrong!"

"I assume things aren't going well since you've taken to talking to yourself."

Niki looked up to find Adam standing nearby, his eyes sparkling in amusement. She placed the magazine on the chair next to her, then stood up, trying to look unperturbed. "You assume wrong, Adam. Things are going quite well."

Adam held out his hand, and as she stepped forward, he took hold of her elbow. "Come on into my office and tell me just how well everything is." He still seemed to be mocking her.

As the door closed behind her, shutting them away from the watchful eyes of the secretary, Niki tilted her head back and looked up at Adam. She felt the usual quickening of her pulse as she gazed at his handsome face. The skin on her arm seemed to burn where he touched her even though the sleeves of her dress and her coat separated their flesh. Why was it that she could feel so attracted to the man at the same time she was so irritated with him? How could being with him make her so happy and so miserable? If only she knew how he felt about her. If only she believed he cared for her, then maybe . . . But Adam remained, for the most part, aloof and a trifle condescending. It was perhaps the greatest bit of acting she would ever do, not to reveal her own confused feelings for him.

"I don't have a lot of time," Niki said as she separated herself from his distracting nearness, moving over to stand by the window. "I've got to get back to the theatre."

The twinkle in Adam's eyes faded. He went to his desk and sat down in his high-backed chair, swiveling around to look at her. "Well, then you'd best tell me why you've come." He was all business now.

"We're going to need more money for costumes. Harry thinks a thousand will do everything we need."

"Are you sure it's necessary?"

"I . . . Yes, I'm sure. Harry doesn't seem to think we can do without them."

"Hmmm." Adam turned back to the desk and pulled a file from a drawer. He scribbled some figures on paper, stared at them silently for a moment, then flipped the front of the file closed again before twirling around to look at her once more. "All right."

"I can have it?"

"Yes. I'll send someone over with the draft this afternoon."

"Thank you, Adam."

He stood up. "I'm just doing my job."

His nonchalant reply stung. "Of course," she said stiffly as she headed for the door before he could rise. "I won't trouble you any further."

"Niki, wait!"

She paused, her hand on the doorknob.

He crossed the room in just a few strides, his hands alighting on her shoulders. "You are coming to Aunt Taylor's for Christmas, aren't you?"

"I'm not sure," Niki whispered.

"She's counting on you."

Niki resisted the urge to turn around. She wanted to see the same thing in his eyes that she imagined she heard in his words, but she knew she couldn't bear it if it weren't there. "I'll do my best," she replied, her voice cracking as she pulled open the door and rushed out.

Taylor sent Roger with the car to the theatre on Christmas Eve. He had stopped first at her apartment, and picked up Eddie, who now waited for her in the back of the car, face scrubbed and hair slicked back. As Niki stepped outside, she poked her hands deeper into her fur muff, shivering as the icy wind whipped her skirts.

Roger hopped quickly out of the automobile and held the door open. It had been a long time since she'd seen him, but he smiled and nodded as if it had been only this morning since he'd last taken her someplace. "Evenin', Miss O'Hara."

"Good evening, Roger," she replied as he

helped her inside. "It's good to see you."

Roger nodded crisply, then closed the door.

Niki looked at Eddie. Her smiled broadened. He was dressed in a new suit, and it was clear he was uncomfortable in it. Still, there was a gleam of excitement in his returning gaze.

"Are you looking forward to tonight?" she asked, already knowing the answer.

He bobbed his reply with enthusiasm.

"So am I," Niki said as the car started forward. "So am I."

They moved slowly through the snow-covered streets, giving Niki ample time to mull over the anticipated reunion with her grandmother. Niki had clung stubbornly to her insistence that she remain on her own until she was performing on Broadway. When they spoke to each other over the telephone, Taylor often asked her to come back, considering she was so close to reaching that goal, but Niki always refused. Now, with the play opening on the first of January, it would have been silly not to comply with her grandmother's request to at least join her for Christmas. Besides, Niki missed her. She missed everyone at White House.

Taylor Lattimer, wearing a gown of silver and powder blue, her hair sprinkled with sparkling gems to match the glittering diamonds that circled her throat, met Niki and Eddie at the door. She clasped Niki's hands firmly, looking her granddaughter over from head to toe before pulling her close for a tight hug.

"Oh, my dear, you don't know how good it is to see you."

"I think I do, Gram. I've missed seeing you, too."

Taylor kissed her cheek before replying, "You have too much of my stubbornness, I'm afraid."

"If I could, I'd be just like you in every way, Gram. Stubbornness and all."

Taylor kissed her again, then turned her eyes on the boy at Niki's side. "Can this be Eddie?" She held out her hand for him to take. "Why, you've grown nearly a foot since I've seen you last."

"Not really so much," he answered.

Taylor dropped a kiss on the top of his head. "I've missed you, my boy."

Eddie's chin quivered. "I . . . I wanted to say how sorry . . . I didn't mean to . . ."

"It wasn't your fault, Eddie. No one ever blamed you. It was an accident, that's all."

"Mrs. Mulligan blamed me."

"No, Eddie. She knows how wrong she was to say the things she did." She squeezed his hand. "Now, no more talk like this. Come into the drawing room, both of you."

Niki followed Taylor and Eddie inside. A fire blazed on the hearth, spreading a welcome warmth over the room. As they came into view, Travis looked up from his place on the sofa.

"Niki!" he cried as he jumped to his feet, rushing over to envelope her in a tight embrace. He picked her off the floor and swung her around in a circle. "You look wonderful, Niki," he said as he put her down again.

Her joy grew with every minute she was in the house. Looking at her brother, she thought she could burst with happiness. "Oh, Travis, you look wonderful to me, too! I've missed you so much!"

"Well, if you've missed me so much, why haven't you come to see me?" he scolded.

"I couldn't, Travis. Really, I couldn't."

Taking her by the hand, he turned her to face the others waiting in the drawing room. Conrad had come to stand beside Taylor and Eddie. Anne Houseman was seated on the sofa, next to the spot where Travis had been only moments before. Behind her, leaning against the piano, was Adam, dressed in white tie and tails. He touched his forehead in greeting, as if tipping an imaginary hat.

"Come and sit down," Travis urged as he pulled her toward the grouping of sofas and chairs. "Anne and I both want to hear about this play of yours."

Reluctantly, she dragged her eyes away from Adam's steady gaze. "Please. I'd rather not talk shop tonight. I'd rather hear about you."

"What's to tell? I keep busy at the bank during the day, and I spend as many pleasurable evenings as possible with Anne." His eyes caressed the young woman as he spoke her name.

Niki felt an unpleasant pang of jealousy, unable to keep the thought from flitting through her mind that she wished someone felt that way about her.

Conrad gave three short coughs to draw everyone's attention in his direction. "I think this is as good a time as any to let everyone know my important news." Assured that all eyes were watching, he placed his arm protectively around Taylor's shoulders. "It's my great joy to announce that this beautiful lady has finally agreed to do me the honor of becoming Mrs. Cheavers."

There was a moment of silent surprise before Niki was on her feet again and rushing to throw her arms around her grandmother, Travis not far behind her.

"Gram—Mr. Cheavers—that's wonderful news! I couldn't think of a better Christmas present!" She kissed them both. Staring up into Conrad's joy-filled face, she said earnestly, "There's no one I'd rather have as a member of my family. I know you'll always make Gram very happy."

"Thank you, Niki. It's important to know

that you approve." He shifted his glance toward Taylor who was watching with loving eyes. "I don't think she would have gone through with it if you didn't."

"Aunt Taylor?" Adam stepped up beside Niki and placed his hands on Taylor's shoulders as he leaned forward to kiss her cheek. "I'm very happy for you." He turned and offered his hand to the groom-to-be. "Mr. Cheavers, welcome to our family."

A mantle of joy surrounded Taylor, and happiness shone from her face, so bright it seemed to add a light of its own to the room. She took hold of Conrad's arm and leaned against him, a gesture both possessive and submissive, one of trust and reliance. It seemed to Niki that her grandmother looked as young as any of the women in the room at just that moment. Seeing the special beauty that love had brought to Taylor's countenance made her wish more than ever to be loved and to love like that. She glanced covertly at Adam as he stood at her side, congratulating Conrad, and wondered again if what she felt for him just might be love.

But if I did love him, wouldn't I be aglow like Gram instead of confused and miserable? she wondered, feeling her heart tighten.

"I think this announcement deserves a toast," Travis said. "Let's have some champagne and celebrate."

As if she'd been waiting just for that moment, Pearl stepped into the room carrying a silver tray with a chilled bottle of champagne and six glasses. She set it on the coffee table in front of the white brocade sofa, and everyone moved to circle the table and take a glass. It seemed only natural, with Travis and Anne standing together as a couple and Conrad and Taylor doing the same, that Niki and Adam would find themselves side by side. Silently, Adam took up the bottle of sparkling wine and poured it into the glasses that were held out to him. Niki's was the last before his own, and he paused before filling it. Though she somehow sensed that his eyes were beckoning her to look up at him, she kept her gaze locked on the empty goblet, noting the slight shaking of her hand as she waited, and at last the bottle was tilted and her glass filled.

"A toast." Travis lifted his glass skyward. "To Taylor Lattimer and Conrad Cheavers. May they find happiness as man and wife, and may the love they share spread to those around them."

"Hear, hear!"

Glasses clinked together. Bubbles tickled Niki's nose. Her eyes watered. At last she looked at him through bleary eyes and found him staring at her, ever so sternly.

How I wish he could smile at me for a change, she thought as she turned away.

Devil take his cold, unfeeling hide!

Soon after, they went into supper, and then it was time to exchange presents. For a while, Niki's thoughts were relieved from the confusion that Adam's nearness caused as she watched Eddie opening packages. The boy was astounded by the number of presents bearing his name. He opened each one with great care. No matter what was inside, he studied it with grave and wondering eyes, then went to thank the giver with profuse gratitude. It was all the more special for Niki when she remembered the previous Christmas Eve. He had been alone and cold. She had been alone and cold. Together, when she had been too stubborn to join Gram and Adam and Travis here, she and Eddie had formed a little family of their own, sharing the joy of Christmas just by being with each other.

Remembering, she wondered if that sparse Christmas Eve wasn't even more special than this one with all its bright lights, pretty wrappings, and expensive gifts.

"This is for you, Niki. From me."

She took hold of the small box, wrapped in silver paper. Surprise was written in her violet eyes as she looked at Adam.

"Go on. Open it."

Carefully, Niki removed the festive wrappings and lifted the lid. Lying on top of the fluffy white cotton that lined the box was a brooch. She lifted it from its shelter, staring with wonder at the tiny figures of a man and woman waltzing. Whatever hand had made this brooch had great talent; Niki could almost believe the figures were real.

"Adam . . . it's beautiful," she whispered, still staring at the gift.

He sat beside her on the sofa and replied softly, "They reminded me of a waltz I had one night on the veranda at Spring Haven."

"You still remember that?" Her heart was racing. "It . . . it seems a very long time ago. Like it happened to different people."

"They *were* different people, Niki."

If she'd looked up then, she would have seen everything she had ever hoped for in his tender gaze. But she didn't look up. Instead, her attention was drawn toward the tree by Eddie's shout of delight.

"A puppy!" He hopped to his feet, carrying the ball of black fluff over to Niki. "Look, Niki! Look at him! Isn't he super? And he's mine. Gram says he's all mine!"

"That's wonderful, Eddie. Oh, he *is* cute. What are you going to call him?"

"Gee, I don't know. Gram, does he have a name?"

"Not yet, he doesn't," Taylor replied.

"Niki, will you help me think of just the right name for him? After all, he'll be living with us. You need to like his name, too." Eddie pulled her up from the sofa and dragged her across the room toward the tree.

"Of course I'll help. Let's see. What do you suppose would be appropriate . . ."

For the time being, the brooch was forgotten.

Adam stood in the entry hall, smoking silently, listening to the laughter floating out from the drawing room. It was a close family scene he had left—Taylor, the matriarch, with Conrad's arm draped protectively over her shoulder; Travis and Anne, young lovers with the world at their feet; Niki, full of joy and a lust for life; and Eddie, the little orphan who nobody had wanted until Niki spied him in the slums. Adam didn't know why he'd felt compelled to leave their midst. He shouldn't feel like an outsider, but he did. He leaned against the banister, blowing rings of smoke into the air.

I'm feeling sorry for myself again, he thought with disgust. It's a most disagreeable habit I've gotten myself into.

"Adam? Why ever are you standing alone out here?"

She was dressed in a flowing creation of red chiffon over white satin. He was amazed by the narrowness of her waist and acutely aware of the feminine swell of her breasts. Her dark-chocolate mass of hair was worn up, revealing a delicate throat that cried to be kissed.

"I . . . wanted a cigarette."

Niki came nearer. "We wouldn't have minded your smoking."

He couldn't understand her. He would *never* understand her. But then, he couldn't even understand himself when he was around her.

She beckoned to him with her hand. "Come on, Adam. Gram's wondering what happened to you."

He ground out the cigarette in the ashtray on the table beside him. He wanted to ask if it was only Taylor who cared where he was, but he didn't . . . couldn't. Mutely, he joined her and they moved back toward the drawing room.

Niki paused just before reaching the archway. "Adam, I . . . I really do want to thank you for the beautiful brooch. I'll cherish it, honestly I will."

He gave no thought to what he was about to do. He simply, instinctively, gathered her into his arms and lowered his mouth to hers. The kiss was as sweet as honeydew, yet it sent a fire like lava surging through his veins. He wanted more. He was starving for more. He longed to go on holding her, to press her soft form even tighter against him, to feel her respond to his embrace. He was almost drunk with desire. He released her mouth and opened his eyes, hoping beyond hope that he would see his love returned in her face.

Niki's hand darted to her lips. "Adam!" she whispered breathlessly. "Whatever made you do that?"

Because I love you, he wanted to answer, but he couldn't. He wasn't ready to tell her. Not yet. Not until he believed she might love him in return.

"Mistletoe," he replied, pointing at his excuse hanging over the doorway.

Taking her firmly by the elbow, he propelled her into the room, avoiding any further discussion regarding the stolen kiss.

CHAPTER 18

Her palms were sweaty. She could barely hold the eyebrow pencil. It was awful. Simply awful! She couldn't remember a single line! It was all a blur. She would never make it through this. Oh, if only she had listened to her mother, she would be safely at home back in Idaho, watching the snow falling through the big picture window in the living room while a fire crackled and popped in the fireplace. Instead, she was sitting before a large mirror, bright lights glaring at her deathly pale face as she tried to apply her stage make-up.

Beyond her dressing room, an audience was gathering. An opening night audience, waiting to see what was hoped would be the first big hit of the year. They had come to see a new actress in a new play with a new director. They wouldn't be easy to please. No audience ever was. They wanted their money's worth. Could she give it to them?

There was a knock on her door.

"Yes?"

The door opened and a stage hand stepped in, carrying a box filled with red roses. "For you, Miss O'Hara."

"Thank you, Charles." As he set them on the counter, she plucked the card from the box.

To the first great star in the O'Hara family. Love, Mother and Father.

"Thanks, Ma," Niki whispered, a tear threatening to fall and streak her make-up.

Harry burst into the room, clapping his hands. "Well, how's my leading lady?" He bent to kiss her forehead but kissed only the air as he moved off across the room again, pacing the floor. "We've got a big crowd, Niki. We're going to be a hit. I can feel it in my bones. There's nothing that can stop us now! My name's going to mean something on Broadway. Look out, Frohman. Look out, Belasco. Harry Jamison's on his way up, and you'd better make room for him!" He was back beside her now and, looking at her reflection in the mirror as he gripped her shoulders, said, "And here's the gal that's going to do it all for me. Niki O'Hara. The most beautiful lady to ever grace the stage."

She felt sick to her stomach. "Oh, Harry," she pleaded hoarsely, "please do shut up. You're making me nervous with your chatter."

Harry laughed. "Why, don't you know it's tradition for the star to be nervous on opening night?'' He spun around and hurried toward the door. "I've got a thing or two to see to before curtain time. See you at Rector's, my love. This is your night to shine.''

Long after the door closed, she sat staring at herself in the mirror. "I've got to do it. *I've got to.* This is what I've lived for, dreamed of. I've *got* to be good!''

It was a dismal pair that waited—not at Rector's, the restaurant of theatre people and their bedazzled patrons—but at Niki's. They waited through the night for the papers and the reviews of their play, but they already knew how the critics would judge them. The audience had already given its review.

Harry sat by himself in the corner, twirling his hat around and around, twisting the brim until it was just a mishappen piece of felt. He didn't speak, not even when Niki asked him if he wanted more coffee. He simply shook his head, still staring at the floor, and went on twirling and twirling his hat.

At last, the papers came.

"You look, Niki. I haven't the nerve.''

"Sure. They can't be all that bad, Harry.'' She flipped through the pages.

"Winter Season," said The New York Times, *opened last night at the Hudson*

Theatre, and, if the fates are merciful, will close tonight . . . One bright spot in this miserable play, written and directed by Harry Jamison (a name, I predict, which will soon be forgotten) was the leading lady, a newcomer to the stage by the name of Niki O'Hara. It is this writer's sincere hope that he will see more of Miss O'Hara in vehicles more worthy of her promising talent . . .

The New York Herald: *. . . Miss O'Hara struggled valiantly to overcome the shabby writing and direction that went by the name of* Winter Season *. . .*

The Sun: *. . . Miss O'Hara, showing promise of great things to come . . .*

Niki couldn't stand to read anymore. She let the papers fall in a pile on the floor and looked across the room at Harry. His eyes were dulled by disappointment and failure.

"Well, they loved *you,* Niki, my dear," he said, trying to add a smile to his words. "I'm happy for you."

She got up from her chair and went to him, kneeling by his side and resting a hand on his arm. "They just didn't give you a chance. Not every play is a hit. Your next one . . ."

Harry grabbed her hand, his desperation exposed. "You'll do my next play, won't you, Niki? The critics want to see you again, and if you're in one of my plays, at least it'll have a chance . . ."

The knock at the door rescued her from replying. She took her time in answering, giving herself a chance to calm her frayed nerves. How could she tell Harry that she felt almost the same as the critics about the play? She had tried to tell him that there were faults with *Winter Season*, but he wouldn't ever listen. He was her friend and she was terribly fond of him, but did she want to do another play with him?

"Adam!" she exclaimed. "I didn't expect to see you here."

"Good morning, Niki." He was carrying a box of red roses. He held them out to her. "I'm sure your place is full of these by now. You were tremendous."

She shook her head. "Hardly. Come on in. I'll get you a cup of coffee."

"Thanks. I'd like that." Adam removed his hat as he stepped into the apartment. A slight frown replaced his smile when he caught sight of Harry. "Hello, Jamison."

"Morning, Bellman. Has Niki's investor come to demand his money back?"

"Harry, really!" She handed Adam his cup, then sat nearby. "You'll have to excuse Harry. He's had a rather bad night."

"Bad night!" Harry cried, jumping to his feet, his apathy dispelled by her understatement. "Bad night? It was a disaster! Niki was the only good thing anyone saw in that play, from beginning to end. Well, I'm not as bad a director as they think I am. Next time I'll choose a better play, and with Niki in it, *I'll* be as famous as they predict *she'll* be.''

Niki cringed.

"You've got to be kidding!" Adam asked, incredulous. "Niki's not going to be in any more of your plays. This one may have flopped, but she'll have the pick of directors after what she showed last night."

Harry's face was turning red right up to the roots of his sandy hair. He pointed his finger at Adam. "Who gives you the right to say what she'll do?"

"*I* give me the right," he replied, getting to his feet. "Someone has to have the good sense to make sure she does what's good for her."

Like a forest that had gone too many months without rain and then had a careless match thrown in its midst, Niki's temper ignited in response to Adam's words. "Now see here, Adam Bellman. You have no right to say what I will or will not do, whether it's for my own good or not."

"I'm sorry, Niki. That didn't come out like I meant it to. I only meant . . ."

"If I want to go on being in Harry's plays, I'll go on doing it. I didn't butt heads with my own mother to get here so I could have my life run by the likes of you!"

"Oh, you didn't, did you?" Adam could have borne Niki's anger—perhaps he deserved it. It was Harry's smirk that made his blood boil. "So is that your decision? To do another Jamison play?"

Niki was caught by the trap of her own hot temper. Only moments before she had been searching for a way to tell Harry she wouldn't work with him again, friend or no friend.

"That *is* what you're going to do, isn't it, Niki?" Harry asked, his faded blue eyes pleading for her affirmation.

If only Adam hadn't forbidden her to do so. "Yes!" She looked at Adam defiantly. "Yes, Harry, I'll do another play with you."

There was a steely glint in Adam's blue eyes as he glanced from Niki to Harry. "All right. If that's what Niki wants, but as manager of the funds for this new production, I must insist on approval of all aspects of the play—approval of scripts, of the theatre, of the other actors . . ."

"But . . . but then it wouldn't really be my play," Harry protested.

Adam shrugged. "You're welcome to do it without the aid of Niki's benefactor."

"Adam, you know that's impossible." Niki's anger had drained, leaving her feeling only confused at the tangled mess the morning had developed into.

Adam put his hat back on, nodded curtly to Harry and to Niki, then stepped to the door. "Let me know when you've decided on the script. I'll be interested to see what you've come up with."

As the door closed, Niki's anger flared again. "Damn your tough hide, Adam Bellman!" she cried as she picked up a nearby vase and flung it at the door. Shocked by her own uncontrolled display, she whirled around and ran into her bedroom, slamming the door, too, as she went.

Adam heard the crash of shattering glass as he descended the stairs, and a smile returned to his handsome face. His spirits lifted; he began whistling. He didn't know why he felt so good. After all, the girl he loved was probably proclaiming her hatred for him at this very moment to a man who had stayed the whole night unchaperoned in her apartment. But something told him this was his chance.

He may have sworn at one time that he'd never let another woman hurt him as Christina had, but there was no way he was going to give up Niki. Compared to these feelings, what he'd felt for Christina was nothing. He loved Niki more than he had ever loved anyone or anything in his life. Maybe he should have just taken her in his arms and proclaimed his love, but he still couldn't bring himself to do that. He had to win her love. He had to know beyond a doubt that she cared for him too. There were times—rare though they might be—when he thought he saw a glimpse of something special in her eyes. Now was his chance to be sure.

"By the time this play is over, Niki O'Hara, you'll either love me or hate me, but you won't be indifferent to me."

Adam was right about that. There was no way that Niki could have ignored him. And though she was loath to admit it, she was glad he was involved. The play Harry came up with had more flaws than *Winter Season*. Adam took a quick look and rejected it at once, then announced he would find the right play himself, even if he had to hire his own writers. Harry sulked for a while, but Niki was greatly relieved.

Weeks later, auditions began for *Another Day*.

"He won't do, Niki," Adam whispered from his seat behind her.

Harry cast an affronted glance over his shoulder before whispering to Niki, "Just *who* is the director here?"

"You are, Harry," she replied, "but you have to admit that Adam is right in this case. That fellow's all wrong for the part of Aaron."

Niki watched as a myriad of emotions played over Harry's face, ending with resignation.

Poor Harry, she thought. It's not turning out the way he always thought it would.

She did feel badly for him. After all, they

were friends. Oh, she knew that Harry was ambitious and that his initial interest in her had been primarily for his own gain, but they had shared too many dreams and too many hardships over the months they had known each other not to be friends now. They understood each others' passion to succeed in the theatre, Niki as an actress, Harry as a playwright and director. They understood the pain of rejection, the meager meals in a cold apartment, while all the time the dream kept burning, refusing to die out.

Yes, she felt bad for Harry, but all the same, she was glad Adam had taken charge. Though she couldn't say it aloud, she was grateful for what he was doing for her, no matter what his reasons. She knew, of course, that his reasons were financial. He couldn't let Niki's mysterious benefactor throw good money after bad.

"Tucker Thorpe? You're next."

Hearing the familiar name, a name that brought back fond memories of Mrs. Whitman and those first months in New York, Niki shook off her musings and watched as Tucker stepped on center stage.

"That's Aaron," she said aloud, starting to rise. "He'll be perfect for the part."

Harry's hand on her shoulder pressed her back in her seat. "Are you a director now, too?" Harry asked sarcastically. "We already have one too many as it is."

"But, Harry . . ."

He looked away from her, calling out, "Go ahead, Mr. Thorpe. Let's see what you've got."

Tucker got the part.

Over the following weeks, Niki found occasion to wonder if Adam was ignoring his other clients. It seemed he as at the theatre nearly as much as she was. Strange how much better things seemed to go when he was there, too. The acting seemed more professional, crisper. The lighting seemed brighter. The story came to life in a new way. Oh, he could be very irritating— changing this, ordering that—but it always seemed to be for the better. Of course, it infuriated her that he was always right.

And then there were those rare times when he complimented something she'd done. It was like the applause of thousands, bringing a rosy glow to her cheeks as pleasure darkened her violet eyes. She couldn't understand herself.

The opening of *Another Day* was only three weeks away, but something even more important was on Niki's mind as she entered the theatre that morning in March. In about twelve hours, she would be standing beside her grandmother while Taylor exchanged wedding vows with Conrad, and Niki was more nervous than she had been on her first opening night. Taylor had insisted on just a small affair, family and a few friends, but it seemed to Niki that she had a million and one things to do and no time to do them in.

Rehearsals went badly all morning, and her patience disintegrated with each passing minute.

"Listen, Niki. If we can just get this scene right once, we'll quit for the day." Harry ran his fingers through his hair as he peered at the floor. "All right, let's try it again from Tucker's farewell line."

"Ellen, you've got to go back with me." Tucker grabbed her by the shoulders and whirled her around.

"I can't, Aaron. It's wrong! Our worlds don't mix."

He pulled her closer. "Then we'll make them mix."

He kissed her, and she ran over her next few lines in her mind. When he released her, she placed a hand over her heart and backed away, shaking her head. "Aaron, I can't think when you do that. Please, you must go without me."

"Niki," Harry interrupted, "you don't *sound* like you can't think. You don't *sound* like you care if he kisses you or not or if he *goes* or not!"

The last hold on her nerves snapped. She stamped her foot on the floor like a petulant child. "Harry, I'm sorry, but I just don't know what you *want* of me! I'm doing the best I can, and if that's not good enough then you can jolly well . . ."

"Excuse me."

Adam's soft-spoken entrance onto the stage broke into her tirade.

"Could I make a suggestion?" he asked, looking at Harry.

The director sagged into a seat on the front row. "Why not?"

Adam turned his eyes back on Niki. "I think she has told you exactly what the problem is. She doesn't know what's expected of her."

He walked across the stage and stopped in front of her. There was a hint of a smile on his lips but not in his eyes. They met hers with a serious gaze which she found unsettling. She wanted to look away but seemed unable to do so.

It was Adam himself who looked away first, turning toward Tucker with an apologetic air. "You don't mind if I show you what I mean, do you, Tucker?"

"Not at all, sir," he answered, backing off stage. "Go right ahead."

"Thank you. Let's see. I should be standing about here, right?"

"Adam, really . . ." Niki began, but he held up a hand to silence her.

"Please. Just see if this doesn't help."

Niki sighed but took her mark on the stage.

"Ellen, you've got to go back with me."

Adam's fingers closed around her shoulders. He turned her around slowly, his hands sliding down onto her bare arms.

"I can't Aaron. It's wrong. Our worlds don't mix."

His grip tightened. His face clouded as he pulled her up against him. He was so much taller than Tucker that she found herself bending slightly backwards in his embrace.

"Then we'll make them mix," he uttered in a throaty whisper.

She watched his mouth descending slowly towards hers. She held her breath. Just as they touched, he drew her up even tighter against him. All thoughts fled from her mind. She seemed to be spinning and whirling, and her own arms encircled his neck as she fought to save herself from being swept away by whatever storm it was that raged about her.

At first his kiss was tender, his lips soft against her own, but as it lengthened, she sensed a change, a desire for more, a demand for more. Instinctively, her heart leapt in response. She pressed herself even closer to his hard, lean body. A slight parting of her lips allowed an involuntary moan to escape.

Abruptly, he released her, and she staggered backwards, her breath coming in little gasps. Her heart raced in her chest until she thought it might burst. She placed her hand over her breast, and in doing so, remembered that it was her line.

"Adam, I can't think when you do that . . ."

A smile crept onto his face. His blue eyes twinkled. "I think you're supposed to say *Aaron*, not Adam." He winked, then spun around to face Harry. "You see, Jamison, she just needed to be shown. I think she'll have that scene down pat from now on. She's a dynamite actress, you know." With that, he disappeared into the wings.

"Why, of all the . . . " Harry sputtered.

Niki stared after him, her world still spinning, her heart still racing.

CHAPTER 19

"**C**ome in, Niki. I was wondering if you were going to find a few moments for me."

Niki closed the door, staring all the while at her grandmother. "Gram, I've never seen you look lovelier."

Taylor was wearing a gown of midnight blue, the fitted skirt revealing a figure as trim as a girl one third her age. Her silver hair was swept off her neck and capped with a wide-brimmed, matching blue hat, complete with dyed egret feathers. A necklace of diamonds and sapphires encircled her long, white throat, a gift from the groom.

"Everyone's here, Gram."

Taylor moved away from the mirror where she'd been studying her reflection and sat down in a chair near the fireplace. "Sit here a moment, my dear. The guests can wait."

Niki crossed the room, but instead of taking a nearby chair, she sat on the floor and rested her arms on her grandmother's knees.

"I always thought we'd be having a chat like this before *your* wedding," Taylor said softly, a serene smile lighting her face from within. "Life never seems to go exactly as we expect it to."

"You're terribly happy, aren't you, Gram?"

"Terribly so."

Niki laid her head on Taylor's knee, staring into the cold hearth while Taylor's hand began stroking her hair. "What's it like to be so much in love?"

Taylor pondered the question a moment as she looked at her granddaughter's face. "Sometimes it's very confusing, but mostly it's wonderful. Don't ever be afraid to love someone, my dear. You may get hurt, but love is always worth the risk."

They sat in silence, sharing that special closeness that had always existed between them, the only sound in the room the steady ticking of the mantle clock.

Finally, Taylor put a finger under Niki's chin and lifted her head so their eyes could meet. "You've grown up a great deal since we left the ranch. I want you to know I'm very proud of you. You're headstrong and impetuous and you're as stubborn as your mother and father put together . . ."—she smiled—" . . . but you're also loving and generous. I pray God will grant you as good a life as He's given me."

"Thank you, Gram." Niki felt a little misty.

Taylor cleared her throat. "Now," she said, standing up, "let's go get me married off to that nice gentleman who's waiting for me."

Niki got to her feet. Standing on tiptoe, she planted a kiss on Taylor's cheek, then took her arm, and they walked out together.

The guests who waited below were, indeed, few. An outbreak of influenza had prevented Brenetta and Rory from coming at the last moment, but Brenetta had insisted that her mother not delay her plans. Although disappointed by her daughter's absense, Taylor was delighted that Erin had been able to come up from Spring Haven. Anne was there with Travis, and Marc and Sarah, newlyweds themselves, had come, too. Conrad's partner— and Anne and Marc's father—Jonathon Houseman, was there. And, of course, Adam.

As Taylor and Niki came down the stairs, everyone gathered in the entry hall. Conrad left the others and went to the bottom of the stairs to await his bride's descent. She paused on the bottom step, letting her glance trail around the room before coming to rest on Conrad; then she accepted his proffered elbow and allowed him to lead her into the drawing room where Reverand

Marshall was waiting.

Niki took her place on her grandmother's left while Adam stood to the right of the groom. The guests formed a close semicircle behind them, and the ceremony began.

"Beloved, we are gathered here together . . ."

Her grandmother looked as radiant as a young bride, her eyes aglow, a nervous smile playing across her mouth. But there was no doubting the love these two felt for each other.

Covertly, Niki's gaze moved to Adam. He looked so serious, dressed in his dark evening suit, listening to the words the minister was saying. Unbidden, her thoughts returned her to that morning's rehearsal and the kiss that had left her so shaken. Just the memory made her knees quake. She shook herself mentally.

"Do you, Conrad . . ."

What would it be like to be loved by a man, really loved? And if a man did love her, would he be good and kind to her, would the very sound of his voice thrill her?

"Do you, Taylor . . ."

Could she love a man enough to give her life to him, to surrender her own dreams and put his life first?

"What God has joined together, let no man put asunder. I now pronounce you man and wife. You may kiss the bride, Mr.

Cheavers."

Niki's vision was blinded by tears. Her grandmother was so happy, and suddenly, Niki felt very alone and unwanted.

"Hurray!" someone shouted just before a shower of rice fell on the bride and groom.

Then everyone was kissing and hugging everyone else. Corks popped from champagne bottles, and Pearl and Fiona brought in the hors d'oeuvres. Niki lost track of the number of glasses of champagne that she drank as she tried to rid herself of self-pity.

"You don't look as if this is a happy occasion," Adam hissed as he slipped up beside her.

"What do you mean? I couldn't be happier for Gram and Mr. Cheavers."

"Now, now. Don't get your dander up. I know you're happy for them." He patted her back as he spoke. When he stopped patting, he let his hand remain there. "You must admit, they look terribly pleased with themselves."

Niki took another glass from Fiona's tray as she passed by. She sipped some, then hiccupped.

"Too much of the bubbly, Miss O'Hara?"

"Not at all, Mr. Bellman." She flashed him a challenging smile. "Chances are, I can hold my liquor better than you, cousin."

"You're on, cousin." Adam lifted his

glass. "To the glorious state of matrimony."

"Hear, hear!"

They sat in the darkened drawing room, just the two of them. The bride and groom had left on their honeymoon, everyone else had gone to their own homes, except for Erin who had retired to her guest room.

"They really *did* look happy, didn't they?" Niki asked again, for what must have been the fiftieth time.

"They certainly did," Adam answered. "Do you suppose marriage makes everyone that happy?"

The room was spinning just a little. Was it the champagne or was Adam kissing her again? No, he couldn't be kissing her. He'd just asked her a question.

Adam leaned over until his nose was nearly touching hers. "Do you suppose marriage makes everyone that happy?" he repeated.

"I . . . I don't know. I've never tried it."

"Neither have I." There was a long pause. "Say, *you* haven't looked very happy for a while, and *I* wouldn't mind being happier. Why don't *we* give it a try?"

"Give what a try?" She wished the room would stop spinning.

"Marriage. Let's go get married."

"What for?"

"So we could be happy. You'd like to be

happy, wouldn't you?''

"Sure."

"Let's go."

He got to his feet, swaying slightly, then swept her up into his arms and headed for the door. She clasped her hands behind his neck and nestled her head against his shoulder as she drifted into an alcohol-induced slumber.

"Insomuch as this man and this woman have consented . . . Do you, Adam Stone Bellman, take . . . Do you, Kathleen Nicole O'Hara, take . . . What God has joined . . . You may kiss the bride . . .''

Helping hands, unfastening each button. So gentle. So strong. Cool sheets. Lips like fire on her throat. Everything spinning. The champagne or his kisses? Lips so demanding. His or her own? Caresses and tingling skin. A burning desire gnawing at the pit of her stomach.

"Adam . . .''

As daylight tried to force its way past her closed eyelids, Niki snuggled closer into the warm protection that seemed to encompass her. If she didn't open her eyes, she would never have to leave this safe place.

"Niki, I think you'd better wake up."

"Mmm. Not yet," she managed to whisper.

"Niki . . .''

She pressed closer to the warmth, holding off some nagging thought that was trying to disturb her, trying to force her back to the conscious world.

"Niki . . ."

Then it hit her. That was Adam's voice. What was he doing in her room? She opened one eye. Nothing made sense. She opened the other, and slowly, the blur began to clear.

Except for a light covering of hair, his muscular chest was bare. The sheet was pulled up to just above his hips, but she knew immediately he wore nothing beneath the sheet. Her head was lying on his shoulder, the fingers of one hand tangled in the fur of his chest.

She lifted her hand and head and started to slide away from him, but the sheet was caught under his outside leg and, as she moved, it slipped away to reveal her own naked breasts. Niki gasped and snatched the sheet back to cover herself. She looked up at him, her eyes wide with shock.

"Adam, what on earth . . ."

He was wearing what appeared to be a wry smile. "I'm sorry to break it to you like this, my dear, but it seems we've gotten married."

"*Married!*" she cried, again sitting up and again revealing a flash of nakedness before she could haul the sheet along with her. "What do you mean, we're married?"

"Just that. We eloped last night."

Her head was pounding, punishing her. She pressed the fingers of one hand against her temples to try to stop the torture.

Adam reached out and pulled a cord beside the bed. The door opened, admitting a man who managed to hide his surprise at the sight that met him.

"Thomsen, bring me a glass of Seltzer and some tomato juice."

"Yes, sir."

"Adam, who was that? Where is Fiona or Pearl?"

"That was Thomsen, my valet. We are in my apartment, Mrs. Bellman."

If she could just clear her head so she could think. "Where are my clothes, Adam? This joke has gone far enough."

His hand on her arm was like a red-hot andiron. She jumped, her eyes flying open, despite the pain, to look into his.

"Niki, it's no joke. We're married."

She felt a little faint. "You mean we . . ."

He nodded.

"But I don't remember . . ." Her face flushed hot. What *should* she remember?

"Unfortunately, neither do I . . . at least not as much as I'd like to." His voice had become husky as he leaned closer. "Niki?"

The kiss reminded her of last Christmas, when he had kissed her under the mistletoe, sweet and gentle. But she had no clothes on, and the longer his kiss lingered, the more aware she became of that fact.

"Adam . . . stop . . ."

There was a rap on the door before Thomsen entered on its echo. "Your juice and Seltzer, sir," he said as he carried the tray to Adam's side of the bed.

"Thank you, Thomsen. Thomsen, I'd like you to meet Mrs. Bellman, my wife."

The valet was really quite amazing, the way he could control his facial expressions. Only Adam, who had come to know him quite well since hiring him, caught the minute lift of one eyebrow before he bowed. "A pleasure to meet you, Mrs. Bellman." Then, "Would you be needing anything else, sir?"

"Nothing for now, Thomsen. I'll ring for you if we change our minds."

"Very good, sir."

Adam held out the Seltzer water to Niki. "Here. Drink this. It might help."

Dubiously, she accepted. She sipped the water until it was all gone, hoping against hope that the throbbing in her head would subside in short order. Finished, she turned to set it on the night stand, but the small table was too far away to reach without moving out from under the protection of the sheet. Feeling the color in her cheeks rising again, she laid the glass on the bed at her side.

"Adam, I . . . I don't know what to say . . ."

She fell silent and, when he made no

reply, she glanced up at him. Her traitorous mind thought at once how handsome he looked. There was an instinctive urge to nestle against his shoulder again, like she'd been when she awoke. On the trail of that urge came a flash of memory of their night of lovemaking. She hid her burning face in her hands.

"Oh, Adam, I'm so ashamed."

"Ashamed! You have nothing to be ashamed of. We're man and wife. Do you think I'd use you shamefully?"

"But, Adam . . ." Her protest died in her throat. How could she tell him that she was ashamed, not because they had spent the night together as man and wife, but because there were no words of love spoken between them. To her horror, she knew beyond a doubt that if he said he loved her but *wouldn't* marry her, she would have gone willingly to his bed and not been ashamed.

As she had done before, she wondered, *Do I love him?* But this time, her question was answered by another. *Does he love me?* Could she trust her life, her dreams with this man, a man she cared for, hurt over, fought with, but never understood? Did she dare to confess to loving him?

No, in answer to his question, she didn't think he would use her shamefully. If he said they were married, then they were married, but what kind of marriage was it to be, beginning this way? If only . . . if only he loved her.

Adam saw her confusion, her fear, and felt fear of his own. His own memory of the night before was muddled. Whatever had possessed them to elope? Oh, he knew why *he* had. The love that burned in his heart for her was no stranger to him. And the desire to hold her against him, to be joined together with her even for just one passion-filled night had seemed worth any risk. But in the light of day, without her love in return for his, he was afraid he had risked too much. It could be his haste would cost him the very thing he sought. Somehow he had to make her understand that he wouldn't force himself on her as her husband. He would give her more time. More time to learn to love him.

"Niki . . ." He started to reach out to touch her again, but he saw her stiffen and so dropped his hands. "Niki, I know this isn't an ideal way to start a marriage, but we can make the best of it. I'm not a brute."

"I know that, Adam."

"I . . . you'll have a room of your own, and I won't . . . bother you."

He saw her flinch and was awash with cold dread. He must have terrified her last night. Had he treated her badly and couldn't remember? Had he been too rough? Careless? Would she hate him now?

Perhaps he should try another tack. Perhaps, if she knew what he wanted out of life . . .

"You know, Niki, I've got a good practice going now. I'll be able to afford a lot of things that I couldn't before. And, as much as I love the city, I think I'd like a quiet place out on Long Island, for summers and holidays and such." He could see it so clearly in his mind's eye. "Not a place as large as Conrad's. Kind of a quiet cottage where we could relax, be ourselves."

It was a friendly, serene picture he conjured up. He and Niki sitting on a shaded porch while children played in the yard. It was a beautiful dream. Who could resist it?

"When you're not on Broadway anymore and we've started a family . . ."

Her sharp intake of air alerted him to his blunder. He glanced her way and saw her face go white and then red again. Her violet eyes darkened like a roiling sea, and he knew he was in trouble.

"Give up the stage! Why you egotistical, self-centered, peacock, you! If you think just because I had too much to drink and had the bad sense to marry you in that state of insobriety that I'm going to throw away everything I've worked and slaved and starved for, then you've got no more sense than . . . than . . ." She jumped out of bed, pulling the sheet with her and wrapping it around her as she went. "Where are my clothes? I'm getting out of here."

Adam grabbed the blanket off the floor and wrapped it around his waist as he got up to follow her. "Wait, Niki. I didn't mean . . ."

She turned on him with murder in her eyes. "You didn't mean. Of course, you didn't mean. You *never* mean." She poked him in the chest with a fingernail. "I bet I can think of at least a hundred times since we've met that you've said that to me. You probably didn't mean to marry me either, but you did."

In retaliation, he replied sarcastically, "Well, there's little doubt I'll rue that bit of untimely over-indulgence, is there?"

Her palm cracked against his face, followed by a startled silence as they stared at each other. Adam caught a glimpse of tears beginning to swim in her eyes before she turned and fled to the bathroom, locking the door behind her.

CHAPTER 20

"**F**or crying out loud, Niki. Can't you remember any of your lines?" Harry yelled at her from the back of the theatre.

"I'm sorry. I'll get it right this time."

"You'd better. I swear, that wedding seems to have wiped your memory clean."

Niki's eyes widened as she inhaled sharply. The tears came in a sudden rush. Pressing the back of her hand against her lips, she ran off the stage and into her dressing room, leaving behind a confused and befuddled director and cast.

She dropped onto the daybed, sobbing. As angry as she had been with Adam when she left his apartment, she now felt only bereft. Her own wedding and she couldn't remember much more than a blur. It should have been the greatest event of her life, even greater than any opening night. Instead, she had married a man on the spur of the moment while both of them were intoxicated, and not one word of love had been shared between them.

If only they hadn't consummated their union, she could have sought an annulment, but now . . . The evidence was overwhelming against the solution. Divorce? It was such an ugly word. Niki wasn't quite as liberated as she liked to think she was. Besides, she disliked failure of any kind.

So what was she to do about Adam?

"Niki?" Harry poked his head in the door.

She sniffed and wiped her eyes. "Come in, Harry."

"You want to tell me what's wrong?"

"I . . . I can't. Not yet." She blew her nose and gave him a half-hearted smile. "Give me a few minutes, and I'll be out and ready to go. Really I will."

"Okay. We'll take a break until you're ready." He patted her hand and left her alone.

She should have told Harry, but she just couldn't bring herself to do so. Not until she understood her situation better herself.

She didn't have long to wait. The next knock on her door admitted Adam.

He remained by the door, his hat in his hands, his face looking grim. "I won't keep you, Niki. I just couldn't leave things the way they were this morning." He paused, seeming to be searching for the right words. Finally, he spoke. "*I don't want a divorce*, Niki." Each word was clipped and precise. "I may not have been the man you would have chosen had you been thinking straight, but we are legally wed and I'd just as soon stay that way. I'm a fair man. At least, I think I am. I'll be good to you, and I wouldn't expect you to give up your career. You could have a suite of your own." His jaw stiffened. "I . . . would never force myself upon you."

He put his hand back on the door knob. "At least think about it, Niki. If . . . if you think you could live with me under these . . . these arrangements, I'll be at my office. You can call me there." He opened the door, then looked back at her. "I am . . . fond of you."

He was gone as quickly as he'd come.

"And I care for you, Adam," Niki whispered, "but that isn't enough. Do you *love* me?" But the familiar question, Do I love him? wasn't necessary anymore. She knew she loved him and had loved him for a long time. Instead of gladness, the awareness of her true feelings for Adam only made her heartache worse. She wasn't satisfied to be just his wife. She wanted to be his life, to be loved as she loved him — completely. She thought of Gram, and how she had always said the day would come when Niki would fall in love and nothing else in the world would be as important as he was.

How right you are, Gram, she thought, and wished it weren't so true.

The wedding of Taylor Lattimer,

widow of Brent Lattimer of the Lattimer Bank and Trust family, to Conrad Cheavers, well-known New York attorney, took place last night in the former Mrs. Lattimer's Fifth Avenue home. It was attended by only a small number of intimate friends and family members.

A more spontaneous affair seems to have been the wedding, which followed only a few hours later, of the new Mrs. Cheavers' granddaughter, Niki O'Hara, to an associate of Mr. Cheavers' firm, attorney Adam Bellman. This writer wishes both of the newlywed couples much happiness.

Niki's plans had called for her to move into the White House on Fifth Avenue now that Taylor was married and gone. She did so that same afternoon. Adam moved in that night. He took the room farthest away from Niki's.

Erin, a bit overwhelmed by the unexpected turn of events, joined them for their late supper. She sensed at once that this was not an ideal beginning for the marriage she, Pop, and Taylor had all been hoping for. She tried to keep a light conversation going throughout the meal but, at last, gave up and retired to her room where she began packing for her return trip. Though she had planned to stay two more weeks, she knew she would only be in the way while Niki and Adam tried to sort out their new life together.

"How did it get in the paper?" Adam asked once his aunt left the table.

"I don't know. I was as surprised as you are."

"We'll be having guests."

"I know."

"Perhaps the best thing would be if we let people think we had been planning to elope for some time. Let them think we're just like any newlywed couple."

"All right, Adam. If that's what you'd like."

"Yes. I think that would be for the best."

People came, all of them surprised.

"We had no idea."

"Why on earth did you elope?"

"I think it's so romantic, don't you?"

"We always thought you'd make a perfect couple."

There were so many people, bringing their congratulations and their best wishes —Travis and Anne, Marc and Sarah, Harry, Tucker, Grace Jones. So many friends, and they managed to deceive them all. Everyone left believing that they were happy and in love.

Yet all the while they lived like strangers, Niki in her room and Adam in his, meeting in the morning before she left for the theatre and he left for his office, meeting again at supper where they ate mostly in silence, each of them afraid to speak for fear of saying the wrong thing, of upsetting the delicate balance that held them together.

Another opening night, waiting in her dressing room at the Hudson Theatre. Once again she stared helplessly at her reflection in the mirror and wondered at her wisdom in coming to New York. She felt all alone in the world. She felt like dying—and not for fear of going on stage this time.

"Niki?"

She spun around, gripping the back of her chair so tightly her knuckles turned white. "Gram!" She jumped to her feet and threw herself into her grandmother's waiting arms. "Gram, I didn't think you'd be here. What about your honeymoon?"

"Goodness, my child. Where better to spend our honeymoon than watching you become the toast of Broadway?"

Taylor pulled Niki with her across to the daybed where they both sat down. She looked down at her gloves as she tugged them off, her attractive features thoughtful.

"Do you want to tell me about it?" she asked finally.

"I don't know if I can."

"Do you love him?"

Niki felt tears threatening and tried to swallow them back.

"Do you, Niki?"

"I . . . I think so."

"And did you know that he loves you?"

She got to her feet and returned to her dressing table. She picked up her powder puff and touched up her make-up. "You're wrong there, Gram. He's doing the honorable thing after making a grave mistake." She swallowed again, still fighting tears.

Taylor followed her across the room. Standing behind Niki, she took the girl by the shoulders and kissed her cheek, then met her eyes in the looking glass. "I wonder if I'm doing you a favor, minding my own business. But I will." She kissed her again, then walked briskly to the door. "Now get your mind back on this play. I expect you to be devastatingly marvelous tonight, and nothing less."

"Thanks, Gram."

After the door had closed, Niki went to her wardrobe closet and pulled out the dress she wore in the first act. Stepping behind the screen, she slipped it on.

"Miss O'Hara, five minutes," a voice called from the other side of the door.

"Thanks. I'll be right out."

One last look at her hair, and she was off for the wings. Tucker smiled at her as she stopped near his side but didn't speak. Only his tapping toe revealed his own jittery nerves.

Harry appeared beside them. "Well, this is it, kids. Let's knock 'em dead." He put his arm around Niki and whispered in her ear, "Do this one for old time's sake, okay?"

"Okay, Harry. Tonight's for you."

The play was good. Not fantastic, but good. Niki was performing professionally, but something was missing. Then, in the second act, when Tucker, as Aaron, spoke his line about making their worlds mix and pulled her close for their kiss, she came alive and the audience felt it. It wasn't Tucker who Niki felt kissing her. It was Adam. She closed her eyes and melted into her leading man's embrace, all the time thinking of Adam and how she wished they were his arms that held her, his voice that begged her to go away with him. When she opened her eyes and backed away from Tucker, clutching her heart, there was something new sparking her acting. A ripple of excitement moved through the audience and remained throughout the following three acts of the play. When the curtain fell at the close of the final act, the applause was deafening.

Adam stood with the rest of the audience, applauding, waiting for the curtain to go up one more time, watching Niki and the others take more bows, her face alive with triumph and joy. Even as the crowd began to disperse, he stayed by his seat, thinking of how she'd looked, how she'd moved, how she'd spoken her lines. She was beautiful. She was wonderful. She was his wife.

His wife, but they lived in separate worlds.

Adam sat down, a lone figure in the emptying auditorium. He stared into his past with something akin to disgust. When, as a foolish school boy, he thought he was in love with Christina, he hadn't been afraid to say what he thought or felt. Then, as a bitter young lawyer, he had been honest about the way he used women. So why, when he'd finally found someone worth fighting for, was he standing silently by? Sure, she must feel that he had done her a grievous wrong, spiriting her away and marrying her while she didn't know what she was doing, but she must like him, at least a little, to have gone with him. Why was he such a coward when it came to telling her that he loved her? So what if she laughed in his face. Would he be any worse off than he was now?

He got abruptly to his feet and headed for Niki's dressing room, determined to find the right words to say to her. He hadn't thought about the throng of admirers that he would find in the dressing room of a new star.

Niki's room was jam-packed with cast,

crew, and fans. Glasses overflowed with champagne and laughter bubbled forth, spilling into the hallway along with the people who couldn't fit into the dressing room. As Adam made his way through the crowd, he was suddenly reminded of the night, over two years before, when he had laughed at Niki's notion of becoming an actress and what he had sworn he would do if she succeeded.

His wife was surrounded by people. Her cheeks were pink and her violet eyes sparkled. He had never seen her look lovelier. As he stopped before her, her smile vanished. He met her gaze solemnly for a brief moment, then dropped one knee to the floor.

"Niki O'Hara, there was a day when I laughed at your ambitions and I promised that, if a day like this ever came, I would admit my error. So, before all your friends, I confess how wrong I was. You are a great actress."

He thought he saw a look of tender gratitude, but before she could respond, a new group of people pressed forward, separating her from his sight.

"Rector's. We're all going to Rector's," someone shouted.

Adam caught a fleeting glimpse of her dark brown hair moving toward the doorway, but he didn't try to follow. She was with her friends. She had no need of him tonight. He stood his ground, managing to keep from being pulled along with the flow of the crowd. When he was once again alone, he gazed around the empty room, then turned out the lights and started for home.

It was a fabulous night—the party at Rector's, the sharing with her close friends, the joy of success. She should have been giddy with happiness. Instead, she kept remembering Adam on his knee before her. She'd wanted to shout aloud her love for him. She'd wanted to pull him to his feet so she could proudly stand by his side, but she'd been swept away on the tide of success and hadn't seen him again that night.

It was nearly four in the morning when Harry dropped her off at the house.

"Goodnight, gorgeous. Get some sleep. Looks like we're in for a long run."

"I will, Harry. Goodnight."

She let herself in with her key. She thought at first that the house was cloaked in total darkness, the servants long since asleep, but as she laid her coat on the table near the door, she noticed the flickering light of a fire spilling across the entry hall from the drawing room. It seemed strange for a fire to still be burning so brightly. As she reached the doorway, she heard the click of ice in a glass and knew she wasn't the only one still awake.

"Come and join me," Adam called from his chair near the fire as he stared at the orange-red flames.

"I . . . I didn't think you'd still be up."

He glanced at her as she came nearer, but she couldn't see his face in the dark room.

"Would you like something to drink?" he asked.

"No. I . . . think I've had more than enough tonight." A great sadness washed over her as she sat down in a nearby chair. "Have you been sitting here drinking all night?"

He chuckled, a mirthless sound. "I'm not drunk, if that's what you're asking. I've learned my lesson." His meaning did not escape her.

There was a long silence.

"You really were wonderful tonight, Niki."

The hint of sarcasm was gone from his voice, and she knew he meant what he said.

"Harry says we'll have a long run. It is wonderful, isn't it, Adam?" When he didn't reply, she got to her feet. "I . . . I'm rather tired. Goodnight."

She was at the base of the stairs before he caught up with her. His hand on her back caught her by surprise, and she gasped as she whirled around.

"Niki . . . I meant it. You *were* wonderful tonight."

It was nice to hear, but it wasn't enough. Her shoulders sagged. "Thank you, Adam. Goodnight," she repeated.

He took hold of her arms, his grip so tight it bruised her flesh. His voice was harsh, sounding more so because of the darkness that hid his face from her. "I know you don't want to be married to me. I know I was drunk and you were drunk. But how long are we going to live together like this?" He pulled her close against him. She could feel his breath hot on her face. "It's time we made our worlds mix," he whispered, quoting the line from the play as he had before, then his mouth covered hers.

She sensed his anger and frustration in the hardness of his kiss, the bruising force of his lips against hers. She wanted to tell him he was wrong about her not wanting to be married to him.

"Adam . . ."

He wouldn't let her speak. His lips took hers again with savage intensity, an intensity that frightened her. She pressed her hands against his chest, trying to push him away, trying to catch her breath.

"Adam . . ."

"No, Niki. Don't push me away."

He swept her up in his arms and carried her up the stairs. Her heart was racing. She didn't want to push him away. She wanted to hold him close forever. Surely, he must know that.

Adam pushed open the door to her room with his foot, then closed it in the same manner. He carried her over to her bed and laid her gently in the center. In the shadows of the night-cloaked room, she saw him remove his shirt. Her pulse was pounding in her head. She felt weak with desire. She knew he was about to make love to her, and she wanted his embrace, his kisses, his lovemaking more than anything in the world.

The bed sagged beneath his weight. A tiny gasp escaped her lips as his arms twined around her once more, drawing her close against him. His mouth searched her face, moving from her lips to her cheeks, her eyes, her ears, her throat. One hand moved to her hair and began pulling out her hairpins, releasing her abundant tresses. His other hand moved to the bodice of her dress where his fingers struggled with the tiny buttons, all the while his mouth continuing its hungry exploration of her face, at the same time both gentle and bruising.

She sensed his frustration with the buttons of her dress and wanted to help him but was afraid to. She didn't know how to act, how to help him. She yearned for him, yet was hindered by shyness. Suddenly, he solved the problem as he gripped the fabric and rent it down the front. Niki inhaled sharply as the cool air of the room brushed her exposed skin, skin inflamed by his touch.

"You're so beautiful," he whispered huskily in her ear as he moved to cover her body with his own.

"Adam . . ." she moaned.

She was caught in a web of ecstasy. She had no sense of time or space. She knew only his touch, his kisses, his desire, and she never wanted to know anything else again.

A sense of well-being flowed over her as she slowly came awake. Niki sighed, hating to give up the dreams that had wrapped her in happiness once she had been allowed to sleep. Her hand snaked across the sheets but found no one beside her. She opened her eyes.

There was no sign of Adam in her room, no sign that he had been there the night before. Her dress was lying neatly over the back of a chair, her shoes tucked under it. She sat up, drawing the sheet over her naked breasts as she did so. She wondered when he had left her.

She slid her feet over the edge of the bed, reaching for her bedrobe. As she slipped into the silky garment, she caught sight of herself in her floor length mirror and moved closer for a better look. Her hair fell in tangled disarray, but didn't it every morning? No, not like this. Nothing about her looked the same. Her skin had a special glow, as if warmed from inside. Her lips looked red and swollen. She touched them and felt a shock as the memory of his kisses, hard and demanding, washed over her.

A knock sounded at her door. She whirled around in joyous expectation.

"Yes?"

It was Pearl. "I've brought you some coffee, Miss O'Hara."

"Thank you, Pearl. Is Mr. Bellman at breakfast?"

"No, miss. He was up and gone long ago. It's nearly noon."

"Noon? I had no idea I'd slept so long. Draw me a bath. I must get dressed. Have there been any calls?"

Pearl beamed from ear to ear. "The telephone has hardly stopped ringing, Miss O'Hara. And the papers have some wonderful things to say about you, too."

"Well, bring them up to me. I'll read them while I'm in the tub."

"Right away, Miss O'Hara." Pearl turned toward the door, then looked back. "Oh, I nearly forgot. Mr. Bellman asked that I give you this note."

Niki took the envelope from the maid. "Thank you, Pearl."

She waited until the door had closed before opening it, removing the white note paper, and reading the crisp handwriting.

Niki, I have used you badly and hope you

can someday forgive me. I'm not sure if I can forgive myself. I have been called out of town on business and may be gone for quite some time. When I return, I think we should decide if there is a future for this marriage of ours.
   Adam

Niki read the note twice, then crumpled the paper in one hand and let it fall to the floor.

CHAPTER 21

Niki held onto the car door as they bounced and jolted their way over the country road. A tiny frown furrowed her brows, and she pinched her mouth, determined not to complain. She felt BJ's eyes on her often but pointedly ignored him, staring out at the passing countryside. She was thankful that he held his questions. She wasn't sure she would have any answers for him yet.

She glanced back at Eddie, riding alone in the rumble seat. He didn't seem to mind the rutted, dusty road they were traveling. His amazement at the great expanses that surrounded him was written across his youthful face. Never had he imagined so much space with no one else around. The trees. The mountains. The valleys. It was all so strange and so wonderful—and rather frightening to a city kid.

"You look great, Niki. Never thought you'd grow up so pretty."

She finally glanced at her big brother, granting him a whisper of a smile. "Thank you, BJ."

Another mile or two passed before he spoke again. "Ma's probably wearing a hole in the floor with her pacing. She was awful surprised to learn you were coming home."

"So was I."

Overhead, the tiny green leaves of the white birch applauded their passing. A deer, hidden in the dense foliage, lifted her head and listened as the automobile puttered along, the doe's large ears twitching as cautious brown eyes watched for signs of danger. Seconds later, secure in their own safety, a mother skunk and her young family sauntered across the road as the dust settled behind the car, their tails lifted haughtily in the air.

Slowly, the Idaho mountains began to work their magic, stealing away the tension that had become such a part of Niki, erasing the frown and easing the pain in her temples. Without realizing it was even happening, she began to smile, an honest smile that came from way down inside.

"It's even prettier than I remembered," she whispered.

"You ready to tell me what brought you home?"

She shook her head. "Not yet, BJ." She glanced his way again. Other than a big hug and kiss at the station and telling her that everyone had missed her, BJ had let her travel in thoughtful silence. She appreciated his sensitivity.

As they crested the last rise that led to Heart's Landing, Niki reached over and touched BJ's arm.

"Stop for a moment."

Niki got out of the car and walked away from the automobile, pausing to stare into the valley that cradled her home. Though the house was still concealed by a veil of trees that rose up from the mountains, she caught a glimpse of green meadows and, in the distance, the promise of white fences and a red barn.

Eddie's hand slipped into hers. "Are we nearly there?" he asked.

"All of it," she replied without really answering, her free arm sweeping in a grand gesture. "Everything you can see is part of Heart's Landing. We're still too far away, but pretty soon you'll see the cattle and the horses."

"Niki. Could I sit up with you for the rest of the way?"

She looked down at him, her street-wise little urchin, and saw the slight tremble of his chin. Taken from his city environment, he no longer seemed so tough or so much older than his years. She ruffled his hair. "Of course you can. We'll be crowded, but we won't mind." She smiled. "You're going to like it here, Eddie. I promise."

Eddie nodded bravely.

They returned, hand-in-hand, to the car and climbed in, Eddie sitting on Niki's lap.

BJ looked at them thoughtfully, then pressed down on the accelerator, and they rolled down the hill on their way home.

Niki leaned forward in anticipation as they neared their destination. Her view of the house was obstructed by the fences and outbuildings until they were almost upon it. When she could at last see her girlhood home, she burst out laughing. There couldn't have been a single soul on Heart's Landing who was doing what they should have been doing at that time of day. They were all there on the front porch, looking as if there was no room to move an inch without bumping into someone else. As the car stopped in its own flurry of dust, the dam burst, and people poured onto the lawn and surrounded the car.

Brenetta was the first one to reach for the door. Tears glittered in her tawny eyes, but she was smiling. "Niki."

Niki bit back her own tears as she helped Eddie to the ground and then followed him. "Mother."

If Niki was afraid that the disagreements of the past would still prove an insurmountable barrier, she was mistaken. Brenetta pulled her into a tight hug, her tears now spilling freely down her cheeks. "Oh, my baby girl. It's so good to have you home."

Rory was the next to grip her to him. Behind the face that tried so often to hide his deep-felt emotions, Niki could read her father's joy . "Kitten, we're awfully proud of you."

"Thanks, Da." She wiped away her own tears as she turned to take Eddie's hand. "Mother. Father. This is Eddie, the little brother I found in New York. Eddie, these are my parents, Mr. and Mrs. O'Hara."

Rory extended his hand toward Eddie. "I'm very glad to meet you, Eddie."

"I . . . I'm pleased to meet you, too, Mr. O'Hara."

"Eddie," Rory said with a shake of his head, "how would it be if you called me Bear? Mr. O'Hara sounds a bit stuffy, and I'd like us to be friends."

"Bear? Where'd you get a name like that?"

"That's my Indian name."

Eddie's eyes grew wide. "Indian name? Are you a . . . an *Indian*?"

"On my mother's side of the family," Rory answered with a wink. "Come on. I'll show you where you'll be bunking and tell you about it."

The boy looked up at Niki who nodded her encouragement. "Go ahead, Eddie." She glanced at her father before he and Eddie walked away, her thanks written in her eyes.

All of a sudden, she was deluged with people again—family and ranch hands and neighbors—all of them welcoming her home with love and acclaim.

* * *

She awoke before sunrise in a room as familiar to her as her own reflection in the mirror. She lay quietly in her bed, listening to the pre-dawn call of the meadowlarks and the killdeer, savoring the peace that filled the house before the day began. Dropping her feet to the floor, she padded over to the window to gaze down at the corrals across the barnyard. She pressed her forehead against the cool glass.

She was safe. For at least a little while, she was safe. No worries. No cares. She had reached a friendly harbor, and here she intended to stay.

Then she thought of her parents. They hadn't pressed her for an explanation last night, but she knew she would have to tell them something soon. She would have to try to explain to them why she had run away from a successful play—the culmination of her dreams, the result of hard work and determination—why she had left behind everything that she had yearned for, now that she had attained them, and come home so abruptly. How was she going to explain the mess she had made of her life?

Suddenly Niki whirled away from the window and rushed to her dresser. Inside she found an old pair of denim jeans and a white cotton blouse. A worn pair of riding boots waited on the floor of the closet as if she'd never been away. She discarded her satin and lace negligee, slipping into her old clothes. She glanced at her reflection in the mirror and wondered at the changes a few years had wrought. The blouse was pulled taut across her breasts and the jeans fit snugly about her hips. It was a woman's figure in girl's clothing and was somehow more provocatively revealing than the lowest of decolletages she had seen on Broadway. With a shrug, she turned from the mirror, grabbing a jacket from its hook in the closet before leaving her bedroom.

The house and its inhabitants were still slumbering as Niki made her way silently down the stairs and escaped to the outdoors. She ran across the yard to the corrals, climbing the fence for a better view. Her eyes darted from one enclosure to another until she found the object of her search.

"Raja," she whispered.

She jumped down, hurrying toward the horse's pen. At the sound of her footsteps, the copper gelding lifted his head, his eyes alert, his ears cocked forward.

"Raja!" she called softly.

The horse nickered a reply as he came toward the gate.

Niki slipped through the fence slats and threw her arms around the horse's neck. "Raja, do you know me, boy?"

The animal nickered again, this time bobbing his head up and down as if in affirmative reply.

"I knew you would."

She reached for the halter hanging on the corner post and slipped it over his muzzle, fastening it behind his ears. Raja shook his head, making the rings on the halter jingle, then shoved his mistress with his nose as if to say, "Let's go."

"Okay. Okay," Niki agreed with a laugh.

She led him out of his corral and into the barn where she looped his lead around a post, then left him to enter the tack room. She emerged carrying a saddle, a heavy pad, Raja's bridle, and a brush. Dropping the tack for a moment, she whisked the dirt from the gelding's shiny coat, noting the sleek muscles beneath the skin. Someone had kept him in excellent condition during her absence.

Laying the brush on a nearby shelf, she lifted the saddle and pad from the barn floor and tossed them easily onto his back, smiling at her own agility. "At least I haven't lost my touch," she said aloud. Raja turned to look at her dubiously.

The sidesaddle might be fine when wearing a dress and riding in Central Park, but here in the mountains of Idaho it would have seemed a ridiculous object. It was as natural as breathing to place her boot in the stirrup and swing her right leg over the saddle. Niki turned Raja's head toward the barn door and tapped her heals against his sides.

The cool morning air kissed her cheeks and tugged at her loose hair as she cantered down the road away from the ranch house. The troubles that had haunted her days and nights in recent weeks seemed far removed. The breeze blew all thoughts from her mind. She rode for the pure joy of it, allowing Raja to choose his own pace and his own path. They left the road that brought car-bound visitors into the valley, following the less civilized trails that led up the mountainside. She enjoyed the rhythmic movements of the horse beneath her thighs, sensing the wild freedom that was barely contained by the iron bit in his mouth.

The sun was beginning to warm her hair when Niki finally pulled back on Raja's bridle, bringing him to a halt on a high ridge. She dismounted and walked to the edge of the bluff. She hooked her thumbs in her back pockets as she stared down at the main house and other buildings that were just a small part of Heart's Landing Ranch. She realized now, more than ever before, how much a part of her this place was. She loved it.

Niki sat on the hard rock earth, hugging her knees to her chest. She would have been content to remain so, enjoying her stroll through childhood memories, but the present could only be held at bay just so long before it won in its demands to be recognized.

"Hi, sis. Got room for company?"

She didn't look up as BJ joined her on the ground, just continued to stare out over the valley.

"Ready to tell someone?"

Niki started to shake her head, but she stopped herself. She had to tell someone. If she kept it all to herself, she was going to go crazy. She nodded. "Yes. I'm ready." She turned her eyes on him. "You've got to promise you won't say anything to the folks, BJ. I don't think I'll tell them everything I'm going to tell you."

He returned her gaze. "Agreed."

"I'm sure everyone was surprised about my marriage."

"A bit."

"Well, no one was more surprised than I was. It was an . . . an accident, BJ. Neither one of us meant to . . . wanted to marry the other."

"An accident?" BJ's eyebrows lifted.

"I know that's hard to believe, but it's true. I don't want to say any more about it than that." The firm line of her mouth warned that she would brook no more questions on that subject. "We . . . Adam and I . . . haven't even had what you would call a *normal* marriage, except on the surface. For the sake of appearances."

BJ's look was grim. "Doesn't sound like a very happy existence to me."

"It wasn't." Niki bit her lip thoughtfully. "Adam made it clear, though, that he didn't want a divorce. I suppose it wouldn't be very good for his career. I thought I could learn to live with it. I thought my own career would be enough. Only . . ." She broke off, the valley below turning into a blur as she stared out through her tears.

"Only what?" BJ asked gently.

"Only I didn't expect to fall in love with him." Her quiet reply was tinged with bitterness.

BJ put his arm around her shoulders. "Is it so bad to be in love with your husband?"

"It is when he doesn't love you." She dashed away her tears with an angry swipe.

Her brother chose not to interrupt the silence that fell between them as Niki fought to control her raw emotions.

With a sniff, she finally continued. "I was so excited when my play was a hit. I thought for a little while—such a *little* while," she added in a whisper, as if talking only to herself, "that he might be able to grow to care for me, maybe even love me."

Niki looked at her brother again, her beautiful face ravaged by an inner pain that darkened her violet eyes to ebony. It revealed too much. It hurt BJ just to look upon such desolation.

"He went away over two months ago, BJ. On business, he said. I don't know where he went. I haven't heard from him." Gripping her arms over her chest, her fingernails unconsciously bit into her own flesh. "Not a word in over two months."

"Have you checked with his firm? Did you ask where he'd gone?"

Niki could only shake her head. "How could I do that? The happy newlywed, letting everyone know that she doesn't know where her husband is, that she hasn't heard from him in all those weeks. I couldn't do it. I had to go on pretending that everything was all right. Being in the play helped. I was busy. My nights were full."

"So why did you leave the play and come back home?"

It was the question she'd been dreading. Could she tell her brother—no matter how close, how loving—something so intimate?

"Tell me, Niki," he pressed, the deep resonance of his voice speaking his concern.

"He . . . we . . . we didn't usually share a bedroom, but . . . the night before he left, he . . . we . . ." She swallowed. "I'm pregnant, BJ, and I'm not sure that I should have the baby. It wasn't made in love, and I . . ." She lifted her haunted face toward him. "How can I bring a child into this world, into a home, without love?"

BJ's own face had darkened in anger. He

grabbed his sister by the shoulders and dragged her to her feet. There was little of the compassion remaining that he had held for her only moments before. He gave her a rough shake. "Niki, you listen to me. I don't care what's happened between you two. I don't even care if he raped you, though I think that term is a bit strong for what most likely happened. Niki, I wouldn't care if you were unmarried. You've been living too long in New York, and your brain's gone soft. No O'Hara's going to have an abortion. That's butchery and you know it. You'll have that child, and if you don't want it, I'll take it for my own and raise it."

Niki gasped. One hand flew to her mouth as her eyes widened in horror. He was right. She must be crazy. She didn't want to murder her child, *Adam's* child. "Oh, BJ, help me," she sobbed, and began to cry in earnest.

He pulled her againts his broad chest and held her as the weeks of pain and fear and bewilderment were let loose, soaking his shirt with a flood of tears. "It's okay," he crooned gently as he stroked her head. "Everything's going to be fine, sis. You'll see. You're home now. You're home."

CHAPTER 22

Adam hadn't meant for it to happen this way, but somehow one day turned into two and then days turned into weeks and weeks into months without his calling or writing. What could he have said anyway? Sorry that I got you drunk and married you? Sorry that I forced myself upon you?

He dismissed the cab and stood on the sidewalk, staring up at the white exterior of the house he now thought of as home, home because she lived there. The hour was late afternoon. Would she be at home or at the theatre? Maybe he should have let her know he was coming.

Boston had been a nightmare for Adam. He hadn't been able to keep his mind on his work. He couldn't rid himself of the shame he felt. He kept hearing Niki saying his name in protest as he carried her up the stairs. He kept seeing the torn dress that he had ripped off of her in his haste. She must hate him now. His chance of teaching her to love him had probably been shattered by his own stupidity.

He picked up his valise and started up the walk. He kept trying to think of something to say to her. There had been a million things whirling around in his head on the trip down from Boston, but now his mind was blank. At the door he paused. Should he use the key in his pocket or should he ring the bell? Was this still his home or was he merely an unwelcome guest come to call?

"You've made a muck of this from the very beginning," Adam muttered.

He rang the door chimes.

Mrs. Mulligan opened the door. Her stern face broke into a rare smile. "Mr. Bellman, as I live and breathe. You're home, sir."

Adam stepped inside, placing his hat in her outstretched hand. His eyes darted to the drawing room, then to the stairs in hopes that Niki would materialize.

"We've all missed you, sir," the housekeeper continued as she hung up his hat.

"I've missed all of you, Mrs. Mulligan." He stepped deeper into the entry hall. "Is Mrs. . . . is Niki still at home?"

The troubled silence caused him to turn and look at the woman. Her brows were drawn tight above her eyes.

"What is it?" he demanded.

"Could it be you don't know, sir?"

"Know what, Mrs. Mulligan?"

"Miss O'Hara's left New York."

"Left New . . . what are you talking

about, Mrs. Mulligan? Her play's still on Broadway. How could she leave?"

"She left the play, too, sir. There's another actress playing her part . . . and not very well either, I might add."

It was like a bad dream repeating itself. The last time he left the city on business he had returned to find her missing from his life. And now it was happening again.

Adam rubbed a hand across his forehead. "Where did she go, Mrs. Mulligan?"

"Back to Idaho, sir. She and the boy. Up and left just over a week ago." She headed toward the dining room, shaking her head. "And it wasn't a peaceful departure, either, with that Harry Jamison standing here, yelling at her that she couldn't just up and go like that. But she did. Packed her bags and left." She turned and looked back at him. "Sort of like you did, sir," she added as she disappeared through the doorway.

Adam gazed up the stairs toward Niki's bedroom. It seemed he had the answer he had come for. He turned on his heel and walked back to the door, snatching his hat from the top of the coat tree and picking up his valise.

"No, Mother. I . . . I'm not going to get a divorce, but the marriage is over all the same."

Niki sat on the couch, twisting a handkerchief in her hands. Brenetta was seated in a chair across the room from her. Rory stood behind his wife, one hand on her shoulder, the other resting on the back of the chair.

"Can't you tell us a little bit more, kitten?" her father asked.

"I'm sorry, Da. There isn't any more to tell. We made a mistake, and both of us have known it from the very beginning. I've come home to have this baby, and when I can, I'll return to the stage. With any luck, I'll have a career left to go back to."

"And what about the child's father?" Brenetta queried softly. "Will he have any say in its upbringing?"

It seemed her heart would be crushed by the hand of pain that squeezed it. "No. He doesn't want anything to do with either of us. I told you. He walked out of my life and won't be back. There's no love lost between us. There's just nothing. It's over and I've faced it. I'm all right, really."

Rory patted Brenetta's shoulder, then came across the room to sit beside his daughter. He placed a strong arm around her and pulled her head against his chest. A dry sob escaped her lips as she threw her arms around his neck and buried her face in his shirt.

Her parents exchanged a worried glance. Taylor had written them about Adam and Niki. She had said the marriage had been a bit premature but that the two were very much in love and she believed they would work out the differences between them, given enough time and patience. She had told them what a fine, caring man Adam was. Somehow, Taylor's description didn't match Niki's statement that he didn't want his own child.

Brenetta wished her mother and Conrad weren't in Europe right now. Taylor would have been able to help sort things out; Brenetta was sure of it. Her mother always seemed to have so much insight when it came to Niki. Much more so than she did.

Niki pulled away from Rory, turning a weary face up to meet his eyes. "It . . . it isn't that I care about Adam. It's just that I'm ashamed to have come home this way. I'm sorry I've made such a mess of everything, Da."

"Don't be silly," he growled, his own sorrow making his reply sound gruff. "We all make mistakes. What counts now is what you do from here on in. You've done right to come home."

As Niki laid her head against her father's chest once more, he exchanged another worried glance with Brenetta, knowing they were both thinking the same thing. Was Niki telling the truth about Adam, or did she feel more for him than she would admit, even to herself?

Days had a way of slipping away without

hardly knowing they'd been and gone. At least, that's how it seemed to Niki. With time, she was able to teach herself some tricks to ease the pain. Tricks such as only remembering the happy times she had spent with Adam. If his face forced itself into her thoughts, then she would summon up memories of him beside the river at Spring Haven, with his pant legs rolled up and a fishing pole flung over his shoulder. Or she would imagine him as he had been on their ride in Central Park. She blanked out their arguments, the harsh words they had exchanged, and as she did so, it seemed that those happier moments spent with him multiplied. They might have been brief, but there were so many of them. A quick smile. A laugh. A kiss. These were the things she would always remember. These were the things she would share with their child as he or she grew up.

The doctor Brenetta insisted Niki see had agreed that she could continue to ride—if she were careful—for another couple of months, and Niki took advantage of his permission. She spent long days astride Raja, wandering through the high mountain country. Sometimes she would dismount beside a clear stream in an open meadow and bask in the warming summer rays, letting the sun turn her complexion to a golden brown. Other days she would search out the canyon where the bald eagles made their nests, watching the magnificent birds as they soared overhead in search of prey.

Occasionally, Eddie went with her, but often he was too busy. The boy had made quick friends with Pepe, one of the ranch hands, and was fast becoming a cowboy. He took to riding as if he'd been born to it, and Pepe was teaching him to rope. Eddie had even learned to walk in that long, easy stride that characterized the men who worked the ranches of the West.

"I think he may be more of an actor than I am," Niki said with a laugh, watching the boy saunter across the yard behind Pepe.

Brenetta looked up from her sewing and joined in Niki's laughter. "He really is an amazing little fellow, Niki. We're awfully glad to have him here with us. But you'd best keep an eye in him. Next thing you'll know, he'll be trying to smoke cheroots just like Pepe does."

"I'll box his ears if he does," Niki replied, her fond tone belying the stern words.

"You're going to make a wonderful mother."

Niki turned around and sat on the porch rail, one hand moving to her still-flat stomach. "I hope so, Ma. I hope I'm as good a mother as you've always been to me."

"Why, Niki," Brenetta whispered, "I think that's the nicest thing I've ever heard. Thank you."

"I wasn't saying it as compliment, Ma. I mean, not just to make you feel good. I mean it." She leaned forward, her violet eyes clouded with worry. "Look at the mess I've made of my own life. How can I be responsible for someone else, someone that will be so dependent upon me?"

Brenetta set her embroidery aside and joined her daughter, placing an arm around Niki's back. "Do you think you're the first expectant mother to ever feel that way, my dear? Every woman worries about it, whether it's her first or her tenth. And the worry doesn't stop when the children aren't little anymore. A mother goes on worrying about them all their lives, wondering if she's done the right thing, said the right thing, and all too often she hasn't. But they survive despite the mistakes, and one day, a mother looks at her children and realizes she's done all right, that she can be proud of them." She placed a soft kiss on Niki's cheek. "Just like I'm proud of you."

"But you still have to worry about me, don't you?"

Brenetta smiled. "Yes, Niki, I still have to worry about you."

The sound of cantering hooves drew their attention to the road leading to the house. It didn't take much effort for Niki to recognize the rider. Tom Call had come to see her often since her return home. Tom was the foreman of the Lazy Starr, her sister and brother-in-law's place.

"Mornin', Niki, Miz O'Hara," he called as he jumped from the saddle.

"Good morning, Tom. Nice to see you again so soon." Brenetta could barely conceal her amusement. She patted Niki on the back, then walked across the porch toward the front door. "If you'll excuse me, I've got to see Cook for a moment."

Tom pushed his dusty hat back on his head. His green eyes twinkled in his tanned face. "I wondered if you'd mind if I joined you on your ride today, Niki."

"Not at all, Tom. I'd like the company." Niki stepped off the porch. "I was just about to saddle up."

"I'll do it for you."

Niki nodded and they fell into step as they crossed the yard.

As she watched him lead Raja from his corral, Niki wondered what she was going to do about Tom. It was plain to everyone that he was interested in courting her. She probably shouldn't spend any time with him at all, but she enjoyed his quiet presence and was grateful for his friendship. She had explained to Tom that, though her marriage hadn't worked out, a divorce could damage her husband's career, and so she had decided not to pursue that avenue. This news didn't seem to sway him, nor did the news that she was pregnant. He seemed willing to wait and see what might happen in the future. In the meantime, he would settle for her friendship.

Adam was staring out the window of his office, his thoughts far from New York, when his secretary buzzed him.

"Your ten o'clock appointment is here, Mr. Bellman."

He sighed, bothered by the interruption. He wished he hadn't agreed to meet with this woman who had refused to leave her name, saying only that it was most urgent that she meet with an attorney. "Show her in, Betty."

As the door opened, he rose from his chair, assuming the professional facade he had learned to wear in front of clients.

The woman breezed past Betty, then waited for the door to close. Her hat and head were covered in a veil of bright yellow lace, the weave heavy enough to hide her face from view. Her gown of lemon-colored lawn draped a profoundly feminine figure. In an almost sensuous movement, the woman reached up and untied the veil at the back of her neck, then lifted it slowly upwards.

"Hello, Adam."

"Melina!"

She walked toward him, holding out her gloved hand for him to take. "I wondered if you would remember me."

He was surprised by her warm regard.

After all, their parting had been somewhat less than congenial.

As if reading his mind, Melina's mouth turned down in a pout. "I hope you've forgiven me for my bad behavior, Adam. Something as silly as our argument shouldn't stand between good friends, should it?"

"I suppose not," he replied, his skepticism clear. He indicated with his free hand for her to be seated. "What's brought you to New York?"

Sitting in the chair across the desk from him, Melina tugged off her gloves and laid them in her lap before speaking. "Father is here on business, and I came along for the fun of it. It looks like we'll be here several weeks." She glanced at him, her deep brown eyes pleading skillfully for his cooperation. "I don't know a soul in New York, Adam, and with Father off with his cronies, I'm quite bored. I was hoping you would consent to have dinner with me."

All his instincts warned him against accepting her invitation, but he was lonely. His days and nights were filled with Niki's memory. He couldn't rid himself of her. He needed an escape. "You know that I'm married," he said gruffly.

"My goodness. Does being married mean you can't have dinner with an old friend from down home?" She seemed to be laughing at him, though she wasn't even smiling.

"No," he replied. "No, it certainly doesn't. I'd be pleased to take you to dinner, Melina. How about tonight?"

"Wonderful. We're staying at the Waldorf Astoria. I'll be ready at seven."

Tom helped her down from the surrey. Music floated on the gentle evening breeze from the back of the house. The Anderson summer barbeque was an institution for natives of the area, and few people ever missed it. During the day there were rodeo events, and in the evening there was dancing. Friends came from miles around, those from farthest away staying with the Andersons until the close of festivities allowed them to return home.

Niki had spent much of the day watching the roping, riding and branding competitions, cheering on Rory and BJ and the other men from Heart's Landing. Even Eddie had competed against other boys his age, and though he didn't win, he had given a good show of the skills he had learned. When the July sun began to torture those crazy enough to stay out in its sweltering rays, Niki had returned home to rest, fighting the nausea that unsettled her stomach so often these days. When she awoke from her nap, she had taken a cool bath, then put on the new calico dress Brenetta had purchased for her, just for this occasion.

"You're pretty as a picture," Tom had told her when he arrived in the fringe-topped carriage.

"You look quite smart yourself, Tom Call," she'd replied.

And he did. His sandy hair, bleached lighter by the sun, was combed back from his face. The dark jeans and bright red shirt looked good on his lean, muscular form. There would be plenty of girls envious of her tonight.

Tom led her around to the back of the Anderson's large house. The grounds were lit by hundreds of Japanese lanterns. Rows of long tables were covered with food, and the delicious odor of barbequed beef teased their noses and made their mouths water. Niki felt starved, her queasiness of the afternoon forgotten.

"You sit here, and I'll get you a plate of food," Tom told her.

Waiting beside a whispering birch tree, Niki let her eyes wander, smiling as her gaze met with the glances of friends and acquaintances. By the time Tom returned with a plate stacked high with food, she had been joined by several others, and they were all talking and laughing and carrying on in high spirits.

As evening deepened, the black velvet sky dotted with glittering stars, the music began in earnest. Couples began dancing on the lawn, the women's skirts whirling above the ground.

"Will you dance with me?" Tom asked.

"I'd love to dance," Niki replied. She picked up the corner of her abundant skirt and held it in her left hand.

"I'm not very good," he apologized.

Hesitantly, they began to waltz. He was right. He wasn't very good. He stumbled over her feet several times, and his face was soon flushed with embarrassment.

"Oh, Tom," Niki laughed, hoping she wasn't being cruel. "I think we'd better sit down before we hurt one another."

He nodded, rewarding her with a sheepish grin. "Guess I should stick to ropin'."

Niki sat down in a nearby chair, her amusement lighting her face.

"Hey, Call. Come here a minute." A group of cowboys stood on the edge of the dancers, one of them waving at Tom.

"Do you mind, Niki?"

"No. You go on ahead."

She watched him walk away.

"Your husband's terribly good looking."

Niki looked at the girl who had spoken. She was about seventeen-years-old with a pretty face and excited hazel eyes. Niki opened her mouth to reply that Tom wasn't her husband . . .

"I wish I could meet someone like him," the girl continued.

The stranger's words jolted her. Her eyes

returned to Tom, standing with his back-slapping friends, their good-natured laughter drifting over the heads of the dancers to reach her ears.

What was she doing here with him? He should be with someone like this girl sitting beside her, a girl free to love him and be loved. He wasn't her husband, and what's more, she didn't want him for a husband. With a sharp clarity, she remembered the waltz she had danced with Adam on the veranda of Spring Haven. On the heels of that memory came the pain, the pain that she'd thought she was over, that she'd fooled herself into thinking she was immune to. She felt faint.

Turning to the girl, she said, "He's not my husband. He's just a friend." She got to her feet, a gigantic effort hiding her sudden sickness behind a smile. "I . . . I have to leave. When Tom comes back, will you please tell him I've gone home?"

Only sheer will steadied her steps as she went in search of her family and someone to take her home.

CHAPTER 23

Adam waited for Melina in the lobby of the Waldorf Astoria. Tonight they were attending a party hosted by friends of Judge Howard's. Adam didn't much care where they went as long as it kept him up late and he could have a few drinks. Anything to get him through another night. Once he was at his desk again in the morning, his work would keep his mind engaged sufficiently enough to keep his thoughts off Niki.

Melina stepped from the elevator. Her exceptional beauty, combined with the amount of skin her dress left exposed, drew eyes from all around the lobby. When she spied him, a slow smile replaced the seductive pout she habitually wore. She glided toward him, her sequined gown, the color of rich coffee, clinging to her figure from bust to ankle. The long train of the skirt was fastened to her left wrist, and in her hand she carried a pearl-handled fan.

Adam rose to meet her, accepting the kiss she brushed over his lips without response.

"Adam, darling, I'm sorry I was so long. I had a terrible time with the buttons on this dress. My maid was no help at all." She dropped her eyelids, her dark lashes brushing her cheeks. "Perhaps next time I should ask you to come up and help."

He took her arm without comment and guided her skillfully toward the door of his waiting automobile. He was oblivious to the staring eyes all around them.

It wasn't that Adam wasn't aware of the talk that must go on when people saw him with Melina. It just didn't matter to him. Though she would certainly be willing enough to share his bed, he had no interest in accommodating her in that regard. The gossip wouldn't change the truth. At the same time, she served him a useful purpose. She kept him from dwelling on the happiness that had eluded him. Adam had enclosed himself once again in his protective shell, but Melina was one woman who wasn't a threat to him. He knew her too well for what she really was and knew nothing she could ever do would hurt him.

The party was held in a grand mansion in the midst of "Millionaires Row," a section of Fifth Avenue facing Central Park where many of the richest men in the world built their homes. Twenty-five steps led up to the front doors, doors that were standing open now to receive the stream of elegantly attired men and women who were descending from their automobiles and climbing the steps. The house itself was ablaze with lights, glittering like the diamonds that encircled the throats of so many of the women in attendance.

Adam helped Melina from the car, then offered her his arm. He couldn't help but note the gleam in her eyes as she stared at the house.

"Be careful, Melina. Noticing money is very gauche. You must always act as if it means nothing to you at all."

She sniffed. "It only means nothing to those who have so much, darling."

Adam laughed, and they started up the steps.

Judge Howard was watching for them and met them just inside the door. He introduced his daughter and her escort to their host and hostess, then drew them further into the house, pointing out people of note to them. The guest list read like a who's who in the world of high finance.

"Adam," the judge said, "you won't mind if I steal Melina from you for a few minutes. There are some people I'd like her to meet."

"Not at all," he replied, spying a servant with a tray filled with champagne glasses. "I won't wander off."

Drink in hand, Adam lounged against a wall and watched the comings and goings. It was quite awhile before he realized that he was the object of someone's watching as well. He swung his eyes around the enormous room—just one of many that were filled to overflowing this night—until he met the gaze of a rather stern looking woman in her mid-forties or so. Her graying brown hair was pulled back in a no-nonsense chignon at the nape of her neck, but her black lace gown suggested style if not the immense wealth he expected in this company.

Seeing she was caught in her staring, she nodded in his direction. When he didn't move or look away, she walked toward him, holding out her hand as she stopped. "You must excuse me. I was trying to remember where I know you from. My name is Ella James."

"Adam Bellman." He accepted her hand, noting the firm grip she returned.

"Bellman . . . hmmm. I could have sworn I knew you. Have we ever met?"

"I'm sorry, Mrs. . . ."

"Miss," she corrected.

"Miss James. I don't believe I've ever had the pleasure." His tone was rather dubious.

Ella James laughed. "I apologize, Mr. Bellman. I believe what I've just done sounded like a line from a bad novel. I am not an old maid in search of a husband. I truly do think I should know you. I just can't think from where."

"Adam, darling. I've been looking everywhere for you." Melina materialized suddenly at his side, hooking her arm possessively through his.

Pointing with his glass, he introduced the two women. "Miss James, this is Melina Howard. Melina, Miss James."

"How do you do?" the two women said in unison.

Miss James, her stern but handsome face still looking puzzled, nodded once again. "It was a pleasure chatting with you, Mr. Bellman. Glad to have met you, Miss Howard. Do forgive me." With that she moved away, disappearing into the crowd.

"My goodness, Adam. Couldn't you have found someone with a little more . . . *class* to visit with while I was away?" She tugged at his arm. "Come on. I want to mingle."

Adam grabbed another drink from a passing tray. "Lead on, Melina," he replied as he gulped it down.

The Sun, *Miss Ella's News About Town: When the cat's away . . . News has it that a beautiful new actress, recently the toast of Broadway, has left town to visit her family in the West, leaving behind her handsome husband, almost in the midst of their honeymoon. This same husband, an attorney by profession, has been seen in recent weeks in the company of a gorgeous*

*blonde companion of Southern persuasion.
Could there be trouble in paradise?*

Melina sat in her satin-sheeted bed, her
back propped by many down pillows and
read the morning paper. Her eyes scanned
the gossip column, but she had to go back
and read it again several times before she
could believe it. Ella James was Miss Ella.

She began to laugh and continued until
tears streaked her cheeks. Oh, this was too
good. Adam and she linked romantically in
the *New York Sun*. It didn't matter that
there was nothing scandalous going on between them. Anyone reading the paper
would believe that Miss Ella knew more
than she was saying. What marvelous
revenge against Niki O'Hara. Too bad she
wasn't here to read it herself.

The door of her bedroom opened, and
Melina's maid, Esther, came in bearing a
silver coffee tray. "I've got your mornin'
coffee Miss Lina."

"Leave it here," Melina said, indicating
the table beside her bed, "and then start
my bath. I'm going to visit a friend and
want to be on my way before noon."

"Yes'm."

Sipping the hot brew, Melina browsed
over the delightful column one more time,
wondering if anyone had dared to tell Adam
about it. Probably not, but even if someone
had, his response had most likely been dis-

appointing. The man had become so remote, and when he wasn't being remote, he was being sarcastic.

"I wonder why I even want to be with him," she said aloud. "He really is disagreeable so much of the time."

Melina knew why. He had scorned her once, tossed her aside for another woman, but she hadn't given in. He was a challenge to her now, something to be conquered, a prize in a great contest. Her desire for him was like a drug in her veins. She needed him, needed to be near him, touching him. In the years since Adam left Atlanta, Melina had been miserable. She had looked for him in every man she was ever with but had never found anyone to take his place. She was addicted to him.

Melina wasn't fooling herself. She knew she wasn't the kind of woman that men wanted to marry. No. When that day came, they always looked for the innocent ones— or at least the ones who let men *think* they were innocent. Someone like Niki O'Hara. Of course, that was just part of the challenge. Melina didn't like to lose, and she didn't intend to lose. The sun wouldn't rise on the day Melina Howard couldn't handle a twit like Niki O'Hara.

"Damn that girl!" Melina exploded, slamming her cup down on the table and sloshing coffee over the rim. "Whether Adam likes it or not, I'll make sure he never goes back to her.''

The auditorium was black as ink. The stage lights glared so brightly that they hurt her eyes. She wished she could see her audience. The stillness frightened her. It was as if something evil lurked just beyond the stage. Her feet were as heavy as lead. It was so hard to get out on the stage. She fought to drag one foot in front of the other. She was going to miss her cue. Her heart beat quickened. Something . . . everything was going wrong.

Music began playing. A waltz. A beautiful waltz. Adam was beside her, dressed in white tie and tails. He was so terribly tall, so wonderfully handsome. His hand in the small of her back guided her as they began to dance around the stage, whirling and spinning and turning and turning . . . and turning . . . and turning . . . and turning . . .

She was so dizzy. His arms were no longer there to support her. He was gone and she was alone in the center of the stage. Alone except for whatever evil thing it was that waited for her out in that terrible darkness. Waiting. Waiting for her.

Niki awoke with a scream. She sat up, clutching the sheet to her breast. Moonlight spilled through the window and splashed across the floor, but it still seemed too dark—dark enough to hide the evil thing of her dream.

"Niki! What is it?" Rory burst into her room, switching on the light.

"Oh, Da," she whimpered.

Her father sat on the bed beside her and took her in his arms. "A nightmare?"

Niki nodded against his chest, her voice still caught in her throat.

Rory stroked her hair. "Well, it's all right now. I'm here. Nothing's going to hurt my baby girl."

"It was so terrible, Da." Niki looked up at him, her eyes as round as saucers. "Something bad is going to happen. I know it. I just know it."

"Not a chance, kitten."

Brenetta joined them as Niki was speaking, and she, too, hurried to allay Niki's apprehension. "Your father's right, Niki. Sometimes pregnancy causes all kinds of fanciful thoughts and dreams. Don't allow yourself to get carried away with premonitions and such." She kissed Niki's forehead. "Now you lie back down and get to sleep."

Niki took hold of her mother's hand. "Will you stay . . . for just a little while?" She felt silly, as if she were six years old again, but she couldn't bear the thought of being alone just yet.

"We'll stay, kitten," Rory answered. "Both of us."

The darkness wasn't so bad with her

parents still in the room, and despite the lingering fear, Niki was able to drift back to sleep, this time, thankfully, into a dreamless sleep.

The Sun, Miss Ella's News About Town: It is becoming more and more evident to this reporter that the public isn't being told the whole story regarding a certain actress's reasons for taking a leave from her show to visit her family out West. Instead of absence making the heart grow fonder, her charming husband seems to have forgotten her altogether, so brazenly is he escorting one blonde belle about town.

"Mr. Cheavers' office."

"Hello. Is Mr. Cheavers in?"

"I'm sorry. Mr. Cheavers is still in Europe on his wedding trip."

"Oh, dear. I thought they would have returned by now. This is dreadful."

"I'm his secretary. Is there something I can help you with?"

"Well, I . . . You see, I'm a friend of Mrs. Cheavers' daughter, Brenetta O'Hara. I need desperately to get in touch with her, but I've lost her address and I was hoping to get it from Taylor. I guess I'll just have to wait until she returns from Europe, only it was *so* important that I get in touch with Brenetta soon."

"Ma'am, I believe Mr. Cheavers has that

information in his address book. Can you hold the line while I check?"

"Oh, could you? That would be wonderful. I'd be eternally grateful. I'll hold on."

". . . Hello? Yes, I have that address for you. Do you have a pen?"

Melina wrote down the address, smiling all the while. When she hung up the phone, she walked across the living room of her hotel suite, waving the paper back and forth in front of her face as she pondered her next move. Pausing in front of a gilded mirror, she grinned maliciously.

"You really have a delightfully wicked mind, Miss Howard," she said to her reflection. "It's a good thing you have no aspirations toward sainthood."

Flicking her full skirts behind her, she swung around and crossed quickly to the desk beneath the window. There, carefully laid out on the surface, were the clippings from Miss Ella's gossip column and the photograph Melina had arranged to have taken the night she and Adam went to dinner after the theatre. She picked up the photograph. What a nice couple they made, Melina leaning against Adam's shoulder as she whispered something in his ear. It would have been better if he had been smiling, but Adam rarely smiled any more, unless he was being sardonic.

Melina shrugged. It didn't matter. The photo showed enough to have the effect she desired.

She sat down at the desk and pulled out an envelope. She took her pen from its holder and began writing. *Niki* . . . She paused. Should she use O'Hara or Bellman? O'Hara, she decided. She didn't want to encourage any lingering sense of possession that Niki might feel. After all, the purpose of this whole thing was to destroy whatever good feelings Niki might feel toward her estranged husband.

And, Melina thought, *to hurt her, to destroy her if possible.*

Once that was accomplished, Melina would be able to concentrate one hundred percent on changing Adam's mind about their future together.

She slipped the newspaper columns and the photographs into the envelope. Then, as a last thought, she scribbled on a piece of pale blue stationary, *From a friend. Thought you should know.*

CHAPTER 24

Summer had ushered in a hot dry spell, and the road leading to Heart's Landing swirled up a cloud of dust so high a visitor was announced long before he arrived. So it was that the O'Haras were waiting expectantly on the porch when Harry Jamison stepped from his rented automobile.

"Harry!" Niki exclaimed as she hopped off the porch, hurrying to throw her arms around his neck and plant a big kiss on his cheek. "Harry, it's so good to see you."

"Not half so good as it is for me to see you." He held her at arm's length. "Niki, you're unbelievable. You're as beautiful in levis as you are in chiffon and diamonds." He tweaked her cheek. "You look radiant, kiddo. The climate here must agree with you."

Niki hooked her arm through his and propelled him toward the porch. "It does, Harry." She lifted her free arm. "Harry, this is my mother, Brenetta O'Hara. Ma, this is Harry."

"How do you do, Mrs. O'Hara."

Brenetta, squinting into the sun, smiled and nodded. "Netta to my friends, and I hope you won't mind if I call you Harry."

"I'd be pleased if you would."

Niki tugged on his arm again. "Let's get inside. That sun is hot enough to fry an egg."

A small fan sat on a table in a corner of the parlor, offering some relief from the heat. Niki led Harry to a chair placed directly in the fan's line of fire, then hurried to the kitchen to bring him an iced tea. With a director's eye, he scanned the room, taking note of the grouping of family photographs on the mantle over the fireplace. The room was comfortable, homey. It wasn't just the summer weather that gave warmth to this room. It echoed with the memories of love that had been shared within these walls.

"You have a lovely home, Mrs. O'Hara," he said.

"I thought we'd agreed on Netta."

"Excuse me. Netta."

Brenetta smiled again, and Harry thought, She's as beautiful as Niki, even if she must be close to fifty.

"Thank you," Brenetta said. "My parents built this house. It's the only one I ever remember. I wouldn't want to live anywhere else, although there was a time when I thought I would. I'm glad I came to my senses."

Harry pointed at the photographs. "Are all those members of your family?"

"Yes, these are our sons, BJ and Travis. I believe you've met Travis?"

"Yes, in New York."

"This is Starr, our oldest daughter, and her husband and family. And this is a picture of my father, Brent Lattimer." She handed him the silver framed photo.

"He was a mighty handsome man."

"Yes, he was, wasn't he? And a good man, too."

"Sounds like you were very close."

Brenetta accepted the photograph back, her expression wistful. "We were. It took me a long, long time to resign myself to his death. Life in this country can be harsh."

"Ma, are you boring Harry with stories of our family?" Niki carried the tea tray into the room, setting it on the coffee table near the sofa.

"Not at all," Harry protested. "Your mother was just telling me about her father."

Niki nodded. "I've always wished I could have known him. I've grown up on tales of Grandpa Brent and how things were here when he and Gram first came west." She handed Harry a tall glass of iced tea. "Now tell us why you've come and how long you can stay. You know, you're the last person I would have expected to see driving up that road."

Harry looked at her for a long moment

before replying. "I thought I'd stay about a week if your folks don't mind the impromptu company." He cleared his throat. "I could start off with saying I just came for a visit, but to be honest, Niki, I came to try to convince you to come back to New York. I knew a letter wouldn't do any good." He took hold of Niki's hand, his eyes pleading with her. "We need you, Niki. The play's just not the same. Oh, the crowds are still coming and the critics still like it, but the public wants you back. They miss you . . . I miss you."

Niki stared down at her hand, clasped within his. Neither of them noticed Brenetta as she slipped quietly from the room.

"Harry, I'm sorry. It wasn't fair of me to leave you that way."

"Well, I'll admit I wasn't too happy when you told me you had to come home for a visit, right when then everything was going so good, but I sure didn't expect to get a letter telling me you wouldn't be back at all." His grip tightened. "Is it because of Adam?"

Niki's glance darted up to meet his gaze, then she hopped to her feet, pulling her hand free. "No! No, it's not because of him. I couldn't care less. I don't want to talk about him. Adam and I are through."

"Oh?"

Sparks flashed in violet eyes. "You don't

sound as if you believe me. Well, it's the truth. Our marriage was a mistake from the very start."

"Are you going to get a divorce?"

"No."

"Why not, if it's really over between you two?"

Niki walked across to the mantle, her eyes moving slowly from one photo to the next. "Because of my family," she whispered.

"Your family?" Harry got up and followed her across the room. "You mean they don't approve of divorce? I know you were raised a Catholic, but you weren't married by a priest. Can't you . . ."

"Not this family, Harry." She turned around, a look of serene joy on her face. "I'm going to have a baby."

Harry looked as if he'd just been slugged. "A . . . a baby?"

Niki nodded.

"You're going to have a *baby*?"

"My goodness, Harry. You make it sound so . . . miraculous. I'm not the first woman this has ever happened to, you know."

"I know, but . . . a baby." He sat down in the nearest chair, still looking overwhelmed, even dismayed. He stared at the floor. "I guess you really won't be coming back to the play."

"I'm sorry, Harry."

Suddenly, he threw off his dark looks. He

got to his feet. "Whatever is wrong with me? You're going to have a baby." His arms wrapped around her and he kissed her soundly on the lips. "It's wonderful. I couldn't be happier for you."

"Thank you, Harry," she replied before she returned his kiss. "And I hope you'll want me back as your leading lady once the baby's born."

He raised an eyebrow, then squinted at her. "I don't know . . . I'm not sure how you'll be as the matronly type." His smile told her he was joking with her.

"Come on, Harry. I want to show you around the place. And I have a million things I want to ask you."

"Okay. Lead on, little mother."

Niki was truly enjoying Harry's visit. He was as awestruck with her rugged Idaho mountain home as Eddie had been. They rode together every day, and they visited late into the night, sitting on the porch after the sun had gone down. Harry was relaxed and at ease, and she decided she liked him better here than she had in New York. In the city, they had shared the struggles and the ambitions, the hard work and the disappointments of trying to make it as actress and director. When they first met, Harry had been almost desperate to succeed, and sometimes that desperation had made him just a little unlikeable. Now he had succeeded. They both had. Their futures in the theatre were promising, even with the unexpected interruption caused by Niki's pregnancy. For the first time, they were taking the time to get to know each other beyond the theatre and beginning to form a friendship based not on their shared dreams but just because they liked each other as people.

The week seemed to be flying by, and Niki knew she was going to miss Harry when he was gone. The day before he was scheduled to return to New York, they decided to pack a picnic lunch and ride up to Niki's favorite meadow.

As they were preparing to leave, BJ arrived with the mail. Dropping everything else on the stand near the door, he carried a large envelope over to Niki. "Thought you might want to open this. It's from New York."

"New York?" Niki took the package and turned it over in her hands. "I wonder what it is?"

"Why don't you open it? It's the easiest way to find out," BJ replied, poking her in the ribs.

"Oh, get out of here," she hissed, but with a smile.

Niki carried the envelope across to the window in the living room and slid her fingers under the flap to open it. She peeked inside. "It's some newspaper clippings and a photo." She dumped the contents onto the desk.

It was Harry who first realized something was terribly wrong. The frozen expression on her face, the almost imperceptible shake of her hands as she held the newspaper. He was walking toward her when she looked up. Her eyes, always so expressive, revealed such total devastation, it frightened him.

"Niki?"

He reached her just as she crumpled forward, the papers fluttering to the floor.

Darkness whirled around her. Her pulse pounded in her head. She was sinking into a deep crevasse, tortured by a hot pain that crashed and ebbed like waves in the rising tide. She was afraid. Terribly afraid. She wanted to cry out, but only a weak moan escaped her parched lips. She thought she must be dying and almost welcomed the notion. At least then she could escape the horrible pain that sought to tear her in two. She gasped as the molten agony ripped through her again, and this time she sank too deeply into the darkness to think any more about dying. Or even about living.

"I'm sorry, Mrs. O'Hara. There's nothing I can do. She's going to lose this child, but I'll do all in my power to save your daughter's life."

* * *

She was rising up out of the dark pit. The pain was gone. But she was tired. So terribly tired. A weariness that gripped every part of her body. She didn't want to wake up. She only wanted to sleep. Perhaps forever.

"Niki? Niki, open your eyes, dear. Niki."

As if from miles away, her mother's voice beckoned to her, and she reluctatntly obeyed. It seemed such a long, long way back to consciousness.

"Rory, come here. I think she's waking up. Niki?"

She wanted to speak, but it seemed too difficult.

"Kitten? It's your da. Wake up and look at me, Niki."

Why must they wake her up? Why did they sound so worried? Couldn't they just let her sleep? Didn't they know how tired she was? She whimpered in protest.

"Oh, Niki, please," Brenetta whispered. "Please open your eyes."

"Mother." Her voice sounded so strange. Her eyes fluttered, then closed tight. "The light . . . It's too bright."

"Close the blinds, Rory." Her mother's arm slipped under her head. "Here, Niki. Take a sip of this water."

It tasted good, so cool on her scratchy throat. She opened her eyes again. The harsh daylight had been shut out of the room, making her parents only shadows in the dim light.

"Ma. What's wrong?"

"You've been sick, dear. Awfully sick. But you're going to be all right now. You just need lots of rest." Brenetta kissed Niki's forehead. "Here. Have another drink."

They hid the truth from her for several days while they nursed her bit by bit forcing her back to health. But one afternoon she awoke and knew without anyone telling her what had happened. Her mother was sitting near her bed. Exhausted herself, Brenetta was dozing.

"Ma?" Niki whispered.

Brenetta was alert at once, bending close to the bed.

"I lost the baby, didn't I?"

Her mother smoothed the hair away from Niki's forehead before answering. "Yes."

"I almost died?"

"Yes, dear."

"I wish I had."

"Oh, Niki." Brenetta moved over to the bed and gathered her into her arms. "Never say that. There'll be other babies."

But not Adam's baby. Now she would never have Adam's baby.

"Hello. Is Niki allowed visitors yet?"

Niki could sense her mother's relief at the

interruption. "Come in, Harry."

Niki lifted her head from Brenetta's breast and watched Harry step closer to her bed. He looked almost worse than she felt, as if he hadn't slept for weeks on end.

"Harry, I thought you would've left by now," she said as he stopped at her bedside.

Harry reached down and touched Niki's hand. "How could I have until I knew you were well again?"

Brenetta got up from the bed. She helped Niki sit up a little higher, fluffing the pillows behind her back, then said, "I'm going to get her something to eat. You'll stay with her, won't you, Harry?"

"Of course."

Niki watched as he sat down in the chair, pulling it closer to the bed. She studied his face—the dark circles under the eyes, the strained lines around his mouth. "I guess I gave everyone a scare," she said lightly.

"You most certainly did," Harry responded with a smile.

"Harry?" The lightness was gone. "It's true, isn't it? About Adam and Melina?"

"Well, I . . ."

"You've seen them together, too, haven't you?"

Harry leaned closer. "I don't think this is the time, Niki. Let's talk about it later when you're stronger."

"No. I want to talk about it now. I want to know the truth."

"All right, Niki. It's true. I've seen them together myself."

"Harry?" She seemed to shrink into the pillows. "I lost the baby."

"I know, love."

"Oh, Harry. I wanted that baby so." Tears began to streak her pale cheeks. "I've lost him. I've lost him."

"Go ahead and cry, kiddo," Harry whispered, shifting, as her mother had done, to the edge of the bed so he could hold her. "Cry it out. I understand."

A violent thunderstorm brought relief from the heat wave that had gripped the area for weeks. Niki got out of bed and went to the window, clad only in her white cotton nightgown. She leaned against the window sill, watching the bright flashes of light that streaked across the rolling heavens. A wind gusted through the valley, and she could hear the horses nickering in the corrals.

Life was so strange. A decision, once made, affected her life forever. If she had never gone to that play in San Francisco as a girl, she might never have wanted to become an actress. If she hadn't insisted on going to New York, she might never have met Adam. If she hadn't taken that ride into the slums, she wouldn't have found Eddie. If she hadn't drunk too much after Gram's wedding, she wouldn't have been pregnant with Adam's child. If she hadn't left New York, perhaps . . .

"Adam," she whispered into the wind, but his name was whipped away from her.

She could have done so many things differently. She had never done the right thing when it came to Adam. She should have told him about the baby. He had told her he didn't want a divorce, that he would treat her fairly. He would have been kind to her and he would have loved the child. She never gave him a chance. She never gave either of them a chance. She just ran away and now there was Melina at his side. The thought crossed her mind that he might have been seeing Melina all along, but she knew that it wasn't true. Adam might not have loved her, might have been unhappy, trapped as he was in their charade of a marriage, but he would never have been a philanderer. No, it was Niki's absence that had given unspoken permission for Melina to fill that vacant spot where Niki should have been.

The rain began, lightly at first, then in torrents. Niki stepped back from her open window, escaping the fine spray that the gusts of wind forced through the screen.

"It's time I start over," she said aloud.

She felt a little stronger, just by speaking the words. She couldn't change the mistakes that she'd made. They were done. What might have been with Adam was in the past. She couldn't bring back the baby she had lost either. She must make a new start, and to do that, she would have to leave the past behind her.

She went to the maple secretary that stood against the wall near the door. Dropping open the cover, she sat down as she pulled a sheet of stationary out of its nook. She stared at the blank paper, listening to the receding thunder as the storm moved beyond the mountains. Then she began to write.

Dear Adam . . .

Dearest Adam. My dear, dear Adam. She swallowed the lump that formed in her throat.

As I'm sure you know, I am at Heart's Landing. I had to find some place that I could think, and it has done me good to be at home, at least for a short while.

I have had time to do a lot of thinking, to try to sort things out . . .

CHAPTER 25

. . . And so, Adam, I think you must agree that the best thing for us would be to dissolve this marriage. Since you are an attorney, I will leave the details up to you. I will not contest any decision you make. If you need any papers signed, you can send them to me here.

Sincerely,
Niki

So, at last it had come. Adam turned away from the letter lying on his desk and gazed without seeing out the window. Despite everything, he had hoped she would never ask for a divorce, even if they lived the rest of their lives at opposite ends of the continent.

He leaned back in his chair and rubbed his eyes. He was tired. Too many sleepless nights. Too many hours during the day when his thoughts slipped to Niki . . .

"Adam, darling. Have you forgotten our luncheon? I've been waiting for you for nearly an hour!"

He swiveled around as Melina barged into his office, feeling all the more weary with her here.

"Get your coat. We're already late."

"I'm not going, Melina. You'll have to go alone."

"Alone!" she exclaimed, her eyebrows lifting in surprise. "I wouldn't think of it. Now, come on with me."

Adam's glance was grim as he stood. "I told you I'm not going, Melina. Please leave without a fuss."

"I can't believe you're doing this to me. What will people think if I show up without you? Everyone knows we're a couple."

A cold glint shown in his eyes. "I couldn't care less what people think . . . and we're *not* a couple."

Melina gasped, her hand flying to her cheek as if she'd been struck. "Adam, what's come over you?"

In a lifeless monotone, he answered, "I'm sick. Sick and tired. Of my life. Of this office. Of this town. And most of all, of you, Melina. Now you have your answer. Get out."

Outraged, her pretty face was distorted as she snarled, "You'll be sorry for this, Adam Bellman."

"I'm already sorry, Melina."

"You're a fool. You could have had me. I'm the right woman for you. I know how to please you. But you just go on mooning over that little chit." She stepped closer to the desk. "Well, I've got news for you, Mr. Bellman. She won't ever come back to you."

Adam sank once more into his chair. "I already know that. She's asked for a divorce."

"A divorce?" Delight replaced anger. "But, you'll be free. There's no reason we can't go on seeing each other." She came around to stand beside him, lifting a hand to caress his forehead. "Perhaps," she whispered in an intimate tone, "we could see even more of each other now."

Adam grabbed her wrist and held her hand away from him. "Get out, Melina," he growled.

A sinister smile twisted her lips. "All right. Have it your way. I've already had my revenge, whether you know it or not." Melina stepped backwards. "Some night, when you're lying alone in your bed, think of what you could have had."

With a toss of her head, she spun around and was gone.

Adam turned over his clients to a bright young attorney who had just joined the firm. He packed his things and sub-let his apartment, then caught a train to Atlanta. He did nothing about the divorce. If Niki was in a hurry, she would have to take care of it herself. For now, he wanted only to escape to the peace and quiet of Spring Haven.

Erin did what she could to help, but Adam didn't *want* to feel better. He chose to savor the hurt and bitterness, hoping that by facing it, feeling it, he would soon begin not to care at all. He threw himself into a busy schedule, using the money he had made in New York to make many of the much needed improvements and repairs to the manor and grounds. He gave the house and outbuildings a fresh coat of white paint. He purchased curtains for the east drawing room and a new carpet for Erin's bedroom. With a promise to himself to rebuild Spring Haven's fine stable of horses to what it had been in his grandfather's day, he traveled to Atlanta for an auction and returned with a flashy young stallion and two brood mares. To outsiders, he appeared the same. Only Erin knew how his heart ached.

Niki left the house before the sun was up, saddling Raja and heading for the seclusion of the heavily wooded mountains. It was good to be riding again. She felt more like herself. Alive once more. The darkness of the past weeks was beginning to lift, and she even found she was able to smile now and then.

Raja picked his way up the steep deer trail, his hooves digging deep into the rich soil beneath the carpet of needles that lay on the ground. Niki leaned forward in the saddle, dodging the low branches that swiped at her hat and scratched at her arms. Above the piney canopy, the sky was beginning to turn from pewter to azure, and the sun was bringing a sweet warmth to the cool morning.

With a final lunge, Raja broke from the dense trees. From this ridge, Niki could look down into the valley. She could see her home and the barn and the corrals. She could even see the rooftop of BJ's place, though it was set too close to the treeline to see very much. She dismounted and sat on the ground, pulling her legs up against her chest. She let her eyes move in a slow sweep over the big valley, absorbing every detail. It was her way of bidding it goodbye again.

Last night Harry had finally convinced her to return with him to New York and to the play. She had been hiding out long enough. Though Heart's Landing had provided a sweet refuge for her, she knew her real life was waiting for her on Broadway. There was nothing to keep her from it any more.

The familiar pang shot through her heart at the thought of the lost child. But her mother was right. It wasn't quite so bad as it had been. Little by little, the pain was easing, and she could think about what might have been without feeling as if she could die from the loss of her unborn child.

Niki even felt a twinge of excitement at the thought of returning to Broadway. It seemed a lifetime since she had curtsied as the curtain rose for one more curtain call. She could almost hear the applause. Yes, it would be good to be working again.

She got to her feet and swung up onto Raja's back, turning him back down the mountain. She had said her farewell to the valley. Now she would have to tell her mother.

New York didn't seem quite as strange as it had the first time she arrived here. The station, the streets, the traffic. They were all familiar to her. It was good to be back.

Niki glanced at Harry, sitting beside her in the cab. He looked a little tired, but she could tell he was as glad to be back in New York as she was.

As if reading her thoughts, he looked her way. "What a place! It's about time I returned. Not that I didn't enjoy my stay with you and your folks, but it is a bit quiet after this city life."

"I'm awfully glad you were there with me, Harry. I'm not sure I ever told you that before."

"You told me, kiddo." He chucked her under the chin. "Wait til your fans get a load of your bronzed face. There'll be ladies throwing off their hats right and left so they can look like Miss Niki O'Hara."

Niki smiled. "And then they'll all curse me for their freckles."

"Well," Harry chuckled, "at least they'll be talking about you."

They remained silent the rest of the way, arriving at their destination slightly before noon. As soon as Niki had disembarked from the cab, the front door of the house flew open and the entire staff spilled out onto the lawn. The formality of the greeting she had received when she first arrived at White House three years before was forgotten. She found herself being hugged by Mrs. Mulligan and Mrs. Tiffany, Pearl and Fiona. Max and Roger were a bit more restrained, offering only handshakes, but these were warm and firm and no less welcoming than the greetings from the female staff members.

"We've got your room all ready for you, Miss O'Hara. We're so glad to have you back. The place has been terribly gloomy without you and Master Eddie around to liven it up." The housekeeper looked surprised. "Why, where is the boy?"

"He didn't come, Mrs. Mulligan. Eddie has shed his city ways and became a real cowboy."

Harry laughed. "Cowboy is right. I expect that by the time you see him next, he'll have learned to rope and brand and whatever else it is those wranglers do as well as the best of them."

"I'm sure you're right," Niki replied as she stepped inside the house.

Mrs. Mulligan was giving orders, sending Fiona for a tea tray, fussing and stewing over her mistress's comfort, barely giving Niki a chance to get her bearings. It wasn't until she had bid goodbye to Harry and ascended the stairs to her room that unwelcome memories had a chance to assail her, robbing her of the joy of her return, at least for a moment.

The sun spilling in through the window was like a spot-light, highlighting the bed. She couldn't shut out the memory of the night they had spent together in that bed, the night when she had conceived, and the last night she had seen Adam. Niki dropped her purse in the lounge chair and moved toward the bed. Her heart felt tight; her mouth was dry. She had to blink away the sudden moisture that formed in her eyes.

"No!" she cried. "I won't do it. I won't get all melancholy. It's done. Finished. It's just me now, and that's how it's best."

It was an ecstatic city that welcomed back Miss O'Hara to Broadway. Dignitaries filled the boxes at her first return performance, and the applause called her back time and again for another bow. It was a thrilling and exhilarating experience. She had been so nervous, afraid she would mess up her lines or forget everything altogether. But it had been incredibly easy. It was more like being herself than acting out a part in a play.

The critics raved about her, too, and she was a "must" guest at every party. With such popularity, Niki found it nearly impossible to get home before sun-up. She would fall into bed, out almost before her head hit the pillow, and sleep until early afternoon. When she awoke, she would take a long, luxurious bath and then read her mail. By the time she was dressed, Harry would be there. They would share a light dinner at her place, then go to the theatre together. Her life was busy and exciting and it left little room for thinking about the empty void in her heart.

"Niki, guess what?" Harry cried as he burst into her dressing room.

She turned from her mirror, her powder puff still held above her nose. "I have no idea. Tell me."

"There's a producer here from London. He's here to look us over . . . and if he likes us, we may be on our way to England some time soon."

"Harry, you're joking. London?"

"You wouldn't mind a few months abroad, would you? If you would, I'm sure we could get your understudy back."

Niki tossed her powder puff at him.

"Don't tease me, Harry. You know darn good and well that I'd be the first one on the ship."

He strode across the room, placed a hand on each shoulder, and pulled her to her feet. "Then you'd better go out there and give them the performance of your life. It's in your hands, kiddo."

"Well, thank you for not putting any pressure on me," she replied with a wry smile.

Harry chuckled, then dropped a kiss on her cheek before leaving her alone in the dressing room.

England! How wonderful. To be able to take *Another Day* to London would be grand. Maybe she could even visit some of the places her mother had told her about from her own stay overseas when she was a young girl. And Niki would be there with so many friends—Harry and Tucker and the rest of the cast. Yes, it would be a real treat.

A knock on her door broke into her musings.

"Come in," she called.

Her visitor was preceded by an enormous bouquet of flowers, all different kinds— roses and carnations and iris and daisies. Niki had never seen anything like it. They held her gaze for several seconds before she lifted her eyes to her guest.

"Niki O'Hara, you've made quite a name for yourself," Melina said as she laid the flowers on the dressing table. "I hope you don't mind my barging in on you this way, but I was afraid I wouldn't be able to catch you after the show and I did want you to know how excited I am by your success."

"Thank you, Melina." Her reply sounded more like a croak.

"Well, you're certainly not the little girl I first met at Adam's party at Spring Haven. You've become a lovely woman. My goodness. It's a wonder this room isn't filled with eligible young men, clamoring for your attention."

Niki turned back to her mirror and continued with her makeup. "They wouldn't be allowed in here so near to show time, even if that were true."

"And I won't keep you either, darling. I just wanted you to know that I was here." She moved toward the door. "Give your best tonight. Kind of a send off for me."

"Really? Are you leaving New York?" Niki looked at Melina in the mirror, a false sweetness in her voice.

"Yes. My father and I are going back to Atlanta in the morning. His business is finished at last. Besides, there's nothing much to occupy my time now that Adam has gone back to Spring Haven." She smiled innocently. "Of course, you knew that, didn't you? Well, good luck tonight." With a swish of her skirt, she was gone.

That woman! How I hate her, Niki

thought, grinding her teeth. She would love to take a swing at that insufferable smile.

" 'Oh, I have nothing to do now that Adam's gone,' " she mimicked, leaning close to her reflection in the mirror. With raised eyebrows and puckered lips, she continued, " 'But then you knew that, didn't you, *dahling.*' " She shuddered.

Niki rose from her makeup table and slipped out of her dressing robe. Turning before the floor length mirror in the corner, she smiled in satisfaction. The sleek black gown showed off her trim figure to perfection.

"You're not going to get to me, Melina Howard," she whispered. "I know all about you and Adam, and I won't let it bother me another second. If all the more he wants is the likes of you, then he can have you with my blessings."

She could almost believe it herself.

Perhaps it was her anger at Melina, but Niki really did give the best performance of her life that night. When Harry came to her dressing room afterwards, he brought the London producer with him.

"Miss O'Hara, I'd like you to meet George Thatcher. Mr. Thatcher, our star, Niki O'Hara."

George Thatcher was a rotund man in his mid-fifties, with graying hair and a handlebar mustache. Holding his top hat in his left hand, he held out his right toward her. "Miss O'Hara, it is a great pleasure to meet you. You are everything the papers have been saying."

"Thank you, Mr. Thatcher," she replied, accepting his handshake. "It is very gratifying to hear such praise from someone like yourself."

"Nonsense. It's merely the truth."

Indicating the sofa, Niki said, "Please. Won't you sit down?"

He shook his head. "If you don't mind, Miss O'Hara, I'd prefer to take you out someplace. Perhaps for supper?"

Niki glanced at Harry and could see his excitement. He was already prompting her reply with a vigorous nod. She looked back at Mr. Thatcher with a smile. "If you'll give me a few minutes to change, I think Harry and I would like that very much."

Harry opened the door. "George, let's you and I go back out to the lobby while we wait for Niki. It'll give us a minute or two for a smoke while we get better acquainted."

"Miss O'Hara," George Thatcher said, excusing himself.

Just before Harry closed the door, he shot an exaggerated wink in Niki's direction, leaving her laughing as she began changing out of her costume.

CHAPTER 26

"Pearl, have Roger come up for this trunk. I think I've finally got everything in it."

"Right away, Miss O'Hara."

"Oh, and Pearl, have you seen my white muffler? I can't seem to find it anywhere and I'm sure to need it when we sail tonight."

"It's downstairs with your other luggage, miss." Pearl paused, then added, "Where you told me to put it about half an hour ago."

Niki looked up at her maid, giving a futile shake of her head. She sighed as she sat on her chaise lounge. "I guess I'm a bit overanxious. I'm just so afraid I'll forget something, and . . ."

"Miss O'Hara, why don't you just relax? It's only a few hours before Mr. Jamison will be here for you. Fiona and I will take care of things. And you can be sure that Mrs. Mulligan won't let anything go undone that needs to be done."

Niki shook her head again. "I really have

been acting terribly, haven't I? Fussing and stewing needlessly. I'm going to do just as you say. I'm going to lie here and rest. Maybe I'll even take a nap. Thank you, Pearl."

Sleep was the last thing Niki would be able to do. How could she fall asleep when in just a matter of hours she would be on her way to London aboard an ocean liner? She was both excited and terrified. So many dreams coming true. So many wonderful things happened to her. It didn't seem possible.

She was startled from her thoughts by Fiona's squeal, followed by the sounds of commotion coming from downstairs. Niki jumped up from the lounge and hurried out into the hall. She halted at the top of the stairs, not sure at first what was going on. Then, the sea of jubilant servants parted and she spied her grandmother. Taylor looked up at just the same moment.

"Gram," Niki whispered in disbelief.

Taylor, wearing a dress of brilliant blue with a tight skirt, elaborately draped, held out her gloved hands toward Niki, her eyes sparkling. "Niki," she called.

Niki flew down the stairs, straight into her grandmother's arms. "Oh, Gram. I never expected to see you. When did you get back? Where's Conrad? How was your trip? Did you know I'm going to London?"

"Slow down, Niki. Slow down."

"I'm sorry, Gram. Come into the other room. Mrs. Mulligan, bring us some tea, please."

They sat down on the sofa in the drawing room, Niki's eyes never leaving her grandmother's face. Taylor looked even younger than she had when she had left on her honeymoon. Her cheeks glowed with a natural rose blush, and her blue eyes revealed true happiness.

"You look wonderful, Gram. I don't have to ask how things are with you and Conrad."

Taylor smiled. "No, I don't suppose you do." She squeezed Niki's hand. As she removed her hat, she asked, "Now, what is this I hear about you leaving for London?"

"That's right. The whole cast of *Another Day* is going to England. We leave tonight on the *Mauretania*. The show has been such a hit in New York, and now George Thatcher is taking it to London."

"Is Adam going with you?"

"Adam?" She said his name a little breathlessly. "But, Gram, I thought you knew. Adam and I have separated. We're going to get a divorce."

The color in Taylor's cheeks paled. She stared hard at Niki, forcing her granddaughter to drop her eyes to her lap in discomfort. That penetrating gaze had always been able to see too deeply.

"My dear," Taylor said at last, "I think

you'd better tell me what's happened while I've been away."

"Nothing happened. Not really. We were never right for each other, Gram. Neither of us were happy." Niki got up and walked to the window looking out on Fifth Avenue. "I guess Adam was more unhappy. He left and didn't come back."

Niki fell silent when she heard Mrs. Mulligan coming with the tea tray. Taylor thanked the housekeeper, then poured two cups. Niki didn't turn around, so she carried it to her.

"Go on," Taylor prompted as Niki took the cup.

Niki swallowed the lump that had risen in her throat. "I . . . may as well tell you. You'll know sooner or later. I went to Heart's Landing for a while. I went because I was pregnant."

"Pregnant? But, Niki . . ."

"I *was* pregnant, Gram. I'm not anymore. I lost it."

"Oh, my dear."

Niki's jaw stiffened. "And while I was losing the baby, Adam was escorting Melina Howard all around New York." She turned and marched back to the sofa, her chin held high. "So now you know why I'm getting a divorce. And I'd prefer not to talk about it any more."

The shock of Niki's news was written on Taylor's face as she followed her granddaughter back to the couch. "But, Niki, this doesn't sound like either of you. I can't believe Adam would desert you, knowing you were pregnant with his child. And he loves you. I can't believe he would see another woman, especially with his wife in a delicate condition."

"He never knew I was pregnant."

"Never knew?" Taylor echoed, incredulous. "Niki . . ."

"Halloo!" Harry stood in the doorway to the drawing room. "Why, Mrs. Cheavers, I didn't know you were back from the continent." He entered the room and bowed smartly as he stopped before her.

"How do you do, Mr. Jamison. It's nice to see you again."

"I suppose you've already heard about our trip?" Harry sat beside Niki and threw his arm over her shoulder. "This is a big day for us."

"Niki was just telling me about it. Seems I returned almost too late. To say goodbye, I mean."

"Excuse me, Harry," Niki said as she got to her feet. "I still have quite a few things to see to before I'll be ready to leave." She hurried out of the room, driven by a desire to escape her grandmother's piercing gaze.

It wasn't long, though, before Taylor's knock announced that she had followed Niki up the stairs to her room. The stern look on her face promised she would bridge no interruptions to what she had to say.

"Kathleen Nicole," she began, in her no-nonsense voice, as she closed the door, "I have a few things to say to you and then I'll say no more about it. I know you love me and will forgive me for interfering. I can't say I know exactly what's gone on between you and Adam since I left, and I know that your marriage didn't start out exactly right either, but I do know that you were in love with him—and from the look of you, you're still in love with him—and too stubborn and foolish to tell him so. And I know that Adam has been in love with you practically from the first moment he set eyes on you back at Spring Haven."

Niki shook her head in denial.

"It's true, Niki, though I'm not surprised you're too blind to see it or that he's been too afraid to show it. It's true, and if he's been seeing another woman, I have to believe that some of it is your fault because love like that doesn't disappear so quickly."

Taylor walked toward Niki, her voice softening. "My girl, I know what I'm talking about now. A misunderstanding nearly ruined my life. Because I was stubborn and foolish and too blind to see the truth, I thought your grandfather didn't love me and I nearly lost him for good. You might not get the second chance that I did. Don't throw Adam away. He's a good man and he loved you very much. I would stake my life on it that he still does."

Taylor hugged her granddaughter, then returned to the door. "Now I know you have a show to go to in London, but if you're smart, you'll give your husband a call and try to sort things out before you go." She opened the door. "I'll go down and keep Mr. Jamison company."

Adam rode slowly along the edge of the cotton field. The sun was already riding low in the sky, and Erin would have dinner waiting for him. Still, he wasn't in any hurry to reach the house. He had little appetite, and the evenings always seemed to stretch on forever. At least during the day, he could keep busy, what with the remodeling and building, working with the horses, checking the fields, and planning next year's crops. But the evenings were too quiet, leaving him too much time to think, and thinking, to a man with a troubled heart, could only lead to more trouble. His moods swung like a pendulum, causing him to snap at Erin over the littlest things, and then to hate himself for doing it. He knew his aunt understood what was bothering him, which only made things worse.

The truth was he wasn't getting over Niki. He couldn't rid himself of her memory. She was constantly with him. As he worked with his new horse, he would envision her riding in Central Park. As he worked in the fields, he saw her rehearsing on the stage. In the evenings, sitting in the drawing room with Erin, he remembered those evenings he spent at White House with Niki and Aunt Taylor and Travis, and how lovely Niki always looked. When he woke up in the morning, he was flooded with the memory of her as she looked the last time he had seen her, curled up in bed, her thick brown hair spread in a tangled mass over the pillow.

The phone was ringing as he came in the door at the back of the house. Erin was just picking it up as he came into the hall.

"Hello? . . . Niki, what a surprise. How are you? . . . Adam? Yes, he . . ."

Adam lifted a hand to stop her, shaking his head. He didn't want to talk to Niki. She could only be calling him about one thing—the divorce. And he hadn't done anything about it.

Erin frowned at him, holding the receiver toward him, but Adam turned his back and walked a few steps away.

"I'm sorry, Niki. Adam isn't here right now. Is there a message I can give him? . . . London? But that's . . . that's wonderful. . . When will you be back? . . . I see . . . No, we're fine, dear. Adam's been working very hard at fixing everything up. You really should see it . . . Of course, dear . . . All the best to you, Niki. Bon voyage."

Erin set the phone back on the table. "You should have spoken to her, Adam."

"Bon voyage? Where's she going?"

"If you'd taken the call, you could have found out for yourself," his aunt scolded. Relenting, she replied, "Yes, Adam, she's taking a trip. The show's going to London. She wasn't sure how long they would be over there."

Without further comment, Adam turned and headed up to his bedroom, sensing that Niki had just taken another step away from him.

Niki stared at the black telephone, wishing she could have seen the other end of the line. She was certain that Adam was there, that he had been standing near Aunt Erin and had refused to speak to her. If only she could have heard his voice, maybe she could believe that her grandmother was right. Now, even if it were true, it was too late. By the time she returned from London, the divorce would be final. Adam might even be married to Melina by then.

No, Taylor was wrong about Adam. He hadn't ever loved her. As for her still loving him, Niki wouldn't let herself think about it.

Niki took up her purse from the table and headed for the stairs. Harry was waiting for her in the entry hall. Taylor had left not long before, promising that she and Conrad would be at the dock to see her off. It had been Taylor's parting glance that had convinced Niki to make the call to Adam, if for no other reason than as a favor to her grandmother.

"I'm ready to go, Harry," she called to him as she descended the stairs. "Are you?"

"I am, indeed," he replied in an exaggerated tone of voice. He crooked his arm for her to take and led her toward the door. As they left behind the bright lights of the house and walked through the dusk to the waiting car, he added softly, "It's a grand adventure we're starting, Niki O'Hara. Are you happy?"

"Of course I am," she replied, then kissed his cheek. "How could I help but be happy?"

The *Mauretania,* sister ship of the *Lusitania,* was berthed at its North River pier, awaiting its customary midnight departure. This floating palace would take five days to cross the Atlantic, five days in which her passengers would live in grand luxury on a scale even grander than the best Swiss hotels.

Niki and Harry arrived at the dock, finding numerous farewell parties already in full-swing. The ship was festooned with paper streamers. Laughter and music filled the night air. Niki wondered if she would really get to see her grandmother again before they left. It seemed impossible to find anyone in this crowd.

The interior of the ship was even more wonderful than she had imagined. Grand staircases, modeled after those found in old Italian palaces, led from one deck to another, and the grille of the electric lifts resembled fifteenth century wrought iron-work. The dining rooms, paneled in straw-colored oak, had cream and gold domes reminiscent of the Chateau de Blois. Everywhere there was elegance at its finest and most tasteful—in the grand saloon and the smoking room and the lavatories and the state-rooms—everywhere.

Unbelievably, Taylor and Conrad found them as they were making their way through the throng along the promenade.

"Niki," Taylor cried as she hugged her granddaughter. "I was beginning to think we'd have to get off the ship without ever finding you."

"I'd about given up on seeing you, too, Gram." She turned to Conrad. "It's good to see you again, Conrad. You've made Gram so happy." She kissed his cheek.

"Not nearly as happy as she's made me. It was a lucky day for me when she came to New York again."

Niki reintroduced Harry to her step-grandfather, then took Taylor by the arm and began walking with her along the deck, the men following behind.

"Gram, I want you to know that I did as you said. I tried to call. He wouldn't speak to me. You were wrong, Gram."

Sounding unconvinced, Taylor replied, "Maybe so. Maybe so."

With a blow of her siren, a forlorn sound filled with longing, the *Mauretania* eased out of her berth at midnight and began her journey down the North River. Niki stood on the deck, waving her white handkerchief, long after the dock had been swallowed up by the night. Along with hundreds of others, she leaned against the rail and watched the twinkling lights of the New York skyline receding from view. Soon she would be out of sight of land. She was a little frightened at the thought.

"Come on, Niki. You're shivering," Harry said to her. "We'd better go inside."

After one more glance at the lights of the city, she let him pull her away from the rail.

"I guess I am a bit cold and tired," she admitted. "You won't mind if I just go to my room, will you?"

"No. In fact, I think it's a good idea. You'll feel more like enjoying yourself tomorrow if you get a good night's sleep." At her door, Harry placed a finger under her chin. "Don't start dredging up all the old feelings, Niki. It'll just make you keep hurting longer. Your grandmother's a dear, but she's wrong this time."

Niki choked back unwelcome tears. "Thanks. You're a good friend, Harry."

He leaned closer and kissed her gently on the mouth. As he released her lips, he said. "Yeah. A good friend. And this good friend says you should get some sleep." He opened her door for her. "Goodnight, Miss O'Hara. See you at breakfast."

"Goodnight, Harry."

Strange how a person can be so tired and still not sleep. Long after Niki had shed her dress and slipped between the sheets of her bed, she lay staring at the ceiling. She could hear the sounds of revelry continuing elsewhere aboard ship, but it wasn't the noise that kept her awake. For some reason, she kept recalling the haunting wail of the ship's siren as they left port, and along with the sad cry, Adam's name kept flitting through her heart.

CHAPTER 27

It was a strange feeling, waking up to the slap of waves against the sides of the mighty ship and the steady thumping of the engines. Though Niki had never been at sea, she seemed to have been born for it. She wasn't the least bit sick to her stomach. In fact, she was ravenous. Since it didn't appear that Harry was going to show up at her door before she starved to death, she decided to go looking for him.

The response to her knock was barely audible. "It's open."

She peeked inside. Fully clothed, Harry was lying flat on his stomach across his bed. He lifted his head only slightly to see who had come in.

"Harry," she gasped, "you're positively green."

His answer was a low moan as he lowered his head again.

"I don't suppose you want any breakfast."

His groan left no question that the thought of food at this moment could not be tolerated.

Niki couldn't stop the smile the crept onto her lips. "Well, I'm hungry enough for both of us. You rest, and I'll check on you a little later."

In the dining room, she looked around for other cast members and soon discovered that Harry wasn't the only one stricken with seasickness. Only Tucker was there to share breakfast with her. Together, they ate enough to make up for those who were still in their cabins.

By noon, the sun was out, and though the air was brisk and the ship still rolling in moderate seas, Harry was feeling good enough to join Niki on deck.

"You should have been a sailor," he grumbled, irritated by her glowing good health.

Niki laughed. "And you should stick to dry land. I was beginning to wonder who was going to direct our play once we reached England. By the color of your face this morning, I didn't think it would be you."

"Ha ha. Very funny."

"Now, don't be grumpy, Harry. We still have several days left to enjoy." She kissed his cheek, sobering. "I *am* sorry you're not feeling well. I don't mean to be cruel."

"I know. And I don't mean to be such a grouch just because I'm seasick and you're not." He paused, then added, "Even though it is extremely unfair."

They laughed together.

The ballroom of the *Mauretania* was ablaze with lights, doubly bright because of the mirrors and crystal that filled the room. The band was playing a waltz as Niki and Harry entered on the second night of their voyage.

Niki was dressed all in white, a gown of chiffon draped low on her back and fitted to reveal her shapely figure. A diamond and amethyst choker encircled her long, white throat, and brilliant earrings dangled from her earlobes. A whisper of perfume made men's heads turn as she walked past; her beauty held their gazes after the fragrance had disappeared. Harry, looking dashing in his own right, didn't allow her to sit down but led her directly onto the dance floor.

"You didn't think I'd pass up this opportunity to hold you in my arms, did you?" he murmured in her ear as his hand in the small of her back drew her closer.

They began to move to the music, twirling their way around the room. Harry's eyes held hers in a steady gaze, and slowly it began to dawn on her that Harry wanted more than friendship from her. He was giving her this time, with the words still unspoken, to think about her response. Their relationship had evolved several times over the past two years. Was a romance between them the next logical step?

Niki couldn't help but be aware how nice it felt to be held this way. She wondered what it would be like to kiss him. Really kiss him, not just the friendly pecks they habitually traded. She could laugh with Harry. She could cry with Harry. He knew the pain she had been through. He had been with her when she lost her baby. She had told him about her marriage, and he knew she had loved Adam, though it was doomed from the start. She had no secrets from Harry. Besides, they shared a passion for the theatre. Could she want more in a lover?

They danced the evening through without saying hardly a word, and the longer they danced, the more Niki thought that this was the answer. This was the way she could rid herself at last of Adam's memory. With another man in her life—not just a friend, but a romantic interest— Adam would soon be forgotten. Sure, that was the way to do it. And Harry seemed a logical choice. He was already her friend. What better way to start a romance?

When Harry walked her to her cabin, she was certain he would kiss her goodnight. She wanted him to. She wanted to get on with it, begin exorcising Adam's memory once and for all.

"It's been a wonderful evening, Niki."

"Yes."

"You were the most beautiful woman in

the ballroom."

"Thank you."

"Shall we do it again tomorrow night?"

"I'd like that, Harry."

"So would I." He leaned forward and kissed her lightly on the cheek. "You'd better get some sleep. Goodnight, love."

Not waiting for a response, he was off down the hall to his own cabin. Niki watched him go, feeling let down and relieved at the same time.

Glenrose's servants had retired for the night, but Taylor and Conrad were still up, sipping glasses of wine as they watched the fire crackling in the white marble fireplace of their private salon.

"You're still troubled about Niki and Adam, aren't you?" Conrad asked, seeing the frown that knitted her eyebrows.

Taylor smiled at his understanding. It was as if he could read her mind. "Yes. I just can't believe that Adam doesn't care ... or that Niki doesn't care, either, for that matter."

Conrad set down his glass, then put his arm around his wife. "You've been trying to get those two together for a long time now, Taylor. Maybe it's just not meant to be."

She shook her head at his tender suggestion. She had been wrong about things in her life, but she wasn't wrong about this. Those two were made for each other—if only they weren't so darned blind and too stubborn to admit it to each other.

Taylor laid her head on Conrad's shoulder. "Though a grandmother shouldn't admit it, Niki has always been a favorite of mine. I don't want to see her hurt. I know Adam is the man who can make her happy. Oh, he's not perfect . . ."

"Not like me, huh?"

She chuckled. "No, dear. He's not perfect like you, but he is right for her. He's made mistakes. Plenty of them. They both can take the blame for the state of things." She looked up at Conrad. "I'm so afraid that Niki's going to do something foolish, something that will keep them apart for good, something that will ruin her chance at happiness." Taylor added a warm smile as her deep blue eyes spoke of her love. "Those chances don't come along very often in this life. You have to grab them when you can."

"Well, Mrs. Cheavers, I know you well enough to know you're not going to just sit here and do nothing. What exactly are you going to do?"

"I don't know, Conrad, but I'll think of something. I must."

Gray skies greeted those onboard the *Mauretania* on their third morning at sea. Greet swells caused the liner to roll as if she were a mere twig instead of one of the greatest ships to ever sail the oceans of the world. Few passengers dared to stray from their cabins, most of them succumbing to the weakness in their stomachs. Niki was among the small number of reckless adventurers who chose to wander to other parts of the ship.

She found a deckchair near the promenade and sat down, wrapped in her warm fur coat. For a while, she just stared out to sea, her mind blank. She decided she liked the solitude of the salt-sprayed deck, the wind tugging at her scarf. Even the roiling heavens appealed to her. The air had a tangy smell to it, and she breathed in until she thought her lungs would burst. She felt lighter than air, as free as a bird, as gay as a lark . . . and a million other cliches that she couldn't think of at the moment.

A man's laughter drew her gaze. Hanging onto the rail and walking at a sharp angle to the rolling deck was a tall man in a water soaked jacket, his brown hair plastered against his head. Gripping his arm was a young woman, equally wet from the spray of rough seas. For a split second Niki thought the man looked like Adam, and her heart raced. Then he looked up, and she could see him more clearly. He wasn't nearly as handsome as Adam. His face didn't have that firm jaw or strong brow. His eyes weren't the cool shade of blue nor were his shoulders as broad and strong.

Suddenly, Niki felt sick. Why was she

comparing this stranger to Adam? Why was she even thinking about him?

She jumped to her feet and made her way, as quickly as she could, to her cabin. She paused with her hand on the door, then passed by her room and went to Harry's cabin. If she was with Harry, she wouldn't think about Adam. She wouldn't *let* herself think about Adam.

She knocked, then entered without waiting for a response. Harry was in bed, as she had known he would be.

"What are you doing here?" he asked weakly, opening only one eye to look at her.

"I came to see if I can help you in any way."

"Yes," he groaned. "Let me die."

"Oh, Harry, don't be silly. No one dies from seasickness."

"Then I'll be the first."

She sat on the edge of the bed. "No, you won't, because I won't let you."

Again one eye opened, this time to reward her good humor with a scathing glance. Niki laughed and went to get him a cool cloth for his forehead. When she returned to his bed, he had pushed himself up against the headboard so that he was only halfway lying down.

"What would people think if they knew you were in my room, with me in bed?"

"People who are as green as you are, Harry, cannot compromise the honor of women. Everyone would know I'm only here to nurse you." She grinned. "Besides, they expect unconventional behavior from theatre people. Consider it a publicity stunt."

As the ship pitched in the opposite direction, Harry sank back down on his bed, a low moan escaping his lips. Niki held the cloth against his forehead, forgetting for the time being the thoughts that had driven her to his room.

It was surprising how different the ocean could be from one day to the next. Clear skies and calm water—calm for the Atlantic, that is—promised a more enjoyable day for the passengers of the liner. Though Harry still looked a trifle pale, he was determined not to spend another day of their voyage trapped in his cabin. He was going to sample all the luxuries of this ship before they sailed into Southhampton, and he was going to sample them with Niki.

By the time they met to eat supper, tonight as guests at the captain's table, Niki was exhausted, but it was a wonderful exhaustion. Harry had been at his most appealing all day. He had been sweet and attentive. He had joked with her, making her laugh until her side ached. He had talked about his own childhood, revealing parts of himself she had never known. She felt comfortable with him, and she knew he cared for her.

It was after supper, and after the dancing that had followed, that Harry led her out onto the deck. The sky was aflame with a million stars, each of them sparkling with such individual brilliance that it seemed one alone could have brightened the night. They stood against the railing, silently absorbing the enormity of the sky and sea and the smallness of man and his attempts at mastering the elements.

"Niki?"

She shivered slightly, then turned her head to look at Harry. He was still gazing out to sea. "Yes?"

"Niki, I want you to marry me."

She hadn't expected him to move quite this fast, and she was found speechless.

"I know you don't love me. Not yet, anyway, but you might love me in time. Even if you didn't, I'd be good to you, take care of you, go on loving you." He stepped back from the rail, turning toward her and placing his hands on her shoulders. "Say you'll marry me as soon as your divorce is final. We're good together, Niki. Director and actress, husband and wife. It's a natural."

"Why, Harry, I don't . . ."

His arms went around her and pulled her close. "Say yes, Niki. Say it now."

Why not? Why not be loved by someone? It hurt too much to be the only one doing the loving. Harry wanted her. He wasn't drunk. He knew what he was asking. He was willing to love her even if she couldn't love in return. Wouldn't that drive away the hurt Adam had left in her heart and the bitter taste he had left in her mouth?

"All right, Harry. When I get my divorce, I'll marry you."

He smiled tenderly. "That's the best news I've ever had." He kissed her then, the kiss as tender as his smile had been. His lips moved slowly across her cheek to her ear. "I do love you," he whispered. "You won't ever be sorry."

There was a giant void left in her heart, and nothing she could do was going to fill the void. There was only one man who could heal her wounds. The same man who had made them.

So long ago, that man had held her in his arms, his kisses stirring up frantic butterflies in her stomach. He had caressed her, and a searing fire had possessed her heart and soul.

Now she wanted to feel the same way about Harry, but she felt nothing. She was neither happy nor sad, excited nor depressed. It was as if nothing mattered anymore. She would get her divorce and she would marry Harry. She would be no better and no worse off than if she didn't get a divorce and didn't marry Harry. It just didn't matter, one way or the other.

CHAPTER 28

The March skies had been drizzling all day. Niki stepped out onto the street, umbrella in hand, and began to walk. She was feeling restless and needed to escape her flat.

After nearly five months, the run of *Another Day* was drawing to a close in London. Soon the cast would be packing up and heading down to the states. With the play over, they would each go their separate ways. Someday some of them might work together again, but it would never be the same tight unit that had made up their theatrical family for such a very long time. Niki was going to miss them.

Niki walked for over an hour, up one street, down another, until her hair was soaking wet, despite her umbrella. When she arrived back at her apartment, she was met at the door by her maid, Celia, who gave her mistress a quick glance, taking in her disheveled and very wet condition, and then ordered Niki to shed her clothes and climb into a hot bath.

"You'll have your death, you will, and who'll get the blame for it, I ask you? It'll be me and don't you forget it. Walking in this weather. You Yanks haven't any sense, you haven't. Not a lick."

Celia kept up her scolding throughout Niki's bath. It wasn't until she had Niki settled in a deep chair near the fireplace, clad in a homely but warm terry robe, her feet tucked up beneath her and a warm mug of hot chocolate in her hands, that she left her mistress in peace. A few minutes later she returned with the mail.

"These came while you were out, mum."

Niki sifted through the envelopes. Most of them could be opened later. However, the parchment envelope with Taylor's return address neatly printed in the corner was a welcome sight. She slit open the back and drew out the pages.

The first part of the letter, written in Taylor's flowing handwriting, was news of Conrad's and Taylor's life at Glenrose. It was a happy letter, filled with cheerful prattle, bits and pieces to be shared and cherished. Though most of Taylor's letters said the same types of things, Niki looked forward to them. They made her feel as warm inside as Celia's hot chocolate.

Niki turned another page. Near the top, the words *Spring Haven* seemed to jump out at her, and she slowed her reading.

We went to Spring Haven a few weeks ago. Adam has done some wonderful things to the place. It made me feel very good, almost as if I'd been transported back through time to before the Civil War. Of course, you must know that Adam isn't practicing law at all since he returned from New York. He's made this old plantation his life.

Something I learned which I'm sure you're not aware of—Adam has not done anything about a divorce. It appears he has no intention of getting one. Believe me, my dear Niki, he's not doing this out of spite. Though he might not admit it to anyone, including himself, he's in love with you and can't let you go. If you want a divorce, you're going to have to get it yourself. And if I've got any intuition left at all when it comes to my youngest granddaughter, you're still in love with him. So take some grandmotherly advice. Tell Harry you can't marry him and come back here and fight for this man. You deserve to give it a better shot than you have. Fight for love, Niki. Don't throw it away.

There was more, but Niki didn't read on. *Adam wasn't getting the divorce,* and Gram still insisted that he loved her.

And she loved him. She couldn't lie to herself about it any longer. She loved Adam as much or more than she ever had.

Gram was right about another thing. She hadn't ever fought to keep him. She hadn't ever come right out and said, "I love you," and waited to see what his response would be. Could it really hurt any worse if she spoke the words and he turned her away?

Of course, there was also the matter of Harry. He was always talking about the wedding he was planning for them once they returned to America. Now she would have to tell him there would be no wedding, that she wasn't free to marry him.

"If I'm going to be honest with myself," she whispered, "I may as well admit that I wasn't going to marry him anyway."

There. It was said. She wasn't going to marry Harry.

Niki got up from her chair and crossed her bedroom to stand by the window, staring down at the narrow street below. How different was her life than what she had imagined it would be such a few short years ago. She could remember so clearly her own determination to go to New York and become a famous actress. She had been so certain she could control her own life, so assured of her own importance in the scheme of things. Instead, she had to admit that her life had been out of control for a long, long time. She had lost sight of what she really wanted, of what was really important to her. It was time she took a good, hard look at the choices she had made, and then do something about correcting her own mistakes.

She was going to see Adam. She was going to tell him she loved him. If he loved her, if he wanted to be married to her, she would even give up her career on the stage if that was what he wanted her to do. Even her acting wasn't as important as he was.

And if he didn't want her, she would make a life of her own, on her own. She wasn't going to marry another man just because Adam wouldn't have her. She wasn't going to settle for second best. She would have Adam or she would have no one at all.

Niki spun away from the window, tugging at the knotted belt of her robe. "Celia! Ring for my car!" she called as she pulled a dress from her wardrobe.

The cable from England arrived at Spring Haven while Adam and Erin were sitting down for their mid-day meal.

Play closing. Question about divorce. Urgent I meet with you in New York. Sailing Thursday, April 11, on the Titanic.

> *Niki*

"What are you going to do, Adam?" Erin asked after he had passed the cable to her to read.

"Nothing. If she wants a divorce, she can get one. She has enough reasons. I can't do anything to stop her."

Erin's fork clattered against her plate. "Adam Bellman, you're a fool. Why don't you do something to stop her? You're mad in love with her, and here you sit, saying you're not going to do a thing." She got to her feet. "I'm tired of feeling sorry for you. If you don't fight for that girl, you deserve every bit of unhappiness that comes your way."

"You don't understand, Aunt Erin."

"Try me."

Adam rubbed his hand across his forehead. "You don't know what I did to her. She couldn't forgive me."

"Have you asked her to?"

His cool blue eyes met hers, sparking with something akin to anger, challenging her to say she would forgive him if she were Niki. "Tell me, Aunt Erin, could you love a man who spirited you away and married you while you were too intoxicated to know what you were doing, a man you couldn't be in the same room with for more than five minutes without having an argument? Could you forgive that same man for forcing himself on you when you had told him you wanted nothing to do with him?"

"Adam . . ."

"That's right. I took her against her will." He rose stiffly from his chair. Placing his hands on the table, he leaned toward her, his face revealing his shame and anguish. "And it's as ugly as it sounds. I carried her protesting up the stairs, and I tore her dress from her like a madman. Of course she hates me. I hate myself."

Erin sank into her chair. "Oh, Adam . . . I had no idea." She stared at his clenched fists, his knuckles turning white as they pressed against the ebony surface of the table. "But . . . but, Adam, if you love her, shouldn't you ask her to forgive you? You might be surprised at her answer."

"I thought so once." He moved away from his place at the table as he spoke, beginning to pace the room. "When I returned from Boston, I planned on asking for forgiveness. I was going to make everything right. But she had left me. Because of me she had even left her play, the one she had poured heart and soul into for months. I knew then how much she must hate me. I had done this to her."

Erin followed him across the room, placing a hesitant hand on his arm. "Have you ever considered that you might be wrong? Taylor says Niki loves you."

"Do you think I'd be here if I thought Aunt Taylor were right? If I thought there were any chance at all?" Adam pressed his head against the fireplace mantle and gazed at the cold hearth. "I've tried lots of different ways to make myself forget that night.

I've tried work and whiskey and even seeing another woman, but it's no use. And if I can't forget it, how can she?''

Harry listened in stoical silence. Niki twisted a handkerchief in her fingers, wishing she didn't have to do this to someone she was so fond of.

"You must see it would be a mistake if we married, Harry. I . . . I am sorry if I've hurt you. You've been too good a friend to me.''

A long silence followed before Harry got up from his chair and came to sit beside her on the sofa. She sat stiffly on the edge, afraid that he would try to kiss her, maybe change her mind, and then she would have to be cruel.

"Niki?'' He placed a finger under her chin and turned her head, forcing her to look at him. "It's all right, Niki. I guess I knew all along that this would happen.'' He smiled sadly. "And I'd rather have you as a friend than not have you at all.''

"Oh, Harry.'' She said his name with a sigh of relief. "You don't know how glad that makes me.''

"There's not much point in my hanging around London now that the show has closed. You won't mind if I sail with you on the *Titanic,* will you? I promise I won't be a nuisance.''

Niki took his hand and held it tightly. "I'd love to have your company, Harry. A friend is always welcome."

Dear Gram,

You'll be happy to know that I've come to my senses. I've asked Adam to meet with me when I return to New York. I don't know if we can put things right between us, but it's not going to be because I haven't tried.

I'm sailing for America on April 11 on the maiden voyage of the largest ocean liner in the world, the Titanic. *It's really exciting to be a part of this historic voyage. They say ocean travel will never be quite the same again. To travel so quickly and in such splendor across the Atlantic! It leaves me breathless just to think about it.*

Harry will be coming with me, even though he knows we won't be getting married once we get there. He's been a good friend, Gram, and I'm glad he'll be with me now. I'm terribly nervous about facing Adam.

I'll post this letter right away so you'll have it before I get there myself. Hopefully, the letter won't be crossing the Atlantic on the Titanic *with me. See you in New York.*

Niki

CHAPTER 29

The White Star liner *Titanic*, like her sister ship *Olympic*, was designed to be the most luxurious and steadiest ship on the Atlantic. The walls of the annex to the first class dining room were covered with Aubusson tapestries. The first class lounge was styled after the Palace of Versailles. The trellises of the palm court were covered with ivy and other climbing plants, creating an illusion of being on dry land instead of at sea. The ship's Turkish baths had Cairo curtains and suspended bronze lamps and a marble drinking fountain. There was a gymnasium and a swimming pool (a first for an Atlantic liner) and a squash rackets court.

Niki O'Hara and Harry Jamison were among the 322 first class passengers—including John Jacob Astor, Benjamin Guggenheim, George D. Widener and seven other millionaires—that boarded the *Titanic* on Thursday, April 11, 1912. They were given a passenger list, twenty eight pages in length, on which were also printed details of the ship's routine.

The bars would open at 8:30 AM and close at 11:30 PM. Lights would be extinguished in the grand saloon at 11:00 at night. The smoking room would close at midnight. There was a fine band, led by a musician named Wallace Hartley, that would provide music for entertainment and dancing. While at sea, passengers could send Marconigrams to the United States via Cape Cod. Desk chairs could be hired for the entire voyage for only four shillings.

After Niki and Harry were shown to their separate state-rooms, Niki's in an Italian Renaissance style and Harry's in Old Dutch, they joined the other first class passengers in the lounge.

Niki had chosen one of her most attractive gowns, a sequined evening dress in the same shade of violet as her eyes. Though there were many beautiful women on aboard, Niki was deluged with admirers, both those who knew who she was and those who just appreciated her striking beauty.

"Niki," Harry said as he touched her elbow, "may I introduce our captain?"

She turned. The commander of the *Titanic* looked just as she thought a British sea captain should look—sixtyish, a white beard, shaggy eyebrows, a strong but gentle face.

"How do you do, Captain Smith." She

offered her hand.

"It's a great honor to meet you, Miss O'Hara. I had the pleasure of catching your performance in London last month. You're extremely talented."

"How nice of you to say so, sir."

"I hope you and Mr. Jamison will join me at my table for supper one night before the voyage is over?"

Niki inclined her head. "That would be *our* pleasure, captain."

Captain Smith touched his forehead as if tipping an imaginary hat, then moved on to meet his other passengers.

"It gives one a great deal of confidence to be sailing on a ship under that man's command," Niki overheard someone say, and she had to agree.

For four days the *Titanic* sailed on a glass-calm sea. More than once Niki heard someone commenting on the strangeness of it. The Atlantic was never calm for four days at a time. The magnificent liner, all 46,328 tons of her, made 386 nautical miles from Thursday noon to Friday noon, 519 from Friday to Saturday, and 546 miles from Saturday to Sunday.

All the passengers agreed that no one had ever travelled on a more comfortable ship. Everything was handled with great panache. Niki and Harry went for swims in the swimming pool, Niki when it was open for women and Harry when it was open for men. They rented the squash racket court, though Niki quickly proved that it wasn't a game for her. They dined superbly in the first class dining room with dinner service made by the Goldsmiths and Silversmiths Company of Regent Street. They danced nightly until the band packed up their instruments. Then they, too, went to their state-rooms and collapsed exhausted into their beds.

Niki sometimes wondered if she had done Harry a favor, allowing him to accompany her back to New York. She wasn't so self-centered that she wasn't aware of his continuing love for her. Being together, day in and day out, on a ship that seemed designed just for lovers had to be making things more difficult for him, especially when he knew she was thinking about Adam. She had tried their first night at sea to decline from dancing, but Harry wouldn't hear of it.

"It will make the time pass all the more quickly," he had told her.

And he had been right. The days seemed to race by as the liner glided through the tranquil waters.

On Sunday morning, Niki went out on the deck for her morning stroll and discovered that the temperature had dropped rapidly during the night. It was much too cold to remain outside. After breakfast, she returned to her room, read a few chapters of a novel she had found in the ship's reading room, then took a nap. The rest of the day passed in equally peaceful pursuits.

Niki wore one of her fur coats to dinner that night. She hadn't been able to shake the cold all day. She was gladdened by the thought that they were only about forty-eight hours from New York. A strange foreboding had joined the chill in her bones. She was looking forward to reaching dry land.

She took coffee with Harry after dinner. She was silent as they listened to the band as they played their after-dinner selections. She sensed that Harry was watching her closely. She knew he was puzzled by her strange mood but hoped he wouldn't question her. If he did, she knew she wouldn't be able to explain it to him. She didn't understand it herself.

As the band began playing "The Tales of Hoffman," Harry got up from his chair and came to stand behind her. "Come on," he said as he held up her coat.

She slipped into her fur and let him lead her outside. She pulled the collar tighter around her throat. There was no wind, other than the artificial breeze created by the passage of the ship. Still, Niki thought she had never felt so cold.

"Can you tell me what's troubling you tonight, kiddo?" Harry asked as he leaned against the rail.

"I don't know," she answered honestly. "I just feel very frightened all of a sudden."

"Nervous about seeing Adam?"

"I . . . I suppose that's it."

Hearing footsteps, they both turned their heads as the ship's officer walked passed them.

"Evenin', ma'am, sir," he said, touching the brim of his hat. He stopped and gazed out over the water. "Quite a night, isn't it? I've been twenty-six years at sea, and I've never known so calm a night . . . nor one so black." Again he touched his hat. "Don't stay outside too long. This air's enough to chill your blood."

The officer was right. It was a black night —so black and so clear that Niki could see the stars setting on the horizon. Where the sky met the sea the line was so clear and definite that as the earth revolved and the sea's edge came up and partially covered a star, it simply cut the star in two, the upper half continuing to sparkle as long as it was not entirely hidden, throwing a long beam of light across the sea.

In the background, Niki heard the Reverend Mr. Carter leading the evening Sunday service in the hymn "For Those in Peril on the Sea." She shivered uncontrollably.

"I'd like to go to bed, Harry," she whispered.

* * *

Adam sat in his big chair in the library, staring over the top of the book that rested on his knees as he chewed on the stem of his pipe. Soft music was playing on the phonograph. His aunt Erin was sitting across from him near the lampstand, embroidering a tablecloth, her eyes squinting over the delicate stitches.

Though earlier it had been warm, the April day scented by the budding of spring flowers, it cooled quickly with the setting of the sun. Adam closed the windows after supper, then lit a fire in the library before choosing a book from the shelves, a book that remained unread in his lap.

Although it was not quite half-past eight, he considered going to bed. He couldn't seem to concentrate on anything. Maybe he would be able to sleep. He closed the book and laid it on the stand next to his chair.

Erin looked up from her needlework. She removed the wire-rimmed glasses that perched on her nose. "Is something wrong, Adam?"

"No. Just can't get into this book."

He got up and walked over to the window, pushing the draperies aside to look out at the evening sky. There was no moon, and though a million stars twinkled overhead, they were helpless against the blackness of night that had enveloped the earth. The dark seemed sinister to him, as it had when he was a very small boy and wanted a light left on in the hall outside his room. He let the drapes drop back into place.

Erin put her embroidery aside. "What's *really* wrong?" she asked.

"I don't know, Aunt Erin. Just feel kind of strange this evening. Must be the change in the weather."

His aunt didn't look satisfied with his answer. "Adam . . . does this have anything to do with Niki?"

Everything in his life seemed to have something to do with Niki. Never a day went by that he didn't see her face in his thoughts, think her name in his mind. He couldn't pretend to Aunt Erin. Something about Niki was troubling him, though he couldn't put his finger on it.

Then, as if he'd made up his mind up days ago instead of just seconds, he answered calmly, "I'm going to go to New York, Aunt Erin. I'm going to meet with Niki."

"And what is it you plan to say to her? Are you going to give her that divorce?"

"Not without letting her know the truth first." He turned back to the window and pushed the drapes aside once more. "If it isn't too late," he added.

In Latitude 41 degrees 46 minutes North, Longitude 50 degrees 14 minutes West, at approximately 11:40 on Sunday evening,

April 14, 1912, the *Titanic* veered to port to miss an iceberg. Her starboard plates were ripped open about ten feet above the keel for a distance of 300 feet, one-third the length of the vessel. Those below, whether crew or third class passengers, felt the sensation of impact more strongly than those in first class; the lookouts didn't feel it at all. The engines were stopped. The atmosphere was perfectly still. The ship came to rest without any indication of disaster. The iceberg had disappeared. There was no hole in the ship's side through which water could be seen to be pouring, nothing was out of place, there was no sound of alarm, no panic.

It was the absence of the throbbing engines that awakened Niki from her troubled sleep. For four days she had lived with the vibration of the engines, a vibration most noticeable when she reclined in her bath or lay in her bed, and she had grown so accustomed to it she had ceased to be conscious of it until it was silenced. She turned on a light and sat up in bed, listening. Everything was so still. Too still.

Niki took her fur coat from the chair where she had dropped it upon returning to her cabin and put it on over her nightgown. Pushing her dark hair back from her face, she stepped into the passageway. Others had been awakened, either by the collision with the iceberg (although they didn't know that then) or by the silence, and their doors were opening, too. Glances were exchanged, then shrugs. A few people wandered toward the stairs, talking softly.

Niki remained near her doorway for a moment. Suddenly, she felt a fresh wave of cold foreboding wash over her. Something was terribly wrong. She turned to her left and hurried toward Harry's cabin.

"Harry! Harry, wake up!" she called as she knocked on his door.

The door swung open, revealing Harry, still clad in his finest evening attire. "What is it?" he asked, stifling a yawn. "I fell asleep in my chair, and the next thing I know, you're pounding on my door."

"Harry, something's wrong with the ship."

"With *this* ship? I doubt that, Niki, but if you're worried, let's go have a look."

Niki tried to be reassured by what Harry said. Of course, he had to be right. The *Titanic* was the greatest ship ever built. She was even touted to be unsinkable. What could be wrong? Niki was just letting her imagination get the better of her.

As they climbed the stairs leading to the deck, Niki felt there was something strange about them. It was a curious sense of something being out of balance, as if she couldn't put her foot down in the right place. She gripped the rail and ascended them as quickly as possible.

Just as they reached the deck, there was a swooshing sound, then a flash of light as the sky was illuminated by distress rockets. The light shed by the rockets also revealed the faces of men and women, up until now who had been merely curious, in all states of dress and undress. It was the first real indication that something was amiss.

"Women and children to the lifeboats, please. All women and children to the life-boats."

Niki glanced at Harry, her eyes wide. "We're going to sink," she said breath-lessly.

"Nonsense. Just precautionary."

Though Harry's words were meant to reassure her, Niki could read the doubt on his face. In truth, the ship was sinking rapidly.

"Take me back to my room," she told him.

Harry shook his head. "If they want the women and children in the lifeboats, then that's where you're going . . . even if it is a waste of time."

"I mean to go, Harry, but even if we're only there for a little while, it's going to be terribly cold. I want to get some more of my coats. There's bound to be plenty of people who won't think of them."

"You've got a good head on your shoulders, Miss O'Hara. Come on."

There was no mad dash for the lifeboats. Many women refused to leave the security of the decks to get into lifeboats and be lowered seventy feet into the darkness, just as a precautionary measure. They much preferred the safety of the *Titanic*, a ship known to be unsinkable. Those more than willing to fill the lifeboats were the third class passengers and stokers who had come from below where they had seen, firsthand, compartments flooded with sea water. They were not as complacent about the sinking ship as their first and second class shipmates. However, too few of these found their way from steerage to the boat deck.

By the time Niki and Harry returned, carrying all of her coats and two blankets, the band had assembled on the first class desk outside the gymnasium and were playing ragtime. Music drifted through the calm night air, making her think of a picnic she had attended last August in Central Park. It had been late in the evening and she and Harry had sat by the lake, listening to the band playing in the background.

The lifeboat, designed to hold seventy people, was less than half full, but Niki was the only woman around at the moment.

"Come on, miss. We've got to lower this boat," a steward said to her.

She took hold of Harry's wrist. "Come with me, Harry. There's room for you."

"Sorry, kiddo. I think I'd better stay here and try to help some of the other womenfolk find their way to the boats." He chucked her under the chin, then tenderly kissed her cheek. "Don't worry about me, Niki. I've got a great future as a director on Broadway. I'm not about to miss the last boat out of here if she goes down."

Niki was starting to cry. "Harry . . ."

"Get in there," he ordered, a bit gruffly. "You're holding up the show. You're an actress. You know better than that." Still holding her hand, he helped her into the lifeboat, then tossed all her coats in after her. "Keep warm, kiddo. I don't want a leading lady with the sniffles."

Her last glimpse of him as the boat was lowered was as he waved, a bright smile on his face.

Though the first lifeboat launched from the *Titanic* had had to be lowered seventy feet to the sea, the one that carried Niki touched water in about one-third that distance. Even so, the business of launching a lifeboat over the side of a liner was not simple. The ropes were new and balky and the winches situated against the deckhouses were not being used. It was a perilous trip down to the water, an ordeal of jerking and tipping as first one end, then the other was let down too fast. Niki breathed a prayer of thankfulness when the pin was released to set them adrift.

Orders were shouted and the crewmen began to pull on the oars. Niki choked back the lump in her throat and brushed tears from her eyes, then started passing out the coats and blankets she had brought with her. There was a boy of about seventeen seated beside her, clad only in an undershirt, but he refused her offer of a fur-lined coat, passing it instead to the shivering young Irish girl beside him.

As they pulled away from the stricken ship, Niki twisted around to look back at her. The black outline of the *Titanic* was bordered all around by stars. Every five minutes another rocket soared overhead to explode with a loud crack and a shower of light. Despite all this, the *Titanic* looked almost normal. Almost, but not quite. The water was almost to the captain's bridge, and the stern was high out of the water.

Then, as those in the lifeboats watched, the ship tilted slowly up until she stood almost vertically in the water. Now motionless, her tilting was followed by a stupefying noise, as if everything heavy in the ship, engines and machinery included, was torn loose from their bearings, falling the length of the ship (which was now the height of the ship) and smashing everything else on their way to the bow.

Like an upright column, the mighty ship stood for four minutes. Then, sinking a little at the stern, she slid slowly forward through the water and dived down into the sea.

CHAPTER 30

Niki watched in horrified silence as the Titanic slipped into its watery grave. The threat of being swamped or sucked in after the ship proved to be a myth. The sea remained eerly calm.

And then she heard the lamentations of hundreds of voices, screaming for help in the icy waters.

"We must go back," she said, softly at first and then louder. "We must go back and help them."

"We can't miss. We could still be swamped," one of the oarsmen answered.

"But there are people back there who need help. We could save another thirty lives, maybe more."

"Don't listen to her," a matronly woman cried, clutching one of the oars which she began to ply in the water herself. "We might be sunk by someone climbing into the boat."

"Dear God, listen to yourself. You might have been one of those left behind. Go back, I tell you! Go back!" She was screaming hysterically now.

"My son . . ." one woman sobbed.

Another joined Niki's plea of mercy for those drowning in the darkness. "Please, go back. My husband is out there. Go back."

"Those aren't cries of drowning people. Those are cheers," one of the crew interjected. "They've all been saved. Those are hallelujahs from the other lifeboats. Just keep rowing. There'll be a rescue ship here before we know it."

But there was no amount of denial that would convince Niki that the cries were anything other than what she knew them to be, nor could she shut out the dreadful chorus from the darkness that continued, in pitiful diminuendo, for nearly an hour, even though she covered her ears with the thick collar of her coat, all the while tears tracing her cheeks.

The grisly night wore on. The lifeboat, lacking water or provisions of any kind, bobbed gently in the twenty-eight-degree water. Animosities began to break out among the survivors, mainly between the women and the crew. Understandably, the mere presence of these men was a source of bitter resentment to so many new widows. When a stoker drew a bottle of whiskey from inside his coat and tried to take a swig, a woman grabbed it from him and threw it overboard, scolding him soundly for drinking in front of ladies. She never stopped to think that the alcohol might have restored some circulation in his limbs and to those he might have shared it with.

Niki seemed oblivious to the dissension around her. Her tears were gone now. She was remembering Harry as he had stood on the deck, waving to her as her boat was launched over the side. She knew now that he had never intended to seek a spot in one of the few remaining lifeboats. He had gone down with the ship, with the hundreds of other doomed souls who had found themselves without a means of escape. If only she had known, she would have forced him to come with her. She would have refused to leave until he got into the boat, too. If only she had done things differently, he might still be alive.

Before the *Carpathia* arrived, the first ship on the scene in response to the *Titanic*'s distress signal, Niki had retreated from these painful thoughts. Her mind and body were numb.

Out of more than twenty-two hundred passengers and crew members onboard the *Titanic,* barely more than seven hundred survived that fateful night. The *Carpathia* arrived in the predawn darkness, firing rockets as she came. To the survivors, her blazing portholes were a glorious antidote to the terrors of the night. During the long process of locating the lifeboats and embarking the survivors, the sun came up, tinging the white ice an orange-pink, a spectacular sight under normal circumstances.

Niki allowed someone to place a sling under her arms, and then she was hoisted up the side of the *Carpathia*. Someone tenderly led her into the first class lounge where they wrapped her frozen limbs in several blankets. A cup of steaming coffee was placed against her lips, and she sipped obediently. Yet she was really unaware of the ministering hands or the kindness of the passengers of the rescue ship. She was too numb. She had blocked out the horrors of the past hours, locking them away in some dark corner of her mind where she wouldn't have to look at them ever again.

"Miss, could I get your name, please? Is there someone we should notify that you're all right?"

Her blank eyes stared right through the man speaking to her. After a few moments, he moved on, unable to bear the emptiness he saw in her dark violet eyes.

"Mrs. Mulligan, is there any word?" Taylor hoped beyond hope that the housekeeper's answer would be positive and that the news would be good.

"Not a thing, Mrs. Cheavers. We've heard nothing."

Conrad closed the door, then took his wife

by the arm and propelled her into the drawing room. He was worried about Taylor. Ever since news of the sinking of the *Titanic* had first reached them, she had been beside herself. It didn't help that the news reports couldn't seem to make up their minds what had really happened. First they had heard that all the passengers were in lifeboats and awaiting the arrival of the *Olympic*. Then the steamer *Virginian* was reported to be towing the *Titanic*. Then the *Titanic* was reported to have foundered but no lives were lost.

Taylor had aged in the two days since word had reached them about the disaster. He hadn't known what else to do for her, so he had brought her to White House, hoping that somehow she would be reassured here as she hadn't been at Glenrose.

After he had seen his wife settled, Conrad went to the White Star Line's office at 9 Bowling Green where the list of names of survivors was read aloud by the chief clerk as he stood on top of the booking office counter. Niki's name was not among them. At the New York American, the latest news was posted on the side of the building. A large crowd milled around in the street, watching as a man wrote the names of prominent personages rescued—Mrs. J.J. Astor, the Countess of Rothes, and Miss Elizabeth Shutes. Niki's name went unmentioned. Conrad began to fear the worst. He didn't know if Taylor could stand Niki's death, should it come to that.

"Have you learned who she is?"

"Can't get a word out of her. She wouldn't eat if someone wasn't here to be sure that she does. Doesn't seem to care what happens to her."

"There must be someone waiting for her that'd appreciate hearing she's all right. Let's ask around. Maybe some of the other passengers can give us a name."

"We'll be at Quarantine by tomorrow night. We'll need to know something by then."

"It's a shame. A girl as pretty as her. I'd hate to have to leave her in some hospital without anyone to claim her, but I suppose we'll have no other choice if she doesn't come round."

The loud pounding on the door brought Conrad and Taylor quickly out of bed. Cinching his robe tightly around his stomach, Comrad hurried for the stairs, but Mrs. Mulligan beat him to the door.

"Who is it?" she demanded, her voice displaying her displeasure at being awakened in the wee hours of the night.

"It's me, Mrs. Mulligan. Adam Bellman."

She opened the door a crack and peeked out, then stepped back as she pulled it open the rest of the way. "Mr. Bellman, sir."

"Mrs. Mulligan, have you . . ." Adam stopped when he saw Conrad midway down the stairs. "Conrad, what have you heard?"

Conrad shook his head. "We don't know anything about Niki."

"Adam." Taylor was standing on the top landing. "I'm so glad you're here." She came slowly down the stairs, holding onto the rail the entire way down.

Adam hugged her, feeling as worn and frightened as she looked.

"Let's go in and sit down," Conrad suggested gently.

"I was coming to New York," Adam told his aunt as they settled on the sofa. "She cabled me to meet her here. I wasn't going to come and then . . ." He ran his hand through his disheveled hair. "Then Sunday night I . . . I knew I had to be here. I was already on my way when the news reached me."

"She's going to be all right, Adam. She's got to be."

Adam put his arms around Taylor and held her tight. It helped to think about someone else instead of dwelling on the chances of his own loss. "Of course, she is. That's why I'm here. To be with her when she gets back."

"Yes, I know who she is. She's Niki O'Hara, the Broadway actress. Is she all right?''

"Looks as if her mind's snapped. It's a pity, it is.''

"Miss O'Hara? Miss O'Hara? Do you remember me? We met on board our first day out. Miss O'Hara?''

On Thursday evening, four days after the sinking of the *Titanic,* the *Carpathia* arrived at Quarantine. A flotilla of chartered tugs, crammed with newspapermen, surrounded the ship and followed her upriver, crying out for details. People by the tens and thousands lined Manhattan's western shore from the Battery to 14th Street to watch the ship come in. At 9:30, the ship tied up, and down her gangplank came the first of the survivors. A human chain of police and company personnel held back the crowd. People wept openly.

Passengers with passes went to the appropriate overhead custom letters to meet relatives. Recognition was sometimes difficult; many survivors were wearing bizarre costumes, clothing made from steamer rugs and ship's blankets and such.

Niki, her eyes still empty, was taken to a quiet room to wait until someone came for her. A stewardess remained, holding her hand and talking softly, trying as she had so often in the past four days to draw Niki back to reality.

* * *

Adam pressed his way through the crowd. "Excuse me. Let me through, please. Excuse me."

He hadn't been able to get close enough to see her get off the ship. It seemed impossible to find anyone who could tell him where she might be. There must be someone who could tell him something.

"Excuse me. My wife was a passenger on the *Titanic*. How do I find out where she is?"

Leaning against a wall, he saw two women clutching each other, sobbing uncontrollably. He looked away. He had to keep looking. He couldn't allow himself to think that his news might be the same as theirs. Time and again he stopped someone, someone that looked as if they might be able to help him, and time and again he was met with a shake of the head or a shrug.

"Sorry, sir. Lots of people can't find the ones they're looking for. Lots of 'em will never be found."

He was growing angry. Angry at his own futility. Frustrated by his inability to do anything, change anything. Still, he wouldn't give up. She had to be here. She had to be.

It was nearing midnight when he clamped his hand down on the shoulder of a weary looking man in a rumpled officer's uniform.

"You've got to help me," he said. "I'm

looking for my wife. She's young and petite. About twenty-one. She's got long, dark brown hair, and violet eyes. She's very pretty. Have you seen her?"

"Do you mean Miss O'Hara?"

"You know her? You've seen her?" Adam's grip tightened and he unconsciously shook the man. "Where is she? Is she all right? Take me to her."

"Please, sir," the officer protested, pushing away from Adam. "If you'll come with me, I'll show you where she is."

He'd found her. She was alive. She was alive after all. He didn't have to be afraid of that thought any more. She was alive and waiting for him.

Adam followed the uniformed fellow along several corridors before he paused to open a door and enter a small room. Adam nearly ran him down before he could get out of the way.

Niki was sitting on a wooden chair against the back wall of the room. Another young woman sat beside her, holding her left hand.

"Niki." He dropped to his knees beside her chair, clasping her limp hand and bringing it to his lips. "Niki, thank God you're all right. You're safe. You're safe." His arms went around her and he hugged her close. "Thank God," he whispered. "Thank God."

"Sir?" A hesitant hand touched his

shoulder. "Sir, I don't think she can hear you."

"What do you mean?" Adam asked as he released his hold and leaned back from Niki.

She sat straight and stiff. Her eyes were wide and staring, her face without expression. Adam took her chin and turned her head toward him. Her eyes looked right through him as if he weren't there.

"Niki?"

He moved his hand in front of her face. There was no response.

His gaze still on Niki, Adam got to his feet as he asked the stewardess, "What's happened to her? What's wrong?"

"We don't know, sir. She's been like this ever since she was found. It wasn't until yesterday that we even knew who she was. It's the shock most likely. Our doctor did what he could but . . ." She paused, then added, "She'll be all right in time, I'm sure."

Adam sank to his knees again and drew her back against him, pressing her head against his shoulder.

"Niki. Niki, come back to me. I love you."

CHAPTER 31

Sunshine spilled in golden radiance into her bedroom. The window was open to the fresh spring breeze, and birds could be heard chirping in the tree just outside. Niki reclined on her chaise lounge, wearing a frilly pink dressing gown. Not that she had chosen it. Pearl had dressed her in it after her morning bath. It was a routine that was followed every day in a house cloaked in sadness.

Three weeks had passed since Adam had returned from the docks with Niki in his arms. Three weeks and there had been no change. Niki was here, but not here. She ate when she was fed, drank when a cup was placed to her lips, walked where she was led, but her mind was still shut off from the reality of life.

Adam spent hours beside her, talking to her, pleading with her to hear him. He combed her hair and rubbed her feet and told her little stories about himself as a boy. And in the night, after she had fallen asleep, he watched her from a nearby chair, gazing in haunted wretchedness.

"How is she, Pearl?" Adam asked as he entered the bedroom.

The maid glanced at her mistress. "The same, sir." She shook her head, then left him alone with his wife.

As he sat beside Niki's chaise lounge, he tried to smile, but it was only a poor imitation. His face was drawn. Dark circles rimmed his eyes, and their usual blueness was dulled by sleepless nights. Still, he always smiled when he spoke to her, hoping that somehow a bit of cheerfulness would help when nothing else had.

"Good morning, Niki," he said as he leaned close to kiss her cheek. "I've got some news for you."

He wondered what she saw as she stared blankly into space.

"We're going to take a trip. We're going back to Spring Haven." Adam took hold of her hand, squeezing it, wishing she would squeeze back. "Remember when we went fishing at my secret spot? We'll go again. It'll do you good. Lots of sunshine and fresh air. And it's quiet. You'll get a lot of rest and you'll get well."

The Bellmans had built Spring Haven from nothing more than a family farm, back when the country was young and impertinent. It had grown into one of the state's greatest plantations, surviving many family tragedies and even civil war. To those who had left it to make homes elsewhere, Spring Haven had remained a touchstone, a place where you always belonged, where you could discover yourself again. Here it was that Adam brought his wife.

True to its name, the plantation was in vibrant bloom as befit the season. The air was perfumed by magnolia blossoms, honeysuckle and roses, alazeas and violets and pansies. Colts on spindly legs romped in the lush paddocks behind the stables. A litter of kittens squeaked and mewed in their nursery beneath the porch. The sky was blue and cloudless; the days were warm and peaceful.

The journey back to reality was not an easy one. There were no cries of the dying in her hiding place, no fear or pain. It was much safer there. She was not required to feel or think. She was untouchable. Yet something—or someone—kept calling her, forcing her from the dark corner of refuge she had found in her mind, and though she tried to resist, she was drawn back toward the light of day, back to the land of the living—and the land of the hurting, the crying, and the dying.

She was seated in a white wicker chair in the midst of the formal gardens. How long she had been staring into nothing she didn't know. The awareness of all that was around her crept upon her slowly. Perhaps it was the scent of the flowers she noticed first, or maybe it was the kiss of the sun on her hair.

Or maybe it was Adam's deep voice that reached her first. He was lying on his back in the grass, talking about the time he had tried to climb the large oak tree at the end of the drive and had fallen and broken his arm.

She lowered her eyes to look at him, savoring the warmth in his voice, the mussed look of his hair, the casual sprawl of his strong, masculine form. She closed her eyes, wanting this moment to go on. She felt safe and secure and cared for. She was glad she had come back.

Then the peace was shattered. In a violent wave of memory, she was swept back to a night of frigid seas and starry skies and sinking ships and great lamantation from those without hope. Silently, she began to weep for those who were lost that night, especially for Harry, who had loved her and died.

Adam shifted onto his side and, resting his elbow on the ground, placed his palm against the side of his head. "You know something, Niki . . ." he started to say.

Then he saw her face. Her eyes were closed and there were tears running down her cheeks. He was almost afraid to move.

"Niki." He breathed her name like a prayer.

She choked back a sob.

"Niki!" He was up on his knees, gathering her into his arms, crushing her against his chest. "Niki. Niki."

His fingers became tangled in her hair. His shirt was dampened as she continued to sob out all the pain she had been hiding from. He wanted to laugh and cry at the same time. Though she hadn't said a word to him yet, he knew she was back. She was here with him. He was holding her and she was holding him back, and he was never going to let her go again.

The river of tears seemed unending. She cried until there were no more tears, and still she sobbed, dry, racking sobs that tore at her throat and her heart. Adam carried her to her room while Erin summoned the doctor. A sedative was administered and finally she found peace in slumber.

When she awoke, she was alone. Daytime had passed its reign into the hands of night, and Niki's room was cloaked in darkness. She pushed herself up against the headboard. Even without light, she recognized her room at Spring Haven. She didn't know how she had come to be here or why, but she was glad she'd been brought here.

Niki threw off the covers and padded over

to the French doors leading onto the balcony. She opened them, welcoming the cool breeze that brushed her hair back from her cheeks. She didn't understand all that had transpired since the night the ship sank, but she knew she was over the worst of it.

She leaned against the outside wall, folding her arms and closing her eyes. She was remembering Adam and the way he had held her as she cried. Could it possibly mean what she hoped it meant? Did he care —*really* care—or was he merely being kind?

"It's been a long time since I waltzed with anyone on this balcony. Would you do me the honor?"

"Oh!" she gasped, her eyes flying open.

Adam held out his arms to her. As natural as breathing, she slipped into them. Slowly, they began to waltz, turning and turning and turning around the balcony. Niki's head was thrown back so she could look up at his face, though it was hidden in shadows. She wished she could see his eyes, read what was in them. She wished she could know ahead of time what his response would be when she told him she loved him, had always loved him.

Suddenly, he stopped. He released her and stepped back so abruptly she nearly lost her balance. It seemed as if he had already answered her silent question. She started to turn away.

"Niki. About the divorce . . ."

Here it was. Her hopes dashed forever.

"I'm not going to give you a divorce. If you must have one, you'll have to do it on your own."

She shook her head as if to clear her ears.

"I know you told me to do what had to be done, but I can't."

"But, Adam . . ."

"I'm not going to argue with you, Niki." There was a long, struggling pause before he continued in a near whisper. "I love you. I love you enough to let you go, if that's what you want, but I want you to stay. I'd like a chance to start our marriage over again. Do it right this time . . . if you can forgive me for what I've done."

"Forgive you?" she echoed, her heart racing.

He lifted a hand toward her, then dropped it to his side. "No. No, I don't suppose you can believe I love you after all I've done."

"But, Adam . . ." This time she was the one to reach out. She took hold of his upper arm and held on tight. "Adam, that's all I've ever wanted to hear . . . that you love me." Tears of joy and disbelief glistened in her eyes as she said softly, "I love you, too."

There was another breathless pause before he gathered her up against him. His mouth touched hers with a tender yearning that made her legs weak. Her arms wound about his neck, and she returned his kiss, the smoldering passion she had held in check for so long spreading like a fire through her veins. With a sweep of his arm, he lifted her feet off the floor and cradled her like a child. Even in the darkness, she could sense the desire in his eyes.

"She was right," Niki whispered, pressing her hand against the curve of his neck.

"Who was right?" came his throaty response.

"Gram. She always said I'd know in my heart when the right man came into my life and that, when he did, nothing else would be as important to me as he was. I didn't really believe it . . . then."

She brushed her lips across his, then laid her head against his shoulder again. To the east, storm clouds had gathered, and Niki heard the faint rumble of thunder. But in her heart, the storm that had raged for so long was silenced.

"I believe it now," she whispered against his throat as Adam carried her into the house.

PULSE-POUNDING HISTORICAL ROMANCE BY BESTSELLING AUTHOR KAREN ROBARDS

2024-6	**FORBIDDEN LOVE**	$3.50 US, $3.95 Can.
2046-7	**ISLAND FLAME**	$3.50
2047-5	**SEA FIRE**	$3.75

Please send me the following titles:

Quantity   Book Number   Price

_____   _____   _____

_____   _____   _____

_____   _____   _____

_____   _____   _____

If out of stock on any of the above titles, please send me the alternate title(s) listed below:

_____   _____   _____

_____   _____   _____

_____   _____   _____

_____   _____   _____

                         Postage & Handling   _____

                         Total Enclosed $_____

Please include $1.00 shipping and handling for the first book ordered and 25¢ for each book thereafter in the same order. All orders are shipped within approximately 4 weeks via postal service book rate. PAYMENT MUST ACCOMPANY ALL ORDERS.*

*Canadian orders must be paid in US dollars payable through a New York banking facility.

FOR THE FINEST
IN CONTEMPORARY
WOMEN'S FICTION,
FOLLOW LEISURE'S LEAD

2143-9	**AMERICAN BEAUTY** Maggi Brocher	$3.50 US, $3.95 Can.
2155-2	**TOMORROW AND FOREVER** Francesca Macklem	$2.75
2167-6	**BED OF ROSES** Rochelle Larkin	$3.25
2188-9	**DUET** Wendy Susans	$3.75 US, $4.50 Can.
2196-X	**THE LOVE ARENA** Pat Gaston	$3.75 US, $4.50 Can.
2207-9	**PARTINGS** Maggi Brocher	$3.50 US, $4.25 Can.
2217-6	**THE GLITTER GAME** Kaye Hill	$3.75 US, $4.50 Can.
2227-3	**THE HEART FORGIVES** Barbara Riley	$3.75 US, $4.50 Can.
2230-3	**A PROMISE BROKEN** Jennifer Peters	$3.25
2249-4	**THE LOVING SEASON** Rebecca Burton	$3.50
2250-8	**FRAGMENTS** Lou Graham	$3.25
2257-5	**TO LOVE A STRANGER** Jean Howell	$3.75 US, $4.50 Can.

Thrilling
Historical Romance
by
CATHERINE HART
Leisure's
LEADING LADY OF
LOVE

PULSE-POUNDING
HISTORICAL ROMANCE BY
BESTSELLING AUTHOR
KAREN ROBARDS

Make the Most of Your Leisure Time with
LEISURE BOOKS

Please send me the following titles:

Quantity	Book Number	Price
_____	_____	_____
_____	_____	_____
_____	_____	_____
_____	_____	_____
_____	_____	_____

If out of stock on any of the above titles, please send me the alternate title(s) listed below:

_____	_____	_____
_____	_____	_____
_____	_____	_____
_____	_____	_____

Postage & Handling _____

Total Enclosed $_____

☐ Please send me a free catalog.

NAME_____
(please print)

ADDRESS _____

CITY_____ STATE _____ ZIP _____

Please include $1.00 shipping and handling for the first book ordered and 25¢ for each book thereafter in the same order. All orders are shipped within approximately 4 weeks via postal service book rate. PAYMENT MUST ACCOMPANY ALL ORDERS.*

*Canadian orders must be paid in US dollars payable through a New York banking facility.

Mail coupon to: **Dorchester Publishing Co., Inc.**
6 East 39 Street, Suite 900
New York, NY 10016
Att: ORDER DEPT.